THE YUKON QUEEN

BOOKS BY GILBERT MORRIS

THE HOUSE OF WINSLOW SERIES

The Honorable Imposter
The Captive Bride
The Indentured Heart
The Gentle Rebel
The Saintly Buccaneer
The Holy Warrior
The Reluctant Bridegroom
The Last Confederate
The Dixie Widow
The Wounded Yankee
The Union Belle
The Final Adversary
The Crossed Sabres
The Valiant Gunman
The Gallant Outlaw
The Jeweled Spur
The Yukon Queen
The Rough Rider

The Iron Lady
The Silver Star
The Shadow Portrait
The White Hunter
The Flying Cavalier
The Glorious Prodigal
The Amazon Quest
The Golden Angel
The Heavenly Fugitive
The Fiery Ring
The Pilgrim Song
The Beloved Enemy
The Shining Badge
The Royal Handmaid
The Silent Harp
The Virtuous Woman
The Gypsy Moon
The Unlikely Allies

CHENEY DUVALL, M.D.[1]

1. The Stars for a Light
2. Shadow of the Mountains
3. A City Not Forsaken
4. Toward the Sunrising
5. Secret Place of Thunder
6. In the Twilight, in the Evening
7. Island of the Innocent
8. Driven With the Wind

CHENEY AND SHILOH: THE INHERITANCE[1]

1. Where Two Seas Met
2. The Moon by Night
3. There Is a Season

THE SPIRIT OF APPALACHIA[2]

1. Over the Misty Mountains
2. Beyond the Quiet Hills
3. Among the King's Soldiers
4. Beneath the Mockingbird's Wings
5. Around the River's Bend

LIONS OF JUDAH

1. Heart of a Lion
2. No Woman So Fair
3. The Gate of Heaven
4. Till Shiloh Comes
5. By Way of the Wilderness

[1]with Lynn Morris   [2]with Aaron McCarver

GILBERT MORRIS

the YUKON QUEEN

BETHANYHOUSE
Minneapolis, Minnesota

The Yukon Queen
Copyright © 1995
Gilbert Morris
2005 edition

Cover illustration by Dan Thornberg
Cover design by Josh Madison

Published by Bethany House Publishers
11400 Hampshire Avenue South
Bloomington, Minnesota 55438

Bethany House Publishers is a division of
Baker Publishing Group, Grand Rapids, Michigan.

Printed in the United States of America

Library of Congress Cataloging-in-Publication Data

Morris, Gilbert.
    The Yukon queen / by Gilbert Morris. — 2005 ed.
       p.   cm. — (The House of Winslow ; 1896)
    Summary: "To fulfill his promise to a dying man, Cass Winslow locates the man's daughter and takes her with him in search of Klondike gold"—
Provided by publisher.
    ISBN 0-7642-2961-3 (pbk.)
    1. Winslow family (Fictitious characters)—Fiction. 2. Klondike River Valley (Yukon)—Fiction. 3. Gold mines and mining—Fiction. 4. Women gold miners—Fiction. I. Title. II. Series: Morris, Gilbert. House of Winslow.

    PS3563.O8742Y85   2005
    813'.54—dc22
                                   2005020512

To Ronnie Root,

Hey, partner, this one is for you!

Every now and then I go to the closet where I keep all the good memories and pull out one that I like. I've just about worn out those that feature you, because those were good times for me.

I'd like to be able to go back and crowd into that little radio station and do a *Sam and Jesse* script—then go to the Awful House and eat greasy steaks with you again.

We can't go back to that, but as the old song says it—

Thanks for the memories!

GILBERT MORRIS spent ten years as a pastor before becoming Professor of English at Ouachita Baptist University in Arkansas and earning a Ph.D. at the University of Arkansas. A prolific writer, he has had over 25 scholarly articles and 200 poems published in various periodicals, and over the past years has had more than 180 novels published. His family includes three grown children. He and his wife live in Gulf Shores, Alabama.

CONTENTS

PART THREE
DAWSON

PART FOUR
KLONDIKE JUSTICE

THE HOUSE OF WINSLOW

★ ★ ★ ★

THE HOUSE OF WINSLOW

★ ★ ★ ★

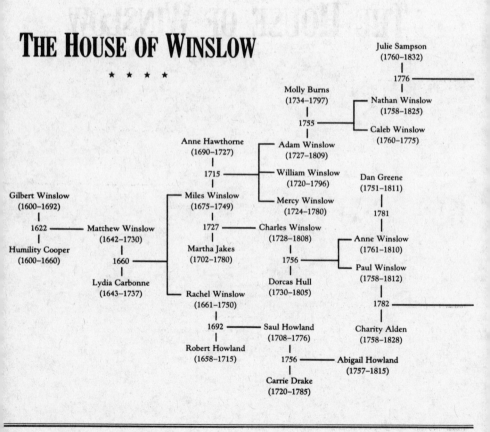

Julie Sampson
(1760–1832)

1776

Molly Burns
(1734–1797)

Nathan Winslow
(1758–1825)

1755

Caleb Winslow
(1760–1775)

Anne Hawthorne
(1690–1727)

Adam Winslow
(1727–1809)

1715

William Winslow
(1720–1796)

Dan Greene
(1751–1811)

Miles Winslow
(1675–1749)

Mercy Winslow
(1724–1780)

1781

Gilbert Winslow
(1600–1692)

1727

Charles Winslow
(1728–1808)

Anne Winslow
(1761–1810)

1622

Matthew Winslow
(1642–1730)

Martha Jakes
(1702–1780)

1756

Paul Winslow
(1758–1812)

Humility Cooper
(1600–1660)

1660

Dorcas Hull
(1730–1805)

1782

Lydia Carbonne
(1643–1737)

Rachel Winslow
(1661–1750)

Charity Alden
(1758–1828)

1692

Saul Howland
(1708–1776)

Robert Howland
(1658–1715)

1756

Abigail Howland
(1757–1815)

Carrie Drake
(1720–1785)

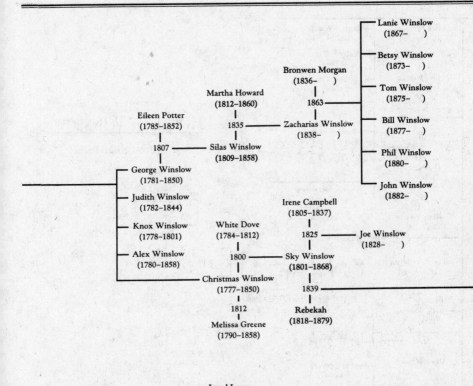

Lanie Winslow
(1867–   )

Betsy Winslow
(1873–   )

Bronwen Morgan
(1836–   )

Martha Howard   1863 —————— Tom Winslow
(1812–1860)   (1875–   )

Eileen Potter   Bill Winslow
(1785–1852)   1835 —————— Zacharias Winslow   (1877–   )
                                   (1838–   )
        1807 —————— Silas Winslow   Phil Winslow
                     (1809–1858)   (1880–   )

George Winslow   John Winslow
(1781–1850)   (1882–   )

Judith Winslow   Irene Campbell
(1782–1844)   (1805–1837)

Knox Winslow   White Dove   1825 —————— Joe Winslow
(1778–1801)   (1784–1812)   (1828–   )

Alex Winslow   1800 —————— Sky Winslow
(1780–1858)   (1801–1868)

        Christmas Winslow   1839 ——————————
        (1777–1850)

             1812   Rebekah
                                    (1818–1879)
        Melissa Greene
        (1790–1858)

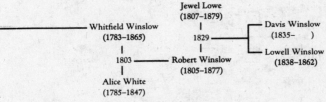

                    Jewel Lowe
                    (1807–1879)
                                        Davis Winslow
Whitfield Winslow   1829 ——————   (1835–   )
(1783–1865)
                                        Lowell Winslow
        1803 —————— Robert Winslow   (1838–1862)
                     (1805–1877)
Alice White
(1785–1847)

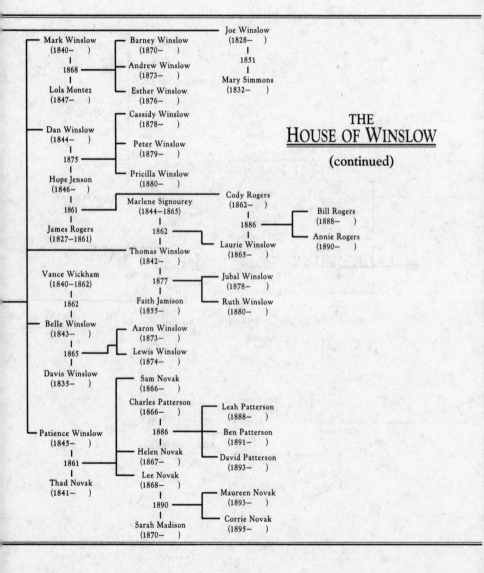

THE
HOUSE OF WINSLOW
(continued)

Mark Winslow
(1840–)
|
1868
|
Lola Montez
(1847–)

Barney Winslow
(1870–)

Andrew Winslow
(1873–)

Esther Winslow
(1876–)

Joe Winslow
(1828–)
|
1851
|
Mary Simmons
(1832–)

Dan Winslow
(1844–)
|
1875
|
Hope Jenson
(1846–)

Cassidy Winslow
(1878–)

Peter Winslow
(1879–)

Pricilla Winslow
(1880–)

Marlene Signourey
(1844–1865)
|
1862
|
Thomas Winslow
(1842–)

Cody Rogers
(1862–)
|
1886
|
Laurie Winslow
(1865–)

Bill Rogers
(1888–)

Annie Rogers
(1890–)

James Rogers
(1827–1861)

Vance Wickham
(1840–1862)
|
1862
|
Belle Winslow
(1843–)
|
1865
|
Davis Winslow
(1835–)

1877
|
Faith Jamison
(1855–)

Jubal Winslow
(1878–)

Ruth Winslow
(1880–)

Aaron Winslow
(1873–)

Lewis Winslow
(1874–)

Patience Winslow
(1845–)
|
1861
|
Thad Novak
(1841–)

Sam Novak
(1866–)

Charles Patterson
(1866–)
|
1886
|
Helen Novak
(1867–)

Lee Novak
(1868–)
|
1890
|
Sarah Madison
(1870–)

Leah Patterson
(1888–)

Ben Patterson
(1891–)

David Patterson
(1893–)

Maureen Novak
(1893–)

Corrie Novak
(1895–)

PART ONE

GOLD FEVER

★ ★ ★

December 1896—August 1897

CHAPTER ONE

A GATHERING OF WINSLOWS

★　★　★　★

"Richmond—twenty minutes to Richmond!"

A tall man in western dress had been speaking quietly to a woman beside him, but at the shout of the conductor, he broke off and turned to stare out the window. Farther back in the car a man's voice said, "Malvern Hill out there yonder. . . ."

A chill touched Dan Winslow at the base of his skull. The engine uttered a hoarse bellow, and black smoke swept by the window and obscured his view, depositing a layer of fine cinders on his right shoulder. The narrow-gauge engine picked up speed, and at the sharp staccato *clickety-clack* of the wheels the tall man's eyes narrowed to slits.

There was nothing unusual in the landscape to cause such a reaction. A plateau lifted from the level of the track, rising about one hundred fifty feet to a crest crowned with second-growth pine and oak. Between the pasture and the top of the hill a herd of fat red cows dotted the expanse of brown winter grass. They were fenced in by rail fences, and midway up the hill sat a sturdy two-story house of white clapboard framed by a red barn on one side and a clump of cone-shaped haystacks on the other. A ribbon of white smoke rose lazily from the chimney, forming a curling streak against the iron gray December sky of 1896.

The scene was a typical picture of a Virginia farm at Christmas—and yet something about it had stiffened Winslow's back. Hope noticed instantly the tension in the corded muscles of his neck and his clenched fists.

"What is it, Dan? Is something wrong?"

Dan kept his eyes fixed on the hill—and as he did, a strange thing came to him. A memory that he had deliberately kept buried suddenly surfaced in his mind. It all came back with intense clarity. He could see Malvern Hill as it had been the last time he had seen it—at five in the afternoon of July 1, 1862.

Through half-closed eyes, Dan saw again the long lines of Confederate soldiers marching forward up the slope. Not being a man of much fancy or given to great imagination, he was shocked at how vividly the scene came back to him. He remembered looking down the line, seeing his men begin to fall, struck down by the guns ranked along the top of the hill. He could hear long-suppressed echoes of soldiers' dying screams, and the smell of blood and dust seemed to fill his nostrils.

"Lieutenant Howe—he's shot in two, Dan!"

"We can't help him, Corporal—we've got to take this hill!"

"Ain't goin' to do it, Dan—they's too many cannon waitin' fer us—!"

And then Dan remembered how a bullet had struck his best friend, Steve Bolton, in the mouth, taking off the back of his head. Dan closed his eyes quickly, his breathing gone ragged—but suddenly a hand closed on his arm, and Hope's voice broke through the memories.

"Dan—what is it, dear?"

With an effort Dan shook his head to clear it of the bitter memories. When he looked around he saw that not only his wife, Hope, but his three children—Cass, Peter, and Priscilla—were watching him with obvious concern. He shook his shoulders together in a firm gesture and managed a faint smile. "Just a bit of a shock from an old memory—I'm all right now."

Cass, his older son, was an astute young man of eighteen. Glancing out at the landscape, he murmured, "Malvern Hill—that was the last battle of The Seven Days. Were you there, Dad?"

"Yes. I was there," said his father solemnly. Dan forced himself to look out once more, then when he turned to face them, his tanned features were strained—an unusual thing, for he seldom manifested such a quality. "The last time I saw that hill, it was covered with five thousand men, some of them dead and others dying." His long lips clamped together for a moment, then he added quietly, "A lot of them were alive and were moving. It—it looked like the field itself was *crawling*."

Peter, the seventeen-year-old, who had his mother's light brown hair and slight build, leaned forward and said, "Did we win the battle, Dad?"

"Nobody won at Malvern Hill, Pete. General Lee thought it was the last chance to cut the Union Army off—but the Yankees had the high ground. We found out they had more than a hundred cannon—and long lines of infantry with good muskets. The barrage of gunfire was so heavy I saw men leaning into it as a man leans into a strong wind."

Priscilla shook her honey-colored hair and gave a wide-eyed stare at her father. "I'm glad you didn't get killed, Daddy."

Cass laughed suddenly and pinched her on the arm. "You goose! If he'd gotten killed, none of us would be here!" She aimed a slap at him, which he fended off; then he looked at his father with an odd expression. "Something to think of, isn't it? If just one of those bullets had hit you—none of the three of us would ever have been born."

"Why, of course we'd have been born," Peter argued instantly. He was a logical young man with a keen delight in metaphysics— which his brother Cass despised. Patting his mother on the knee, Peter nodded confidently, saying, "We'd have the same mother but a different father."

Dan sat quietly as Cass and Peter argued, and finally Hope leaned close, pressing against him. At the age of fifty-one and after having four children, she still had the slim figure of a young girl and her blue-green eyes sparkled as she whispered, "I'm glad I got you—instead of that other fellow Peter's talking about." She always had the ability to lighten his moods, and until the train pulled into the station, she kept him occupied with questions about the family reunion they'd come to Richmond to attend.

"I got a letter from Belle," Dan said as the passengers began gathering their belongings to get off the train. "She and Davis and the boys will meet us."

"That ought to give us some status," Hope smiled. "I'll bet the president of the college doesn't come out to meet every visitor."

Davis Winslow had been a minister serving churches in Richmond and Washington ever since the end of the Civil War—but he was also the founder and first president of Bethany Bible College located in Richmond.

Dan stood up, a tall man, still lean and strong at the age of fifty-two. He had a full head of thick reddish brown hair, slightly curly and only lightly sprinkled with gray. Years in the saddle under the hot sun on his ranch had kept him fit. Plucking up one of the bags, he said thoughtfully, "Belle did all right—married to a college president." He grinned crookedly at Hope. "All you got was a broken-down cowpuncher."

Hope reached up and smoothed Dan's hair back from his forehead. "I got the pick of the litter," she nodded firmly. "Now, let's go meet the Winslow clan!"

★ ★ ★ ★

Aaron Winslow leaped out of the buggy before the wheels stopped turning and spoke roughly to the two saddled horses tied to the rear. "You two—settle down!" It was a typical act, for he was an impetuous young man. At the age of twenty-three, there was still a trace of immaturity on his well-shaped face. He had a certain grace in his movements, however, which one does not expect in a man of six feet one. Reaching back, he helped the dark-haired woman down, urging, "Come on, Mother—the train's pulling in right now!"

Belle Winslow gathered her full skirt and waited until Davis got out. When he came to stand beside her, she said, "We've got time, Aaron. You and Lewis go ahead—I want to speak to your father."

"You two have more *secrets*!" Lewis Winslow was no more than five feet ten and possessed none of Aaron's muscular grace. His intelligent brown eyes crinkled suddenly. He had a sharp humor that popped out from time to time. "I'll bet the college board would like to know how you two carry on! I saw you kissing Mom in the peach orchard yesterday, Dad!"

Davis Winslow had grown heavier than when he had courted Belle Winslow, the famous Dixie Widow. His present duties kept him from getting enough exercise, though Belle kept at him.

"You watch your phraseology, young man," Davis warned sternly. "Now, do as your mother tells you."

Lewis turned to follow Aaron but paused long enough to ask, "Was Uncle Dan really a gunfighter, Dad?"

"Well, more or less—but that was years ago when he had to fight for his ranch."

"Gosh! A real gunfighter in our family!"

As Lewis whirled and raced after Aaron, Davis smiled at Belle. "I told you to stop kissing me in public. I've warned you about this unbridled passion that possesses you when I'm around."

Belle Winslow sniffed. "As I recall, *you're* the one who did the kissing." She was a beautiful woman, looking much younger than her fifty-three years. Her hair was black, her eyes violet tinted, and her skin was still the envy of much younger women. She looked after Lewis and smiled. "He has a mother who was a famous spy for the Confederacy—but he's more impressed with his uncle's gunfighting!"

"Well—it looks like your fame is going to take a backseat for a while," Davis shrugged. He put his arm around her as they moved along. "I don't care what people say. I'd rather hug you than be president of any college!"

Belle was pleased and murmured, "You *do* have your moments, Davis Winslow!" The two moved toward the platform where the train was huffing in, exhaling great plumes of steam. Quickly she said, "Did Elton Harvey talk to you?"

A frown creased Davis's brow. "About Aaron and his daughter? Yes, he did. I'll have to speak to Aaron."

"I wish you could take a stick to him!"

"At twenty-three, I think it's a little late for that." Davis helped Belle down the steps that led to the platform, then added, "Aaron has got to grow up—and he's got to leave respectable girls alone. Bad enough to run after some of the cheap women as he does."

"Wait until after the reunion," Belle said quickly. "Aaron just sulls up when either of us tries to talk to him. Maybe Mark or Dan can talk some sense into him."

"I can't understand him, Belle," Davis complained sadly. "He's been a rebel since he was twelve years old. Nothing like Lewis, is he?"

"None of us are like anyone else. Look at Patience and me. We are as different as night and day! Oh, look—there's Dan!"

The two moved forward and Belle threw herself into her brother's arms with a squeal. "Why, you good-looking thing, you! Look at him, Davis—he's not a day older than the last time we saw him!"

"Belle—you're still the same—beautiful as ever!" These two were very close, and for a moment they stood regarding each other fondly. Then Dan said, "We'll talk—but these are our sons, Cass here—and this is Peter—and our daughter, Priscilla."

Belle and Davis greeted the three, admiring them properly, then Davis said, "And this is Aaron, our oldest son—and Lewis, our younger."

Lewis at once moved forward and said, "Did you ever meet Wyatt Earp or Bill Hickok, Uncle Dan?"

Dan grinned, his teeth very white against his tanned skin. "Met Hickok once. A more vain old bore I never hope to see! Most of those 'legends' were pretty sorry, Lewis."

Aaron greeted his cousins, taking time to bend over Priscilla's hand and murmur, "Why, I didn't know I had such a beautiful young relative! Lewis, we'll have to take special care and keep the young romeos fought off of our cousin." He made a fine picture in his gray suit, shiny black boots, and sweeping black hat. He helped his mother and Priscilla into the buggy, supervised the loading of the luggage, then said, "Cass, you and I will have to ride to Belle Maison. You're probably a better rider than I am—but I'll try to keep up."

The two young men mounted the extra horses that Davis had brought along. As the buggy left the station, Cass's horse tried to buck its rider off. Cass sat easily in the saddle, got the horse's head up with a firm jerk on the bridle, and said, "Here—now!" The sorrel quickly recognized the uselessness of such behavior and placidly followed the buggy.

"You're a good rider, Cass," Aaron noted.

Cass shrugged, saying, "About all I'm good at, I guess." He caught the look of surprise on his cousin's face and tried to smile. "Well, I've done nothing but ride a horse since the day I was born. Hard not to when you grow up on a cattle ranch. But you've been to college and done a lot, my dad tells me."

Aaron shook his head and said nothing. The young man's remark had brought a look of frustration to his features. When they cleared town and were on the muddy road leading north, he said, "Why, I had to go to college, I guess. At least, my parents expected me to go. I hated to disappoint them—but looking back, I think it would have disappointed them less if I'd never gone."

Cass was surprised and said so. "But—you've had good jobs, and you've traveled a lot. You don't know what it's like growing up on a ranch, Aaron!"

"From what I've heard, it sounds exciting, Cass," Aaron said. "I've envied you, growing up in the wild West."

Cass shook his head, protesting moodily, "It's awful! You're stuck out in the country a million miles from a town. Every day the same thing!"

Aaron twisted in the saddle, examined the young man, and smiled sardonically. "Sounds like my job in the bank—every day the same." He shook his head, adding, "They're all the same. Guess man's born to be bored. And it's worse for a preacher's son."

"Why—how is that?"

"People expect you to be holy—which I'm not!"

Cass suddenly laughed. "Well, darn! It sounds like you and me are both mavericks, Aaron. I've been a pain in the neck to my folks since I was sixteen."

"I started earlier, Cass—and I've had time to do worse." He caught Cass's look of astonishment and shrugged. "I'm the prodigal son, Cass. I've left my father's house—and I've done some things that make eating with hogs look almost respectable." He leaned forward and stroked the horse's neck, then straightened up, a bitter glint in his eyes. "I'd like to do something—but be blamed if I know what. Anything but work from eight till six for the next forty years!"

As they rode behind the buggy, the two men discovered that they had much more in common than either had expected. Both were young, restless, and filled with some sort of rebellious spirit that would not let them rest. Finally they approached a large white house behind a long circular drive. Pulling their mounts to a stop, Aaron said, "That's Belle Maison—you've never been there?"

"Nope," said Cass, taking in the impressive plantation spread out before him.

"Well, it's a fine place. Our aunt Patience married a Yankee, and to everyone's surprise he turned out well. In fact, everybody in the country admires Thad Novak." For a few moments they sat atop their horses in the drive as Aaron spoke of the home place, then he said, "Look, Cass, you and I, we can have some fun while you're here. We'll go into Richmond and paint the town red! I just paid my debts—so it's time to run them up again."

"Hey, that's good of you, Aaron!" Cass was feeling good, and as he dismounted and looked around at the magnificent plantation, he thought, *I wish I never had to go back to herding cows again! Maybe I can get a job and stay here with Aaron!*

★　★　★　★

"Fasten me up, Thad—we've got to hurry!"

Thad Novak had just tied his black bow tie after much effort. It was crooked and gave him a lopsided look, but he gave up on it and turned to Patience, who was struggling to button the back of her dress. It was a new dress made of muslin in a paisley pattern of coral and white, and she said with exasperation, "It's too *young* for an old woman like me!"

"Yep, you're an old relic, you are," Thad grinned. Stepping behind her he fastened the remaining buttons, then turned her around and put his arms around her. "Mrs. Methuselah—all of fifty-one years old." He studied her carefully, then said, "I'd better get a wheelchair to get you down the stairs."

"Oh, you fool!" Patience had to laugh. She kissed him lightly, then stood back to look at him critically. She had practically forced him to buy new clothes for the reunion and now gave him her full attention. "You know, for an old fellow of fifty-five, you're not a bad-looking man." Thad was wearing loose-cut fawn-colored trousers and a brown brocaded waistcoat. He had a tucked shirt with a detachable collar, a new invention which he *hated!* Patience reached up and straightened his tie, then said, "You look very nice." A pixieish expression filled her dark blue eyes, and she added, "If you drop dead from fright while making your speech, we won't have to do a thing to you—except put a lily in your hand!"

"Pet! What a thing to say!" Thad whirled her around and gave her a resounding slap on the bottom. When she yelped and begged for mercy, he turned her back around, and she saw a troubled expression clouding his dark, wedge-shaped face. "Pet, you may be right. I'd rather face a firing squad than try to make a speech."

"You'll do fine, Thad. After all, you are the master of Belle Maison." Seeing his agitation, Patience took his hands in hers and looked him squarely in the eyes and said, "If it hadn't been for you after the war, we'd have lost it all. The Winslows are forever in your debt for hanging on to our heritage."

"I don't know about that," Thad muttered. He had married Pet and thrown himself into the work of bringing the plantation through reconstruction. It had been a grueling task, for the North had imposed harsh measures in the South after the death of Lincoln. The Winslow men had scattered, going out to make their way in the world. They had all done well, he reflected. "But Mark is the oldest son—and a success, too. Vice-president of a railroad and all. And Davis, president of a college." Thad shook his head, ticking off the Winslows. "And Tom, a colonel, and Dan owns a big ranch. They're all somebodies—"

"Stop that, you hear me, Thad!" Pet's eyes narrowed and she shook him almost violently. "They're successful and we're proud for them. But *you're* the one who stayed here and poured your life into this place. I'm proud to be a Winslow—but I'm even more proud to be Pet Novak!"

Thad blinked in surprise. He had always been in awe of this family. In fact, in many ways he felt himself inferior to the colorful Winslow siblings. Thad stared at his wife for a long moment, then said huskily, "Well—I'm glad to hear you say that, Pet. I—I was feeling pretty doggone common."

"Nonsense! Now, let's round up all our branch of Winslows." She laughed suddenly, adding, "My brothers and my sister may be famous—but we're more successful than any of them at the one thing that counts." When he gave her a quizzical look, she punched him in the side, saying, "We've got as fine a crop of children as any of them—and grandchildren, too! Now—let's go roust them out!"

They left at once, recruiting Sam, their oldest son. "You'll have to help with the grandchildren, Sam," Pet said instantly. "If you won't marry and have children of your own, you'll have to help with the brats of others."

Sam Novak was a slight young man, dark featured as was his father. He was thirty and had never married. At the age of seven he had announced that he intended to be a minister. As he matured into a young man, he had remained true to his calling. He had become a successful evangelist but now was bound for the mission fields in China.

"Well, I'll whip the rascals if they need it," he shrugged. "You look like an actress, Mama," he added, a droll light in his brown eyes. "Vanity, vanity! I'm shocked to see my own mother giving in to such things."

"Wouldn't hurt you to dress up, Sam," Thad put in. He was tremendously proud of this son of his but covered this up by such remarks. "You look like you're going out to pick cotton."

"I'm hoping to shame the rest of you into more sedate dress." He eyed his father, then said, "You do look nice, though."

"Go help Helen. She'll never get those children dressed in time."

"All right. What about Lee and Sarah?"

"I'll take care of them—you go on."

Sam moved along the hall and banged on a door at the end. When it opened, he said, "Hello, Charles. Mama sent me down to help with the kids."

Charles Patterson was the husband of Sam's sister, Helen. He was a successful lawyer, but not particularly good with children. He stood there rubbing his wild thatch of reddish hair for a moment, then grinned. "I can handle a judge and a jury, but your sister and our children are much harder. Come on in, Sam. I'd appreciate the help."

When he entered, Sam was swarmed at once by David, age three, Ben, age five, and Leah, age eight. He threw himself into getting them dressed while carrying on a conversation with his brother-in-law at the same time. The children idolized him, and he loved them as if they were his own. Finally the inner door opened and Helen emerged. She was wearing a dress made of magenta silk satin overlaid with pink lace flounces. Over it she wore a stole of green satin, offset by white gloves. "Oh, Sam, you can't wear those old clothes!"

"If they're good enough to preach in, I guess they're good enough to eat dinner in."

"But—we're going to have photographs made!"

"Then they'll show me as I am." Sam grinned and grabbed Ben's hand, pulling it out of his pocket. "You little pickpocket! Stop that!" He rose and said, "Well, I guess we better go." He eyed Helen's dress and grinned. "You look fine, sis. But that dress cost enough to send a preacher into the heart of China!"

"I'll give you the cost of it when you leave, Sam," Charles said quickly. "I'm proud to have a missionary in the family."

They left and discovered that Thad and Patience had just managed to get their son Lee and his wife Sarah in motion. Lee was a tall man of twenty-eight with the strong Slavic features of his father. Sam spoke to him at once. "Ready for the session, Lee? Here, let me hold Corrie." He reached out and took the one-year-old, and at once Maureen, who was three, put up such a howl to be held that he scooped her up in his free arm. "Now, hush, will you, sweetheart."

"Sam, you're a natural-born father," Lee said, winking at Charles. "I think you ought to marry a widow with six kids."

"Lee—don't tell him that," Sarah warned. She was a small, pretty woman with a wealth of auburn hair. "He's so impressionable he just might go out and do it!"

"You can talk later," Thad broke in. As he looked over his family, a surge of pride rose in him. "Lord, there's a bunch of us Novaks!"

"Well—we're not all here *yet*," Lee grinned. He laughed aloud as everyone looked instantly at Sarah—who blushed richly. "Yep, got to repopulate the world, as the scripture says."

Thad and Patience gave each other a surprised look, then congratulated their son and his wife. As soon as Helen and Charles had done the same, Thad took a deep breath. "Well, God bless us every one, as Tiny Tim said. Now I'll have something to say in this blasted speech."

"Pour it on, Pa," Sam grinned. "Before we leave, let me take up a collection for Chinese missions!"

"I'll do it!" Thad nodded emphatically. "Now, let's get down there—I can't wait to hear what I've got to say!"

CHAPTER TWO

OUT OF THE PAST

★ ★ ★ ★

"We had some good times in this room when we were growing up, didn't we, Tom?"

Tom Winslow cast a quick glance around the ballroom that had been decorated for the Christmas holidays. It was a large room that took up half of the lower floor of Belle Maison. It was thirty feet wide and nearly sixty feet long, with tall windows that allowed bars of pale sunlight to enter. "Sure did, Mark. I wonder how many of those girls we romanced in here still remember us?"

Mark laid his glance on this younger brother of his, admiring the erect, strong figure that years in the saddle had produced. A thought came to him and he smiled. "Remember Lily Beaufort, Tom?"

"I sure do," Tom said ruefully. "You and I nearly knocked each other's teeth out over that wench!"

"I hurt for a week," Mark said softly, letting the memory run through him. "It was right out there, wasn't it—just past the big elm? But just think, Tom, Lily's a grandmother now, a white-haired old lady—not the saucy young woman she was before the war."

"That's right, isn't it, Mark? Hard to think of her like that. Well, we're all getting older. Those days seem almost like a dream now. But God's been good to us. I don't know any other family with three boys in the Confederate Army who didn't lose at least one." He glanced over toward where his wife, Faith, was sitting with their married daughter Laurie. "Good to have grandchildren, Mark. Laurie and Cody have been a real joy to Faith and me."

As the two men spoke of days long gone by, from across the room, Sam Novak came to stand beside Cody Rogers and his wife, Laurie. Cody looked young for his years, his blond hair still long as it had been years earlier when the three of them had traveled with Buffalo Bill Cody's Wild West Show. "Been a long time since our days on the road with Colonel Cody," he said. "You two like to go back to show business?"

"I've got all I can do to handle Bill and Annie," Laurie said at once. At the age of thirty-one she was almost as slim as she'd been when she was a trick rider. She hugged the two children who stood with her, then remarked, "I hear you're going to China as a missionary, Sam. I think that's fine!"

"Be a little more exciting than a Wild West Show," Cody grinned. There was a grace about him as he spoke. "Watch out for wild animals."

The three stood there for a time, and finally Sam said, "How do you divide the kids up among the grandparents?" When they stared at him, he laughed. "Well, you have two sets claiming them, don't you? How do you settle it?" He referred to the fact that Laurie was the daughter of Tom Winslow by his first wife, while Cody was the son of Hope Winslow by her first husband.

"We let both sides spoil them to the limit, Sam," Cody grinned. "We do have a time trying to explain it all to strangers. I reckon they think Laurie and me are living in sin or something—wait a minute, I think Thad's about to wind himself up for his speech. Here, you, Bill, and Annie—sit down with me and your mother!"

As Thad stood up, there was a scurrying around as those who were standing and talking found their places. He waited until they were all seated, then started to speak—but a loud voice called out, "We're ready, Thad—turn your wolf loose!"

Everyone laughed, and Thad scowled at Aaron, who grinned back at him. "If you're all through with your rude remarks, Aaron," he said firmly, "I'll ask you all to keep still. I'm as nervous as an old maid on a Mississippi River gambling boat as it is!"

Mark spoke up at once. "Let's have a little respect for the master of Belle Maison!" Applause punctuated his remark, and he sat back, saying, "Go to it, Thad!"

"Well, I wish you were making this speech, Mark," Thad said slowly. "You're the oldest son of Sky Winslow—and when I finish my few remarks, you've got to come and give us a *real* speech." Thad took a deep breath, then continued, "The first time I came to this place—Belle Maison—I was unconscious. I'd nearly froze to death, and if it hadn't been for a big slave named Toby I would have died. . . ."

For the next twenty minutes Thad related the story of how he'd come to Virginia as a poor boy and had become a part of Sky Winslow's family. He was not a public speaker, but as he told the story, including how the war had decimated the South, all of the older Winslows felt drawn into the simple history. Finally Thad said, "I guess the best thing that ever happened to me was to come to this place and be a part of the Winslow family. I'm proud of you all!"

He sat down and applause rocked the room. Thad's face reddened and Pet clung to his arm fiercely. "You did fine! Real fine, Thad!"

Mark rose and stood for a moment looking around at the familiar faces turned toward him. "Back in the days when I was helping build the Union Pacific across this country, I never thought I'd be standing here looking at all the Winslow clan. . . ." He spoke clearly, a big man with rock-solid purpose in every word and deed. He outlined the history of the family, not leaving a one out, and concluded by saying, "One thing I want to give you today. I want to read a passage from an old book—most of you have it, I think." He picked up a thin book bound in black leather and held it gently in his big hands. "*The Journal of Gilbert Winslow*," he said quietly. "He was one of those who came to this land to find something better. Those of you who've read his journal know he wasn't a man of faith when he left England—but you will remember that he found God. I want to read you what he wrote when his life was nearly over. He was one of those arrested and tried during the Salem witchcraft trials. When he wrote this passage, he was sick and dying." Opening the book, Mark began to read:

May 6, 1692. When I left England years ago, I did not expect to die in a prison, nor did I expect to be charged with witchcraft. But God is in all things, and He knew about this before I boarded the *Mayflower*. I am glad that my dear wife, Humility, has gone to be with Jesus, for though I can endure this place, it would have broken my heart to see her suffer! Hard enough for me to see my son, Matthew, and his wife in this place.

The executions continue. We got word this morning that Giles Corey, that saintly old man! was pressed to death last night. They piled huge stones on him, and when they commanded him to confess that he was in league with the devil—he whispered, "More weight!" He was a fearsome man, Giles Corey, and is now in the arms of Jesus.

I have been praying that Matthew and Lydia will be spared, but as for me, the martyr's crown does not seem so frightening now as it did when I was younger. Now I would wish that my descendants would be men and women of faith and courage.

My hand trembles so that I cannot write—but if any of my name read this in some far-off time, let me beg you a favor. If life presses you, and you are tempted to weaken and give up your faith—remember Giles Corey! Cry out when life puts heavy burdens on you, "More weight!" That would please God—and it would please your ancestor—Gilbert Winslow.

Mark closed the book and looked out over the still faces. He saw tears in his wife's eyes, and she was not alone in the emotion that swept over those gathered in the ballroom. "No one could say it better than that, I think. And now, let me follow the biblical pattern and call the roll of the House of Winslow:

> Gilbert begat Matthew,
> And Matthew begat Miles,
> And Miles begat Adam,
> And Adam begat Nathan,
> And Nathan begat Christmas,
> And Christmas begat Sky,
> And Sky begat the five of us you see here."

Mark motioned to his sisters and brothers, intoning, "Sky

Winslow begat Mark—and Thomas—and Daniel—and Belle—and Patience . . .

"I wish our father and mother—"

"Hold on there!"

Mark was startled by a rasping voice that cut across the room and turned at once, along with everyone else in the room, to see a man standing just inside the double doors. Blinking with anger, Mark said, "Sir, this is a private meeting. Please have the courtesy to take yourself outside!"

The newcomer was an elderly man, evidenced by his long, scraggly white hair and his weathered wrinkled face. He was stooped and thin, but his eyes were bright blue as they met those of Mark. He was wearing a worn brown coat that was too large for him and a pair of shapeless black pants stuffed into a pair of cowhide boots with run-over heels. He clutched a scruffy wide-brimmed hat in one hand and peered from under bushy white brows around the room, seemingly pleased by the disturbance he had created.

Mark cleared his throat and glanced toward Tom and Dan for support. "Old timer, my brothers will show you out. I'll be glad to talk to you—"

"Now, Mark, I thought you wuz sort of givin' a toast to all the younguns of Sky Winslow."

Taken aback by the old man's use of his first name, Mark stammered, "Why—why that's right, but what's that got to do with you?"

A sly light glinted in the amazingly youthful blue eyes. His lips curved up in a grin under his walrus mustache and he chuckled rustily. "Well, I reckon you left one out, didn't you?"

"Left one out?" Mark looked more bewildered than ever. "Why—all five of us are here."

"Wal, thet's as may be—if I don't disremember, Sky Winslow had *six* children."

For one moment Mark Winslow stood as still as if he had been turned to granite—then he cried out, "Joe!" With an agility that belied his age, Mark dashed across the room to grasp the shoulders of the old man, peering down and saying, "It *is* you—Joe Winslow!"

Tom gave a start, glanced wildly at Dan, then the two stood

up and moved at once to greet the newcomer. Dan grasped one thin shoulder and Tom took the hand that Mark wasn't holding, and the two of them beamed down at their half brother.

"*Who* is he?" Cass asked his mother. "I never heard of him."

"He's Sky Winslow's son from his first marriage," Hope whispered. "I never met him, but your father spoke of him for a long time. I thought he'd died."

Joe Winslow blinked as he was surrounded by the tall men. "Wal, now you fellers are *big*—look just like Pa, all three of you!"

"Joe, where in the world have you been?" Mark demanded. "I've tried to find you several times, but my letters never caught up with you, I guess."

"Aw, I meant to write, Mark, but you know how it is. I never was much for writin', anyhow. But I got the one about this here reunion, and I thought if I was ever going to see all of you, it'd be now."

"Come along, Joe," Mark said. "We'll fix you a place. Guess you could stand some good cooking?"

"Don't eat much, but shore is good to see you, Mark." Joe Winslow allowed the three brothers, joined at once by Belle and Patience, to seat him. He nibbled at the food they put before him but seemed more interested in the young Winslows. He kept asking questions, and everyone was amazed at how sharp he was. After being told the name of any one of the family, it seemed to be fixed in his memory. Once Lola said, "Joe, we're giving you too many names. I know how confused I get when I'm introduced to a lot of people."

"Why, I'm pretty good at names and faces." Joe shrugged his frail shoulders. "Fer instance—" He looked around the room and pointed at one table. "Thet's your boy, Andy, and your girl, Esther. And you got a boy named Barney who ain't here. And over there's your wife, Tom. Her name's Faith and that's your younguns—Laurie, Ruth, and Jubal. And Laurie's married to Hope's first son, Cody. An' the grandkids is called Bill and Annie—named after Buffalo Bill and Annie Oakley." Joe Winslow obviously enjoyed the open-eyed stares of amazement he received, and went on to complete the list.

"There's Dan and Hope and their kids—Cass, Pete, and Priscilla. Davis and Belle and their kids—Aaron and Lewis. And of course, Thad and Patience and their younguns—Sam, Helen, and Lee."

"That's amazing!" Mark leaned back and stared at his half brother with admiration. "But you always did have a fantastic memory."

Joe sat back and his eyes grew thoughtful. "I think a lot about Ma—your ma, Rebekah," he said finally. "She took me in like I was her own. I remember how when we was growin' up, she never made a mite of difference between her own younguns and me. I still miss her, even to this day, I do. Pa, too, of course."

Mark cleared his throat. "When he died, Joe, one of the last things he said to me was, 'I do love Joe—keep praying for him, Mark.'"

"Pa said that? I'm glad you told me, Mark. Means a lot to me."

"Tell us about what you've been doing, Joe," Patience spoke up. She had met her half brother only once, when she was six. He had come for a brief visit to Virginia, but she still remembered him, and Sky had read his son's letters to her. "I know you went to the gold fields."

"Aye, Patience, I did—and not just *the* gold fields—I went to all of 'em. Been my downfall, prospecting."

"Dad told me once you could have been rich—but you kept wandering around looking for the really big strike," Dan said.

"Yep, he had me right," Joe admitted. "Like about a thousand other prospectors, I reckon. I should have stayed home and been with my family like you boys—but I was too fiddle-footed for that."

"How is your family, Joe?" Mark inquired.

"Lost Mary, my wife, two years ago," Joe said abruptly. "I was off in Nevada on a fool prospecting trip. The kids had to bear it all alone." He shook his head sadly. "Got four kids—and Mary had to just about raise them all alone. I wasn't much of a husband or a dad."

Cass had been listening avidly to all this—as had they all. Clearing his throat, he said, "Uncle Joe, did you ever hit a big strike?"

"Not yet, boy—but I will!" Joe grinned at the expressions of doubt on every face. "That's the way it is with men like me. Gold fever don't never let up. I'm sixty-eight years old, but when the news of the next big strike comes—I'll be part of the stampede, you bet!"

"What if there's not another big strike?" Aaron asked, leaning forward, his eyes intent on the old man. It was like seeing a resurrection of sorts. "Maybe there won't be another strike."

"Always another strike, Aaron," Joe said firmly. He peered at the young people who were watching him intently and shook his head. "Don't want to think about it. Mark, you remember Dad talking about old Horace Orwell, the man who lived outside Portland?"

"Why, sure I do."

"I met him once on the way to town on a Saturday afternoon. When I asked him what he was up to, he said, 'Going to town to get drunk—and do I dread it!' " Joe waited until the laughter died down, then said, "Reckon that's the way I feel about huntin' for gold. I can't stay away from it—but it's brought me nothing but grief and disappointment."

"Well, it's time to eat," Mark said. "But first we have to get some photographs of this family. Are you ready, Mr. Catton?"

"Ready, sir!" A man in a long white cloak had entered the large room, and at once he began directing the session. The family was blinded as periodic flashes of powder illuminated the room, and the air was filled with the giggles of the younger people, who loved it all.

Finally Catton said, "Now, we need one good shot of the older folks."

"All *six* of us," Mark grinned, taking Joe firmly by the arm. "Come along you 'older' folks."

The photographer arranged them carefully, seating the four men, with Pet and Belle standing stiffly beside them. "Hold it—!" The flash exploded and Joe blinked and said, "Well, now, I sure didn't mean to add my mangy old carcass to the picture making."

But Belle patted his arm fondly. "Who knows, Joe? When our great-great-grandchildren see this picture, you may be the one they point out." She smiled, adding, "They may say, 'That's Joe Winslow—he made the big strike when he was in his sixties!' "

Joe patted her arm and smiled. "Don't know about that, Belle, but I know Davis hit gold when he found you!"

Across the room Ruth, the daughter of Tom and Faith, had

drawn Priscilla and Esther aside. "This is so much fun," she said. "I wish we didn't all live so far apart. It's nice to have family near—and we're all split up, scattered all over the country."

"Why don't you come to New York for a visit, Ruth?" said Esther at once. "And you, too, Priscilla. I could show you the city. Why, we could have a wonderful time together."

"And then you could come out west to visit us," Ruth broke in. "We could teach you to ride and shoot just like a real cowgirl!"

The three excitedly made plans, then they all proceeded to besiege their parents with pleas to let them have a visit. When there seemed to be no objection, Esther smiled. "I'm going to buy a pair of divided skirts tomorrow—and you two will have to buy fancy ball dresses."

Mark later said to Dan and Tom, "It'd be a good thing if those three did get together. Let's work on it."

★   ★   ★   ★

Christmas came, with mountains of food, colorfully wrapped presents, a tree decorated with strung popcorn and candles, a taffy pull, and lots of singing.

"I wish it didn't have to end," Cass said to Aaron a few days before he and his family were scheduled to leave. The two had been joined by Jubal, and they all dreaded going back to their routines. "I'd just as soon get thrown in jail than go back to looking at the backsides of beef critters!" Cass moaned.

Aaron eyed his cousin speculatively. "Then don't go back," he said matter-of-factly.

"Why—I *have* to, Aaron!"

"I've been thinking about you a lot, Cass. You and I are a lot alike. I had to leave my home—and you can do the same."

"And do what?"

"Hit Uncle Mark up for a job," Aaron shot back. "I'm surprised you didn't think of it yourself. He's vice-president of the Union Pacific. They hire people all the time."

"Sure, Cass," Jubal nodded. He frowned and then sighed. "I get so tired of divinity school, I think sometimes I'd rather lay track! Looks like a man could be a preacher without learning Greek. How many Greeks am I likely to meet?"

"Why—I *could* do that," Cass said slowly. "Must be *something* I could do for the railroad."

"Sure—and Uncle Mark likes you," Aaron said. "Even if he didn't, he'd do it for your dad. He thinks Dan Winslow is the finest man there is—except maybe for Tom. Why, he even offered me a job, but I didn't take it."

"Why not?"

"Oh, I didn't want to make a mess with Mom's brother. But you can bet he'll give you a fair chance."

"Well, I guess I'll try it—but I'd rather go hunt gold with Uncle Joe."

Aaron grinned, for all three of them were taken with the old man. "Me, too—but he said himself that hunting for gold is for idiots."

"Guess I might qualify, then," Cass grinned faintly. "But he's had a full life, hasn't he? I'd rather hear him tell his tales of the gold camps than eat."

"Sure, he's had some great times—but now he's old and worn out. And broke, too, I guess." Aaron lifted his eyebrows, adding, "Get the money, Cass, then you can buy all the fun you want."

"No, that's not right," Jubal spoke up instantly. "You know better than that, Aaron." He had grown fond of this tall relative of his and hated to hear him talk like that.

"Doesn't sound like you got that from your father, Aaron. He doesn't believe that," said Cass.

"No, I didn't." Aaron spoke curtly, and Cass realized that he didn't want to talk about his family. "Go see Uncle Mark, Cass. Maybe you'll get a job close to me and we can see each other often."

"Those girls have been pestering the folks to let them visit. Don't see why we can't do the same," Jubal said. "I'd like an excuse to cut loose from college and run around the country for a while."

"If we find any adventure, Jubal," Aaron smiled, "you'll get a slice of it."

With the holidays coming to an end, Cass knew his parents would be anxious to get back to the ranch, so he wasted no time. That same day he cornered his uncle and when they were alone said, "Uncle Mark, I want a job."

"Why, I thought you'd want to stay on the ranch, Cass." Mark actually was aware of the young man's unhappiness because Dan had told him of it more than once. He'd even offered to help Cass, but Dan had been hesitant, asking him to wait.

"I'm not a rancher, Uncle Mark," Cass said. He stood before his uncle, a sturdy six feet with tawny hair and blue-green eyes. There was a stubbornness in the set of his jaw, and now he made his case. "Oh, I can do the work—but I don't *like* it—not like Dad and Peter do. I—I know I sound like an ingrate, but don't you think some men are cut out for something different?"

"Yes, I agree with that. Seen too many men make the mistake of trying to force their sons into their own mold." Mark studied the boy, then asked, "What sort of job do you think you could handle, Cass?"

"Why, I don't know, sir," Cass shrugged. "I'm strong and I'm pretty good with books. Dad wanted me to go to college—and I guess I should have taken his advice and gone. But I'll work hard if you'll give me a chance."

"Of course I'll help you, Cass," Mark said at once. "We can always use a good man. But you'll have to talk to your parents. I couldn't do anything without their consent."

"I'll talk to them right now, Uncle Mark!"

Actually Dan and Hope were not too surprised by Cass's request, for they had been expecting this willful son of theirs to leave the ranch sooner or later. He was a stubborn young man, and once he set his mind, he usually got his own way. They put him off at first, but after a long talk with Mark, Dan said to Hope, "I think it's best to let him have a go at it. He's set on it, and I know Mark will do his best for him."

"I know you're right, Dan," Hope answered. "Maybe after a while he'll find ranching isn't so bad. Let the world rough him up a bit, and I pray he'll come back to us."

When they told Cass that he had their permission, he almost exploded with excitement. "I'll do fine—you'll see!" he promised them. "I—I know I haven't been a good son, but now I'll put my whole heart in this job for Uncle Mark!"

The next day Cass left with Mark and his family, headed for New York. After he was gone, Dan and Hope walked slowly around the big white house. They were sobered by Cass's decision, but Hope said, "When Laurie left home, Tom and Faith were just as worried as we are. But look how well that turned out. She found our Cody and they are as happy as any couple can be."

Dan turned to her, putting his big hands on her shoulders. "You'd find something encouraging to say if the world were burning up, wouldn't you?" He pulled her close and the two clung to each other. "Know what I thought when I saw you the first time?"

"No. What did you think?"

"I thought you were the best-looking woman I'd ever seen."

"Know what I thought when I first saw you?"

"You thought, *That's the best-looking man I ever saw!*"

"Oh, no I didn't," she corrected him. "I thought, *That's the most stubborn man I ever laid eyes on! He'd make a woman miserable!*" Then she pulled his head down and kissed him firmly. "And I was right, too!"

"That I'd make you miserable?"

"No, that you're the stubbornest man alive!"

Dan laughed, then the two turned and walked hand in hand toward the house. "You've been real good for me, Hope. Just like your name." For a few moments Dan didn't say any more, but when they reached the house, he said, "We'll have to pray for Cass, won't we?"

"Yes. He's never been alone—this will be his first time away. And he's got the wrong idea that money will bring happiness. I don't know where he got it, but it's there."

"God may have to shake him some to set him straight—but we'll see him serving the Lord one day. I've got His promise on that!"

CHAPTER THREE

NEW YORK

★ ★ ★ ★

From the time Cass Winslow arrived in New York, he was dazzled by the size and splendor of the city. After the endless horizon of the empty plains of Wyoming, he was stunned by the furious activity of the metropolis.

A few days after the trip back from Richmond, Mark and Cass were sitting in the parlor talking before dinner one night.

"Sure is a lot to see here, Uncle Mark," said Cass.

"Well, we're glad to have you here. And Lola and I would like you to stay with us—"

"I appreciate your offer," interrupted Cass, "but a man has to make his own way. I don't want to take advantage of your hospitality. I need to find a place of my own to start."

Mark tried to press the issue but could tell Cass felt awkward about his offer to stay with them. "Well, you know you're welcome here anytime," said Mark as he stood up.

"Thanks, Uncle Mark."

"Let's go on into the dining room. Your aunt has quite a meal waiting for us."

Later that night when Lola and Mark were in their room getting ready to retire, Lola said, "Mark, I'm a little worried about this arrangement. Do you think it's wise to let Cass make his own way? He could stay here with us. We've got plenty of room."

"I thought as much, but when I mentioned it to Cass, I could tell he was embarrassed. It would be a little uncomfortable, I suppose, living under the stern eye of your boss. He'll be all right. I'll have Andy show him around and check on him from time to time. I gave him an advance so he'd have a little cash. He'll be fine."

The next day Mark Winslow took the day off from his busy schedule and helped Cass settle in. He'd taken Cass to a rooming house, obtained a room for him, then said, "Go exploring for a few days, Cass, see what's here. We'll put you to work after you've had time to look things over."

Cass could hardly wait for his uncle to leave, and as soon as possible, he left his room and began to explore his new world. He walked the streets for hours, stunned by the crowds that flooded the sidewalks. "Gosh, there's more people on *one* street here than there are in all of Wyoming!" he muttered.

He came to the East River, to the Brooklyn Bridge, and lifted his eyes to the huge cables that formed a mighty and intricate web, spanning the river. A cab driver who was leaning against his cab took in the young man's wide-eyed stare and said, "She's a hummer, ain't she now?"

"Sure is!"

The driver was a short, thickset man with an Irish brogue and a sharp gaze. "Aye, I don't think there's nothin' like her, sir. 'Tis the longest suspension bridge in the world." He gave a little speech informing Cass that the bridge was not big enough. "Already too small to carry the traffic. Couple of other bridges now— not as fancy as this one, begorra. Yer new to our fair city, I take it, sir?"

Flattered at being called "sir," Cass stood for a time talking with the cab driver, then invested a little cash in a ride around the city. The driver, whose name was quite euphonious—Mick McGonigal—kept up a running patter, pointing out all the sights. "Now that's the Flatiron building," he announced. "Twenty stories tall, she is!"

Cass craned his head to look upward at the rising skeleton of steel girders. Men were walking along the narrow strips of steel as carelessly as if they were wide sidewalks. "I wouldn't do that for a million dollars!" he exclaimed.

"You wouldn't? Aye, sir, I doubt that," McGonigal argued. "I'd do almost anything for a million dollars—and so would most men."

"Well, maybe I would," Cass grinned at the Irishman. "But I'll bet they don't get paid that much, those fellows up there." As they rode along Cass asked question after question, such as, "Where do all the people here get water? Back home we can take it out of a river—but I don't think I'd want to drink out of that river I just saw."

"Why, no, me boy, we got aqueducts!"

"You got—*what* kind of ducks?"

McGonigal stifled a laugh, saying, "Tunnels, I mean. They bring in three hundred million gallons of fresh water a day." He kept up his patter, and after a long drive pointed his whip. "There's something for you to see, now!"

Cass looked to his left and gasped as an ornate tower rose majestically above the skyline. It capped a huge structure that featured a walkway shielded by an endless series of graceful pillars spanned by arches. "What's *that*?" he asked.

"Madison Square Garden," his guide spoke proudly, waving his whip and pointing out the fine features as though it were his own possession. "The swells, they'll be having the Annual Horse Show this week. A box will cost you $35,000, sir. How many would you like?"

"For one place to sit?" Cass was scandalized. "None, I guess."

"Well, you might like to go up on the roof."

"The roof?"

"Oh, it's a grand sight. A garden with all sorts of plants." McGonigal turned and winked at his fare, a lewd smile on his face. "There's a statue of a young lady wearing no more than a grape! Oh, it caused quite a stink at first—preachers up in arms all over the city. Like to go for a look?"

"Well, I reckon not. I've got to write my mother telling her what all I've done—and I don't think she'd much relish hearing that."

The sun sank behind the facade of the tall buildings as they went along, the streets growing as dim as any canyon in Wyoming. Suddenly there was a blinding flash of light, so sudden that Cass gave a startled cry. "What's that!"

McGonigal laughed aloud. "No fear, sir—it's just them new-fangled 'lectric lights. Ain't they something, now?"

Cass blinked like an owl coming out of its hole into dazzling sunlight. "Why—you could read a book by those things!" He was so fascinated that he had the cabby drive around for an hour just to see them. The lights threw their beams on the walls of buildings so that he could read the signs urging people to vote for William Jennings Bryan for President. When he finally got out of the cab and paid the fare, he said, "Thanks for the tour, Mick. We'll do it again for sure!"

★ ★ ★ ★

For two days Cass explored New York, poking into the crowded tenement section of lower Manhattan, the most crowded spot on the face of the earth, with over one thousand people per acre. He was horrified by the verminous firetraps and the noise and stench of the place, and turned his attention elsewhere.

Wanting to please his uncle Mark and keep his promise to his folks, Cass threw himself into his work. He had been given the grueling task of keeping track of thousands of Union Pacific cars as they were shifted all over the country. "I know it's tiresome, Cass," Mark sympathized with him one day, "but anyone who goes up in the railroad business has to learn how the Union Pacific works."

"Sure, I understand," Cass had responded—and he had applied himself. But for a young man who had wandered over the wide plains of Wyoming, the crowded, stuffy office soon closed in on him like a prison. Day after day he stared at pages of numbers until his eyes ached, and within three weeks he was heartily sick of the job. To ease the boredom of it all, each day as soon as quitting time came, he began going out and throwing himself into the night life of the city.

It was Lola who first noticed his restlessness. One day when she had stopped by the railroad's offices, she said, "Well, Cass, how'd you like to see how the rich and famous live?"

"How's that, Aunt Lola?"

"I've got invitations to one of Mrs. Astor's balls tonight. Mark and I don't attend, but you might find it interesting."

"Who's Mrs. Astor?"

Lola laughed at him. "She'd be crushed to hear you never heard of her, Cass. She happens to be the wife of John Jacob Astor, the wealthiest man in the country. They have a huge house with a ballroom that seats four hundred guests—so the people who are invited are called 'The Four Hundred.' You ought to go. It'll be something to see, or so I'm told."

With the mounting dissatisfaction of his job, Cass was ready for something of this nature. "Sure, I'll take it in, Aunt Lola. Maybe I'll give the joint a little class!"

When he arrived at the ball that evening, an arrogant doorman stared at him with distaste, but Cass grinned and handed him the invitation. "I'll try not to brush up against Mrs. Astor," he joked, but the man simply glared at him.

Cass entered, and for the next two hours he watched the spectacle of wealthy people engaged in throwing as much of their money away as possible on the most mundane affair to be imagined. The ballroom was full of people, all dressed in some sort of costumes. Jewels glittered on the necks and fingers of the women, who wore brilliantly colored dresses—and the men's attire was just as outlandish. One man appeared in a suit of gold armor, which Cass heard was worth $10,000. Other courtly dancers tripped over their swords as they moved across the glossy dance floor.

"I like your costume." Cass had been watching the dancers, when a voice at his elbow brought him around. When he turned, he found himself facing a woman in her early twenties wearing a brilliant green dress, cut rather low. A necklace of green stones graced her smooth neck, and two huge diamonds winked and flashed from her earrings. "Where did you get such a realistic western outfit?" She eyed his gray trousers, cavalry-style shirt and high-heeled boots with interest.

"Why—it's not a costume," Cass said. "I didn't know this was a costume affair, so I just wore what I always wear."

"Really! Are you a cowboy?"

"Well, I have been—up until a few weeks ago." For the next

few moments, Cass found himself telling this attractive woman about his new life, then finally he shook his head. "I'm pretty out of place here, I reckon. My uncle is Mark Winslow—he's vice-president of the Union Pacific Railroad. I just came to see the show."

The woman laughed at his choice of words. "Well, my name is Lorraine Jennings. What's yours?"

"Cassidy Winslow—but everyone calls me Cass."

"Well, Cass," Lorraine said, taking his arm possessively, "you are going to dance with me—no argument!" She pulled him to the floor, and when he awkwardly put his arm around her, she said, "Now tell me, do you wear a gun and shoot people out west. . . ?"

The next two hours flashed by for Cass. He'd never met anyone like this young woman! She was fascinated by the West, so he elaborated on the romance of life on the range. She listened avidly and finally said, "Come along—I've got to show you off!"

"I'd just as soon not," Cass mumbled, but it was useless. Lorraine soon had gathered a group of younger people and had introduced Cass with fulsome praises. "He's a real cowboy from Wyoming—he didn't wear his gun tonight, but he does when he's riding the range. . . ."

Cass was soon swamped by questions, and as he answered them awkwardly, Nellie Follet whispered to Lorraine, "He's a dream, isn't he? Like one of Gibson's men!" Charles Dana Gibson's drawings of handsome, clean-cut young men and shapely young women were the rage. "He makes the other men look pretty pale and weak, doesn't he?" gushed Nellie.

Lorraine eyed Cass, taking in the tall, strong figure and the smooth, clean-cut jaw. His hair was an unusual tawny color and was longer than the eastern cut. He had deep-set eyes and high cheek bones, which with his strong chin and muscular neck made him look absolutely masculine. "You leave him alone, Nellie," Lorraine smiled, tapping her chin thoughtfully with one forefinger. "I have plans for Mr. Cassidy Winslow. . . !"

★　★　★　★

Once Cass had been caught in a stampede of wild cattle, an experience he never forgot. And the hectic pace of keeping up with Lorraine Jennings had some of that same frantic effort. Lorraine was the daughter of Simon Jennings, who had made his fortune in bicycles. Cass had seen pictures of this novel form of transportation, but was somewhat shocked at the craze that took hold in the city and throughout the nation. The pneumatic tire made the sport of cycling possible, and a million bicycles rolled out of Jennings' factory each year.

There seemed to be no end to the demand for bikes, and Diamond Jim Brady, financier and philanthropist, gave Lillian Russell, the famous singer known as "The American Beauty," a gold-plated, jewel-studded bicycle, and then bought a dozen gilded ones for himself. Bicycle races were organized, and famous stars, including the beautiful Anna Held and Eugene Sandow, "The Monarch of Muscle," promoted the two-wheelers.

"Maybe you could herd cattle on bicycles in Wyoming," Lorraine prompted Cass. "You could start a whole new form of cattle ranching." Cass had a ludicrous picture of punchers roping a thousand-pound steer from one of the fragile machines, and declined to become the western dealer for Jennings' bicycles.

Lorraine had nothing to do, and her prize "cowboy" brought her much attention. She delighted in showing Cass off, and practically every night for weeks, the two moved among New York night life socializing. They attended performances by Minnie Fiske, the fine tragedienne acting in the plays of Ibsen, and they rolled with laughter at the antics of Lew Fields and Joe Weber as the pair regaled music hall audiences. And at a performance of "The Girl I Left Behind Me," a drama about an Indian uprising, Lorraine quickly silenced Cass when he protested that the Indians he'd seen were nothing as ideal as the ones on stage.

Cass was captivated by the girl, and she was fascinated by his background. He fell promptly in love with her, despite warnings from both his uncle and his aunt. As for Lorraine, she enjoyed the novelty of the young westerner—and allowed him to kiss her and returned his kisses with an eagerness that deceived Cass.

One Saturday afternoon, Lorraine told Cass she wanted to show him Coney Island. It was a "slumming" expedition for Lorraine, who loved to see how the "lower classes" lived. She had actually forced Cass to take her to the tenement district once, where she had been shocked by the deplorable living conditions. But after having distributed money to some street children, she seemed to feel she had done her part to help alleviate the suffering of the less fortunate.

The pair rode a brilliantly lit trolley, and when they got to Coney Island, they went at once to Steeplechase Park, where they rode the Scenic Railway, the Giant See-Saw, and then settled down in a gondola in the Canals of Venice.

As the boat entered a long, dimly lit tunnel, Cass seized Lorraine and kissed her. She protested slightly but returned his kiss for kiss. She was soft and enticing in his arms, and he groaned, "Lorraine—I can't stand this! I love you so much! You've got to marry me."

"I know, dear, I know!" Lorraine held him tightly, then whispered, "Oh, Cass—you're such a dream! But what would we do? Papa would cut me off if I married a man out of our social standing."

The words took him by surprise. And as the gondola slowly emerged from the tunnel, Cass began to realize that these weeks with Lorraine had not meant to her what they had for him. He had never felt so taken with a woman as he had with Lorraine. Yet for her, Cass was something new and exciting that had crossed her dull social path, and she had been caught up in the moment of it. She had let her emotions run, yet deep inside knew the social boundaries she could never cross.

Yet Cass tormented himself in the fashion of young men. He had never thought of getting married in Wyoming, but something in the fairy-tale world that Lorraine inhabited seemed to dull his good sense. He well understood that people like the Jenningses were as far from his reach as the moon—but he could not tear himself away from her.

They wandered all afternoon along the boardwalk, past the bathing houses, dance halls, shooting galleries, freak shows, and eating houses, and Cass soon wearied of it.

At last they strolled down to the beach where women were elegantly garbed in bathing suits made with as much as ten yards of cloth. "I've got to get me a suit," Lorraine pouted. "But Papa would clap me up forever at home if he heard about it."

"Guess he won't hear about it if you don't tell him," Cass shrugged. He started to leave with her on his arm but found their way blocked by a pair of grinning young men, both tall and hulking. "Guess we need to get by," he said, his eyes narrowing.

"Aw, now, cowboy, where's your six-shooter," one of them replied. He reached over and seized Lorraine's arm, saying, "Sweetie, why don't you let your cowboy go play with his horsie? You can come with us—we'll show you a good time."

Cass's years on the range had honed his instincts about tough situations. He knew instantly that the two were out for trouble and acted at once. Planting his right foot, he drove his fist squarely into the grinning face of the loud man and was pleased to see him go down flat on his back. "Hey—" yelled the other man and threw himself at Cass. He was a big, muscular young fellow but had no fighting skills at all. Cass stood off and pounded him at will. The fight, however, had attracted several of the ruffians' friends. They came running up, and soon Cass was overpowered and knocked to the ground. If a policeman hadn't arrived almost at once, he'd have taken a bad beating, but the arrival of the law sent the bunch scurrying away.

"You hurt?" the policeman asked.

"No, but I was about to be—thanks for your help."

Cass had been in numerous fights, but for Lorraine it had been a traumatic experience. When they got back to the boardwalk, Cass found a cabbie and helped Lorraine in. She was pale and silent as they drove toward her house, and finally she said, "Cass, I was so frightened!"

"Why, it was just a fight, Lorraine," Cass grinned. "Been in lots worse out west."

She shook her head and said no more, and when she got out of the carriage, she was still silent.

"What's wrong?" Cass asked, standing before her.

Lorraine didn't quite know what was wrong. She had been carefully protected from the "masses," and the fight had opened her eyes. The world of Cass Winslow and of his "sort" had been fun to dabble in, but now she was ready to go back to her own. And she knew that she couldn't take him with her.

"Dear, Papa is taking us all for a long trip day after tomorrow.

This will have to be goodbye for a time."

Somehow Cass knew that she was lying. There was nothing in her face to tell him this, but he had learned something about her in the weeks they had spent together. She was speaking to him in the same tone she used for head waiters and other servants. Anger raced along his nerves and he suddenly reached out and kissed her roughly. His lips were demanding and she pulled away with a gasp, her eyes wide with alarm.

"I guess you're telling me you're tired of me," Cass said, an edge in his voice. "You throw your toys away when the new is gone, don't you?"

"Let me go!"

Cass considered her plea, then released her. He turned and walked stiffly away, ignoring her cry, "Cass—Cass!" His confusion and anger led him straight to a saloon, where he got thoroughly drunk.

The next morning he arrived at work late. He was pale and his hands trembled so violently that his supervisor, Mr. Vining, eyed him narrowly. Cass looked up at him so defiantly that the man walked away without a word but filed the incident in his mind. *He may be the nephew of the vice-president*, Vining thought, *but I'm the man he has to satisfy!*

★   ★   ★

A little after three, Cass's supervisor came to him. "Mr. Winslow wants to see you in his office—right away."

Cass stared at the small man, a bitter smile curling his lips. "Been doing a little talking, Mr. Vining?"

Robert Vining was small, but not without courage. He looked up into the eyes of the tall young man and said defiantly, "I got tired of covering up for you, Winslow. You're not doing your job— and it's my responsibility to point that out. I've tried to talk to you, but you haven't listened."

Cass stared down at Vining but felt no anger. "That's right. I've been pretty worthless. You should have tied a can to me long ago." He thought of the weeks that had passed since Lorraine had given him the brush-off and added, "Took some nerve for you to go to the boss about his nephew."

"Look, Cass, you'll get a hiding from Mr. Winslow—but I'm willing to try again. Tell him I said so—it might make a difference."

Cass was touched by the man's offer but shook his head. "That's decent of you, Mr. Vining—but we both know that I'm not cut out for this kind of work." He opened his desk drawer, pulled out a few things, and shoved them into his pockets. Then he stuck his hand out, and when Vining took it with surprise, Cass grinned. "Next time you're in Wyoming, stop by and I'll give you a free ride on a nice horse. So long—"

Cass then turned and walked out of the office. When he got to the end of the hallway, he stopped in front of the large door to his uncle's office. With a new resolve, he knocked.

"Come in."

Opening the door, Cass entered the ornately decorated room from which Mark Winslow managed the railroad. He came and stood in front of the large desk where his uncle was busy at work.

Without preamble, Cass said the same thing he had just told Vining. "I've had it with New York, Uncle Mark. It's a nice sideshow, but no place for a fellow like me."

Mark looked up from the pile of papers and shook his head regretfully. "This is my fault, Cass. I should have helped you more." He was worried about the thing and slapped his hands together in an abrupt, angry gesture. "Lola told me I should have spent more time with you—and looking at it, I see now that you need to be outside. You're like I was at your age—need to be active. Let's try again—"

"Thanks, Uncle Mark—but I've made up my mind about this." The corners of Cass's wide mouth were drawn down in a faint scowl, but he managed to laugh slightly. "I'll tell Dad you did your best—but I've got to get away from here."

"There's more to it than the job, isn't there?" Mark shot the question suddenly. "It's that young woman—Lorraine. She hurt you pretty bad, I guess."

But Cass refused to answer directly. "Let's not get into all that, Uncle Mark. I—I've just got to have some time. I wish now I'd spent more time with you and Aunt Lola and Andy and Esther. Maybe I'll come back—when I grow up!"

Mark tried to reason with Cass but two days later found himself putting Cass on a train bound for Wyoming. Mark was in a gloomy mood when he got back home, and he threw himself into a chair. "Well, I made a proper hash of that, Lola!"

"It wasn't your fault, not altogether." Lola came to stroke his hair, sitting down on the arm of his chair. "I should have been more thoughtful—we both handled it badly."

"I hope Dan and Hope will understand." Mark shook his head doubtfully. "Wouldn't blame them if they got upset with me."

"He's young. You were probably like him when you were eighteen."

"I was in a shooting war with Robert E. Lee when I was not much more than twenty," Mark replied. He took her hand and forced a smile. "Marse Robert didn't allow much foolishness from us—and then after the war I got you—and you didn't allow *any* a'tall!"

She leaned down and kissed him lightly, then stood up. "I think of Barney—how he almost threw his life away when he was in prizefighting. I—I hoped we could have kept Cass from making that same mistake."

Mark stood and took her in his arms. He knew she was worried about their nephew. "Barney came out of it. And Cass, he'll find himself. It's tough to be young, but nobody can do it for you." After a moment's silence, he added, "He'll be all right when he gets back to the ranch with his family. . . ."

It wasn't until weeks later that Mark and Lola discovered that Cass never made it to Wyoming. He had dreaded the thought of going back, defeated—and at some point on the trip west, he made a decision.

I'll go to the coast, he decided. *Lots of opportunities for a young man there. Maybe I'll run into Uncle Joe—*

Impulsively, he bought a ticket for San Francisco and a few days later stepped off the train filled with a new determination to make his life a success. "There's big money here—and I've got to find a way to get it! No matter what my folks say—it's money that makes the world go round."

He was not quite so young as to imagine that he would make his fortune and go back to make Lorraine Jennings understand that Cass Winslow was not a man to tamper with—but his desire for riches was the most vital thing in his soul as he stepped on the soil of the West Coast for the first time.

"I'll make a pile—or die!" he said grimly, then turned and walked away from the huffing locomotive toward his future.

CHAPTER FOUR

AN ALLEY IN SEATTLE

★ ★ ★ ★

San Francisco was a fascinating city in the year 1897—perhaps too much so for Cass Winslow. He found a room and, as he had done in New York, took a few days to get the feel of the town. He saw at once that he was more fitted to the spirit of San Francisco than he had been to New York. The East had given him a cramped feeling, but in the first day he sensed there was a raw freedom to be found in San Francisco.

As he roamed around the harbor, where a forest of tall masts rose from all the anchored vessels, he thought of shipping out on one of the sailing ships. The lure of exploring distant lands around the globe was strong, and he even went so far as to talk to some of the bronzed sailors about signing on. One of them, a hulking Swede, eyed him with frosty humor and told him bluntly, "The sea ain't for most people, sonny. It's a hard life, and make no mistake! Plenty of bad food and low pay—and dangerous. Many a shipmate of mine is cradled in the deep. Better get a safe job ashore."

"But I'd like to see the world," Cass argued.

The Swede laughed and downed his beer. "Get rich, sonny, then go first class!"

Cass cast a rueful grin at the sailor. "I just tried that in New York. It didn't work out too well." He downed the rest of his beer, then stared at a huge schooner. "Being a sailor can't be much worse than punching cows—there's got to be something better than that!"

"I just know the sea—and I'll never live on land," the burly Swede answered slowly. He lifted his eyes and gazed at Cass with a sense of fatality in his pale blue eyes. "Man's got to die—and he's got to eat dirt until he does." Then he laughed roughly and drank off the rest of his beer. Wiping his lips with his sleeve, he shrugged his massive shoulders. "Maybe you ought to go prospecting. A few got rich back in forty-nine. Most of 'em didn't, though—most of the old sourdoughs died sick and broke."

Cass left the saloon and wandered along the docks. The words of the sailor seemed to lodge in his mind, and he thought of Joe Winslow. *He's tried all his life to get rich—and never made it.* But there was a youthful exuberance in him, brought on by the fresh sea air. He turned from the harbor and decided to spend the day roaming the city. The fact that it was built on a hill fascinated him, and when his legs grew tired, he got into a cab, ordering the driver to give him a tour of the city, especially where the wealthy lived.

"Show you where the nabobs live, sir?" the driver grinned. "There are some houses here that'd put Solomon's temple to shame! Seems like some of them who hit it rich can't find ways quick enough to spend their money!"

Cass spent the rest of the day riding down streets lined with elaborate mansions, all erected as a testimony to the power of wealth. Just seeing them seemed to fuel his dream for success. Finally, as the sun dipped low over the harbor, he ordered the cabbie to take him back to where he was staying.

After Cass paid his fare, he stepped out of the carriage and went straight to his room. He sponged off in the basin on the nightstand and then went to bed. For a time he lay there, listening to the sounds from the street below as they floated up. From far away the hoarse bellow of a foghorn laid its rough voice on the night—a sound that was somehow foreboding to Cass. He tossed in bed for a time, but sleep seemed to have fled. Finally he rose and went to stand beside the window, looking down at the amber lights that traced the streets meandering down to the harbor.

The salt tang of the sea breeze was refreshing, and he thought of the days in Wyoming when he'd followed herds, breathing the dust-laden air that had lined his nostrils and coated his lips and throat. Again he thought of going to sea, but he remembered the sailor's words and knew that such a life was not for him. Leaning out of the window, he let his eyes rest on the flickering reflection of the stars on the sea. They seemed to wink at him, tiny diamond-bright specks on the dark blue mass of water that stretched out before him.

A restlessness welled up inside him, and his lips tightened as he thought, *I've got to find my way! I can't spend the rest of my life trying on jobs like a man tries on a coat!* He blinked angrily and ran over in his mind the time he'd spent in New York—and the image of Lorraine Jennings came to him. For an instant he could almost smell her perfume and sense the satin of her cheek! Then he swung away from the window and threw himself on the bed, a rash streak sweeping over him at the memory.

"I'll get the money—and then we'll see!" he muttered into the darkness. "Somehow I've got to get rich!" For a long time he lay there wrestling with his thoughts and finally drifted off into a troubled sleep, dreaming of Lorraine—and of a life filled with riches.

★　★　★　★

The mountain of dirty dishes that rose before him seemed to mock Cass. Earl Browder, the ill-natured owner of the Gay Paree Hotel, made things worse. "You takin' a vacation, Winslow? Get them dishes washed—and fast!"

Cass gritted his teeth, longing to sweep the dishes to the floor with a magnificent crash—but he decided against it. He was flat broke and needed this job even though he hated it. "Yes, sir," he muttered and began to scrape the leftover food from a plate into a five-gallon can. He had always thought that range work was the worst sort of labor, but two weeks of washing dishes had changed his mind. Plunging the dish into the steaming water before him, he muttered, "I'd rather herd cattle anytime than be a pearl diver!"

Around him rose the continual babble of voices, highly flavored with the shrill tones of the Chinese cooks. The smell of the kitchen turned his stomach, and he remembered how on his first day on the job, he'd been forced to escape into the alley and vomit. Sweat ran down his face, caused by the unbearable heat. The wood-burning stoves glowed with a fierce heat, and the steaming water he was forced to plunge his hands into blinded him.

From his right a voice broke into his misery. "How'd you like a nice walk along the beach, Cass? A little fresh air?"

The speaker was a short, thickset man of thirty with dark brown eyes and a thatch of black hair that fell over his forehead. The sound of old Ireland filled the man's voice, and he grinned at the misery on Cass's face. "And a nice pitcher of cold beer? Faith, that would set you up!"

Cass gave the speaker an annoyed glance. "Shut up, Mike," he groaned. "This is bad enough without you making it worse."

Michael Rooney was scrubbing at a blackened pot with a lackadaisical motion. He had arrived two days earlier and had become an irritating factor to Cass from the start. There was a cheerful quality about the Irishman, despite his obvious poverty, and Cass soon grew weary of his optimistic remarks. Rooney held the pot up as if it were a polished jewel, examined it carefully, then plunged it back into the steamy water and began scrubbing it again.

"I'll tell you what would be worse, me boy," Rooney said. "To be in Ireland digging spuds—now *that* would be worse!"

"I don't see how." Cass tried to ignore the irrepressible comments from Rooney as he washed pile after pile of dishes. Finally there came a break in the dull routine. He left the kitchen and stepped out into the alley for a breath of fresh air. But he found Rooney beside him and sighed as the Irishman lit up a pipe. "I don't see how you can be so blasted happy—washing dishes for pennies!"

Rooney sent a wreath of smoke spiraling into the air as he regarded his companion. He was a curious man by nature and had managed to ferret out most of Cass's background. Cass had made the mistake of telling him how he'd left the ranch to get rich, and there was a teasing note in Rooney's voice as he said, "You picked a bad time, me boy, to try to make your fortune. You're too late for the gold rush—and too early for the next thing that draws men to a fortune."

"And what will that be, Mike?" Cass asked wearily.

"Oh, we'll know it when it gets here," Mike said airily. "But now's the wrong time to get rich."

"How do you figure that?"

Rooney was a sharp-witted fellow. He had little education, but he was clever and read more than most. And he had the ability to take what he read and transform the bits and pieces into a rough sort of philosophy. He loved to talk and now leaned back and began to expand on the political and social factors that were shaping America.

✗ "They call these times 'The Gay Nineties'—and I guess there's lots goin' on, Cass. We got Buffalo Bill to entertain us with his wild Indians. We got Mark Twain to make us laugh with his witty stories. We got the Gibson girl to look at—not to mention Lillian Russell and Little Egypt." Rooney leered at Cass, winking broadly at the reference to the belly dancer who had become famous by maneuvering her anatomy in dances never seen before. Then he sobered and shook his head. "But it's not the good time that people want to believe, not in a million years!"

Cass stared at Rooney in surprise. It was unlike him to make such pessimistic statements. "What's wrong with you, Mike? This pearl diving getting you down?"

"I've done worse," Rooney shrugged. "But I'm telling you this ain't no gay nineties, Cass. The rich are getting richer and the poor are gettin' poorer. We got a few millionaires here and there, and the rest of the country is full of paupers. Why, this morning in the paper—right on the front page—there was a story about a rich girl who committed suicide. And just below that was another story about a poor girl who starved to death in a tenement!"

"I guess things have always been like that, Mike."

"Sure, but we're in the worst depression anyone can remember," Rooney said stubbornly. "There ain't enough work—which you ought to know, Cass. You never thought you'd wind up washing dishes in a third-rate restaurant, did you?"

Cass glared at Rooney, muttering, "I'm getting out of here, Mike!"

"And goin' where?" Rooney demanded. "Back to the cows in Wyoming?"

"No!"

"Where then? There's no work back East."

It was a question Cass had asked himself almost constantly since he had arrived in San Francisco. His small store of cash had quickly vanished, and he'd found no suitable work. The job at the Gay Paree was hateful, but he'd been hungry and desperate. He'd given up his room, sold his clothes, and was now reduced to a rickety bed for twenty-five cents a night in a dilapidated rooming house. He had thought longingly of the clean room that had been his in Wyoming, and of his mother's good cooking—but pride ran strong in him. He would never go home, he'd pledged himself doggedly—not until he'd made his fortune!

"You two—get back to work!"

Browder burst out of the door, a scowl on his broad face. He was a big man who took pleasure in bullying his employees. "I don't pay you for gabbin'! Now get back to those dishes—it's all you two are good for!"

Cass might have let the insult pass—but Browder made the mistake of shoving him roughly. Anger flared up in Cass instantly, and he turned to face the big man. "I don't need any help," he said evenly.

Earl Browder was the sort of man who had to prove his toughness. He had beaten one young man badly two days after Cass had started work, and now a look of gray pleasure crossed his face. "Cowboy, you ain't out on the range now! Get inside—" As he spoke Browder seized Cass's arm and swung him around.

Cass went with the pressure, and as he came around he gave Browder a chopping blow in the throat. Instantly Browder began choking and wheezing. Cass stood back and waited, and as soon as the big man got his breath, he said, "I don't let any two-bit hotel owner push me around. Pay me off!"

"I'll pay you off!" Browder yelled and threw himself toward Cass. But Mike Rooney stuck his foot out, and when the owner fell sprawling, he calmly kicked him in the head. The blow made a *clunking* sound, and Rooney observed, "I think we'd best not wait for our pay, Cass. Let's go."

The sudden and casual violence of Rooney's act took Cass by surprise. He looked down at the figure of Browder apprehensively, but Rooney laughed harshly. "He'll be okay. If I'd kicked him anyplace except his head, it might have hurt him. But he's got a head like a billiard ball." He stooped down and rolled the still figure over, then plucked a leather wallet out of Browder's inner coat pocket. Opening it, he extracted several bills, put the rest back, then replaced the wallet.

"You can't rob him, Mike!"

"Just taking what he owes us." Rooney handed half the bills to Cass, then added, "We'll have to get out of town. He'll have the police on us for sure. Let's get our stuff."

"Where will we go?" Cass asked as the two walked out of the alley.

"Wherever the first ship out is heading for—that's where we'll go."

Four hours later they were standing on the rail of the *Jennie Ware*, a small freighter bound for Alaska, but due to touch in at Seattle on the way. The captain had agreed to give them passage for a small fee, and as San Francisco faded into the fog, Rooney slapped Cass on the back. "Well, me boy, maybe it'll be Seattle where you'll make this fortune you're so greedy for."

"I wish you'd go with me, Mike."

"Well, now, I've always wanted to see them mountains of ice— so I'll take a quick look at Alaska. Maybe then I'll come back and settle in Seattle."

Cass watched as the fog closed in, then he turned to face Rooney. "You don't want to get rich, Mike?"

"Vanity, vanity, all is vanity," Rooney shook his head. "Gold is yellow, all right, but you can't spread it on bread like butter. Did ye never hear the story of the poor fellow who got some magic so that everything he touched turned to gold?"

"No, but I wouldn't mind having a touch of that kind of magic!"

"Why, it'd do you no good, Cass! You couldn't enjoy a gold steak—and what good would a gold woman be? Give me something warm and soft!"

Cass dropped his head and stared down at the deck as the sting of a memory suddenly surfaced. The foghorn bellowed, drowning out the slapping of the waves against the sides of the boat. When the horn finally faded, Cass grinned roughly at his friend.

"I'll take a hard golden woman anytime, Mike. You could always melt her down and get the cash!"

★ ★ ★ ★

The day the *Jennie Ware* sailed into Seattle the sky was gray with rain clouds, and a slight drizzle was falling. Cass and Mike stood on the deck watching the busy stevedores on the docks as the crew cast the anchor.

Seattle clung to the side of a steep cliff as had San Francisco. But it didn't take long for Cass to discover that there were few other similarities. The weather, for one thing, was completely different. For the first month he lived there, it rained every day. It was never a downpour, but he walked around in a never-ending drizzle, so that even when he was inside he never felt completely dry.

"We had a drought here last year," one of the original citizens nodded confidentially when Cass complained. "Yep, it lasted almost the whole day!"

Cass, accustomed to the hot sun of Wyoming, caught a cold almost immediately and could not shake it off. Along with it came a raspy cough that made his chest so sore he felt as though he were torn in two every time one of the terrible spasms wracked his body.

He had managed to find a job loading freight on ships, but the competition was stiff. Every morning he would go down to the dock where the dockmasters chose men for the work. Sometimes Cass got chosen, but more often than not the jobs went to friends of the boss. He quickly discovered that the way to get hired was to stick a slip of paper in one's hatband. This was the token that a man was willing to pay a kickback to the foreman. It grated on his nerves, and for several days he refused to bow to the custom. But his money was almost gone, and finally he put the slip in his hat and was chosen at once.

The work was hard, especially when he was assigned to work in the dark holds of the ships. Down in the stygian darkness, he worked long hours struggling with the cargoes. Sometimes it meant wrestling with the fresh-cut beams from sawmills, which were all sticky with gum and sap. After a few grueling hours, his hands had become raw, and his lungs were chilled with the damp, stuffy air of the hold. Other cargoes were even worse, but he had no other choice.

After work one night, he left the ship with his pay in his pocket, tired to the bone. His steps dragged as he moved along the string of saloons that lined Skid Row. It got its name back in the early days when loggers had skidded the huge logs down to the sea at this spot. The town had grown up around them, and now the street was lined with brothels, saloons, gambling halls, and cheap rooming houses.

Cass ignored the cries of the shills who stood outside the saloons calling, "Come on, give us a bet!" He had no cash to spare. He was barely making enough for his room and board, so he ignored them and slowly made his way along the muddy street, his head down with fatigue.

He had found a boardinghouse several blocks from the main part of town, rough and unpleasant, but cheap. The owner, a small man with a ferocious beard, provided better meals than most, and at least the bed was free of bedbugs.

Entering the house, Cass nodded politely at the wife of the owner, a tired-looking woman with gray hair. "Hello, Mrs. Tatum," he mumbled.

"Supper's almost ready."

"I'll wash up." Cass went out on the back porch and stared down at the single pan used by the other nine boarders. It was ringed with grime, so he chose to wash directly under the pump. The water was cold and the raspy bar of lye soap gave forth little lather. He had not shaved in three days and felt dirty as he always did when he failed to shave. Turning to the towels hanging limply from nails driven into the wall, he started at their condition, then did his best with his shirt and filthy handkerchief.

The table was filled when he went to the dining room, and several of the men nodded to him, while others ignored him. It was not a friendly bunch, but Cass was so tired he didn't care. He filled his plate with beef stew and greens, topped off with a huge chunk of corn bread. To wash it down he had a mug of thin milk. But he ate little because his head was hurting and his lungs had a tight feeling.

He carried his plate and mug to the kitchen, tossed them in the dishpan filled with warm soapy water, then climbed the stairs to his room. Stripping off his clothes except for his underwear, he lay down on his cot and closed his eyes. The headache pounded like a white-hot spike being driven from temple to temple, and soon he started coughing.

"Must be coming down with something. . . ." he muttered, dreading the thought of another wakeful night. He hadn't slept well for two nights and now he felt worse. The three men who had cots in the room came in later, waking him, so he got up and got a drink of tepid water.

"Feeling bad, Winslow?" Felix Myers asked. "Heard there was cholera going around. You better not have that. They say it's mighty contagious."

"Just a cold, I guess. Nothing to worry about."

But the next morning, Cass could hardly get out of bed. The headache was worse, and his bones ached. *Worse than getting piled by a bronc,* he thought, his mind cloudy from the bad night's sleep. He forced himself out bed, donned his dirty clothes, and went down to breakfast. But he had no appetite, so he rose and left the table after a few bites.

"Can't load lumber on a breakfast like that, Winslow," Felix warned. "Better go see a doctor."

But there was no money for a doctor or for medicine, so Cass slowly made his way to the docks. With the slip in his hat, he got the job, but by ten o'clock knew he couldn't make it. "Sick——" he muttered to the foreman. "Got to lie down. . . ."

"Well, be gone with you, and don't come back until you're able to work!"

For the next three days, Cass stayed in bed, managing to eat a little, but his fever raged dangerously high. On the third day, the owner came and demanded the rent. When Cass confessed he didn't have it, Tatum cleared his throat. "Don't mean to be hard— but I'm not running a hospital, Winslow. Some of the men are complaining—'fraid they'll catch whatever it is you got. Gonna have to ask you to move on."

Cass stared at him but could see it was useless to argue. "All right," he said wearily. He threw his pitifully small store of belongings into a sack and left the house. His knees were weak and his head hurt so badly he had to make an attempt to focus his eyes. After inquiring around, he found a place to stay for two nights, but then his money was completely gone and he had to leave there too.

He slept the next night in a stable, but the owner told him to move on in the morning. He had had little to eat and was light-headed and moved only with extreme effort. When dark fell, Cass stumbled into an alley, lay down, and fell into a comalike sleep. He dreamed wildly, nightmarish visions intermingled with pleasant dreams of home and family.

His fever came back, and when the sun cast its rays across the harbor in the morning, he tried to get up but fell against the wall, sprawling helplessly. His mouth was dry and the pain in his head blotted out all thought. He thought he was dying, but somehow it didn't seem to matter much.

"Well, now, young fellow—what's this?"

Cass felt hands on his forehead and managed to open his eyes a little. He saw a blur of a face and managed to whisper, "I'm—sick!"

"I'd say so. Now, let me give you a hand. . . ."

Cass tried to stand and almost cried out with the pain in his joints. He had no strength left in his weary body, and as he sank back to the ground, the calm voice said, "I'll get some help. You can't lay out here like this."

Cass tried to answer, but he was unable to frame the words. He was vaguely aware of the voice, and the next thing he knew, he felt strong hands lifting him. Then everything went black as he slid into a pool of darkness.

★　★　★　★

A strong light caused him to awake, slowly lifting him out of confused darkness. He shut his eyes and rolled his head to one side to avoid the glare.

"Well, now, you've decided to live, have you?"

Opening his eyes cautiously, Cass saw a man sitting beside him. He tried to speak, but his lips were dry. "Water—please!"

"Shore—now, guess you can drink out of a cup this time." The man poured water from a pitcher into a cup, then turned back to the bed. "Be better if you sit up—won't spill so much that way."

The water was tepid, but Cass had never tasted anything better. "Thanks," he muttered after draining the cup three times. His thirst quenched, he lay back and looked around the room. "This your place?" he whispered.

"Shore. My name's Fletcher Stevens—but folks call me Fletch." He was a dark-skinned man with gray hair and dark blue eyes. He wore a tattered denim shirt and a pair of equally shabby trousers held up by black suspenders. "I was getting a mite worried about you, Winslow."

"You know me?"

"Found your name on a letter in your stuff. You got any people close?" When Cass shook his head, Stevens leaned forward and felt Cass's forehead. "No fever. Guess you're going to live."

"How long have I been here?"

"Let's see—three days, I make it."

Cass was feeling stronger. His pounding headache was gone, and he slowly sat up in the bed. "You make a living taking care of sick men?"

Fletch grinned. "I guess I make as much at that as I do at anything else. You hungry?"

"I could eat a whole cow!" Cass was suddenly aware that he was ravenous. "But I've got no money—as you know."

"Won't break me—a few eggs and biscuits."

Twenty minutes later Cass finished the last of his meal, sopping white gravy with a morsel of a biscuit. He washed it down with a few swallows of milk, then sighed. "Never was so hungry in my life!" He was sitting at a table across from Stevens and now gave his host a curious look. "You take in many like me, Fletch?"

Stevens grinned rather shyly. "Don't fall over many men in your shape, Cass."

"I owe you something—I think I'd have died if you hadn't taken me in."

Fletch shook his head, saying at once, "You'd do the same for me, I reckon."

"Maybe so—but you didn't know that when you picked me out of the alley."

"Don't always have time to get a fellow's references," Fletch shrugged. "Don't worry about it, Cass." He began to clear the table, and asked casually, "You're not from these parts?"

Fletch finished the dishes, poured two cups of coffee, then sat down and listened. Cass leaned back and gave a brief history of the past few months. When Cass was finished, Stevens shrugged. "Hope you make that fortune, Cass."

"When I was going under—in the alley—I didn't think too much about that. I just wanted to stay alive." Taking a swallow of the coffee, Cass studied the features of the man who'd rescued him. Fletcher Stevens had been a handsome man at one time— was still not bad looking. He had patrician features, including high cheekbones and a long English nose. There was a gentleness in his blue eyes, but his features somehow had a vulnerability that Cass couldn't pin down. *He looks like he's been hurt pretty bad—and never got over it,* he thought to himself.

"How about you, Fletch? Do you have a family?"

Stevens at once looked down at his hands. "Did once," he said quietly. Then he got up and pulled his coat from a hook on the wall. "Going to get some fresh grub. Won't be too long."

When Stevens was out of the room, Cass thought about the abruptness of the man's response.

"Somebody's left their hoof prints all over him," he said out loud. "He's not crying about it—but he's hurt pretty bad." He rose to his feet, waited until the dizziness subsided, then thought, *Maybe I can do something for Fletch. I owe him a lot.*

CHAPTER FIVE

GOLD FEVER

★ ★ ★ ★

The razor-keen double-bitted ax cut into the thick base of the towering spruce. Cass yanked the ax back and saw a tremor run through the huge evergreen. Instantly he whirled and ran yelling "Timber—!" as loudly as he could.

Reaching the safety of a clearing punctuated by broad stumps, he wheeled and watched as the spruce began to lean. There was something majestic in the fall of the giant trees, and he watched with awe as the massive tree picked up speed, moving ponderously at first, then hurtled downward. It struck with a force that rocked the earth, sending dust upward in clouds—then it settled down and lay still.

Cass moved forward to begin trimming the large branches, but seeing Bud Tyler coming to help, he remarked, "Know what, Bud? Every time I chop one of these big ones down, I feel like a murderer."

Tyler stared at Cass blankly. He was a tall, lanky man of thirty who had done little but chop down trees all his life, and Cass's words caught at him. Pulling a plug from his pocket, he bit off a chunk and settled it in his jaw. "Whut kind of crazy talk is that, Cass? It's only a tree."

Running his hand along the rough bark, Cass considered the fallen giant, then murmured, "This tree was here when Columbus discovered America, Bud. When Washington was camped at Valley Forge with one of my ancestors in his little army, this tree was a hundred feet tall. All these years it's been growing—and now it's just a piece of dead wood."

"Know whut, Cass?" Bud said. "You got *notions*, thet's whut you got!" He loosed a stream of amber at a beetle, hit it squarely, and watched with satisfaction as the bug fell over on its back, legs waving wildly. "Notions—and that kind of thinking ain't good for a man!"

Cass laughed and lifted his ax. "You might be right, Bud. Well, let's get this thing trimmed." He moved quickly, the ax slashing branches from the tree. He thought of how awkward he'd been when he'd first hired on the timber crew. He'd cut firewood all his life, but the lumberjacks used their tools so expertly that at first he'd despaired of ever mastering the ax. Day after day he'd gone to bed with aching muscles and blistered hands. But as the weeks had slipped by, he'd toughened up, recovering completely from his illness. His cough was gone now, and he felt invigorated breathing the mountain air. The hard work on the range had given him a resilience, so that although he had not yet become as skilled as his fellow workers, the foreman had grudgingly admitted, "Well, for a cowboy I guess you're a pretty good timber man, Winslow!"

Now as Cass lopped the branches from the giant spruce, he took pleasure in the ease with which he could put in a long day in the woods. He thought also of how fortunate he'd been to meet a man like Fletch Stevens. Not many men would have been so generous as Fletch. He had kept Cass in his shack until he fully recovered from his illness. When Cass had protested that he had no way to pay for his board, Fletch had laughed. "Why, I guess you'll find work when you get up and about. Don't worry about it, Cass."

A warm feeling came over Cass as he sheared the last limb, and he thought, *I guess I wouldn't have made it if Fletch hadn't taken me in. Got to make it up to him somehow. . . .* Then the woods boss appeared, shouting, "All right—let's get to the house and get those axes ready for tomorrow!"

Cass ended the workday as always, by honing a sharp edge on his ax; then he piled into the wagon. The loggers had put in a hard day that would have sent a city man to the hospital, but they yelled and joked all the way back to town. Cass was often the butt of many of the rough jokes, but he was used to tough men doing hard jobs and managed to hold his own.

When he got to the small shack and opened the door, the smell of hot cooking filled the room. Fletch looked up from the wood stove and grinned. "I figured you'd get here in time for grub," he said. "Go wash up and we'll have chow."

"Don't get your hand too close to me, Fletch," Cass grinned. "I'm hungry enough to eat a bear!"

Fortunately for Cass, Fletch was a good cook. When the two sat down, Fletch picked up a platter, saying, "Here, get yourself around one of these steaks, Cass—and I've got apple pie, so save room for it."

Cass ate like a starved wolf, downing the succulent steak, two huge baked potatoes that he soaked with fresh butter, a plateful of butter beans, and endless fluffy biscuits. Fletch ate little himself, but watched with amusement at the younger man's appetite. "I remember when I used to eat like that," he observed as he cut the third slice of apple pie and plopped it down before Cass. "Food tastes better when you're young." He picked up his cup, sipped the scalding black coffee, and his eyes grew remorseful as he added, "I used to go out to the garden when I was a kid, pick the biggest white onion I could find, and eat it like an apple. Like to do that again."

"Plenty of onions left, Fletch."

"Not the same somehow."

Cass looked up quickly, noting that Stevens was looking rather sickly. He had not been feeling well lately and his mood was sober, almost sad. Cass had noted a strong streak of fatalism in Fletch the last few weeks and wondered why. *Seems like he's just sort of given up—and he's not that old*, he thought, but aloud said, "Let's go out and take in the town tonight, Fletch."

"Too tired. And you'd better watch yourself. The gamblers and the fancy women make their living off young fellows like you."

"Oh, they won't get much from me," Cass said firmly. He ate the last bite of pie, downed the hot coffee, then wiped his lips with his sleeve—then laughed abruptly. "My ma would beat me with a carpet beater if she caught me using my sleeve for a napkin. I'm losing all my manners—what few I had."

"You ought to go home, Cass." Stevens was watching the young man carefully. He was not a man who'd made many close friends, but somehow young Winslow had come to mean a great deal to him. Being a man who could see himself clearly, Fletch realized that he was seeing the young man as a reflection of his own troubled youth. He leaned forward and said, "It's not too late for you, Cass. From what you've told me about your family, you're losing a lot by leaving them. You could have a fine ranch. Go be with your people. . . ."

Cass shifted uncomfortably on the rough chair. "Sure, I've thought about that—but it's just not for me, Fletch."

"Why not?"

"I've got to make it big—and on my own." A restlessness swept over Cass, and he rose and walked to the window. Outside the darkness had washed over the street, and he stared at the amber ring that marked the streetlight. Bugs circled the aureole, darting and dodging toward the flickering flame, and occasionally one of them would get too close, hit the flame, and shrivel instantly. Finally he turned and leveled his eyes on Fletch, his voice urgent as he tried to explain. "I got this thing in me, Fletch. Sometimes I think it's the devil himself! Can't really explain it, but it's like I—I'm driven to make it big!"

"Lots of men have that kind of devil," Fletch shrugged wearily. "I had it myself when I was your age."

"You know how it is then!"

"Sure I do—and I know it's a devil that leads you down a road with no good end." Fletch struck the table abruptly with his fist, making the dishes clatter. "What if you got rich? You think that would silence that devil? Not a bit, Cass! Money never brings a man peace—never! It just makes him greedy for more!"

A desperate need to explain himself to Fletch rose in Cass— but he had no words to describe the thing that drove him. He stood there, his tall stature illuminated by the flickering kerosene lamp, then shook his head. "I can't go back. Maybe I should, but I just can't!"

The two faced each other, and a bitterness rose in Fletch. He'd come to the end of his own life and had found it empty. Looking back over his past, he said regretfully, "A man has to make his own mistakes. He rides down a pretty dark road and once in a while the path forks. If he goes one way, he maybe finds what will give him peace. But if he goes the other way, he can't go back and take that path again. No way a man can see down the road—wish I could go back to a few of those forks—I'd do it all different."

"Well, you may be right," Cass admitted. He felt a sharp grief for the man who sat before him. Stevens had no hope left. *He made his mistakes—and he's given up.* "Well, come on and we'll see the sights. I need a keeper, and you're elected." He slapped the thin shoulder of his friend, adding, "Come along, Fletch—I don't want you sitting around feeling bad."

"All right." Fletch rose and the two men cleaned the dishes, then left the shack. As they left, Fletch said self-consciously, "Didn't mean to preach at you, Cass. Just want to see you do well."

"Sure," Cass said. "I guess I need some preaching, Fletch. And I don't have to worry about getting rich. At the rate I'm going, it would take about nine hundred years for me to get my first million!"

★ ★ ★ ★

An abrupt and harsh staccato sound brought Cass out of a deep sleep, gasping and flailing his arms wildly. "What—what's going on!" he cried. The furious knocking continued, and a light bloomed in the room as Fletch struck a match to light the lamp. Cass rolled off the bunk, demanding, "Who's that trying to knock the door down? Is the place on fire?"

Fletch shook the match out, a grim look on his gaunt face. "They're not burglars anyway—too much racket for that." The two left the bedroom and went to the main room, where Fletch reached up on a shelf nailed to the wall and plucked down a Colt .44. Cocking it, he stepped to the door and called out, "Who the devil is it? What do you want?"

"Open the door, Fletch! It's me—Bud Tyler!"

Lowering the revolver, Fletch stepped back, disgust on his face. "That lout! He doesn't have to wake the dead to get you out of bed for work!"

He slipped the bolt, and the big lumberman rushed into the

room, his face alive with excitement. "Gold! It's the big strike!"

A thrill ran along Cass's nerves at those words, and he leaped to seize Bud's arm. "What's that? A gold strike!"

But Fletch groaned and walked back to replace the gun on the shelf. "Another one? That's about the tenth one this year. I'm going back to bed."

"No, it's the real thing, Fletch," Tyler insisted. "Feller came into town last night—rode all the way from San Francisco."

"The strike was there?" Cass groaned. "I should have stayed there instead of coming here!"

"No, it ain't in California like in forty-nine," Bud said, shaking his head fiercely. "It's way up north—in Alaska! Some place called the Yukon. This feller, he said a ship come into San Francisco loaded down with gold! Feller said everybody was headed north to stake out claims."

"We've got to go to San Francisco—" Cass said.

"No, there ain't no need of that," Bud insisted. "They wuz *two* ships that left all loaded with gold—" He put his head back and let loose a wild howl, then pounded Cass on the back with his massive hand. "The name of the other ship was the *Portland*—and she's coming to dock this mornin'—right here in Seattle! Come on, fellers—we got to get down to the harbor!"

Cass made a leap for his clothes, pulling them on with haste. As he shoved his feet into his boots, he saw that Stevens was not making any sign of getting dressed. "Aren't you going, Fletch?"

"I've seen these things before, Cass," Fletch shook his head. "It's another wild tale—but you go on down with Bud. You can get some excitement out of it for a while. Beats working in the woods, I guess."

But Cass hardly heard his partner's words. The excitement of it all and the fantasies of gold had already gripped him. He ran out the door with his boots unlaced and his shirt unbuttoned. "Come on, Bud—let's go!" he cried, and the two young men left at a dead run.

Fletch Stevens walked slowly to the door, watching the pair as they were joined by other men, all running toward the harbor. He leaned against the frame of the door, slumped and feeling tired. *I can remember a time when I would have beaten them all to meet that ship.* His shoulders sagged and he turned and walked over to the cabinet above the sink. Pulling down a bottle of raw whisky, he sat down at the table and poured a clear stream into a mug. He swallowed it, shuddered violently, then slowly closed his eyes and put his head on his arms.

By the time Cass and Bud reached the harbor, a mass of yelling, shoving men had bunched up in front of the squat vessel with *Portland* outlined by peeling paint on the bow. The gangplank had been lowered and men were disembarking to the cheers of the crowd.

"Why—there must be five thousand men here!" Cass exclaimed.

"Everybody who can walk, I guess," Bud agreed. "Look—those bags they're carrying—that must be gold!"

Cass stared at the voyagers, all of them dressed in the roughest of clothing. They all looked weary and gaunt, but their eyes gleamed as they struggled under their burdens. Most of them carried what appeared to be huge fat sausages over their shoulders, and it was apparent that the weight of the sacks was enormous.

"Show us the gold! Show us the gold!"

A wild cry went up from someone, and the crowd took it up, chanting at the top of their lungs. A rough-looking individual carrying a leather grip tightly bound with three straps stepped to the wharf—and at the last step, the handle broke, sending the grip down on the wooden plank with a loud thumping noise. The owner stared at it, then lifted his head and laughed wildly. "I'm John Wilkinson—the richest hobo in the world!" he screamed. Then he began unfastening the straps, shouting, "Show you the gold? Yes—I'll show it to you!" He got the last strap free, then pulled a box from the huge grip and opened it. Plunging his hands into it, he lifted what seemed to the crowd to be yellow sand, but mixed with large rocks.

"There it is—gold and nuggets—that I dug with me bare hands out of the earth!" Wilkinson shouted. "Yellow gravel—but men will kill for it and women will sell themselves for it!"

A huge miner behind Wilkinson stepped off the gangplank, looked over the crowd and grinned, exposing blackened teeth. "There it is—all you got to do is go pick it up." He laughed and shouldered his way through the excited crowd.

"Come on, Bud," Cass cried. "Let's get him to tell us about the strike." They were joined instantly by a mob that practically pinned the big miner to the wall of a warehouse. His name, he announced—taking a mighty pull at a bottle that one of his admirers offered—was Nils Anderson.

"I left my family two years ago—borrowed three hundred dollars to go prospecting. My wife's had a hard time, I don't doubt—but I've got a hundred and twelve thousand dollars—and she'll never want for anything again!"

His words ran across the crowd like wildfire, and Cass spoke up. "Tell us about the strike, Mr. Anderson—where's the gold?"

"Yeah, and how do you get it out of the ground?" Bud cried. "I'll go today to get what you've got!"

"It don't hop out of the ground, lad," Anderson said, a grim look crossing his weathered face. "Ye'll freeze in winter and burn in the blasted summer. And ye'll live on beans and flapjacks until ye hate the sight of 'em. . . !"

As Anderson outlined the hardships that prospecting entailed, Cass could hardly contain himself. He felt that devil of a drive gather new strength inside him. He listened avidly as the speaker told of how the *Portland* had been jammed by the gold the miners had dug out of the earth—some in boxes and packing cases, some in belts and pokes made of caribou hide. He actually saw some gold brought ashore in jam jars, medicine bottles, and tomato cans—and gold held in blankets tied with straps and cord, so heavy that it took two men to hoist each one down the plank!

"Must be nigh unto three *tons* of gold on this old scow!" Anderson shrugged. "And there's lots more where this came from." He shouldered his heavy poke and moved away, followed by an admiring crowd that never stopped firing questions.

"We better get to work, Cass," Bud finally said. "We're liable to get canned if we don't."

Cass stared at the young man as if he had said something stupid. "Are you crazy, Bud?" he said. "This is the biggest thing that's ever happened to me—and you want me to go back to chopping wood?"

"Well, you can't go to the Yukon *today*, can you?" Bud shot back. He turned and left, an injured expression on his face, but Cass scarcely noticed. He was intoxicated with the promise of wealth, and all day long he joined the mob that followed the new heroes, hanging on their words as if they were from scripture.

When he finally got back to the shack, he found that Fletch was not impressed with the news of the gold strike. He had gotten drunk and by now was very edgy. "In the first place—most of the gold will be gone by the time new men get there. And how would you go, Cass? You can't *walk* to Alaska—and you can bet that the rates for passengers on ships headed north will skyrocket!"

Cass argued that there *had* to be a way. Long into the night Cass and others who stopped by talked excitedly about the strike. Fletch ignored them and began to drink again, but when Cass mildly rebuked him for it, he snapped, "*You're* the one who's drunk, Cass, not me! Gold fever—it's worse than the plague!" He took a swallow of the whiskey, then stared at Cass with disillusionment in his eyes. "You'll find out—it's like everything else in this world. The big fish will get the gold—and the rest of you will die as poor as the day you were born!"

★ ★ ★ ★

In the days and weeks that followed, Stevens' gloomy words seemed to haunt Cass. The country went mad—or so it seemed—over gold. In Seattle before the week was out, streetcars had to stop running because the influx of thousands of gold seekers had filled the streets. Men sold their businesses and bought passage to Alaska, leaving everything they had behind. Clerks by the dozen quit their jobs, and the Seattle *Times* lost most of its reporters. Salesmen simply walked away from their jobs, half the police force handed in their badges, doctors deserted their patients, and the mayor of Seattle, W.D. Wood, didn't bother to return home from his business trip to San Francisco. He simply wired his resignation and joined the stampede.

Cass continued to work for a while. He knew it would take money to buy passage and supplies to get to the Yukon. Yet every hour he toiled in the woods, he thought of nothing but the gold fields. Soon it began to affect his work. Finally his boss came to him one day and laid him off. "You're going to get killed—or get somebody else killed, Winslow! Come back when you get this crazy gold fever out of your system!"

And Cass discovered that Stevens had been right about the

matter of getting to the gold fields. The price of riverboats tripled, and many were shipped north to use on the Yukon River. Prices shot up, and Cass watched in despair as those with cash bought their passage.

He lost weight and could not sleep. Driven by an almost insane desire to get to the Yukon, he finally made a desperate venture. He took the little cash he had saved and headed for a saloon one night, hoping to make a killing at poker. Instead, he lost everything and left the saloon as miserable as he'd ever been in his life.

That night as the two men ate, Cass moaned, "I've *got* to get to the Yukon, Fletch—I've just got to! It's the one chance in my life to make it big—and I'm missing it!"

"You're young, Cass. There'll be other chances."

"No, not like this one. Remember what you said—that a man comes to a fork in the road—and if he chooses the wrong one, he can't ever go back."

"But, Cass—"

"I can't ever come back to this place, don't you see that, Fletch?" Despair etched a shadow on Cass's face, and he clenched his fists. "Nothing will ever be right if I don't make this one."

"Life's more than gold, Cass."

"Is it?" Cass grunted. "I don't think so."

"Look at your dad. From what you've told me, you think it's all his money that makes him what he is?"

"Well—no, of course not—but I'm different from him," Cass said defiantly. "When he was a young man he had to take chances—lots of them. When he got out of the Civil War, he didn't have a dime to his name. He took a bunch of half-wild cattle up to Wyoming and had to fight for everything he had! He told me once that if he hadn't come when he did, he doubted that he'd ever have had a ranch!"

Fletch was silent—but he had been for the past two days. His face was stretched, and he was feeling worse than he let Cass know. "I guess you'll have to wait for another chance, Cass," he said finally. He got up and moved across the room, but before he reached the sink, the dishes fell from his hand.

Cass jerked at the sound and stared at the other man. "Never saw you drop—" He halted abruptly, then leaped to his feet as

Stevens began to stagger. "Fletch—what is it?" He managed to catch the older man, but only barely. Lowering him to the floor, he saw that Fletch's eyes were closed and his face was as pale as chalk. Fright ran through Cass, and he cried, "Fletch—what's wrong?"

But Fletch was trembling in every joint. His eyes opened suddenly and Cass saw they were rolled back in the man's head. He picked the sick man up and carried him to his bunk. He ran to get water and washed Fletch's face, but there was no sign that his friend even knew it.

"I'll get help!" Cass said and left at once. He got one of Fletch's friends to stay with him, then went to get a doctor. When he finally found one—an elderly doctor whose name was Muldrow—he had to practically threaten him with violence to get him to come and take a look at Fletch.

An hour later, when they returned, Fletch was no longer trembling. Dr. Muldrow sat down beside the still form, listened to his heart, then rolled the man's eyelids back. He tapped and probed and finally turned to the men who'd come to see about their friend.

"A stroke—or his heart. Can't say for sure."

"Well, do something!" Cass said insistently.

Dr. Muldrow shook his head. "Not much any doctor can do. He may come out of it—I think he will." He hesitated then added, "But if he has family, you'd better send for them."

"Is he gonna make it, Doc?" Jerry Simmons asked. "He's never been sick that I know of."

"God knows—but I don't. Even if he does come out this time—chances are he'll have another of these attacks." Dr. Muldrow shrugged. He saw the anguish on Cass's face and asked, "You're no kin?"

"Just a good friend."

"Well, he's going to need every friend he's got," Muldrow said, shaking his head sadly. "Keep him warm, and try to get him to eat something when he wakes up." Pulling out a cigar, Muldrow bit off the end and lit it with a kitchen match. He stared down at the still form, his wise old eyes showing little—then turned and left the small shack.

Jerry frowned at the doctor's back. "Cheerful old goat, ain't he, Cass? Well, we'll take turns taking care of Fletch. You want to take the first watch?"

"Sure, Jerry."

Well into the night the two of them sat there reminiscing of old times, until Jerry finally left, leaving Cass alone with the still form of Stevens. He sat down on the chair, looked down at the pale face of his friend, and tried to think how it would be. *No Yukon for me* was his thought, and a sadness went through him. He was a man who hated to lose, and he knew the gold strike was an adventure he'd never be able to have now. Taking a deep breath, he expelled it slowly, then sat quietly watching the face of Fletcher Stevens.

CHAPTER SIX

THE PROMISE

★ ★ ★ ★

The arrival of the *Portland* in Seattle marked the beginning of a behavior known as *Klondikitis* in America. The city seemed almost demented, and the rest of the country was only slightly less afflicted.

Dogs, goats, sheep, oxen, mules, burros, and Shetland ponies, all designed for Klondike packing, jammed the already crowded streets. Horses came in from Montana, many of them bony and worn out. They had been worth no more than three or four dollars but sold for twenty-five and more in Seattle. Mules came from Colorado, and reindeer, whose horns had been amputated, were sold as beasts of burden. Washington elks were brought in by the hundreds, selling for two hundred and fifty dollars apiece.

As for the transportation companies, they were overwhelmed by the migration of gold seekers to the north. One railway company received twenty-five thousand queries about the Klondike, and two thousand New Yorkers tried to buy tickets for the Klondike.

Gold coins that had been hoarded in mattresses were suddenly dug out and spent for tickets to the gold country. Grocers doubled their help; supply stores ran day and night. Factories making dehydrated food could not begin to meet the demands; everyone wanted dehydrated food—eggs, onions, and even dehydrated split pea soup! The stampeders bought milk tablets, peanut meal, saccharine, desiccated olives, coffee lozenges, beef blocks, and pemmican.

By the summer of 1897, a deluge of books, maps, pamphlets, brochures, advertisements, and newspaper reports had poured from the presses. Most of them were filled with half-truths and outright lies—but they were all eagerly received by the greedy public as if they had been handed down from Mount Sinai.

Cass Winslow lived in the midst of the excitement, since Seattle was the center of the maelstrom. Though he was surrounded by all the frenzied activity, he was not part of it. Day after day he faithfully cared for Fletch Stevens, working at night on the docks so that he could take care of Fletch during the day. It took all the resolve he had to keep to this routine, because everything inside him cried out to cast duty aside and throw himself into the mad activity of the gold seekers.

"How's Fletch?" Cass asked as he came in from his job. He was tired and wanted to sleep, but knew that he had to care for his friend before he could get some rest.

"Not too good, Cass." A small man named Harry Tellers had sat with the patient during the night. He had slept in the chair beside the bed and now rose and stretched. Picking up his coat, Tellers shrugged into it, adding, "Didn't sleep good. Had those nightmares again. Well, I've got to go, Cass."

"Thanks, Harry."

Cass slumped down in the chair and glumly drank a cup of cold coffee. It had been a hard night, loading equipment onto a steamer, and he wanted to fling himself on the cot and sleep. But instead he washed his face and went in to see Fletch. He found him awake and said as cheerfully as he could, "Well, you about ready for a good breakfast?"

Fletch Stevens was lying on his back staring at the ceiling. He rolled his head toward Cass, saying, "Not too—hungry. Why don't you sack out? You must be—dead beat." His speech was slurred and broken, and when he tried to sit up, he fell over, his face falling into the mattress.

Cass leaped to help him, lifting him up and pressing him back against the pillows. "Not sleepy, Fletch. Here, you look like a bum. I'm going to clean you up and shave you." Despite the sick man's protest, Cass proceeded to get the old tub filled with warm water. He had never nursed anyone before, but as he continued caring for Fletch he was getting better at it. Since the attack, Fletch had lost the use of his left arm and leg almost completely, so he was confined to a chair. After a quick bath, Cass carefully shaved his friend's bristly cheeks, keeping up a sprightly conversation.

"Now, you look like a man again," said Cass, wiping off the last of the lather. "Here, let's get you in the kitchen. You can direct the construction of the breakfast."

Stooping, he picked up Fletch's slight form easily. Carrying him into the kitchen, Cass set him carefully in an overstuffed chair he'd managed to talk a furniture dealer out of. "Now, let's see if for once I can go through this without burning anything—"

"You don't—have to cook for me," Fletch protested. His cheeks were sunken and his eyes had lost their luster. He hated being sick, hated having to ask for help. But as the young man ignored him and busied himself at the stove, Fletch said, "Guess I can read some of the paper."

"Read it out loud, Fletch. I'm behind on what's happening."

Fletch picked up a copy of the *Times*, using his one good arm rather awkwardly. He found a story that interested him and began to read aloud:

> Prosperity is here! So far as Seattle—is concerned, the depression is at an end. A period of prosperity, far greater than anything known in the past—is at hand. The financial barometer of Dun and Bradstreet declares that the demand— of supplies for shipment to the Klondike region has made— July and August the two busiest months ever. And this is only the beginning. . . .

Fletch read on in a halting voice, with a comment from time to time from Cass. Then when the meal was ready, Fletch dropped the paper, saying, "Guess they believe all that—but I've heard it all before."

"Well, see if I've made these eggs right," Cass said. He no longer mentioned going to the gold fields, for he knew it was impossible. Cass sat down and ate a large breakfast, carefully paying no attention to Fletch's awkwardness with his fork. He spoke of his days on the range, and finally when they were finished, he cleared the table and then asked, "Do you want to go back to bed, Fletch?"

"No, I—I'm sick of it. But you go on, Cass. I'll be—all right."

"I'll just sit for a while." Cass stirred his coffee idly, and the two of them sat there for half an hour. Finally Cass cleared his throat and said, "You have any family at all, Fletch?"

Instantly Fletch turned to face him. "In case I drop dead— you'll h-have someone to write to?" His tone was bitter, but seeing the look on Cass's face, he lifted his good hand in a gesture of apology. "Sorry, Cass. Didn't mean to say that." He sat silently for a moment, then said, "I've been getting some things together. You'll find a letter I want mailed if I don't make it—and some instructions about what little I've got—what to do with it."

"Aw, we won't worry about it," Cass said, "but it's always best to take care of these things."

Fletch stared at the young man thoughtfully. "Like to be going with the others, wouldn't you, Cass?"

"Sure, but some things a man can do—some he can't." It was his standard answer these days to those who inquired about his plans, but there was a tenseness in his lips that revealed the struggle it took to say the words.

"Wish I was a millionaire," Fletch murmured. "I don't think it's what would do you the most good—but I'd send you if I could."

"I'd probably fall in the Yukon and drown."

Fletch saw the strain on the youthful face and said no more. Later he insisted that Cass go to bed. "I'm fine—just bring me my tablet and a pencil."

Cass moved Fletch and his chair to the bedroom, and then handed him the writing material. As he arranged a board across the arms of the chair to serve for a desk, he asked, "Fletch, how do you feel? Any better?"

"I'll never be any better, Cass."

"You don't know that!"

"Yes, I do." Fletch sat back in his chair, his face somber. "I never mentioned it, Cass, but I've had these spells before."

"Why, you should have told me!"

"What for? There ain't nothing anyone can do about it." Fletch picked up a pencil, tested the point, then smiled. "The others were like this one—only not so bad. I've had three of them—and each time it was more serious. The next one will get me, I think."

"Don't talk like that!"

Fletch shrugged, then said quietly, "I've not been a man to think much of God, Cass. Now that I'm about ready to step over—I wish I'd been more in that way."

"Let me get a minister," Cass said at once. He had not been deceived by Fletch's condition. The doctor had warned him that another attack would probably be fatal.

"No, let it go."

"But it's not right to die without God!"

Fletch gave the young man before him a strange smile, asking gently, "What about you, Cass? You could die before sundown. Are you ready to meet God?"

A flush rose to Cass's cheeks and he dropped his head. The silence ran on and finally he lifted his eyes. "No, I'm not, Fletch. I—I guess most of us think we have forever."

"Sure, we all think like that. I did when I was your age."

Cass bit his lower lip thoughtfully. "My folks are Christians—and almost all of my relatives. But I never took their way."

"Not too late, Cass."

The two said no more, and soon Cass left the shack. He had been humbled by the conversation because he admired his parents' Christian commitment deeply. He'd met some who called themselves Christians whose behavior did not match their profession—but he was not fool enough to let this sour him on faith.

The streets were crowded as he made his way to the store, where he made a few purchases. Eggs had gone up to a dollar a dozen, and when he complained, the storekeeper shrugged. "Can't help it, Cass. Whole town's gone crazy, I think. The farmer I buy my eggs from upped his prices. Said the gold seekers are packing eggs in jars of sand—and they don't care how much they pay for them." He handed Cass his change, adding, "Crazy fools. Those eggs will spoil, mark my words!"

"I guess things are a little wild, Mack."

"Wild?" Mack Tomkins snorted and threw his hands into the air. "Wild ain't the word for it, Cass! Have you heard about the visions?"

"The *what*?"

"Why, people are seeing *visions*—visions of gold!"

"Haven't heard about that."

"Right in the paper—listen to this, will you:

> A group of Italian laborers in New York City have seen gold in some sand which they were digging. And a visitor to Victoria, British Columbia, has seen a vision of gold in an outcropping in a gutter near that city's post office. And a farm near Elizabethtown, Kentucky, had been reported as a source of gold lining the ground.

Mack threw the paper down angrily, sputtering, "Did you ever *hear* such nonsense?"

Cass picked up his small sack of groceries, shook his head, and left the store as Tomkins continued his tirade to the rest of his customers. He was as aware of "Klondikitis" as the grocery man. He'd read ads in every issue of the paper that begged for funds to join the race to the Yukon. One of them, he recalled as he moved along the street, had said, "Wanted $700 to go to the Yukon. Will give value and personal property and if successful will give $1000 additional."

Maybe I could put an ad in the paper—but I don't have any security at all. Threading his way along the street, he passed a saloon that had taken advantage of the craze by placing a piano on the sidewalk. One of the highly painted saloon girls was leaning on it, singing in a raucous voice, accompanied by a pale-faced piano player with a cigar clamped firmly between his teeth:

> All you miners wide awake!
> Go to the Klondike, make your stake;
> Get out your pick, your pan, your pack,
> Go to the Klondike, don't come back.
> Ho for the Klondike, ho!

The woman finished her song just as Cass came even with her. She flashed him a wide smile, then reached out and took his arm. "Come along, honey. We'll have a good time before you leave to get rich."

"How do you know I'm not already rich?" Cass grinned.

"Aw, you ain't rich—not in them clothes!"

"Right—and I'm not going to the Klondike."

Cass pulled away and twenty minutes later stepped inside the door to the small shack. "Hey, Fletch—" he called out, setting the groceries on the table. "I'm home."

Usually Fletch answered his call, but there was not a sound from the bedroom. A tiny alarm went off in Cass's head, and he stepped quickly to the bedroom door. It was half closed, and when he pushed it open he saw that Fletch was twisted in his chair, almost fallen. "Fletch!" Cass leaped to the man's side and lifted him upright. As he did, he noticed Fletch's face had the same waxen pallor he'd had during his last attack.

With a groan, Cass picked up the wasted form and laid Fletch carefully on the bed. He got water and washed the pale face, and to his relief Fletch opened his eyes.

"Hey, you gave me a scare!" said Cass, then asked, "Was it another attack?"

"Y-yes." The single word seemed to take all of Fletch's strength. His eyelids fluttered and his breathing, Cass saw with alarm, was very shallow.

"I'll get the doctor—"

"No—" Fletch said in a slightly stronger voice. "No time!" He lay still, then said, "Dead from—the neck down—" He gasped and seemed to try to lift himself. "Hit me hard—Cass."

"Let me go for the doctor, Fletch!"

But Fletch blinked his eyes and licked his lips. "Can't help me—been hoping you'd c-come—before it was too—late." His voice was a wisp of his normal strong tones, and Cass leaned forward to hear. "Get—papers in box—"

Cass turned and picked up the box from the table beside the bed. It contained the papers that Fletch worked on from time to time. "Open it," Fletch whispered, and when Cass had done so, he said, "The picture—my family—"

Cass picked up a faded daguerreotype and studied it. A young Fletcher Stevens stood proudly beside an attractive young woman and a small girl. "Your wife and daughter?" Cass asked.

"Yes." Fletch struggled for a moment, then said, "Help me sit up, Cass." When he was braced against the pillow, a little color came back into his face. "Better. I can breathe better—still can't move my arms and legs, though."

"Where is your family, Fletch?" Cass asked. He had never seen a man die, but he knew the end was not far away. "Can't we get word to them?"

"Martha died four years ago," Fletch said. "She was a wonderful woman. Deserved better than me."

"What about the child?"

Fletch had been staring at the picture, but when he raised his head, Cass saw raw pain in the faded blue eyes. "My daughter. Her name is Serena." His lips drew back in a grimace, and when he spoke, years of regret ran through his tone. "I've been the—world's worst father and husband, Cass! I abandoned them. . . ."

Cass sat beside the dying man, listening to the sad story. He'd known Fletch was a tragic figure, but as he heard the slow, halting tale of failure, only then did Cass understand what lay behind the man. *He never got over leaving them,* Cass thought. *That's why he's had no real joy in him.*

Finally Fletch grew silent. "Getting sleepy—hope I don't—go out before—" His head dropped and for an instant Cass thought he was gone. But when he checked and still heard the labored breathing, he sighed with relief.

"Got to get Doc Muldrow here," he muttered. Rising from his chair, Cass left the house and went to find Jerry.

"Drag him here if you have to, Jerry," Cass admonished him as he left running for Muldrow's office.

Then Cass hurried back to sit beside Fletch—and for the first time in years he prayed. It was a mere fragment—"God, don't let him die like this! Let him at least live long enough to write to his daughter!" It wasn't much, and he felt ashamed at the awkwardness of it—but at the same time, Cass Winslow knew that it was something his father and mother would have approved. Somehow that gave him a measure of peace he hadn't known for a long time.

★ ★ ★ ★

"He's on the razor's edge." Dr. Muldrow shook his head doubtfully. He had come every day for three days, but never had he given any hope. "Never seen such tenacity," he muttered. "He should have been dead by now. What's he holding on for?"

Cass studied the square face of the physician for a moment,

then shrugged his shoulders. "He's worried about his daughter."

"Daughter? I didn't know he had one."

"He hasn't seen her for years. She's in some sort of religious place—a convent, I think."

"A nun?"

"No, not the way I understand it." Cass took a moment to collect his thoughts, then said, "Fletch said that when his wife died, he was in no shape to care for the child, so he made arrangements with this place to take her. I don't understand the conditions, but clear as I can make it out, the girl is deciding what she wants to do. She can either stay and become a nun, or she can leave."

"How old is she?"

"Sixteen years old." Cass shook his head sadly. "Fletch feels he's failed her—which he has, I reckon. But I think he's praying for someone to take the girl in and give her a real home."

"Humph. He's not a praying man!"

"No, he's not, Doc. And he's not praying for himself like most of us would be—but for the girl to make it." Running his hand through his thick mop of tawny hair, Cass looked at Muldrow and asked, "How long has he got?"

"How long? He doesn't have *any* time, Winslow! I can't see what's kept him alive. Never saw such a bad heart!" Muldrow lit up one of his cigars, stood there for a moment, then said gruffly, "Too bad! I'll ask around—see if any family will take the girl."

"Thanks, Doc."

After Muldrow left, Cass moved restlessly around the kitchen. He had slept little for the past three days, for Fletch had seemed to take comfort in his presence. Fletch insisted on Cass hearing the whole story, and as he did, a great pity for the man who'd taken him in welled up inside Cass.

He'd thought of the girl, Serena, how she might be helped. Once he'd said, "I'm sure my folks would take her in, Fletch. Let me write them."

Fletcher had been interested in this and said so. "It may come to that—but I'm hoping God will do something else."

On the afternoon of the fourth day after the attack, Cass walked into the bedroom and found Fletch looking out the window. He was lying flat on his back, and when Cass sat down, the ill man turned and said, "The doc wonders what's keeping me alive, doesn't he?"

"He thinks you're in pretty bad shape, Fletch." Cass sat beside his friend until Fletch dropped off to sleep, then he got up and went to bed himself. He slept poorly; rising before dawn, he went to check on the sick man.

"Cass? Come here!"

When Cass moved to sit down in the chair beside the bed, he saw that Fletch was different. He had been gaunt, and despair had marred his eyes—but now there was a peace in his countenance. "I've been praying all night—and something happened to me, Cass!"

"What was it, Fletch?"

"I—I've not been a religious man—" Fletch said haltingly, his lips forming the words carefully. "Never admired anybody who lived like the devil—then ran crying to God when they came to die." He moistened his lips, then his voice seemed to grow stronger. "All this time, I've been praying for Serena—never once for myself."

"I know that, Fletch—"

"Well, early this morning—I was about to pass out. Thought it was another spell—and it was like somebody said, 'I want you for myself.'" Fletch blinked and tears came into this eyes. "I know you'll think I'm crazy—but I *know* it was God talking to me!"

"No, I don't think you're crazy. My folks—they hear from God all the time."

The room was quiet, and slowly Fletch related how he'd been afraid he was losing his mind, but finally he'd just cried out for mercy. "I just asked God to forgive me—and He did, Cass! I know He did!"

"I'm glad for you, Fletch!"

"Thanks, Cass. But that wasn't all. I didn't pray anymore—but as I was just lying still thinking how merciful God is, something came to me—and I believe it was from God." He smiled suddenly, his face lighting up in a way Cass had never seen. "God told me what to do about Serena!"

"He did?" Cass leaned forward and peered intently into Stevens' face. "What did He say?"

"It was about you, Cass," Fletch said. "God told me that you would be the one who would take care of my girl!" When Cass began to protest, Fletch said in a positive voice, "And that's not all. You're going to the Klondike, Cass!"

The world seemed to stop for Cass, and he could only stare at the face of the sick man, thinking he'd lost his mind. "To the Klondike—how?"

"I've got a little money. Not much, but enough to finance a trip for you. I want you to take it and go to the gold fields."

At once Cass grasped the idea. "Fletch—you mean help your daughter by finding gold in the Yukon?"

"Yes. And I think God is in it." Fletch studied the youthful face of Cass Winslow and said slowly, "I worry about your itch to get a lot of money, Cass. I think it's bad. But this way, you can help someone—and that's good. Will you do it?"

"Do it?—of course I'll do it," Cass exclaimed. "And I'll find gold and see that your daughter never wants for anything!"

"Here—go to the bank. I've already written a check. Draw it all out and put it in your name. Then buy two places on a ship—"

"Two places?" Cass interrupted. "Why, you don't mean for me to take your daughter with me?"

"That's what came to me—and I think it was God."

Cass was stunned by what he had heard. "In the first place, I'm not leaving you. I'll stay with you—"

"I won't be here long," Fletch cut in. "God has let me live just long enough to find Him—and to tell me what to do with Serena. And you must take her with you, Cass—you must!"

Cass gently argued with Fletch about taking the girl. He summoned every argument he could think of about the dangers of the trip, the hardships that had broken strong men—but to all this Fletch simply said, "God is in it—you must take her, Cass!"

*　*　*　*

Finally two days later, on August 2, Fletch died. He went easily, and Cass was beside him till the end. Fletch had asked Cass to take his hand. "I can't feel it, but I want you to promise me— you'll take—Serena—!"

Cass sensed there was no time left. He said slowly, "All right,

Fletch—I promise to take her. And I'll take care of her—don't worry."

Fletcher Stevens opened his eyes wide and whispered, "Thank God—" He lay there for half an hour but didn't speak. Finally Cass saw a movement in the frail body. Seeing that Fletch was trying to speak, he leaned forward, putting his ear close to Fletch's lips. He caught the words ". . . thank you, God—for sending a man—to care for—Serena—!"

And then Fletch seemed to relax, and he was gone.

Cass patted the still hand, then rose and looked down on the face of his friend. For a long time he studied the face. He'd never seen such peace on the features of Fletcher Stevens. Finally he murmured, "I'm not much of a man, I guess, Fletch—but I'll take care of your daughter—if it kills me!"

CHAPTER SEVEN

"I'LL GO WITH YOU!"

★ ★ ★ ★

The huge dog lowered his body and curled his upper lip back to expose a massive set of gleaming white fangs. From his deep chest arose a terrifying snarl that would have frozen the blood of even a strong man—and the girl who crouched before him with open eyes whispered, "No—no—!"

With a swift movement, she whirled and raced across the dead brown grass. She was very fast, and her feet scarcely seemed to touch the ground as she sped toward the gate that swung loosely in the trim white fence. Her cheeks reddened, touched by the sharp August wind. When she cast a look behind her, taking in the enormous animal that was covering the ground with incredible speed, she gasped and threw every ounce of her strength into the race.

Head down and gasping with the effort, she was within ten feet of the gate—and then she uttered a short cry as a set of powerful jaws closed on the calf of her right leg.

"Thor—let go of me, you brute!"

The mighty jaws didn't close all the way—which would have meant a badly wounded leg—but neither did the massive animal turn her loose. The girl was caught off balance and fell to the ground, but as soon as she was down, the dog released his grip and instantly began licking her face.

"Get away, you messy ol' thing!" she scolded, shoving at the mighty chest with both hands. When the dog persisted she beat at him futilely with both fists, crying out, "Let me up—you win!" She began to laugh, her body shaking with merriment, and finally she succeeded in getting to her feet. At once the dog rose on his hind legs and placed both huge paws on her shoulders. Staggering under his weight, the girl avoided getting her face washed again with the red tongue, and then gave the animal a hug.

"You big bully! Don't be so proud of yourself—whipping a little girl like me." Then she grabbed twin handfuls of the charcoal tan fur and yanked at them playfully. "All right, you get your prize. Come on, I've saved some bones from the kitchen for you. You want them—bones?"

"Wuff!" the dog huffed and turned at once toward the gate. He was a massively built Siberian husky. His fur was a charcoal tan color, except for his head and shoulders, which were a darker shade. His fur was thick and his paws were enormous, as was his head. There was an easy sweep to his gait, and though he was by far the largest and strongest dog Serena Stevens had ever seen, he was incredibly fast, able to run down a rabbit from time to time.

Serena opened the gate, and the pair made their way past a series of small stone outbuildings set on the edge of the pasture. A small herd of black-and-white cows lifted their heads from where they were grazing, then lowered them and continued munching on the thin brown grass. A large barn loomed to the left, and Serena greeted a tall man in overalls who was entering the door. "I'll be back to help you with the milking as soon as I can, Seth."

"Take your time, Miss Serena—and don't bring Thor. He makes the cows nervous."

Serena laughed, then leaned down and patted the dog's side. "All right—I won't."

The two made their way to an enormous white house that rose three stories high. It had originally served as a hotel, but the town three miles to the south had never developed, so it now housed a small group of nuns. Serena entered the back door, whispering, "Wait here, Thor—" then quietly made her way down the wide hallway that ran through the center of the house. When she reached the kitchen, she went at once to a large pie-safe, opened the door, and removed a large item wrapped in brown paper. Quickly she turned and left the room, and soon was back outside watching Thor ecstatically crunch the massive bones.

"I saved them for you, and I hope you're grateful. My, what horrid manners you have!" But the dog didn't seem to mind being criticized, because he merely snorted and began to chew on a fresh bone.

"Serena—where are you?"

At the sound of a voice from above her head, Serena flinched. "Here, let's get away—" She grasped the bone that was clenched between the huge teeth, but she could not even budge it.

"All right, I see you down there!" Serena looked up to see a black-garbed nun leaning out the window and staring down at her.

"Why, yes—what is it, Sister Veronica?"

"What are you feeding that animal?"

"Just a few bones I saved from supper last night."

"Sister Margarita was planning to make soup from them!"

"Oh, I didn't know that. I'll save the rest of them—"

"Never mind! I hardly think we'd want to use them for soup after that dog has slavered all over them. Come up here at once!"

"Yes, sister." Serena whispered to Thor, "Now—see what trouble you've gotten me into!" She entered the house and climbed the stairway to the second floor. Her own room was on the third floor, and she wished she could go to it and lock the door. But she knew that was hopeless. Her steps dragged on the worn carpet as she approached the door to the nun's office. When a voice bade her enter after she knocked lightly, she took a deep breath and opened the door.

Sister Veronica was sitting behind her big oak desk. She was a rather pretty woman in her middle fifties but looked much younger. Serena had made the mistake once of asking her why she'd chosen to be a nun when she was pretty enough to catch a man. Even now it seemed that the Mother Superior had not forgotten that remark, because she fixed her large gray eyes on the young woman in a severe manner.

"I will not have you feeding that huge animal our food, Serena!" she said with asperity. "I made a grave error in allowing you to keep him. But how could I know that such a small puppy would turn out to be as big as—as an elephant!"

"Please, Sister Veronica," Serena begged. "I promise I'll be more careful. The Swensons on the next farm save all their left-overs for Thor. I won't use any more of the food from our kitchen."

Sister Veronica drummed her fingers on the arms of her chair as she studied the girl. She let the silence run on, then shrugged. "Very well—but I have a another matter to speak to you about."

"Have I done something else wrong, sister?"

A smile tugged at the prim lips of the nun. "You've been here in front of this desk often enough to suspect so. How many times have I had to discipline you, child?" Then she waved Serena's answer away. "Never mind that." Rising to her feet, she turned and paused to gaze out the open window. She was a woman who knew her own mind—a firm woman who had uncompromising convictions and ruled her group with a resoluteness one finds in generals or admirals.

But this girl was different. *She's been a problem ever since we took her in—I should have sent her away long ago.* She turned suddenly to ask, "How long have you been with us, Serena?"

"Why—four years, Sister Veronica."

"Yes, four years. You've grown from a child into a young woman." The woman let her eyes run over the girl, thinking of how she had changed. Serena Stevens had been an ordinary-looking child when Fletch Stevens brought her to the convent four years ago—but in the last year she had become a beautiful young woman. It seemed the awkward, almost sticklike figure had blossomed overnight. The firm curves of womanhood were revealed by the trim gray dress the girl wore, and Sister Veronica's lips tightened as she thought of what the girl's attractive figure might mean if she were to leave.

Her face is so unusual—I suppose it's those eyes—so dark blue they look almost black— And the smooth complexion, the glossy dark brown hair, irrepressibly curly, forming a crown around the oval face. It was a piquant face, alert as any the Mother Superior had ever seen. *Too pretty—she doesn't know it now—but men will let her know quickly enough!*

"Serena, when we talked last time, I told you it was time for you to choose your vocation. Do you remember?"

"Of course, sister—but I just can't seem to make up my mind."

"You love God. I know that much."

"Oh yes! Who could help that?"

"More than you might suspect," Sister Veronica said tersely. She had grown very fond of Serena but had not seen in the girl any indication that she would fit into the life of the convent on a permanent basis. It took a total commitment to give up one's life as a woman—the joys of home, husband, children—to serve God as a nun. Sister Veronica had held high hopes once that Serena would show this spirit—but it had not happened.

"Can you not give your whole life to God?"

Serena twisted her hands nervously. She had prayed about this matter for months. She had wanted to please Sister Veronica and the others who had been so kind to her—but something inside her made her realize that she would never be able to live the life of devotion they had chosen. Dropping her eyes, Serena shook her head. "No, sister—I would not make a good nun—but I want to serve God in whatever way I can."

"You want to leave this place?"

"I—I must go, I think."

Sister Veronica felt a pang, but she was accustomed to such things. So few were ready to take the veil! She studied the girl, then nodded. "Very well, Serena." She hesitated, and for a moment was tempted to put off what she had to say. There was a rash desire to withhold what she knew must be told—but then she realized she could not forsake her responsibility to the girl.

"Serena, I was hoping your choice would be different." She turned and went back to the large desk but did not sit down. Keeping her eyes fixed on the young woman, she said slowly, "This afternoon a visitor came to see me—and he came about you."

"About me?" Serena never had visitors and could not imagine who it could be. "Did my father send him?" Hope sprang into her face, for she had long dreamed that her father would come or send someone and take her away from the convent.

Sister Veronica hesitated, and her voice was not quite steady as she said, "His name is Cassidy Winslow. And yes—your father is responsible for his visit. I've asked Mr. Winslow to wait in the parlor. Go see him—and when you've finished, come back here."

"Yes, sister!" Serena whirled and left the room, but when she was outside and came to the stairs, she halted abruptly. Her heart was beating rapidly and her breath was short. She had not heard from her father in weeks, and his last letter had said nothing about anyone coming to see her. He had come only twice in all the time she had been in the convent, and then only for brief visits.

Sister Veronica had set forth the decision about becoming a nun very clearly. *I've got to go,* Serena thought. *Whoever it is, he'll have to take me with him!*

When she reached the first floor and moved to stand in front of the large oak door that led to the parlor, her courage almost failed her. She had led a lonely life, for the convent was no place for a young, high-spirited girl. It had been like a lonely exile for her in many ways, despite the kindness of the women. She had learned to keep her exterior calm—but inside she had felt like a captured bird! Now as she stood with her hand on the door, she prayed, *Dear God—take me away from this place—let me go and be with my father!*

Then she took a deep breath, and when she had regained her composure, Serena opened the door and stepped inside. The man who rose from the sofa was much younger than she had expected—and much better looking. He was tall and had a mop of tawny hair, and his eyes were a strange shade of blue-green such as the girl had never seen.

"Miss Stevens?"

"Yes, I'm Serena."

Cass had been expecting a younger girl. This was not an adolescent child such as he had fixed in his mind—but a lovely young woman. *How old is she? Only sixteen? It'll be worse than I thought if she goes—I'll have to fight the men off her!* He let none of this show in his face, however, but nodded politely. "My name is Cassidy Winslow."

"I'm glad to meet you. Won't you please sit down?" Serena sat down and looked at the big man, waiting for him to speak.

Cass felt as awkward as he could ever remember. He knew nothing about the girl, and the Mother Superior had been as suspicious as a detective about him at first. But then he'd told her the whole story and shown her the will Fletch had written. Fortunately, Cass had had the sense about him to get the simple document witnessed by Doc Muldrow and Harry and notarized.

Sister Veronica stared at the large signature of a certain Judge Thomas P. Gallagher at the bottom. She stood in silence for a moment, realizing that her time of guardianship for Serena had come to an end. After a brief word she'd merely said that she'd allow him to see the girl only after she'd talked to her. Standing there now looking at Serena, Cass thought, *Now I don't have any idea what she said—and she's put me in an awful spot!*

"Did Sister Veronica tell you about me?"

"Why, just that you came from my father."

Blast that woman—why didn't she tell the girl? Cass set his hat down carefully on the table beside the sofa. He was wearing new clothes—a dark blue suit, white shirt, and polished black boots. He had realized he couldn't show up at a convent in his ragged clothes. Now he rubbed his hands nervously along the sides of his pants, trying to think of a way to break the bad news to this beautiful young woman sitting in front of him.

Finally he said, "I—I've got bad news for you, Serena."

At once the girl's enormous blue eyes fixed on him. The well-shaped lips trembled as she whispered, "Is—is he not well?"

Cass gritted his teeth, wishing desperately that he were anywhere in the world but under the gaze of those eyes!

"It's very bad—he became very ill a few weeks ago, and—"

When the tall man broke off, Serena knew instantly what he was trying to say. She had not been close to her father, but he had been her only hope of leaving the convent. She had a few fine memories of him, drawn from those days when she was but a child. And now, she understood from Winslow's twisted face, he was gone.

"How did he die?" she asked, struggling to keep the tears from her eyes.

Cass spoke haltingly, giving the girl the facts—and found himself admiring her spirit. Most young girls would have broken down at once. When he came to the end, however, telling her how Fletch's last thoughts had been of her—he added, "The last word he said was—Serena."

At that, the tears could not be kept back. Serena threw her hands over her face, and her shoulders began to shake. Cass was horrified, but he had no earthly idea what to do to comfort her.

When the girl rose, he came to his feet and stood there as she walked over to the wall and leaned against it, her figure shaking from the sobs of grief that wracked her. Her dream of escaping the convent and being with her father had been shattered in a moment!

Cass went to her, touched her, and to his amazement she turned and fell against him! "Now—it's going to be all right," he muttered inanely. He realized that she was so distraught she had turned to a stranger with her grief. Awkwardly he put his arms around her, and she wept with her face pressed against his chest. *Poor kid—she's lost him and she never really had him.*

And while the girl wept, Cass suddenly realized he was holding a very attractive young woman. He was acutely conscious of her body pressing against his—though he knew that she had no such thoughts. It was a disturbing development—one he knew he would have to deal with very strictly if she were to accompany him to the Klondike.

Finally the weeping lessened, and the girl drew back, her face pale. "Here, take this," Cass said, offering her a clean handkerchief. He waited until she was calm, then asked, "Do you want me to come back later?"

"No—I want to know why my father sent you."

"Well, we'd better sit down. It's a long story—and a little complicated."

The two of them sat down, and Cass told her the story of how he'd come to be in Seattle. He didn't spare himself in the telling, and then when he told her of how her father had taken him in, he shook his head. "He was a good man, Serena. No man was ever better to me—except my own father." And then he came to the part that he wasn't sure about. He explained how Fletch had asked him to join the gold seekers in Alaska—and finally he told her how Fletch had asked him to take his daughter with him.

Serena had listened very carefully. Because of the protected life she had lived these last four years, she didn't know men. Yet somehow she realized that her fate lay in the strong brown hands of this tall young man. *He looks worried—but he seems honest,* thought Serena.

He ended by saying, "Serena, it's going to be a difficult and dangerous trip. I think it would be better if you stayed here. I'll go look for gold, and when I make a strike, I'll get the gold and come back. Then we can find a place for you."

Serena Stevens was not schooled in the ways of the world. She had grown up under the care of her mother, and for the last four years—her most formative years—she had had no opportunity to learn what most young women learn.

But now she looked up at Cass and innocently said, "I'll go with you, Mr. Winslow."

Cass stared at her, appalled. He wiped his brow, studied his feet, then asked, "How old are you, Serena?"

"I'm seventeen."

"I—I thought your father said you were sixteen."

"He wasn't very good about things like birthdays."

Cass nodded but seemed troubled. Everything he hadn't expected to happen was somehow happening. He picked up his hat, rounded the crown, then creased it again. Looking up at her he said, "Well, I thought you'd be a little girl. Somehow sixteen doesn't seem so old. But you're not a little girl!"

Something in his eyes and his tone caught at Serena. "You mean you'd take a little girl with you—but not a young woman?"

"You can discipline little girls—spank them if they need it." A gleam of unexpected humor touched his eyes. "I don't suppose you'd put up with that, would you, Serena?"

Despite her grief, Serena was still pert. "I'll try to behave so well that you'll see no need to—spank me."

Cass was at a loss for words. Though he had meant what he had promised Fletch, he had hoped all along that the girl would choose to stay with her present arrangements. *My only hope is to make the thing sound so bad she'll choose to let me go alone.*

That was his plan, but it never got anywhere. He argued for what seemed like a long time—outlining the discomforts and dangers of the trip, but the girl simply watched him with those enormous blue eyes. And when she did speak, it was to say, "I'll go with you, Mr. Winslow."

"Blast it, call me Cass!" he finally burst out. "Serena, you just can't know how bad it's going to be."

"Neither can you. But I know one thing, Cass . . ." She paused and looked directly at him. "It's not going to be any worse than staying here."

"But you've got a nice bed, plenty to eat—"

"That's not enough!" The large eyes flashed and Serena straightened her back. "I've got to leave, Cass. Sister Veronica knows it and I know it. I've been treated very well here—nobody could have been kinder—and I've hated it!"

Cass stared at the girl. "Hated it? Why?"

Serena had listened carefully to Cass's story and now threw it back at him. "Why did you leave your home in Wyoming? Were they unkind to you? No. Didn't you have a nice place to sleep and all you wanted to eat?"

Cass flushed and laughed awkwardly. "You're pretty sharp—but it's different for a man."

"Different how?"

"Well, a man's got to make his own way. A woman's got to catch—"

When Cass halted abruptly, Serena smiled. "Got to catch a man—is that what you didn't say?"

"I guess it was."

"Well, I'm not out to catch a man. And life has to be more than what I've had here. It's fine for those who want such a life—but I'm not one of them! I've got to have some freedom, Cass! Can't you understand that?"

Cass nodded slowly. "Guess I can," he admitted. "But it's not as safe out there as it has been in here."

"*Safe* is a not a word I like very much," Serena said slowly. She lifted her eyes to him and repeated what she'd said at the beginning. "I'll go with you, Cass Winslow. And I won't complain, no matter how hard things get."

Cass made up his mind at once. "All right, we'll do it. Get your things. The train leaves at four-thirty."

Serena turned to leave the parlor instantly, saying as she reached the door, "I'll have to say goodbye to everyone—"

Cass waited in the parlor for a time, then went outside to stand beside the buggy he'd rented. He stroked the nose of the horse, wondering if he'd done the right thing. Memories of Fletch came to him and he murmured, "I hope this thing is of God, Fletch—because it sure doesn't make sense from any other point of view!"

Finally the girl came out, trailed by a covey of black-clad nuns. Amidst hugs and kisses, Serena said her tearful goodbyes to all those who had been so kind to her. Finally Sister Veronica came to stand in front of Cass. Her eyes were moist, but her tone was firm. "God strike you dead if you fail this child, Cassidy Winslow!"

Cass blinked, then grinned. "I'll say 'amen' to that, Sister Veronica." Then he grew serious, adding, "Remember, I promised Serena's father on his deathbed I'd take care of her—and I'll do my best!"

"Then I will say—God give you strength to keep your vow. I will pray for you every day!"

"Thanks, sister." Cass moved to put Serena's small trunk in the rear seat, then put out his hand to help her. As soon as he touched her hand, a sudden bloodcurdling snarl caused him to whip around. He gasped as he faced a huge Siberian husky with an impressive set of fangs. Instinctively he reached to his hip for his gun, but it was stowed in his bag.

"It's just Thor, Cass," Serena said. She stepped between the man and the dog, saying, "Quiet, Thor—it's all right."

Then she turned and said, "I've got to take him. He's all I have, Cass."

"Does he bite?"

A dimple appeared in Serena's cheek and a mischievous light touched her eyes. "Only if I tell him to," she murmured. Then she asked, "Is it all right? Can he go?"

"Sure—just tell him I'm all right. He looks like he could tear a leg off a man."

Serena patted the floorboard of the rear seat, and at once the big dog leaped into the buggy. "Now I'm ready," she said. As the buggy left the grounds, she turned and waved to the nuns who were watching them go. When she turned her face forward, she murmured, "It's the only home I've had for a long time."

"Not too late to change your mind," Cass ventured. "Lots of people aren't going to make it, Serena. That dog of yours—he's going to be all right. Got a little mean streak in him. That's who'll make it—the tough ones."

Serena thought about this, then shook her head. "God told you to take me. He won't let us die."

"I'll do the best I can for you—but I've got a pretty bad record. No blue ribbons on my wall."

The buggy moved smoothly down the road, and Serena thought of the vast distance that lay before them. Then she turned to him and smiled, her eyes fixed on him.

"I'll go with you, Cass!"

PART TWO

SKAGWAY

★ ★ ★ ★

August 1897—April 1898

CHAPTER EIGHT

THE *WILLAMETTE*

★ ★ ★ ★

"Well, here it is," Cass said wearily. Late afternoon shadows were closing over the street as he fumbled in his pants pocket, came out with a key, and inserted it into the rusty lock. As he struggled to turn the key, he was aware that Serena had said little since they had gotten off the train. She had been lively enough on the journey back to Seattle, but all the way from the station she had carefully watched the swarming crowds and the streets that hummed with activity. *Probably wishes she were back in the convent,* Cass thought, *and so do I!*

But he ignored this thought and finally conquered the stubborn lock. Pushing the door open, he entered and set the trunk down with a loud thump on the floor. He'd left the place in a mess. There were still dirty dishes in the sink. The remains of the last meal he and Fletch had shared were still congealed in grease on the stove, and dirty clothes lay strewn everywhere.

"I left in a hurry," he muttered defensively. "Should have cleaned the place up a little."

Serena turned to him at once, saying, "I can do that, Cass. I've had lots of practice." Leaning down she untied the rope she'd fastened to Thor's collar, and the big dog began to sniff around and explore the room. She was wearing the same gray dress she'd worn when they'd met, but with the long journey it was wrinkled and stained. The strain of the trip on her was showing. She was very tired, for there had been only a few snatches of sleep, sitting bolt upright on the train. Her eyes were gritty with lack of rest and she couldn't remember ever being so exhausted. But she knew better than to complain and moved to the sink, saying, "I'll just clean this up."

Cass picked up the trunk and said, "You can do that later. First you'd better get some rest." He hesitated, then moved to the door of the single bedroom. "You can take the bedroom." Moving inside, he waited until she had come to stand in the center of the room. He set the trunk down, saying, "I'll clear my stuff out of here."

"Where will you sleep?" Serena asked.

"I'll find someplace—maybe in the livery stable."

Serena looked up at him and noted that he seemed awkward and ill at ease. "You can't do that, Cass. This town is packed. We'll fix you a place in the big room."

"Well, it might not look right." Cass faltered, then shrugged his shoulders. "I was expecting a younger girl—but I guess I just didn't think."

"We'll make the best of it," Serena assured him. "These aren't normal times. It doesn't bother me."

"It *would* be tough to find a place," Cass admitted. "Fellow next door has a spare wooden bunk I can borrow." He hesitated at the door, his blue-green eyes studying the girl. "Not exactly a convent, is it? But I can put a lock on your door."

Serena looked down at Thor. An impish expression leaped into her eyes and her full lips curved into a smile. "Oh, I think Thor is safer than any lock you could find."

Cass gave the big dog a careful glance, grinned and said, "Right! Well, let me get my junk cleared away, then you can rest up."

But Serena steadfastly refused to go lie down and rest. While Cass went to borrow a bed, she began washing dishes, and by the time Cass returned and had gotten the wooden bunk set up, she'd not only cleaned the room but had started a fire in the small wood stove. An hour later the two were sitting down to a good meal of bacon, eggs, biscuits—and a stack of pancakes.

"Say, it looks like I found a cook for our trip to the Yukon,"

Cass said, stuffing a large segment of a pancake covered with butter into his mouth. He was pleased with the meal and said, "I'm a rotten cook, Serena. Glad to see you're a good one."

"My mother taught me to cook when I was a little girl. And I got lots of practice at the convent." Serena sipped her coffee, happy that she had found something to do. She wanted to prove to Cass that she would not be a helpless female expecting to be pampered. "I'll have to learn to cook over a campfire, though. I've always used a stove."

"Won't be hard for you." Cass ate steadily, then said with satisfaction, "Best meal I've ever had!"

"You were just hungry."

"I was starved—but I know good cooking when I taste it." He watched as she rose and went to the stove. As she came to refill his coffee cup, he spoke what was in his mind. "Tomorrow I'll take you to your father's grave."

"Yes, I'd like that." She spoke calmly, and Cass once again was impressed with the girl's controlled demeanor. Young as she was, there was a certain air about her that he'd rarely seen in a woman. *Must be that convent, I guess—she's not easily rattled. Most girls her age would be nervous in a situation like this.* He sat idly in his chair, talking of the trip to the Yukon. After a few minutes, he noticed her eyes were drooping. "Gosh, I'm getting to be a gabby cuss!" he exclaimed. "You get to bed—no, I'll wash the dishes. That's fair—you cook, I clean."

"All right, Cass." Serena rose and moved to the door of the bedroom, speaking to Thor, who came to her side at once. She turned and said gently, "Thank you for taking us with you—most men wouldn't have been so kind."

Cass felt awkward and embarrassed. "Your da—well, he did a lot for me." He smiled at her, adding, "We'll have some tough times—but we'll make it. Good-night, Serena." When she had closed the door, he rose and washed the dishes, thinking of Fletch and the promise he had made to his dying friend. The room was full of memories, and when he finally pulled off his boots and stretched out on the bunk, he murmured, "Well, Fletch, I'm doing my best. . . ." Then he closed his eyes and within a matter of minutes fell sound asleep.

★ ★ ★ ★

The wood-burning engine expelled twin gusts of steam as it chugged into the station, then with a *chuffing* sound came to a stop. At once the passenger cars erupted as men and women scrambled to the brick pavement. The new arrivals were covered with black soot, and their clothes were wrinkled. They were wearied by their long journey, some of them coming all the way from the East Coast; but though their faces were drawn with the strain of the long trip, their eyes sparkled with excitement. They had come to Seattle, lured by the lust for gold and driven by the mania that caused them to give up everything for the one chance to become millionaires.

Two of the men pulled away from the main stream of passengers and headed for the station agent standing on the platform. The taller of the two asked, "We're looking for a fellow named Cass Winslow. Ever hear of him?"

The station agent gave the young man a sour look. "Think I know everybody in town? No, I never heard of him."

Aaron Winslow stared at the man, then nodded. "Thanks a lot. Appreciate your courtesy." He turned to his companion and said, "Come on, Jubal. We'll float around this burg."

"Sure." Jubal shifted his heavy grip to his free hand. "Guess we'd better get a hotel room, then we can do some looking."

But this proposal proved to be more difficult than either of them had expected. The town had gone wild with the gold strike. Every hotel was bursting with men, restaurants were overtaxed, and they were lucky to get a space on the floor—complete with blankets—at a rooming house on the edge of town.

When they had secured this modicum of shelter, they ventured forth with the purpose of finding their cousin. They passed by "steerers," men who had been hired to lure gold seekers to various outfitting stores. Hundreds sat in the roadways, dressed in gaudy mackinaws, wide-brimmed miners' hats, iron-cleated high-top boots, and heavy wool socks. All of them were waiting for a ship, and they passed the time playing cards and babbling about what it'd be like when they struck it rich.

After several fruitless hours of searching, Jubal said in despair, "I don't think this is going to work, Aaron. We could walk around for a month and not find Cass. Maybe we can go to the steamship offices. If he's bought passage, we can at least know when he's leaving and catch him at the dock."

They made the rounds of the transportation companies, asking about Cass, and at the same time inquiring about fares to the Klondike. What they discovered was not encouraging. None of them had Cass down as a passenger, and the tickets were being sold at outrageous prices. One agent for the *Excelsior* said, "Gentlemen, I've been forced to turn away ten times the ship's passenger list. You'd better be prepared to pay a thousand dollars to get to the Klondike."

When they left the office, Jubal said, "Gosh, Aaron, you have to be a millionaire just to *get* to the gold fields! I don't think we're going to make it." Jubal had joined Aaron almost on a whim. He had been scheduled to return to divinity school, but had decided that the experience of the gold rush might teach him more than theology books. The news of the gold rush had spread across the country like wildfire because of the telegraph. Every newspaper of every major city carried it on its front page. In fact, Jubal and Aaron had known about it long before Cass's letter had reached them. His father, Tom Winslow, had been apprehensive, saying, "It's a dangerous sort of trek, Jubal. Adventure is all right—but you could get hurt or even killed in a thing like this. You're my only son—and I hate for you to risk it."

But Jubal had been persuaded by Aaron and had been happy enough up to this point on their long journey to Seattle. Now he shook his head. "It's too expensive, Aaron. I can't afford it."

But Aaron said, "We'll find a way. Come on, I've got an idea of how we might find Cass." As they moved toward the center of town, he said, "Nobody's heard of Cass—but he's a newcomer. What we have to do is find somebody who knows the fellow he's staying with—Fletch Stevens. He's been here a long time."

"Why, sure! He'll be easier to find than someone new."

The scheme worked better than either of them had expected. They went to the courthouse, where a clerk looked through the records and gave them an address. "Stevens, Fletcher—1202 Oak Street—that's down close to the Sound—ask around."

An hour later they were standing in front of a run-down shack squeezed between a harness shop and a rooming house. Aaron squinted at the faded numbers written on the peeling white paint. "This is it—1202. Bet old Cass will be surprised to see us!" He knocked on the door, and when it was opened by an attractive young woman, he was somewhat rattled. "Ah—we're looking for Cassidy Winslow, miss."

"He's not here right now."

"Can you tell us when you expect him back?"

"He should be home any time. Are you friends of his?"

"I'm Aaron Winslow and this is Jubal Winslow. We're relatives of Cass. We just got into town and need to let him know we're here."

The girl's face showed relief. "Oh, I see. Well, in that case, won't you come in and wait?" She stepped back, and when they stepped inside, she turned to apologize. "I have to be careful— but Cass will be glad to see you, I'm sure. Be quiet, Thor!" She spoke to a large Siberian husky that had forced himself between her and the two men, a menacing growl low in his throat. "He won't bother you now," she assured them. "I'm Serena Stevens."

"Oh yes," Aaron nodded, grasping the situation. He had thought at first that the girl might be living with Cass—or perhaps was his wife. "You're Fletcher Stevens' daughter. Cass wrote me about how he was staying with you. Is your father here?"

Both men saw the flicker of emotion that passed over the girl's face. "No," she answered quietly. "He died recently."

"Oh, I'm sorry!" Jubal said at once. "We didn't know. Perhaps we should call later?"

"No, it's all right." Serena made an attractive picture in her light blue dress. She had just washed her hair and the dark brown curls framed her face in a most attractive fashion. Her lips were long and full and her skin glowed with youth. "Sit down—there's coffee if you'd like some." The two men sat down and she joined them, drinking tea instead. Quietly she told them her story, of how her mother had died and that she'd been separated from her father—then she related how her father had asked Cass to take her with him to the Klondike.

As Serena spoke, Aaron listened carefully. He was a man who had known women, but something about the calm demeanor of this girl puzzled him. Then, when she spoke of her years in the convent, he began to understand her better. *She's a looker—doesn't know much about the world, I'd venture.* He was curious about how Cass had come to agree to such a big responsibility, but even as he pondered the question, the door opened and Cass walked in.

"Well, I'll be—!" Cass halted and stared at the two men, then let out a yelp as the two men rose and came to beat him on the shoulders, crying his name. Finally he broke loose and stared at them. "You're a fine pair! Why didn't you tell me you were coming?"

Serena watched with a slight smile on her lips as the cousins all talked at once. *They're great friends, those three.* Then when Cass turned to introduce her, she said, "It must be nice to have a large family."

Aaron felt a pity for the girl—and a streak of admiration. "We Winslows think so. Don't you have any family at all?"

Cass said quickly, "I guess you could say *I'm* her family, Aaron. Her father sort of left her in my care." He reached over and put his hand on Serena's arm, and smiling down at her said, "Guess I'll be kind of a father to you, do you think, Serena?"

Serena looked up at him, but shook her head. "No, you're too young for that."

"Well, an older brother, maybe." Cass removed his hand abruptly from her arm, aware not only of the softness of its feel but of the grin that both Aaron and Jubal were fixing on him. "Come on—we'll go celebrate. You can get a good meal down at the Palace Restaurant for as little as it costs to feed an African village for six months!"

★   ★   ★   ★

After the peaceful existence she'd known at the convent, Serena's head swam with the clamor and excitement of Seattle. All three of the Winslows were determined to get to the Klondike as quickly as possible, and she accompanied them in their attempts to get equipped and find transportation to the gold fields of the North. Before their first foray, Cass had pulled out a map and placed it flat on the dining table. "Here—if you three are going to the Klondike you may as well see where it is." When they were gathered around, he used a fork as a pointer. "There's where we're headed for—Dawson."

114

"Why—it's in *Canada*!" Jubal exclaimed. "I never knew that."

"Sure—and we'll be under Canadian jurisdiction and law when we get there. Hope it's better than some we had in Wyoming!" He traced a line across the Gulf of Alaska, saying, "This is one way—'The All-water Route.' The ship will skirt around the edge of Alaska and put people off at St. Michael—here. From there it's possible to take a boat down the Yukon River all the way to Dawson."

"Sounds like the way to go," Aaron said.

"It's also called 'The Rich Man's Route,'" Cass added dryly. "Costs a fortune—and the boats are booked up for months."

"Is there a 'Poor Man's Way'?" Jubal inquired.

"Sure—it's called 'The Inside Passage.' Look, we'll get on a ship here, hug the coast, and get off either at Dyea or Skagway. Then we have to get to Dawson down the Yukon by boat."

"It looks closer that way—by 'The Inside Passage,'" Serena commented. She squeezed between Jubal and Aaron, tracing the route with her forefinger. "If it's cheaper, we'd better go that way."

Aaron was acutely conscious of the young woman's shoulder pressing against his arm. "What's it like, Cass—the trip overland?"

"The very devil, I hear." Cass frowned and tossed his fork down. "Oh, some of the promoters make the trip seem like a Sunday school picnic—but the men I've talked to who have actually *been* over the route say it's a killer. But we've got to take our chance. The thing is to get the best outfits and the best transportation."

"Well, let's get at it," Aaron grinned.

After studying the map and making some more plans, the four of them left to buy more supplies for the long journey that lay ahead.

As they walked along the crowded street, Serena noticed that Aaron was the only one of the three wearing fine clothing—a pearl gray suit and a striped shirt with a cravat. *He is very handsome*, Serena thought.

When the four of them stepped off the boardwalk, it was Aaron who offered her his arm in crossing the busy street.

"Don't mind those fellows, Serena," he said in a stage whisper. "Cass is more accustomed to herding cows than escorting young

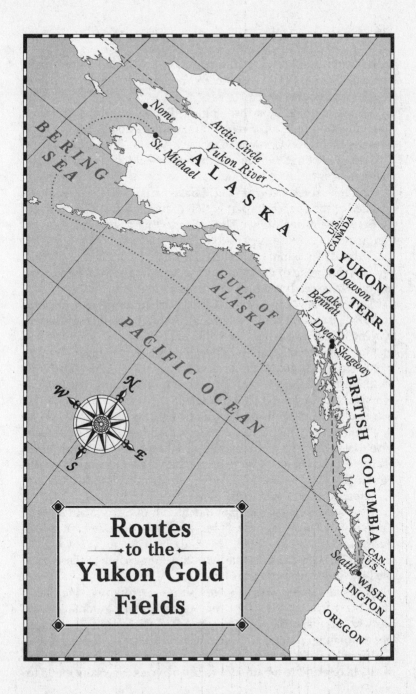

Routes
to the
Yukon Gold
Fields

ladies—and Jubal is a theologian, more interested in the gray beard of Daniel's billy goat in the book of Daniel than in the charms of a young woman."

Serena laughed aloud, saying, "I didn't learn to expect any such attention in the convent, Aaron. And I don't think I'll get much on the trail from what Cass says."

"Don't bet on it, Serena. An attractive girl like you will draw the men—but I'll protect you."

"Who'll protect her from *you*?" Cass demanded. He was a little irritated at the overzealous attention of his cousin and showed it.

Serena said demurely, "Thor will do that." She smiled up at Aaron, adding, "He's very jealous, I'm afraid."

"I don't blame him one bit!" Aaron said. "Well, Thor and I will see to it that none of these uncouth miners bother you. Now, let's get ourselves ready for a great voyage!"

The next few days Aaron and Cass haunted the steamship companies, and on Friday afternoon Aaron came into the shack waving an envelope.

"You got our tickets?" Jubal yelped. "On what ship?"

"A steamship named after a valley in Washington—the *Willamette*. I had to fight two other fellows for them, but we can stop worrying about getting to the Yukon."

"Are the staterooms pretty small?" Jubal asked.

"Staterooms? Jubal, these are for *deck space*!" Aaron stated. "We'll sleep where we can and eat what's put before us." His white teeth gleamed as he slapped the young man on the back with gusto. "We're *pioneers*, boy! No comforts for us until we come back loaded down with gold!"

Cass was studying a map of the interior of Canada but looked up to say in a worried tone, "I hope we have enough cash to get outfits and see us through." He shook his head and scowled. "I thought I'd seen crazy people—but the things some of these people buy—why, it's *outrageous*!"

Serena was leaning over his shoulder to study the map. "You're right, Cass. Why, the promoters are selling automatic gold pans set on a spindle—they're supposed to work like a gramophone, digging gold as they spin around!"

"That's as bad as one of those nutty 'Klondike Bicycles,' " Jubal said. He referred to an attempt to sell bicycles especially made to be used in travel in the Yukon—another fanatic idea that many gullible gold seekers fell for. "Now they're selling 'ice-cycles'— bicycles with a ski in the front for crossing the ice."

Aaron chuckled and shook his head. "Did any of you see the 'boat-sled'? They had one down at the dock this morning. It's some kind of sectional steel craft built to float. Darndest thing I ever saw!"

"What in the world did it look like?" Serena questioned.

"Oh, it had a couple of air chambers, some sails, and a burglar-proof compartment to store gold dust in—not that it'll ever get to Dawson."

"We've got a week before the *Willamette* sails," Cass said. "We'll spend it getting the most we can for our money. At least we won't be buying any crazy things like ice-cycles!"

★ ★ ★ ★

When the *Willamette* sailed out of Seattle on August 14, seventy-five hundred people pressed together on the dock to wish her a good voyage. The ship was actually an old coal-carrier that had been roughly converted into a passenger ship by the Pacific Coast Steamship Company. As nobody had bothered to sweep the coal dust from the ship, the passengers soon became covered with it—the three Winslows and Serena Stevens being no exceptions.

"You look like you're ready for a minstrel show, Cass," Serena said as the two stood on the deck watching the coastline fade. She drew her hand across her cheek, stared at her fingers, and burst out laughing. "I must look about the same."

Cass shook his head in despair. "There must be eight hundred people on this ship, Serena—not to mention three hundred horses."

Serena looked across the deck that was piled high with hay and said, "I'm glad the horses are here—otherwise we wouldn't have all that hay to make a bed in."

Cass stared at the hay, then grinned at her. "Always put a good face on things, don't you? Well, come along and let's see if we can find a place to put down our blankets. I'd say it's going to be a little crowded." He led the way to the mountain of hay, and the two found a hollow spot where they laid out their blankets. "Nice and cozy—with only a few hundred dirty men to share it with," Cass noted. He glanced at Thor and asked, "Will he stay here while we go and get something to eat?"

"Yes—if I leave something for him to guard." Serena pulled a handkerchief out of her pocket and placed it on top of her blanket. "Guard, Thor—guard!" Thor came and stood over the handker- chief, his eyes fixed on the girl. When they moved away, Serena said, "He'll make anyone who tries to take it pretty sorry, I think."

"He'll come in handy," Cass said. "Dogs are selling for as high as five hundred dollars—even for mutts. Most of them won't stand the cold, though. But Thor here, being a husky, will do just fine. Come on—the dining room's down this way."

They soon discovered that the ship only had eating facilities for sixty-five, so they had to wait until several shifts had passed through. When they finally got inside and faced the food that was slung on the table, they found it sickening. The floor was filthy, and the stench of horses and human sweat was overpowering. "Come on," Cass said in disgust after attempting a few bites. "We can't eat this garbage!"

They returned to their little space, where Serena rummaged around in one of her large bags and pulled out a sack. "Go find Jubal and Aaron. I kept some of our supplies out for us to snack on."

In the end, it was Serena's provisions that kept them going. She'd been the only one who'd thought of the possibility of a shortage of food on the ship and had packed two large sacks full of canned goods and crackers. As the *Willamette* lumbered through high waves day after day, the four came together to eat. Serena parceled out the food, and she'd made certain that Thor had provisions too.

One evening just as the sun dipped below the horizon, Aaron found Serena standing at the rail. For once there were few pas- sengers standing there, and he smiled and leaned on the rail, say- ing, "Haven't had a chance to tell you—but we all know you've kept us from starving."

Serena flushed at his praise and tucked a rebellious curl under the blue ribbon that tied her hair back. "Oh, you'd have survived." She was somewhat intimidated by Aaron Winslow. He was a gentleman in dress and manners. Unlike Cass, who had little polish, or Jubal, who was stiff with her, Aaron was easy and could make her smile. She had never seen such a fine-looking man and sensed that he knew much about women. She was a little uneasy in his presence and turned back to watch the choppy gray waves as they slapped against the boat.

Aaron was intrigued by Serena. He'd known many women and had been successful with a majority of them. But there was an innocence and ethereal quality about this girl that drew him. She was attractive, and he was sensitive to feminine beauty. He chatted easily with her, then let his hand fall on her arm. "You look very beautiful tonight," he said quietly. "I suppose you've been told that many times."

"No, not ever."

The simplicity of her reply and the shyness in her large blue-black eyes charmed Aaron. "Well, you should have been. A shame to waste such beauty in a convent." His dark eyes sparkled and he added, "When we get back to San Francisco with a pot full of gold, we'll dress you in silks and diamonds! By George, princes and presidents will fall at your feet!"

"I guess they'd look pretty silly," Serena giggled. But then he put his hand on her back and turned her around. She grew serious and watched him intently. When he leaned forward to kiss her, she didn't know what to do. She was both fearful—and tempted.

"Getting dark, Serena." They both turned to see Cass standing on the deck behind them, his face unsmiling. "I guess it's time to have something to eat."

"Yes, Cass," Serena said, her face pink with embarrassment. She hated that he had seen her practically in Aaron's arms. *He'll think I'm nothing but a loose woman,* she thought in anguish as she hurried away.

Cass stared at Aaron, his lips drawn into a taut line. "Aaron, we may as well get one thing straight. We leave Serena alone."

Aaron had been disconcerted, but he was a stubborn man. "There was nothing wrong, Cass. Don't get tangled up in your own harness."

Cass stared at Aaron steadily. "I think a lot of you, Aaron. But Serena is my responsibility. I'll whip any man who presses himself on her—and if I can't whip him, I'll shoot him."

Aaron was startled into silence. Then carefully he replied, "All right, Cass. It'll be like you say. Maybe I was out of line—but it won't happen again. Jubal and I both have grown very fond of Serena."

Cass didn't speak for a moment, then he smiled. "Fine! Maybe I was too jumpy, Aaron. I'm fond of Serena—but I'm fond of you, too."

Aaron grinned, then stepped forward and slapped Cass on the shoulder. "You confounded gunfighter! I swear I thought I was facing Wild Bill Hickok!"

Happy that the scene had ended pleasantly, Cass said, "Well, he's good, too. Come on, let's eat." The two moved down the deck and the moment passed—though neither of them forgot it for some time.

CHAPTER NINE

CASS MAKES AN ENEMY

★ ★ ★ ★

"Oh, it's so beautiful!" Serena exclaimed as she gazed at the rugged wilderness of the coast. She and the three Winslows had squeezed themselves against the rail of the *Willamette* at the word that their final destination was sighted. Now as the vessel chugged out of the rough waters of the sea into a bay, the four were anxious to get off the crowded ship and onto the shore. "This is Skagway Bay, isn't it, Cass?"

Cass was pressed against Serena very tightly and tried to move away—but the crowd all round them was too great. "Yes. The name comes from an Indian word, 'Skagus'—means the home of the north wind."

"Kind of a chilly name," Jubal murmured. "Guess it gets pretty cold here in winter. Already nippy."

"I was talking to the first mate last night," Cass said. "He said a man named William Moore saw this strike coming a long time ago. He built a cabin at the foot of a pass—called the White Pass. Guess he's in on the ground floor. Bound to be rich if he owns the townsite."

Aaron had remained silent, but now his eyes narrowed. "Look at that beach." When the others turned their gaze to the strip of land where the ships formed a line, he said, "It's not going to be easy, beating all the passengers ashore. There's no dock that I can see."

Cass agreed, adding, "Right—and finding all our gear will be a nightmare. The crew just threw our outfits into the hold—no order at all."

"I tied a bright yellow ribbon to all our bags," Serena spoke up.

"Where'd you get yellow ribbon?" Aaron asked. And when Serena blushed, he laughed. "I'll bet it was your best petticoat."

"Never mind!" Serena gave Aaron a defiant look. "You'll be glad when we start trying to find our outfits."

She was right about that—but just getting ashore proved to be their first nightmare. The long bay was dotted with hundreds of craft, all the way from large, dirty freighters such as the *Willamette* down to slim canoes. A few snub-nosed scows creaking with ponderous loads shuffled back and forth from the boats to the beach—which was a mile away. Serena watched in dismay as men, outfits, and animals were dumped into the shallow sea.

"I feel sorry for the horses," Cass murmured as they watched the frightened animals being swung from the decks in special boxes. When they were clear of the ship, the bottoms opened and the frantic horses were dropped into the water. "I'd like to drop the captain into that cold water!" Cass muttered angrily. He loved horses, and the cruel treatment of the animals on the voyage had sickened him.

Serena reached down and patted Thor's side. The purser had tried to get her to throw him over the side along with the goats, mules, oxen, and other dogs, but she had stoutly refused. Now she said, "Cass, it's so terrible!"

"It may get worse. These men are so crazy with gold fever, they'll do anything to get it."

As he spoke, Cass abruptly recalled how Jubal had warned him and Aaron about that very thing. Cass had been speaking of what he'd do when he was rich, and Jubal had listened quietly, then had said, "Cass, I hope you don't get too caught up in this thing. Any man that puts gold—or anything else—before God is going to lose everything."

Cass had grown irritated with Jubal's preaching and told him they'd all come to get rich. Aaron had slyly reminded the young preacher that Solomon and David had been rich, but Serena had taken Jubal's part. "Jubal's right," she'd said, her chin held high. "Money won't buy happiness."

Cass glanced down at Serena, admiring the gentle sweep of her smooth jaw. Her rich brown curls were blowing in the wind, and her cheeks glowed from the crisp air. She was wearing a simple brown dress, and the breeze pressed it against the curves of her figure. *Can't blame Aaron for admiring her*, he thought, then shook the thought away. "Well, let's see if we can get in one of those scows—I'm ready to get ashore."

After a few minutes of shoving past the other passengers who were gathering some of their belongings, Serena was finally wedged in the prow of one of the boats headed for shore. She held on tightly to Thor, and as soon as the small craft nosed onto the beach, she leaped to the ground, calling, "Come on, Thor!"

Cass joined her, and the two stood staring at the confusion that reigned up and down the beach as they waited for the boat containing Jubal and Aaron to arrive. "Why, it looks like an *anthill!*" Cass exclaimed. The entire beach was a confused mass of swearing men and neighing horses. Off to one side was a tattered jungle of tents, with sheet-iron stoves that sent spirals of smoke upward. Dogs yelped and howled, and the horses neighed piteously as they were driven back and forth. The air was filled with the racket of rasping saws, creaking wagons, and the shouts of angry men.

Aaron and Jubal came to stand beside them, and Cass shook his head. Looking around he said, "This is going to be a chore—look at that mess!"

The others looked at the mountainous piles of goods and saw that there was no order at all. Many of the crew who should have been responsible for unloading the gear had jumped ship to go to the gold fields. Now only a few harried representatives from the various shipping firms were in view, vainly attempting to sort out the confused melee.

"Look!" Jubal said urgently. "Those fellows over there are just taking what they like!"

Cass shot a glance at three men who were throwing outfits onto a wagon they'd drawn up beside the mass of goods. "We'll have to find our stuff, or some birds like that will just haul it off."

The four of them joined the cursing would-be miners, pawing

at the boxes and bags, but it was Serena's yellow ribbons that saved them. One by one they discovered their gear—except for one large box. They split up, and Serena muttered with determination, "We've *got* to find that box. It's got all our clothes in it— oh, there it is!" She ran over to the wagon where the three men had tossed a box on top of the heavy load—and there was a yellow ribbon fluttering from one of its ties.

"I'm sorry, but you've made a mistake," she said to the three men. "That box with the yellow ribbon belongs to me."

The three men halted in astonishment. Two were roughly dressed, but the third man who sat on the seat of the wagon wore better clothing. His eyes swept over Serena, taking in the trim form and the beauty of her face. At once he jumped down and took off his hat. "Your box, you say?" He was not much over thirty, and there was a rakish look about him. He stood just under six feet and was trim and muscular. His hair was black, with a touch of gray at the temples, and he had a pair of direct hazel eyes. "Well, I think you've made a mistake, young lady. I remember tying that ribbon on myself." He turned to ask one of his partners, a hulking giant, "Don't you remember that, Leo?"

"Sure, Brent. I used one of my very own handkerchiefs."

A lean man, an albino, came and stood close to Serena. "Why, we all make mistakes, sweetheart. But a gal as pretty as you— why, we won't take exception." His face was colorless, even his eyes, and there was an aura of evil about the man. He wore two guns, and as he spoke he let his hands brush against the butts in a loving fashion.

"I'm Brent Traphagen," the black-haired man announced. He was graceful as a cat as he came and stood directly in front of Serena. He seemed to expect some reaction from her. "You've not heard of me?"

"No—but that's my box, Mr. Traphagen."

The big man named Leo reached up, taking the yellow strip of cloth between his fingers. "Hey, Brent—this looks like part of ladies' underwear! Whitey, you better check the lady and see if we've got a match here."

A small group of men had stopped their work to observe, and an older man with a full beard said, "Traphagen—call off your dogs."

Instantly Traphagen leveled his eyes on the older man and let his hand rest on his gun butt. "Tyler, you're outgunned. Go away or I'll rub you out!"

Tyler looked at the three, then dropped his head, at which Traphagen laughed. "Now, maybe that *is* your box, miss—I didn't get your name."

Serena's face was pale, for nothing in her past had prepared her to face evil men. She did not wish to give her name, so she turned and tried to leave, but Traphagen instantly took her arm, holding it in an iron grip. "Now, don't get upset," he smiled. "You and me, we'll go to my place and talk about it. Here, just get up on the wagon—"

"Let that girl go!"

Traphagen loosed his grip on Serena's arm and whirled to face the challenge that came harshly. He found himself facing a tall young man wearing rough clothing. He was young, but he had a gun stuck in his belt and held himself ready. Brent Traphagen was no coward, but he liked an edge. Having no idea of the skill of the young man, he hesitated, but cast a look at Whitey Dugan. Noting that the albino was watching the newcomer, he said easily, "Don't know you, do I?"

"Cass Winslow—now what's this all about, Serena?"

"They've got our box, Cass—see the ribbon?"

"Little lady's made a mistake," Traphagen said smoothly. He had a nice smile and used it now. "With all this gear, it's easy to make a mistake. Looks like the lady's made one."

"You're the one making a mistake, Traphagen," Cass said. His temper had risen and he said evenly, "I'm taking the box."

Traphagen ruled men by fear, and the mutter that ran around the crowd was a clear signal to him. *Got to get this fellow down—* He glanced at Dugan and saw that the albino was grinning with fixed lips. *We've got him hipped—when he goes for his gun, Whitey will take him.*

"You're a thief, Winslow!" Traphagen allowed anger to wash across his smooth face. "Get out—or go for that gun."

Men leaped out of the way, frantically scrambling to get out of the line of fire. Cass said evenly, not taking his eyes off Traphagen, "Serena—move away." He waited until the girl had stepped back, then said harshly, "All right, Traphagen, you're tough on women—see how you can handle a man."

Traphagen took one final glance at his two henchmen. Whitey was standing directly behind Winslow like a wire spring, and Leo Ritter stood to Winslow's right with his hand under his coat. Assured that he was covered, Traphagen nodded. "We'll just see—"

But even as he spoke, Whitey felt something cold and hard on the base of his neck. A soft voice said, "You can scratch for it this time, Whitey."

Traphagen wrenched his gaze from Winslow and saw a tall man smiling coldly at him. He had lifted a gun and held it on the neck of the albino. "Jubal—put your gun on that big ape—"

But Jubal had already moved to stick the barrel of his gun into the ribs of Leo Ritter. "Steady—" he said quietly, then reached over and plucked a short-nosed .38 from the belt of the big man. When he had it, he turned and said, "All right, Cass—we've got these two."

Cass stood loosely, his blue eyes glittering in the sun. They were more blue than green now, and there was an indolence in his bearing that suggested a lazy cat. At the same time, the very carelessness of his tall figure warned Traphagen.

"Well, Traphagen, let 'er flicker any time you're ready," Cass murmured.

But Brent Traphagen was not moving. He had a keen brain and knew that he was now facing a man about whom he knew nothing. He was quick with a gun, but something about Cass Winslow kept him very still. His mind raced, and he understood that there was no way he could win this one. *If I get Winslow, one of his friends will plug me—got to ease off!*

"Why, no box is worth a shooting," Traphagen said. He forced a smile, bottling up the raging anger that swelled inside his chest. "I guess you got the best of the argument, Winslow."

The hum of voices rose, and Cass knew the man before him was not used to being faced down. "Sure you don't want to try it?" Cass goaded. "Just me and you, Brent."

Traphagen shook his head. "A man's manners get rusty out here." He turned to Serena and said, "Sorry, miss. I never should have questioned the word of a lady. I'll ask you to accept my apology."

Serena's knees were weak, for she had never been in the presence of violent men. She nodded, saying, "Thank you," but she knew that sudden death had been avoided by a hairsbreadth. Fearfully she looked at Cass, thinking, *He could have been killed!*

"Leo, get the box down for the lady." When the big man had tossed the box down, Traphagen forced a smile. His face was flushed, but he let nothing show in his features as he murmured, "Be seeing you, Winslow."

Cass watched as the well-dressed Traphagen stepped back into the wagon, and when the other two joined him, he spoke to the horses. Whitey Dugan called out, "I'll see you around—" his colorless eyes fixed on Aaron.

Cass turned as Serena came to him.

"You came out of that better than you know," said the tall man with the beard who had been standing off to the side. "I'm Asa Tyler." After everyone was properly introduced, Tyler shook his head. "Never saw Traphagen back down—not ever!"

"Who is he?" Aaron demanded. "He's trouble, I know that—but what does he do?"

"Gambles—lends money. Got plenty of money, but nobody knows where it came from. He pretty much takes what he wants."

Serena stepped forward and put her hand out. "Thank you for offering to help me, Mr. Tyler."

The old man's eyes grew warm. "Why, I wasn't that much help, miss." Then he turned to the three men and warned, "This ain't over, you know. Traphagen ain't gonna forget—and neither will them two thugs who work for him. Dugan's killed three men with them fancy guns of his—and Ritter's a bruiser. Kicked a man to death in a joint in Portland."

"Thanks for the warning, Asa," Cass said. The close brush with violence had sharpened him, and now he asked, "Are you headed for Dawson?"

"Sure—ain't we all?" His wise old eyes studied the group, and he said, "I prospected with a feller by the name of Joe Winslow. Reckon he's any kin?"

"Joe Winslow? Why, he sure is!" Cass exclaimed. "Is he here?"

"If he ain't, he sure as blazes will be," Tyler grinned. "Joe wouldn't miss a strike like this!"

It was with Asa Tyler's help that Cass and the others got their tents up in a better place than most—a sheltered spot half a mile from the beach but with a little privacy. They made camp in the shelter of some skinny firs that shielded them from the view of the masses swarming on the beach.

Serena insisted that Asa stay for supper, and by the time twilight was beginning to close in, the five of them were sitting around a cheerful campfire eating a rich stew that she had concocted out of the tinned meat.

"Girl, come and be my cook." Tyler grinned as he wolfed down the stew. "I'll pay you out of my gold—when I find it, that is."

"Here now, that's a fine thing!" Jubal laughed. "We give you a good supper—and you try to steal our cook." He lifted his mug, drained off the coffee, then said thoughtfully, "That was pretty close today, Cass. Could have gone the other way."

"You got that right, Reverend," Asa spoke up. "Traphagen, he's a bad one. Looks slick, but so does a wolf. Wolves ain't as bad as Brent Traphagen, though." Then he stood up and stretched, saying, "Well, good to have you folks. If I can be of any help, just ask."

"What's next, Asa?" Aaron asked. "I'm ready to start digging for gold."

Tyler laughed softly. "First you got to git whar it is, Aaron. And I reckon thet's gonna be about as hard as gettin' it out of the ground."

Cass looked up from the blaze, his eyes intent. "Getting to the river, you mean?"

"That's gonna be a trouble. Two ways to go—you got a map on you?"

"I'll dig it out," Cass offered. He rose and rummaged through a sack in the tent, then returned with a small map, which he flattened on the ground.

Tyler bent over and the four watched as he touched the paper. "There's the White Pass—right here. It zigzags all over the place, forty-five miles long. That's ten miles longer than the Dyea trail across the Chilkoot—but it's six hundred feet lower."

"Which one you taking, Asa?" Aaron asked.

"Wal—it ain't so easy to decide. The White Pass, I reckon. If the weather don't catch us—that would be the best way to go."

"Mind if we tag along?" Cass asked tentatively. "I don't want to butt in—"

"Shore! Shore! Why, I'll be proud for your company." His seamed face beamed, and he turned to Serena. "You know how to make sourdough biscuits?"

"No—is it hard to learn?"

"Not with a good teacher like me! Well, I should be getting back." He hesitated, then said to Jubal, "Glad to have you along, Reverend. We're goin' to need God on this here trip. Good to know we got one of His own with us!"

Aaron grinned across the fire at Jubal. The rich yellow tongues of flame cast his chiseled face into angular lines, and his black eyes gleamed. "You're our fire insurance, Reverend Winslow. Up to you to keep us from perdition."

Jubal was sitting hugging his knees and staring into the fire. At Aaron's comment he released them abruptly and cast a reproachful glance at his cousin. "No man can do that, Aaron. We all stand alone before God."

"Sure, that's right. I was just kidding. You stick with your guns."

Cass nodded his agreement. "Lots of preachers in the Winslow line, Jubal. I'm glad you're keeping up the family tradition."

After a few minutes both Aaron and Jubal went to their tent to turn in. Asa had said he was coming by early in the morning to check out their gear and help them find what they hadn't purchased in Seattle.

Serena leaned back away from the heat of the fire, enjoying the peaceful moment. The long trip had worn her thin, but now as the wind made a sibilant whisper as it moved through the green needles overhead, she felt the fatigue leaving her. She was tired enough in body, but it was the mental strain that had caused her to lose weight. The uncertainty of the future and the suddenness of her new life pulled at her. Leaning down she picked up a tiny stick, held it over the fire, then pulled it back to study the blue and yellow tongue of flame. It wavered as she breathed on it, and Cass, who was sitting beside her, said, "Pretty nice—all this peace and quiet, isn't it?"

"Yes. I'm soaking it in." She watched the tiny flame until it burned down, then tossed the stick into the fire. For a time she and Cass spoke of the trip. "When do you think we'll leave, Cass?"

"Pretty soon, I hope. If winter catches us, we'll be in poor shape. I'm glad we met up with Asa. That'll be a help." He stretched his arms high, exhaled, then turned to say, "Sorry you had to get involved with that fellow Traphagen."

"Oh, I was terrified, Cass. Those men would have killed you if Jubal and Aaron hadn't come to help."

"Expect so. It was pretty close." He sat quietly, then looked up abruptly. The sky was spangled with myriads of stars. "They look close, don't they? Mighty pretty."

"I wish I knew their names."

"Like sailors do?" He studied the dark blue curtain of the night, admiring the spectacle, then said, "I think sometimes about how people have been looking up at those same stars for hundreds of years—just like we are." Being off the crowded ship had brought a peace to him, and he smiled as he added, "Maybe a cave man and a cave girl sat in front of a fire and looked up at those stars—just like us, Serena." He picked up a handful of loose dirt, let it filter through his fingers, then looked at her with a trace of sadness. "I guess they loved and fought and had children—those two—but they're just dust now."

"Why, you sound so—so *empty*, Cass! I don't like for you to feel like that," she said softly.

Cass turned toward her. He was so close that he could see the pupils of her eyes as they reflected the amber light of the fire. He had been apprehensive about bringing her, but she had never once complained. "Sorry—guess I've got a case of the mullygrubs."

"The—*what?*" Serena stared at him. "It sounds awful—but I guess it just means you get discouraged sometimes."

"Don't you?"

"Sometimes—but not often." She smiled at him and swept the horizon with a quick gesture. "We're caught up in something big, Cass. People from all over the world are coming here—and we're part of it! And I'm glad to be here—to experience the adventure of it!"

Cass was fascinated by her excitement. Without thinking he put his hand on her shoulder and squeezed it. Her lips opened slightly with surprise, and she became very still. Cass had smiled, intending to commend her for her behavior, but he was caught by the clear beauty of her face. She looked at him with trust, her eyes large as he bent his head. Then he kissed her—and her lips were soft and sweet as they yielded under his. There was a wild sweetness in her that brought strong hungers to Cass—but he drew back at once.

"Sorry, Serena. I—I didn't mean to do that."

Serena had never been kissed, and she was confused. "It's all right, Cass. I guess we're entitled to one mistake." She stood up and walked to her small tent they had set up for her. Crawling inside, Serena wrapped her blanket around her and lay down. She had been powerfully stirred by the simple kiss, but when Cass had drawn back, she had felt rebuffed. As she lay there, tears flooded her eyes. *Does he think I'm bad?* she wondered. She had no experience with men, and for a long time she lay there, knowing that she and Cass had passed some sort of mark—that they could never go behind the kiss.

Cass felt as miserable as he'd ever felt in his life. *Fine—that's how you keep your promise to Fletch! Get the girl out of a convent—then start to romance her!* He was a sensitive young man and was powerfully moved by the stirrings that the kiss had brought to him. He had kissed women before, but the touch of Serena's lips had been like nothing he'd known. She was so fresh, so innocent—and that for some reason made her all the more desirable.

Not wanting to wake Jubal and Aaron, Cass grabbed some extra blankets and rolled up in them a little ways away from the fire. He closed his eyes and tried to sleep. But for a long time, the memory of the kiss disturbed him. He vowed angrily, *All right—I made a mistake. I'll be more careful.* Then he remembered how he'd been furious at Aaron's attention to Serena—and this made him feel totally miserable! *I'll leave her alone—and I'll see to it that no other man bothers her!*

Somehow this vow didn't soothe his jangled nerves. For hours he twisted and turned under the bright stars. They seemed to be eyes that peered down on him, and he finally buried his head under his blanket until sleep overtook him.

CHAPTER TEN

Angel in a Red Coat

★ ★ ★ ★

For three such active young men as the Winslow cousins, the constant delays that prevented them from starting at once for the gold fields were frustrating. If it had been up to them, they would have started out the day after they stepped off the *Willamette*—but they soon discovered that this was not practical. Asa Tyler and other men more experienced in the rigors of the trail managed to persuade them to take the time to get their gear in perfect shape before plunging into the unforgiving wilderness.

"I know you young fellers are chompin' at the bit," Asa shrugged. "But it's a sight better to spend a few days gettin' things ready. Many a man I've seen fail because he didn't pack his outfit right."

The "few days" stretched out to "a couple of weeks," but at last, as September wound down, every precaution had been made, and the three Winslow men gathered around the small sheet-iron stove for a last breakfast before hitting the trail.

Jubal had cooked the meal, and now he interrupted Aaron and Cass, who were going over the map for the one hundredth time. "Where's Serena?" he asked. "Somebody go and get her out of that tent before these flapjacks get cold."

Cass turned to face Serena's tent, which was set off from the one used by the men, separated by a few spindly firs. "Serena—

come on!" he yelled. "We've got to eat and get these tents packed!"

"Just a minute—you all go on and eat. I'll be there shortly."

Inside the tent Serena looked down at herself with a sinking feeling. Ever since they'd arrived at Skagway, she'd worn a dress, one of the two she'd brought. But from what she'd heard from Asa and others about the harsh conditions ahead on the trail, she'd come to the conclusion that a woman's clothes wouldn't be adequate. For several days she'd pondered the matter, then had taken the plunge. She'd taken a few dollars and made her way to the general store and purchased two complete men's outfits. She'd been embarrassed by the crude comments made by the owner, but she had ignored him and returned to her tent with her "new clothes."

But now as she looked at herself, she felt a moment of doubt. She wasn't sure what the reaction of her wearing men's garb would be from Cass, Aaron, and Jubal. Her years at the convent had instilled a strong sense of propriety.

"What do you think, Thor?" she whispered. "Do I look too— too bad?" The big dog considered her thoughtfully with his large yellow eyes. Then, opening his jaws in a massive yawn, he put his head down and closed his eyes. Serena giggled and punched him with the toe of her new boot, saying, "I hope Cass and the others take it like you do." She took a deep breath, then lifted the flap and stepped outside. She saw the three men turn to look at her and said hastily, "How do you like my new outfit? I thought it'd make traveling easier."

Aaron said at once, "Fine! Makes a lot of sense. Looks nice, too." He was surprised to note that the snug-fitting tan trousers and the light blue checked shirt set off her figure in a startling fashion—far more so than the shapeless dresses had. He noted the small boots and said, "Surprised you found things to fit you."

Cass was taken aback by the transformation but said grudgingly, "Be easier for you on the trail." He took his eyes from her quickly, saying, "Let's eat and get those tents packed."

It was a quick meal, but Serena didn't forget to commend Jubal for his cooking. "Your pancakes are better than mine, Jubal." She smiled at the young man. "I don't know how you do it. We use the same recipe—but mine are tough as shoe leather half the time."

Jubal's face lighted up at her comment. He no longer felt tense around her. During the days of waiting, he and Serena had gotten to know each other better. The two of them were tied by their Christian commitment, and he realized that he was strongly drawn to the girl—more than he admitted. They spent hours talking about the Bible. Though they each had a different religious upbringing—considering Serena's days in the convent—they never grew sharp with each other over the differences in their beliefs.

Aaron had teased Jubal about the girl once. "Better watch out, Preacher. You might wind up with a wife and a house full of kids."

Jubal had given his cousin a strange look. "A man could do worse. Did you know the Lord favors married men, Aaron?"

"Is that in the Bible?"

"The eighteenth chapter of Proverbs, verse twenty-two. 'He that findeth a wife findeth a good thing—and obtaineth favor of the Lord.' "

Jubal had said no more, but Aaron had watched the pair carefully, and now, as he pulled down Serena's tent, he said, "You have an admirer, I see." When she gave him a startled look, he smiled and added, "Jubal, of course. Haven't you noticed?"

Serena flushed, for she had, of course, noted Jubal's growing attention. But she shook her head, saying, "There's nothing to that, Aaron." But there was an uncertainty in her tone and manner, so that Aaron was even more certain that the two were closer than he or Cass had realized.

★　★　★　★

The trail they found themselves on as they left Skagway was a forty-five mile switchback that wound through bog and mire. It crossed and recrossed rivers, climbed over dangerous mountain trails, and followed canyons and valleys until it ended on the beach at Lake Bennett, where the Yukon River had its beginning.

For two days they trudged along, and if it had not been for the three pack mules they'd bought, they would not have been able to make the trek at all. On the morning of the third day, Aaron said to Asa Tyler, "This isn't as bad as I thought, Asa. We're making good time."

Tyler lifted his eyes to the winding trail that zigzagged ahead, cutting behind a rise of stone outcroppings. "Wal, we made good time for a fact—but this here trail, it's like a woman I had once—she looked good, but there wasn't never no telling when she'd cut loose and have a fit."

Serena, who was walking close behind the two men, laughed aloud at Asa's comparison. "You don't trust women, do you, Asa?"

"Some of 'em have contributed to my education, gal. And this here trail, it's behaving purty well right now—but we'll see how she goes."

At first it seemed that Asa's dire predictions were too gloomy. The next day they passed Devil's Hill, clinging to a slippery slate path scarcely two feet wide. "This thing is like a corkscrew!" Jubal gasped. He was holding the reins of one of the pack mules, and when he looked down at the rocks five hundred feet below, he turned pale.

"Not afraid to meet your Maker, are you, Reverend?" Asa teased.

"No, I'm not," Jubal snorted, giving the lines a hard jerk. "I'm bound for heaven, but I have to admit the *getting* there worries me a little!"

The next day they edged around Porcupine Hill, which was even worse—then came Summit Hill, a thousand-foot climb. The rains had loosened the soil, so that liquid mud streamed down off the mountain like a flood. Huge slabs of granite barred the way, and once a yawning mudhole swallowed up one of the mules of the party in front of them. The mule made such piteous noises that his owner finally shot him in disgust, cursing as he waded out to retrieve the pack.

The death of the pitiful animal seemed like a foreboding sign for evil fortune to fall on the struggling travelers. That night the cold weather hit them like a blow. Torrential rains fell, and by morning, the temperatures had dropped so low that all of them had chattering teeth and blue faces.

"Still think this is a purty nice trail, Aaron?" Asa demanded slyly as they struggled to get the tents struck and packed. Staring up at the peaks ahead, he turned a doubtful face to the four young people. "If any of you can pray, reckon this is as good a time as any to start," he pronounced. "We got here too late. Lots of folks gonna be headed back to Skagway."

"And do what, Asa?" Cass demanded.

"Wait till spring."

Cass stared at the older man incredulously. "You mean—stay all *winter* in that mudhole?"

"Some won't. They'll get on ships and go home."

"Not me!" Cass said adamantly. "I didn't come here to spend six months sitting in the mud at Skagway."

Serena was watching Asa carefully. "Cass, I think we better consider it. If Asa says—"

"I'm going on," Cass said sharply. "If you want to go back, you and Jubal can go. Aaron and I will get through."

But Serena shook her head. "No, we must all stay together. I'll see if I can get a fire started. We'll need hot food to face this cold."

After a quick hot meal, they bundled up in the warmest clothes they possessed, loaded the mules, then moved out. All day long the weather was unrelenting as they slogged through the mud, shivering in the icy rain. They traversed no more than a few miles, and then were forced to make camp. Jubal and Aaron were able to start a fire under a fly that kept the rain from pouring onto it, and Serena threw a meal together. As they sat on boxes, downing the hot food, Jubal said, "Cass, we might *have* to think about waiting until spring. We didn't get over two miles today, and I heard one fellow say it's worse up ahead."

"We can make it," insisted Cass as he tore a cold biscuit in two and chewed it doggedly. He was short with them, and the others remained quiet. Finally just before Serena went to her tent, she came and asked, "Are you angry with me, Cass?"

Startled, Cass stared at her. He had been upset for days by his reaction to her kiss but would not admit it. "No, of course not." He tried to soften his manner, saying, "It's just that this is going to be a tough trip. I tried to tell you, but neither of us knew it'd be this hard."

"I'm not complaining, Cass."

"No—but Jubal wants to quit—and I don't think Aaron will stick it out either. This is just a lark for those two. But for me it's more than that."

Serena studied Cass's face, noting that he looked drawn and

tired. He hadn't cut his hair, and now the tawny locks lay loosely around his ears and on his neck. His lips were drawn tight and his eyes were hooded so that she could not tell what he was feeling. Although she didn't realize it herself, she had put an extraordinary degree of trust in Cass Winslow. Having no family, Serena naturally needed someone to cling to—and since she had left the convent with him, she had subconsciously reached out to him. "I don't want to be a burden, Cass," she murmured softly, lifting her eyes to look at him.

She made a fetching picture, her curly hair forming a soft canopy around her face. She had lost a little weight, her cheeks were slightly sunken, which made her eyes look very large. Her lips were wide, the lower one being fuller than that of most women. And as he looked at her, Cass remembered the kiss under the stars. He was still chafing at himself for what he held to be a breach of faith to Fletch Stevens. "You're no burden, Serena," he said roughly, then seeing that he had hurt her, added more gently, "We'll make it, Serena, don't worry."

"All right, Cass, if you say so." She summoned up a smile, which brought out the dimple in her cheek. "Good-night," she murmured, then turned and disappeared into her tent.

Cass went to the other tent, and Aaron, who had already gone to bed, said, "Cass, I don't want to be a pest, but do you think Serena can take this trail? She's not as tough as you are. Might be better if Jubal did take her back to Skagway."

"She wouldn't go, Aaron. She might be little, but she's stubborn enough for a tribe of Indians. We'll be all right. If we're lucky, maybe the weather will break."

They had no such luck, and the weather didn't break; it only got worse. Soon the trail was filled with those who had given up. It was like a defeated army in retreat—a continuous string of beaten men staggering back toward Skagway. They all had the glazed look in their faces of the critically wounded—staring eyes and half-open mouths and a wobbly gait.

For Cass and those who strove to push on, those in retreat proved to be almost as great an obstacle as the miserable weather. As a gray drizzle shut out the sun, the mud acted as a sort of glue, making a hopeless tangle of men and animals, tents and supplies. Fires sputtered and went out, and shivering men—haggard and whipped—hovered over the dying embers.

During this time of delays, the wretched horses and mules had to stand, often for hours, with crushing loads on their backs, because no one would chance unloading them in case movement might resume. Many of the poor beasts had been doomed to the glue factory, and had been bought in Seattle at outlandish prices. Some had never been broken or ever felt the weight of a pack on their backs before.

One gray afternoon when Cass pulled the group over for a rest, Serena noted that one man had unloaded his animal, a scrawny horse. When she looked closer she saw with disgust that the horse had running sores on its back. The man threw a blanket over the sores and proceeded to reload an enormous heap of gear back on the injured animal.

A young man who apparently was on his way back came to chat with the men. When Serena said indignantly, "That man ought to be shot!" he gave her a guarded glance.

Aaron said grimly, "If we started shooting every man who mistreats his horses, we'd run short of ammunition." Then he said, "This is Serena Stevens—and I didn't get your name."

"I'm Jack London." He was a broad-shouldered man in his middle twenties. He had a pair of bright brown eyes, a shock of crisp brown hair, and a determined jaw. "Glad to know you," London nodded. He motioned up the trail, saying, "Canadian border's up there about a mile. The mounties are checking all the stock. They're shooting animals like that one with the sore back."

"You're giving up?" Cass asked. London didn't look like a quitter. He was strong and had a determined look. "Why not go on?"

"I talked to the chief of the mounties—fellow named Samuel Steele. He says the bad weather has closed the trail ahead. Be closed all winter, he said. Nothing to do but dig in and wait for a break."

Serena asked, "Isn't there another way?"

"Steele mentioned the Chilkoot Pass. It's been crossed this time of year. Steele said that none of us are going to get to Dawson before spring—no matter which route we take."

Stubbornly Cass shook his head. "We're going to go on, London."

A cheerful smile broke across the bronzed face of the other man. "Good luck—but I think I'll see you back in Skagway." He nodded to Serena, adding, "Talk a little sense into these fellows, miss." Then he turned and moved back down the muddy trail.

The four continued their journey, arriving at the Canadian border late that afternoon. A long line of men and pack animals stretched out before them, and they discovered that London had spoken the truth about the border check. The line moved slowly, and dark had nearly fallen by the time they reached the three mounties. "These are policemen?" Serena asked Asa.

"Sure—the best in the world, I'd say," Asa said. "From what I hear, these fellows don't put up with much. I heard about the time there was a riot in one of the towns in Canada and the local law sent to mountie headquarters for help. The sheriff and the mayor met the train that was bringing reinforcements, and jest one mountie got off—and it wuz thet fellow right there, the tall one, if that's Steele. When the mayor asked Steele about the rest of the force, Steele just looked at him and he says, 'There's only one riot, isn't there?' "

Serena fixed her eyes on the tall mountie, interested in the sort of man who would do such a thing. "He's fine looking, isn't he?"

"Wal, I reckon a female would notice thet. Maybe you can flutter your eyelashes at him, Serena," he grinned slyly. "Sort of influence him to let us go through."

"Asa! What a thing to say!" Serena declared indignantly. "You are the most awful man!"

"Been done before," Asa shrugged. "But looks to me like those mounties are turning back everybody."

Cass had grown impatient with the delay, and when he finally reached the checkpoint where the mounties were, he said, "I'm Cass Winslow."

"I'm Steele." The speaker was a big man of magnificent physique—tall, powerful, and deep chested. His kinsmen had served the King of England for three generations. One had fought with Wolfe at Quebec, another with Nelson at Trafalgar. Another had been the tallest soldier in the British army of occupation in Paris following the overthrow of Napoleon. Steele's father had been one of the original Northwest Mounted Police who helped to negotiate with Sitting Bull after the Custer massacre at Little Bighorn.

He had policed the construction of the Canadian Pacific Railway, and now ruled the Yukon territory with an iron hand. His nickname, as Cass would soon discover, was "The Lion of the Yukon."

"I think you'll find our animals sound enough," Cass said aggressively. "We'd like to press on."

Steele had penetrating blue eyes and laid them now on the young man. He was so tall that Cass felt overpowered—which was unusual for him. "I'm sorry, Mr. Winslow, but I'm afraid that you'll have to turn back."

Cass stared at him, and just then the others came forward. "What's the trouble, sir?" Jubal asked respectfully.

"The trouble is that bad weather is closing in. By tomorrow the pass will be frozen over so badly that nobody could make it through with animals."

"We can do it," Cass said defiantly. He lifted his chin, glaring at the tall policeman. "We'll take the risk."

"This isn't America, Mr. Winslow," Steele said evenly. "In your own country, you may throw your life away as you please—but in my country, you'll abide by the laws of Canada." His eyes came to rest on Serena, and he hesitated. "Are you with this party, miss?"

"Yes, I am. My name is Serena Stevens, sir," Serena said. She was wearing a fur hood that framed her oval face, and her smooth cheeks and large blue-black eyes made her most attractive. "We do need to get to Dawson—if there's any way at all."

Steele shook his head and waved a big hand at the men who formed the line behind them. "All these men feel the same, but His Majesty's government is responsible and cares for their safety—even if they don't." He allowed a smile to lift the corners of his wide mouth. "And I would be less than faithful to my commission if I allowed a young lady to endanger herself on such a useless quest."

Cass argued loudly for some time, but finally Asa said, "Cass, if Superintendent Steele says it can't be done, why, that's all we need to know. We'll have to go back."

Jubal and Aaron added their voices, and Cass, his face dark with anger, turned and walked back to his pack animal. Serena, however, stepped closer to Steele and put her hand out. A small smile creased her lips, and as his big hand took her own, she said,

"Thank you, Superintendent. You'll have to forgive Mr. Winslow. His whole heart's in this thing."

"No offense, Miss Stevens." Steele held her hand for a moment, marveling at the ease of manner in the American girl. Englishwomen were more reserved, but he admired her bearing. "Are you related to Mr. Winslow?"

"No, not at all. He was a friend of my father, you see. . . ."

Steele listened as Serena gave him a brief account of her history, then nodded. "Sorry about your father. And I can understand Mr. Winslow's urgency—but, really, Miss Stevens, very few of these thousands are going to get through to Dawson before spring. Even those who leave from St. Michael to steam up the Yukon are going to be disappointed. The river will be frozen over and they'll have to wait just as your people will."

"Well, I'm grateful you were here," Serena said. "If you hadn't been, we'd have gone on and—and come to grief, I expect." The strain of humor that lay in her surfaced abruptly. A dimple appeared and she smiled up at him. "The Bible says there are such things as angels who sometimes come to help us. I never thought angels wore red coats, but are you *certain* you're not my guardian angel?"

The question amused Steele, who grinned broadly. He was a serious man, forced to be so by the rigorous demands of his duty, but he liked a good joke, and coming from this attractive young lady it was doubly good. "I've been called many things, Miss Stevens—but never an angel."

"In any case, thank you so much for your care." Voices of protest from the line of men behind startled her, and she glanced back in alarm. "Oh, I must let these men through! Goodbye, Superintendent Steele. If you get to Skagway during the winter, come and visit. I'll make you some real sourdough biscuits."

"I just may do that." Steele pulled off his hat and the wind ruffled his chestnut hair. "I'll try to perform my angelic duties again in the near future."

Serena returned to find that the men had been watching her with Steele. "Did you charm him into letting us go through, Serena?" Aaron teased.

"I think it would be easier to charm the mountains into doing something than that man," Serena said. She looked back and waved at Steele, then added, "He's handsome enough to be an actor on a stage, isn't he?"

The remark displeased Cass. He jerked at the lead of his mule and said sharply, "Let's get out of here."

"He's jealous of the mountie." Aaron punched Serena gently on the arm. "Good for him, though. A man needs a little stirring up from time to time."

"Oh, don't be a fool, Aaron!"

Aaron looked back at the red-coated officer, then said thoughtfully, "I'm glad he was here. Cass would have gone on, and even I can see it's hopeless. Well, we'll have lots of time to get acquainted, won't we? All winter in Skagway!"

That night they set up the tents, and as the bitter wind moaned around, touching the canvas wall and howling like a banshee, Serena thought of what Aaron had said. *Jealous! Not in a million years—not Cass Winslow!*

After she fell asleep, dreams came—and one of them involved an angel coming into her tent. But strangely enough, instead of the standard white robe angels are supposed to wear, this one wore the scarlet red coat of the Northwest Mounted Police!

CHAPTER ELEVEN

THE SIGN OF JONAS

★ ★ ★ ★

By midwinter Skagway boasted over five thousand inhabitants, many of them without the means either to move forward to the gold fields or to return to the States. Cooped up and frustrated by the hopeless situation, men turned sour and violence began to break out. The saloons proliferated like mushrooms, and the skeleton law enforcement—one sheriff and one part-time deputy—could only stem a small part of it.

Jubal was appalled by the raw greed and reckless attitude toward life that enveloped the town. One Sunday morning he rose early and helped Serena fix breakfast, the two of them intent on attending a service at the small church they had discovered. Aaron and Cass were sleeping late. Neither of them had yielded to Jubal's pleas to attend church. Aaron had laughed at the idea and Cass had grown sullen when Jubal had invited them to go.

"Listen to this, Serena," Jubal said as he studied a newspaper. "You know that Englishman George Buchanan—the one who killed the woman and then shot himself?"

Serena was standing at the small wood stove, turning two eggs over carefully. They were almost worth their weight in gold since the four of them were limited to one each per week. Lifting the bubbling egg delicately, she turned it over, then did the same with the other one. As she slid them onto the plates and came and put them on the table, she nodded. "The Englishman who worked for the Townsite Company? Yes, I remember." She sat down and said, "Ask the blessing before this gets cold, Jubal."

Without hesitating Jubal bowed his head and said, "Thank you, Lord, for this food. In Jesus' name. Amen." He then began carefully cutting his egg into segments, and Serena smiled at him. "You don't waste any time on long blessings, do you?"

"Heard too many long-winded prayers that didn't say anything." Jubal chewed the egg with pleasure, swallowed it, then shook his head. "I don't dirty my plate up for fewer than four eggs back home." He stuffed half a biscuit in his mouth, then picked up the paper. "Listen to what this nitwit of an editor at the *Post-Intelligencer* wrote about the Buchanan murder:

> A man found time amid the hurry and bustle of the mushroom city to become infatuated with a woman. The icy fogs that stole down from the mountains could not chill his heart of fire. He suffered until the flames stole up and touched his brain—made it glow with a dazzling light—and looked on the taunting woman with a murderer's eyes and strove to kill the scornful spirit he could not break.

Jubal threw the paper down and stuffed the remaining half of the biscuit into his mouth, protesting with disgust, "What garbage! This is the kind of stuff people write in those soupy penny novels for silly women to read!"

Layering a biscuit with blackberry jelly from a jar, Serena took a bite. As she chewed, she noted with amusement that the article had not affected Jubal's appetite. She sat there listening as he rambled on about the events of the past week, then when he finally ran down, commented, "We'd better be on our way. I hate to be late."

Jubal rose, and after Serena donned her heavy mackinaw, the two left. They picked their way through the city of tents, avoiding several snarling dogs. Thor, who trotted along beside Serena, would have thrown himself into several of them, but at the woman's sharp command, the husky contented himself with uttering deep-throated growls. Jubal looked down at the huge dog, saying, "If you ever go broke, you can sell Thor for a lot of money. I never heard of such prices as these dogs are going for!"

Serena shook her head, the dark brown hair shaking almost violently. "I'd never sell him—you know that. He's like a friend to me." The cold bit at her lips and ears, and she reached up to lift the hood of the parka. After a moment's silence, she spoke of the dog again. "When I was at the convent, I didn't have any real friend except Thor, Jubal. The Mother Superior wanted me to become a nun, and I tried to go that way. They were so kind to me."

"But you couldn't do it?"

Serena thought about her youth, then shook her head. "It's a good way for some—but it's not for me. When I was growing up my mother and I went every Sunday to a small Baptist church. I was converted when I was only nine, and the pastor of our church was a fine Bible teacher. My mother's grandfather had been a Baptist minister, so I absorbed what little theology I could from her and Pastor Roysten."

Jubal was interested in hearing how she had grown in her faith, so for the rest of their walk he kept her talking about her beliefs. Finally when they arrived at the small white frame building that had been a feed store but had been converted into a church by a handful of faithful believers, he said abruptly, "I've never talked with anyone about the Lord as I have to you, Serena—not even my parents. It's good to share the things of the Spirit with someone."

"It's been good, hasn't it? Cass and Aaron are fine—but they don't know the Lord." Her smile came, and she touched his arm, adding softly, "I would have had a hard time on this trip without you, Jubal."

Jubal blinked with surprise and started to speak, but then the pastor—a tall, raw-boned man named Hosea Carmichael—came to greet them, cutting off what Jubal was about to say. "Come along, you two," he smiled. "Can't start a song service without our best singers." He shook hands with both of them and said as they entered the building, "I'd like for you to take the service next Sunday, Brother Winslow. I'm going over to Dyea to try and help their little congregation."

"Well, I haven't done much preaching—"

Carmichael waved his hand, cutting Jubal short. "You'll do fine—just fine!" Then he winked at Serena adding, "I'll depend on you to keep this fellow's theology straight, Miss Stevens. If he drifts off into some kind of heresy, just sic the dog on him!"

For the first part of the service, Jubal enjoyed singing some of the songs he had grown up with. He also enjoyed standing by Serena, listening to her beautiful voice. Just before the sermon, Pastor Carmichael announced to the small congregation that they would have the pleasure of hearing Jubal Winslow preach the following Sunday. A murmur of surprise went through the small gathering, which left Jubal feeling awkward. Then Hosea Carmichael went right into the sermon, preaching passionately about how a person's heart is where his treasure is.

The service had been sparsely attended, but as Serena and Jubal made their way back to the camp they felt good about it. "I wish I could preach as well as Hosea." Jubal shook his head. "He's never seen the inside of a college—but he can sure touch people's hearts."

Serena knew that the young man was troubled at the thought of his own inadequacy, and as they moved along the frozen path she formed a resolution. *I'm going to get those cousins of his to come and hear him preach even if I have to get Thor to help me drag them here!*

★　★　★　★

Cass shifted uncomfortably on the rough wooden bench. He was squeezed in between Serena and Aaron, the three of them seated on the first row. *Wish we'd gotten here earlier—I feel like I'm in a fishbowl!* He glanced at Aaron, who winked at him and grinned. Leaning over Serena, Aaron said, "I expect the parson will give it to us with both barrels, Cass. After all, he *knows* all our sins—just has to guess at the rest of these folks—oh, look out, here it comes!"

The small group had been singing for the best part of forty-five minutes, and Cass had been taken back to his days as a boy, when he'd sung those same hymns in a small Methodist church. He could almost hear his father's deep baritone and his mother's clear soprano, and it somehow made him feel ashamed that he'd never followed their example of faith. Now he shook his head slightly, because he had come only at Serena's urging. As Jubal rose and moved to stand at the wooden table that contained only a pitcher of water and a single glass, he thought grimly, *If he starts in with hellfire and damnation, I'll walk out of here!*

But Jubal had no intention of such preaching. He was wearing a brown suit and there was something boyish in his countenance. At the age of nineteen he was younger than most of his audience. After the small congregation quieted down, he began, "Paul said, 'Let no man despise thy youth.' I guess that's my only hope this morning, because I see some of you out there who've been serving God longer than I've been alive." Then he straightened up and his gray eyes swept over the small group—all of them roughly dressed men with hard hands, except for three women. Jubal cast a swift glance at Serena, who answered with a smile and an encouraging nod. Taking a deep breath, he began to speak in a clear voice.

"The Lord Jesus Christ is not like any other human being who ever lived. And if Jesus is only a man and not God—then I'm in terrible trouble, for I'm putting every ounce of trust I have in my faith in Him. And this morning I want to put before you the reasons why I'm risking my soul on Him. His claims were awesome. He didn't say, 'This is the truth as I see it.' He said, 'I *am* the truth.' He didn't say, 'I've come to share with you some spiritual bread.' He said, 'I *am* the bread you need.' He didn't say, 'I've come to tell you about spiritual life.' No, He said, '*I* am the light.' And He didn't say, 'I've got a fine doctrine about the resurrection.' He said, '*I* am the resurrection.'"

This was not the sort of preaching that the men were accustomed to, but they were fascinated at the trim young man who stood before them. Cass was relieved that he wasn't going to be subjected to a barrage of scripture consigning him to hell. He listened carefully, unaware that Serena was stealing glances at him, her eyes wide with hope.

"What evidences do we have for believing that Jesus Christ is who He claimed to be? He said clearly, 'To know me is to know God; to see me is to see God; to believe in me is to believe in God. To honor me is to honor God.' And there are many reasons why I believe all of these claims. We have His virgin birth, His preexistence, His sinless life, His mighty works, His ability to forgive sin, His perfect fulfillment of Old Testament prophecies, the teachings of scripture, and His resurrection from the dead. It would take many sermons to deal with all of these—so this morning we

will look at only one of them—His resurrection from the dead."
Jubal opened his Bible and said, "My text will be taken from the
Gospel of Matthew, chapter twelve, verses thirty-eight through
forty-one:

> Then certain of the scribes and of the Pharisees an-
> swered, saying, Master, we would see a sign from thee. But
> he answered and said unto them, An evil and adulterous
> generation seeketh after a sign; and there shall be no sign be
> given to it, but the sign of the prophet Jonas: For as Jonas
> was three days and three nights in the whale's belly; so shall
> the Son of man be three days and three nights in the heart
> of the earth. The men of Nineveh shall rise in judgment with
> this generation, and shall condemn it: because they repented
> at the preaching of Jonas; and behold, a greater than Jonas
> is here.

Closing his Bible and holding it firmly in one hand, Jubal began to speak from his heart. He knew his subject well, and for the
next forty-five minutes, he went through the scriptures in the Old
and New Testaments, speaking with great conviction about the
resurrection of Jesus Christ. His voice was clear as a trumpet, and
once Cass and Aaron exchanged astonished glances. Jubal in all
his talking to them about God had never given any indication that
he was such a dynamic preacher.

"Notice that the Pharisees asked for a sign that Jesus was the
Son of God, the Messiah they all yearned for. But hadn't they had
many signs? Jesus had fed five thousand people with a few loaves
of bread. He had healed lepers and raised the dead. But look carefully at verse thirty-nine—"

Serena had been following in her Bible and now placed it
gently before Cass, who gave her a startled look, then turned
quickly away from the look in her eyes.

"Jesus said that there would be only *one* sign given that He was
the Son of God—and that one sign was the resurrection of His
body. And that's enough!"

Jubal lifted his voice, and his eyes glowed as he cried, "If you
could find the tomb of Buddha, you'd find a body in it. If you
could find the grave of Confucius, that man would be there. But
the tomb of Jesus Christ is *empty*. He is risen from the dead!"

A tide of loud "amens" swept over the small room, and as Jubal continued to preach, Cass found himself profoundly moved by the sermon. Jubal closed by saying, "Jesus is alive—and you have only one hope to join Him in eternity. He said, 'Come unto me,' and He said that those who will come to Him will have everlasting life. . . ."

Jubal invited those who wanted to know Jesus Christ to come forward so that he could pray with them. Several men moved forward, but Cass made his escape as soon as he could. When he was outside, he found that Aaron had followed him. The two men left at once, and when they were halfway back to their camp, Aaron broke the silence. "Well, I feel like I've been skinned—and he didn't say a word about my sins."

Cass nodded somberly. "Know what you mean, Aaron. He's— not what I expected."

"Well, you may not agree with his doctrine—but *he* believes it." When they reached the camp, the two men seemed uncomfortable, and Aaron said finally, "His folks will be proud of him— but I guess I feel pretty small, Cass. I don't know a thing about God—and I guess I'm too far gone to learn." He turned and left without saying another word, leaving Cass to stare after him.

Cass felt moody and depressed, because deep inside he knew he was just as far from God as Aaron was. He'd heard many sermons but had gone his own way. He knew his lack of faith in God was a burden to his parents, but somehow he couldn't seem to find his way. He did know that as long as he lived, he'd never be able to hear the word *Jonas* without thinking of the sermon he'd just heard.

When Jubal and Serena finally returned, Cass said gruffly, "Good preaching, Jubal. Your folks, they'd have been right proud of you." Then he turned and walked stiffly away, leaving Jubal and Serena staring after him.

"He's running from God," Jubal said sadly.

"Yes, and so is Aaron," said Serena. Then she put her hand on Jubal's arm and smiled at him. "But they've heard the gospel. I never heard a better sermon!"

Jubal flushed and started to speak, but somehow could not say what was on his heart. Finally he said, "It helped to see you out there in the congregation, Serena. I—wish you'd always be there."

Serena gave the young man a startled glance. He was looking at her in a peculiar way, and she could tell he wanted to say more. Instead, he said, "We'll talk later," and walked away. Serena stared after him for a moment, then shook her head. A touch of regret in her eyes, she turned and entered her tent. She felt depressed but couldn't fathom why.

CHAPTER TWELVE

TREK OVER CHILKOOT PASS

★ ★ ★ ★

"I'm sick of this mudhole!" Cass snapped, throwing his fork down on the table. He had been sullen and morose for two weeks and now glared defiantly at his companions. "We didn't come here to sit around like a bunch of mummies!"

Serena had gone to the stove to get another round of coffee. Startled by Cass's outburst, she turned to answer him patiently. "I know waiting is hard, Cass—but we don't have much choice." Picking up the blackened coffeepot, she came to fill the cups, saying, "Skagway is pretty bad—but we can stick it out."

"I won't do it!" Cass shook his head stubbornly. His face was drawn and there was a rebellious glint in his eyes. "I'm getting out of here, and I want all of you to go with me."

Aaron shoved his chair back from the rickety table, took a long pull at the strong black coffee, then asked, "I suppose you're still thinking of the Chilkoot Pass?"

"Yes!"

Jubal was worried. He had seen this coming and had talked it over with Serena. Now, one glance at the stubborn set of Cass's face and he spoke urgently. "Cass, we see men coming back every day after trying to tackle that treacherous pass. It's so bad that some of them take one look and give up."

"They don't want to get to Dawson as bad as I do." Cass took a deep breath and gazed around the table, gauging the temper of the three. He had been more affected by the delay than any of the others because the hunger for success ran stronger in him than it did in any of them. For Aaron, the quest for gold was an adventure. For Jubal, it was an opportunity to have a long vacation before returning to college. As for Serena, she was so happy to be out of the convent that she'd be content to sit in Skagway all winter. Cass stood up and looked down at the others, his mind made up. "I'm going to try the Chilkoot. If you three want to wait here until spring, that's all right with me!"

Serena had been observing Cass over the weeks and recognized that he was serious. Instantly she cast an appealing look at Jubal, saying, "We've got to stay together!"

Jubal would have done anything for Serena, so he nodded at once. "Well, it'll be a break in the boredom." Turning to Aaron, he smiled and said, "You've got to come along, Aaron."

The monotony and crowded conditions in Skagway had begun to grind Aaron down, and he sighed heavily. "I guess I'd better go along—just to keep you three from getting lost!"

Cass was elated at their decision. "Let's pull out this morning—I'll start breaking down the tents!"

A frenzy of activity seized the little group, and for the next three hours, they threw themselves into breaking camp. Asa Tyler came by as they were leaving, his eyes growing grim when Cass excitedly told him the plan. "Wal, you got your minds made up," he said finally. "Hate to see you do it, though. That Chilkoot ain't nothin' to fool with."

"We'll be waiting for you in Dawson next spring, Asa," Cass grinned. Then he took the bridle of the lead pack mule and started out. The sun still hung high in the sky, and by dusk they had made good progress. That night as they sat around the fire, Cass was filled with high hopes. It was bitterly cold and they were all wearing furs and heavy coats, but Cass laughed at the hardship. "Anything is better than Skagway for the rest of the winter," he said cheerfully. "We're going to make it, you can put that in the bank!"

Aaron grinned at him, his teeth looking very white against his bronzed skin. "Can't wait to get your pockets full of gold, can you,

Cass? Well, I'm with you there." He moved his head to stare through the smoke at Serena, who was sitting with her knees drawn up, embracing them with her arms. "Not much like the convent, is it?" he teased her. "Bet if anyone had told you six months ago you'd be in the Klondike with three rough characters, you'd have thought they were crazy!"

Serena laughed and smiled at Aaron, saying, "I'd rather be here. Sometimes I got so bored at that place I nearly went crazy. I was always getting into trouble and ending up in Sister Veronica's office for one of her stern lectures. Guess I must be a rough character myself." She removed her arms and threw them around Thor's large neck. He looked up and tried to lick her face. Avoiding the rough caress, she grabbed handfuls of his thick, loose fur and shook him roughly. "Be still, you beast!" she commanded. Thor had a habit of opening his mouth wide so that he seemed to be grinning when he was pleased, which he did then. Serena laughed. "Look at that maw! You've got a mouth as big as a whale's, Thor!"

Aaron smiled at the sight of the huge dog that appeared to be grinning. At the reference to a whale, Aaron looked at Jubal and said, "I've always been able to forget the few sermons that were inflicted on me, but somehow I can't forget your sermon—the one about the sign of Jonas." Picking up a stick, he held it to the fire and it burst into a tiny flame. Staring at it, he seemed to be lost in thought, then shook his head. "Don't know as I understood all you said, Jubal, but it's got me thinking." Suddenly he was aware that the three were watching him curiously, so he rose and said, "I'm ready for bed. I think I'll turn in. It's gonna be a long day tomorrow."

Serena rose to her feet, said good-night, and disappeared into her small tent. When the two were gone, Cass stared across the fire at Jubal. He had developed a firm affection for the young preacher, and now said, "Never did tell you how much your sermon—well, it got to me, Jubal." He grinned unexpectedly, adding, "You'll have Aaron and me at the mourner's bench yet, Parson!"

Jubal flushed with pleasure, saying quickly, "I don't want to preach at you, Cass. You and Aaron and I, we've gotten pretty close, haven't we? Serena, too, of course."

Cass had not missed Jubal's obvious admiration for Serena and now asked, "You're interested in her, aren't you?"

"Yes, I am." Jubal's youthful face was never more sincere. He looked at Cass, saying, "I'm in love with her, I think. Do you think she'll have me?"

Cass was startled at his honest openness and his eyes went wide. "Why, I don't know, Jubal. Hard to tell about a woman—and Serena's had a protected life. She hasn't had any experience with men." Jubal's words disturbed him, and he tried to tell himself that was only because he was responsible for her. The idea grew in his mind, and the more he thought of it, the more he felt uncomfortable.

"What's the matter, Cass?" Jubal inquired. "Don't you think I'd be a good husband?"

"Why, I'm pretty sure you would—but it's a little soon for Serena to be thinking about marriage." Then he shook his shoulders and stood to his feet. "But she's the one you have to ask, Jubal, not me."

Jubal rose and cast a nervous look toward Serena's tent. When he turned to face Cass, he said, "Well, I won't say anything—not for a while. But it's good to be able to talk to you, Cass. And I'm glad that you're thinking about God." He hesitated, not wanting to say too much, but there was an obvious affection in his youthful face as he added, "But nothing in the world would please me better than to see you and Aaron find Jesus Christ." Then he turned and walked to the tent, leaving Cass alone with his thoughts.

Once inside, Jubal took off his coat, rolled into his thick pad of blankets, and began to pray silently, as he always did. He was interrupted when Aaron said, "Pretty good for us Winslows to be together on a trek like this, isn't it, Jubal?" He reached over and punched Jubal's shoulder, saying with affection, "You son of a gun! Got me and Cass all stirred up with your blasted preaching!" He laughed quietly, then sighed, and his voice was serious as he murmured, "Good-night, kid. It's okay for you to pray for me if you want to."

Jubal said quietly, "I haven't waited for permission, Aaron."

★　★　★　★

The town of Dyea proved to be as rough as Skagway, so the four travelers moved through it, stopping only long enough to buy a few supplies. The first few miles of the trail beyond Dyea that led to the Chilkoot were deceptively easy. It was a pleasant wagon road that rambled through fine-looking country of meadow and forest. But as they pushed forward, telltale signs of an earlier stampede became apparent. Serena looked at the items that were strewn beside the trail—trunks filled with frivolous contents stood open, for every conceivable weight had been discarded by the weary prospectors, some even kicking off their heavy rubber boots. Cass learned later that an enterprising Indian had retrieved the footgear and taken it back to Dyea to sell to new arrivals—who also had cast it aside!

Five miles out, the foursome reached Finnegan's Point, which consisted of a few tents huddled around a blacksmith shop, a saloon, and a makeshift restaurant. From the Point, the trail led directly toward the Dyea River, a messy-looking stream cluttered with boulders and masses of tangled tree roots. As they trudged onward, all of them began to pant, for the grade was rising imperceptibly. "Won't be much cooking from here on," Aaron called out, motioning to the barren landscape. "I'd guess this is about the last of the timber. Wish all this blasted rock would burn!"

By nightfall they reached Sheep Camp, which nestled at the base of the mountains. It lay in a deep canyonlike depression that appeared as if it had been scooped out by a giant paw, and by the time they'd set up camp, all four were exhausted. The cold numbed Serena's hands as she cooked a quick meal, and as soon as possible they all wrapped up in their blankets. "Tomorrow, we'll see the way out of this," Cass promised. "The Chilkoot's not too far ahead."

"Why would anyone raise sheep in this kind of country?" Jubal asked drowsily.

"Fellow next to us said it's called Sheep Camp because it's where hunters used to camp to hunt the wild sheep," Aaron said. He shivered and pulled himself down into his cocoon of blankets. "It's *cold*! Never could stand the cold!"

"You've come to the wrong place, then," Cass observed dryly. "We'll see a lot worse, I'm thinking." He thought of Serena and laughed softly. "Wish I had a big, warm dog to snuggle up to!"

The next morning they ate a hasty meal, loaded the mules, and then headed out. The Sheep Camp was so crowded that they had to thread their way between the tents. At one time Thor was challenged by a large black dog—but he easily thrashed the other dog in an off-handed fashion. Dogs and horses were everywhere. They soon discovered that many of them had been cut adrift by prospectors who had given up. Serena's heart went out to the poor horses that hobbled about the camp, starving, their backs raw from wet blankets. In the end they were rounded up and shot, their bodies soon hidden by the falling snow.

When they finally reached the other side of the camp, a scene unfolded itself to the four newcomers that none of them would ever forget: against the snow white face of a mountain rampart that lifted itself against an iron gray sky, a solid line of men appeared to form a human chain. They were bent double under the weight of huge burdens on their backs and seemed to be frozen, they were moving so slowly and deliberately.

Aaron drew a deep breath as he stared at the panorama. "And we've got to go over *that*?" he muttered, shaking his head.

"No other way to get there," Cass answered. He was intimidated at the sight, but refused to let the others notice. "Come on, let's get in line."

Serena kept staring at the awesome sight of the antlike figures crawling up the glittering sheet of ice and was startled when a voice said, "Well, now, it's Miss Stevens, isn't it?" She turned, and her glance fell on a red coat that stood out like a flag against the white background. Superintendent Sam Steele had emerged from the milling crowd and walked over and stood beside her. Looking down on her, he smiled. "I didn't expect to see you here."

"You never came to Skagway, Superintendent," Serena said demurely. "I was hoping you might."

"Call me Sam or Samuel," Steele gently admonished. "And if I'd known you were expecting me, you can depend on it that I'd have come." There was a strength that flowed out of the man, not just in his vigorous manner, but in his calm spirit. He made other men seem smaller than life, and his brown eyes shone with health and determination. As he stood towering over her, Serena felt almost like a child, but he treated her, she noted, with a courtesy that men from the States lacked. She thought perhaps it might be the English influence, but in any case, she warmed to the big man. But Steele, despite his obvious pleasure in seeing her, shook his head and frowned. "Have you heard about the new policy?"

"Policy? I don't think so."

Steele motioned to the Winslow men, who had kept a few paces away as the two talked. When they stepped forward, Steele said, "There's a new regulation in effect. I don't expect you've heard of it. No one is allowed to enter Yukon Territory of Canada without a year's supply of food—roughly eleven hundred pounds."

Cass looked over the mules piled high with gear, then said, "We might not have enough, Steele. You'd send us back if we don't?"

"It's the regulation," Steele shrugged. "I realize it may sound harsh, but people will starve if something isn't done. If this were American ground, you could do as you please, no doubt. But the Canadian government feels a responsibility for all the people pouring into this area."

Steele's statement concealed the fact that he himself was basically responsible for the new regulation. He knew better than the Prime Minister or any of the governors the terrible tragedy that would follow if the masses of gold seekers plunged into Dawson with no reserve of food. He had urged the new regulation, and those over him had listened to his reasoning and passed it. Steele felt a certain satisfaction in that it was successful enough to turn back many who would have perished.

Cass lifted his chin in a defiant attitude. "We'll get the food, Steele."

"Cass, we can't step down to a grocery store and buy supplies!" Jubal protested.

"Then we'll buy it from people who're turning back," he said in anger. "The rest of you set up camp. I'll get the stuff we need."

For two days Cass spent all his time talking and haggling over prices for more supplies from weary men who had given up and were turning back. He was seen only when he returned with his new purchases, then he would disappear on the hunt for more.

Steele was busy with his duties, but he appeared once to ask Serena if she would like to meet his staff and have lunch with them. She went with him, and after the meal, the two of them walked along the base of the mountain. Steele proved to be a man who knew how to listen, and soon he had heard the story of Serena's life from the time her mother had died and she'd been left in the convent until Cass Winslow had shown up and brought her along to the Yukon.

The two had stopped beside a huge outcropping of granite, the knees of the mountains. It formed an L-shaped crook that offered a measure of privacy from the hustle of the camp. "I admire your courage," he said finally. "But I doubt the wisdom of attempting to cross the Chilkoot at this time of year."

"Is it so very dangerous?"

"Well, not so much in terms of life and limb. If a man falls, he slides a bit." Steele was intrigued by the youthful features of the girl. He had never seen such a clear complexion, and her eyes were so dark blue that they almost seemed black. She wore a bulky fur parka, but even that could not disguise the trim curves of her body. But it was the innocence that shone in her face that attracted the tall mountie. He was constantly in the presence of the worst form of society, including prostitutes, and the sight of the youthful innocence and purity that was unmistakably reflected in the features of Serena Stevens drew him strongly.

"Why shouldn't we go on, Sam?"

"It's a matter of the spirit, I think. That pass takes the heart out of strong men. Look at it, Serena!" He gestured toward the long black line of figures, then went on strongly, "You've got to carry a ton of supplies up that pass. The average man can carry about sixty-five pounds. He has to carry it for about five miles, put it down and go back for another load. That's about *thirty* round trips to get the whole outfit moved. From first light till dark it goes on, and those who get in that line seem to lose their humanity. It's called 'The Chilkoot Lock-step.' A man can't get out of line, because if he does, he can't get back in. He can't disrobe or bathe, because the wind cuts you in two!" Steele shook his head in disgust. "You'll see for yourself, Serena—men get filthy, stinking, red-eyed, and sick with fatigue. I hope you'll convince Mr. Winslow to turn back and wait until spring."

"I don't think I can do that. He's very stubborn and determined to go on."

"He wants to be rich that bad?" Steele's displeasure showed in the sudden hardening of his lips. "I can't fathom it—how men will destroy themselves and others for gold. It's worse than a thirst for liquor! Well, let me try my hand. Perhaps the other two men will dissuade him."

But Steele failed, as Serena had known he would. Cass listened to the mountie, but only shook his head stubbornly. "Thanks for your concern, Steele," he said shortly. "But we'll make it."

By the morning of the third day, Cass had collected enough food and equipment to satisfy the new regulation. The small group stood at first light, looking over the mound of food and equipment that had to be moved. "We'll never do it, Cass," Aaron muttered. "It's too much for us."

The mound contained tents, cooking utensils and tools, as well as lime juice and lard, black tea and chocolate, salt, candles, rubber boots, and potatoes. Also included were soap, cornmeal, string beans, extra clothing, as well as all the rest of the gear needed to sustain them for a year without outside aid.

Cass's face was wolf-lean from the trip so far, and there was a steely determination in his eyes as he said, "No, we can't carry it all—but I've hired four Chilkat Indians to help."

"They're pretty well paid, aren't they?" Aaron demanded.

"Thirty-five cents a pound," Cass nodded. "It'll take most of our money, but we've got to do it. The best claims will go to the firstcomers, and I didn't come all this way to lose, Aaron."

Serena saw that his mind was made up, so she said quickly, "We'll make out. God will help us."

Jubal gave her an approving glance and added his agreement. "When do we start, Cass?"

Aaron looked at the other three, shaking his head solemnly. "I don't like it, Cass—but I'll go."

The four Chilkats appeared thirty minutes later—all of them short and square with powerful shoulders and round faces. Cass and the other bearers lashed together the crates, fastened them into harnesses, then shouldered the packs and started off. Serena was amazed at the seeming ease with which they carried the enormous loads. When Jubal helped her with her own pack—the lightest of them all, she said, "I wish I was a Chilkat—at least for the next few days." She glanced down at Thor and laughed. "He's carrying more than I am!" she said. She had rigged a pack for the big dog, and he bore it lightly. Looking up with his lopsided grin, he huffed at her, thinking it was some sort of new game.

"I wish I had four legs like Thor," Jubal said. "Two just aren't enough."

The four of them began the arduous trek, and by the end of the day, all of them agreed fervently with Jubal's statement. Only Thor had any energy left at all, and Aaron moaned, "My legs are *killing* me! I envy that dog, Jubal! He's not even breathing hard."

That night they all shivered from the biting cold as they slept. They rose early, and as they fell into the line of men trudging up the mountain, a flake of snow bit at Serena's cheek. "It's going to snow," she gasped. It was necessary to lean forward up the steep path, and the straps of the pack cut into her shoulders. "We don't need that!"

The weather continued to worsen, and for the next three days all of them felt as if they were enveloped in a nightmare. Steele's words came back to Serena, and she repeated them to the three that night as they sat shivering, dreading the bitter cold that kept them from sleep. "Sam says this trail robs people of their humanity." She bit off a morsel of jerky, chewed it, then swallowed. "I think he's right. I feel like some kind of a machine."

"We'll be over soon," Jubal said. He alone had kept up his spirits, and as they sat there shivering, he seemed almost joyful. "Soon it'll be spring, and we'll think of this—and it'll be nothing at all! Cass will hit it rich, and you, too, Aaron. You'll dig out nuggets big as my boot! And you, Serena, why, you'll be Queen of the Yukon!"

Serena laughed aloud. "I wish the Queen of the Yukon had just one cup of steaming hot chocolate right now! I'd rather have that than a big gold nugget." She leaned over and patted Jubal's shoulder in a playful fashion. "And what about you, Jubal? Don't you get a gold mine, too?"

Jubal shook his head. His face was pale with the cold, but he said, "No gold mines for me, I guess. If I did get rich, I'd like to go to China and start a mission work. God's doing lots of wonderful things over there. . . ."

Aaron listened as Jubal spoke with excitement of how he'd love to go to China, and Aaron finally said, "You'd do it, too, wouldn't you? Cass and me, we're nothing but money-grubbers." There was a strain of envy in his tone as he murmured, "Makes me feel pretty low."

"Me too," Cass said. The trip had sapped his energy, and the gold at the end of the trip now seemed somehow unimportant. He knew that his desire to be rich was merely dormant, frozen by the icy wind that moaned like a demented banshee over the mountain. *Wonder what it would be like to love God like Jubal does?* He pushed the thought away and fell into silence.

Just before they rolled up in their blankets, Jubal said in a hesitant voice, "Would you mind if I said a prayer?" When Cass and Aaron said with some surprise, "Why, go ahead, Jubal," he bowed his head and began to pray.

"Father, the way ahead is dangerous, but you are the God of all times. You know what lies before us, and I bow my head to your holy will. . . ." He prayed for some time, asking for God's favor, then he said in a warm voice, "I pray for my cousins, Cass and Aaron. Oh, God, keep them safe until they find you as their God! Let them not know death until they are a part of the family of God! I know that one day they'll be safe in the household of God, but keep them from harm until that day comes!" Then his voice changed, and he went on in a gentler tone, "And bless my sister, Serena! I thank you for the spirit of Christ that flows from her. Prepare the man she is to marry—and make him a strong man of God!"

Serena's head jerked up as she heard this, and a shock ran through her. But when Jubal finally said, ". . . in the name of Jesus Christ, I ask this!" she rose and went to him. Leaning over, she kissed his cheek, whispering, "Thank you, Jubal!" Then she went to her small tent and wrapped up in her blankets. Calling Thor to her side, she put her arms around him and closed her eyes. She began to weep softly, but didn't know why.

★ ★ ★ ★

Somehow Jubal's prayer depressed Cass and Aaron—or perhaps it was the sudden intermittent storm that fell and raged for the next two days. It reached blizzard proportions as six feet of wet snow was deposited on the peaks. The pass became so treacherous that the packers Cass had hired protested against going on. But Cass was adamant about pressing on, so at dawn on the morning of April 2, the little party started their weary climb. A few other hardy souls plodded along with them, and at noon they reached a natural break in the pass, a flat saucerlike depression, where they threw off their packs and sat down gasping for breath. The snow was swirling around, and Aaron walked over to the edge to stare down. He could see no more than a dozen yards through the swirling snow—and even as he stood there, he heard a sharp crack above him. Startled, he thought at first it was a gunshot, but when he glanced upward, he saw a wall of snow at least forty feet high rushing down at him!

Jubal had seen it also, and he realized that while the rest of them were far enough away from the ledge to avoid the avalanche, Aaron was right in its path. He threw himself forward and reached Aaron, who was staring upward, paralyzed by the enormous wall of snow that was crashing down at a terrifying speed.

There was no time for warning, so Jubal seized Aaron's arm, and with all his strength whipped the larger man back toward the flat section. Aaron went sprawling on the glassy ice. He struggled to his feet just in time to see Jubal lose his balance. Crying hoarsely, Aaron tried to stand up—but to his horror, Jubal was struck by the moving wall of snow and swept over the edge!

"Jubal—!" Aaron screamed and started forward. He was caught and held back, and when he stared around and saw who was holding him, he struck out, yelling, "Let me go, Cass!"

But Cass held on and Serena, her face gray with horror, came to take his other arm. The two of them fought Aaron, but it took the strength of two of the Chilkats who came to help to keep Aaron from plunging into the abyss.

Finally Aaron slumped to his knees and began to sob. Serena held his head tightly against her chest as a mother might hold a hurt child. The shock of the thing held her in a terrible grip. When she looked up, she saw Cass's face twitching. Their gaze locked for a moment, and then he turned away, walking blindly into the storm.

"He's gone, Aaron," Serena whispered, her throat so full she could hardly speak. The wind moaned, a terrible dirge that struck them all to the heart. Serena held Aaron tightly, closing her eyes. "He's gone, Aaron—but he's gone to be with the One he loved the most. . . !

CHAPTER THIRTEEN

"Gold's Not Worth Dying For!"

★ ★ ★ ★

The avalanche covered ten acres to a depth of thirty feet. Rescue parties from the Sheep Camp rushed to the spot, digging parallel trenches in an effort to locate the victims. Aaron, Cass, and Serena threw themselves into the rescue efforts, nourishing a faint hope that Jubal might have survived. It was a terrible time, hearing the muffled cries of the victims who were still alive. As the rescuers frantically searched for survivors, they heard one man calling out his last goodbyes to his friends above, and another could be heard alternately cursing and praying until his voice was finally silenced.

The hours wore on, and the victims buried in their white tombs slowly died, asphyxiated by the carbon dioxide given off from their own breathing. When their corpses were finally lifted out by the rescuers, many of them were still in a running position, as if running in terror from the wall of snow and ice that had trapped them.

More than sixty men had perished, and Jubal was one of these. One of the other parties found his body, and sent at once for Cass and the others. When the messenger had awkwardly given them the terrible news that their friend was dead, Aaron had stared at him, hatred in his black eyes. He had gone to the site without a word, and when Serena had tried to comfort him, he had turned abruptly and stalked away.

The bodies were taken back to the Sheep Camp, and two days later, Jubal's funeral was preached by Hosea Carmichael. The ground had been frozen, of course, and over fifty men had worked in shifts loosening the rocky soil with picks and crowbars to dig shallow graves.

Most of the victims had been buried already, but Serena had insisted on getting word to Hosea Carmichael in Skagway and awaiting his arrival. The afternoon sun emitted a sickly yellowish light over the mourners as the minister took his place at the head of the rough wooden casket. Looking around at the ragged shapes of the men who formed a semicircle, he opened his Bible and began to read. "But now is Christ risen from the dead, and become the first fruits of them that slept . . ."

After reading many scriptures, Carmichael closed his Bible and began to speak of Jubal. Hosea was a rough-hewn man, used to the hardships of the wilderness, but despite this he had tears in his eyes as he stood there. "I do not weep for Jubal Winslow," he said, letting his eyes fall on Cass and Aaron. "He is in the presence of the Lamb of God. No, I weep for myself, for these relatives of his, for those back home who will miss him. We weep because it is *our* loss—not because some terrible thing has happened to our brother. We will miss him, which is as it should be. He was to us a friend, to some a son, a brother, a lover, perhaps, to some young woman. But he is not dead—no, he is alive now as he never was before, for he is now living in the true light. . . ."

Finally he prayed and then nodded to the miners who stood back from the coffin. They stepped forward and took the ropes, slowly lowering the coffin into the raw earth. Then they removed the ropes and stepped back. Carmichael stooped down, took a clump of frozen dirt and dropped it into the grave. "From dust we come, to dust we shall return," he murmured. Next he nodded toward the three who stood at the foot of the grave, whereupon they silently moved forward and dropped a handful of the rocky soil into the yawning hole.

As the clod from Aaron's hand struck the casket with a dull

thud, the tall man straightened as if he'd been shot. Instantly he whirled and walked stiffly away, his head down.

"He's taking it bad," Carmichael said to Serena as he led her away.

Serena hesitated, then nodded. "He feels responsible, Hosea . . ." She related how Jubal had given his life to save Aaron's, and then shook her head. "He blames himself."

"Ah—well, perhaps it will bring him to God. Tragedies like this sometimes do that, you know."

But Serena was silent. Finally she said, "I hope so—but he's not listening to God right now. He's terribly angry and bitter. I tried to talk to him—but he blames God for Jubal's death."

"Bad! Very bad!" said Hosea. "Right now is when he needs God the most."

"He was very fond of Jubal. More than I knew." Biting her lip, she fought against the dull despair that had steeled over her since Jubal's death. "I—I know how he feels, Hosea."

Carmichael was not an educated man, but he was very quick. "You cared for the young man, Serena?"

"No, not in the way you mean. But he was beginning to fall in love with me." The sky was darker now, and as the two moved toward the tent city, she murmured so quietly that he could barely hear the words.

"I'm afraid I'd have hurt Jubal if he'd lived—and I couldn't have borne that. . . !"

★　★　★　★

By the time Cass, Aaron, and Serena made the journey back to the top of the Chilkoot Pass, the fury of the blizzard had abated some. They found a town of sorts, but it was a strange one. The "buildings" were towering piles of freight, and the "streets" were the narrow aisles left between. Most of these were filled up with snow, so they joined the other miners in the task of clearing the narrow avenues.

The mountains of freight provided the only shelter on the mountain against the inclement weather. And everyone spent all their energy trying to survive, which was hard. The only firewood available cost a dollar a pound, and they huddled over their tiny fire that night, shivering and scalding their lips with the strong black coffee.

Aaron was withdrawn, and as soon as he finished the meal, he rolled into his blankets. Cass sat holding his hands up to the flickering blaze, listening to the soft moan of the wind and the howling of a dog somewhere far off. The shock of Jubal's death had dulled his thinking, and now he looked over at Serena and said, "I've got to write Jubal's folks—and I'd rather take a whipping!"

Serena had her arm around Thor. She stroked his thick fur for a time, then said quietly, "I don't think any of us know what to say when something like this happens. Do you know them well, Cass?"

"I haven't spent much time with them. His father is an officer in the regular army. They've moved from post to post all of Jubal's life. But they're fine people—and Jubal was their only son." Cass made an angry gesture with his hand, adding, "How do I tell them, Serena? I—I just can't do it!"

"Yes, you can." Serena spoke firmly, and her eyes caught the reflection of the tiny flames as she leaned forward. "You can tell them that he died saving Aaron's life. You can tell them that he helped you. You said so, you and Aaron. Nobody ever reached you with a sermon like Jubal did that Sunday morning in Skagway."

But Cass shook his head in black despair. "That's not enough, Serena—not for his parents and not for me." He rose and turned away, his face bleak, then stopped and swung around. "Why did it happen? Jubal was just getting ready to live—and now he gets snuffed out like—like he was a bug! God didn't have to take him like that!" He kicked angrily at the snow, then walked stiff legged to take his place beside Aaron, leaving Serena alone in the cold darkness.

The next morning, the three joined the procession to Lake Bennett. They hardly spoke at all, especially Aaron, who seemed to have lost the power of speech. When they arrived at the lake, they found a great tent city had sprung up beside the snow-covered shore. Everywhere they looked they saw every imaginable kind of tent. There were bell tents and pup tents, the square tents and the round tents. They saw dog tents and army tents and tiny canvas lean-tos. There were no "buildings" of any kind, but businesses had been set up in larger tents, including saloons, cafes, bakeries, post offices, and even chapels.

As they moved through the tent city, they noted that every flat place along the beach was filled with mounds of supplies. The noise of the place was deafening as tethered animals added their voices to the din of thousands of men.

And the boats! There were boats by the thousands, many of them still under construction.

"Look at that!" Cass breathed, staring at the beehive activity. "I thought those who'd gotten over the pass would be on the river headed for Dawson."

Aaron looked at the teeming shoreline and shook his head. "Nobody's going anyplace until spring," he said shortly. "We should have listened to Steele. He told us we'd never get to Dawson until spring."

Cass glared at him, wanting to argue, but he realized that Aaron was right. "I guess so, Aaron," he said grudgingly. "Well, we'll just have to wait. We'll have to build a boat anyway, and that'll take time."

Aaron suddenly turned to face the two of them. His face was stiff and his voice was harsh as he spoke. "You two do as you please. I'm going back."

Both Cass and Serena stared at him, and it was Serena who said, "But, Aaron, the worst is over!"

"How do you know that?" Aaron demanded. "Haven't you heard what Asa told us about this river? It's a killer, and I don't intend to die in this God-forsaken place!" His long lips twisted into an ugly shape, and he added harshly, "Isn't one of us enough? Jubal's gone—and for what? A few pounds of yellow gravel!"

"It's more than that!" Cass replied stiffly.

"No, it isn't. And gold's not worth dying for, Cass. I know that now. Don't try to talk me out of it. I'm going back!"

As much as they tried, both Serena and Cass saw there was no reasoning with Aaron. He was bitter and said little for the rest of the day. But the next morning when he was ready to leave, he did speak of what was in his heart. As they were eating the last of breakfast, he put his cup down and said, "I wouldn't be any good to you, Cass. When Jubal went down in that avalanche, something of me went with him." He shook his head and Serena saw that Jubal's death had marked him terribly. "I didn't believe in very much before I came here—and now I believe in nothing!"

"Don't say that, Aaron!" Serena pleaded.

"It's true, why not say it?" Aaron rose and pulled his pack onto his shoulders. "You two can have my share of the supplies." The two rose and he hesitated, then said, "I'll go tell Jubal's parents, Cass. I can do that much."

"I wish you'd stay on, Aaron," Cass said. Then he put his hand out and gripped that of the other man. "But I can see you've got to do it. Go see my folks if you can, try to explain about me."

Aaron tried to smile but couldn't. "I'll do that." Then he turned to Serena and took her hand. "Goodbye, Serena. I wish you'd come with me. My folks would be glad to have you—or Cass's parents."

"He's right," Cass said, turning to Serena. "I think you ought to go with Aaron."

"No, I'm going on with you, Cass. It's what my father wanted."

Aaron stood there studying the girl, and something in her face made him narrow his eyes. But he said only, "Goodbye. Take care—I've lost enough in this accursed place without losing one of you!" Then he turned and walked away, his back straight and his head high.

Serena said softly, "He's terribly hurt, Cass. I don't think he'll ever get over it."

"He won't, and neither will I." Cass looked down at the ground and shook his head. "All this was my idea. If I hadn't come, Jubal would still be alive."

"Don't think like that—there's no answer for the way things happen."

"You should have gone with Aaron, Serena."

"God told my father for you to bring me with you. We'll do what God says."

Cass lifted his gaze and held her eyes for a long moment. The hubbub of voices was all around them, but for that one moment of time they were totally unaware of all the activity. Cass said slowly, "You really think that God is in all this?"

"He's in everything, Cass."

"Even Jubal's death? How can that be?"

"I can't say—but I know He loved Jubal. He loves us all, Cass—and that's why all of us must learn to take whatever comes as if it were from His hand."

"I can't believe that!"

"Not now—but someday, I think you will."

Cass was mystified by her faith, and for one brief instant felt that he had found in this girl some secret that he'd been searching for all his life. He stood there and the sound of the saws biting into the green wood rang through the crisp air. Overhead the gray sky was as blank and expressionless as a sheet of paper, except where a formation of geese made a ragged V far off to the south.

Releasing his breath, Cass said quietly, "Let's go build a boat, Serena."

She smiled and touched his cheek in a tender gesture. She held it there for one moment, studying the angular planes of his face, attempting to read his thoughts. Then she lowered her hand and nodded.

"All right, Cass. We'll build a boat and we'll go to Dawson. Let's see what the good Lord has for us there!"

PART THREE

DAWSON

★ ★ ★ ★

May 1898—September 1898

CHAPTER FOURTEEN

DOWN THE YUKON

★ ★ ★ ★

"I thought that Skagway was pretty bad—but I guess this is worse," said Cass as he stopped to catch his breath.

Serena paused from where she stood by the top of the tree that Cass had chopped down. Her arms ached from cutting the branches with a small ax, and now she stood up and arched her back. "I suppose so—but we'll be out of here soon."

Cass shook his head slightly. Building a boat had turned out to be a grueling task. All around him the air was filled with the crash of falling timber, the tapping of hammers, and the drone of saws from the sawpits. Glancing around, he observed the men who worked furiously. Almost all of them had lost weight, and their stiff new mining clothing they'd bought back in Seattle and other ports was now faded, worn, and patched. Most of them had ragged beards and looked like coal miners from the deep, since the blinding sunshine on the white snow had driven them to coat their faces with charcoal and wear primitive eye-shields.

"Let's take a break, Serena," Cass said wearily. They had risen before dawn and labored to cut trees and drag them down to the shore.

"Let's fix something to eat," Serena suggested.

The two of them quickly built a small fire, and soon the aroma of cooked meat and coffee filled the air. As they sat down on the trunk of one of the trees, Cass studied Serena as she ate a chunk of beef. "You're working too hard, Serena," he said and, leaning over, took her hand and looked at her palm. "I've told you to take care of these blisters," he admonished. She protested, but he ignored her. Procuring some ointment from their small medical kit, he tore a handkerchief into strips and proceeded to bind up her hand.

Serena sat quietly, stealing a glimpse at Cass's face as he worked on her sore hand. They had talked little since Jubal's death. It was as though when he had died something had closed down in Cass. He seldom smiled, and when he did speak, it was in an impersonal manner. Now, however, the touch of his hand on hers seemed to bring back some of the old spirit in him. "There—now you're through chopping wood."

"But we've got to build a boat," Serena protested. She cast a glance at the sawpit that Cass had built and felt a moment of despair. To produce the rough-dressed planks for a boat, the peeled logs were laid on a platform and a line was chalked down the side. One man stood on the platform and held a six-foot saw against the log. Another man stood beneath, grasping the lower handle. With an eye to the chalk line, they guided the saw along the length of the log, but it was a back-breaking job.

The cutting was done on the downward stroke only. The man on top guided the saw and pulled it up, while his partner beneath hauled it down, letting its great hooked teeth cut into the green lumber. The man below always got his eyes full of sawdust, and the operation often caused terrible quarrels.

"I think I can pull the saw up, Cass," Serena said. "We've got to have planks."

"No way you can do that." Cass shook his head. "It takes two strong men." He studied the sawpit, then took a bite of his sandwich. Chewing it thoughtfully, he said, "I could sure use Aaron for this job." He didn't mention Jubal, and Serena noticed it. The memories of the young man were still too painful for both of them.

"How will we get the logs sawn into planks then?"

"Don't know."

Cass's answer was filled with doubt, and the two of them avoided the subject for the rest of the day. Cass went back out and

179

cut and trimmed some more trees by himself. He hitched them to one of the pack mules owned by a neighbor and in the next two days had cut down enough logs to build a small boat. That night as they sat around the campfire, he said, "I'll have to hire some help—but we're about broke."

Serena was sitting beside Thor, rubbing his broad head. Noting the doubt that etched itself on Cass's face, she said timidly, "Cass, there's one way we can get a boat."

"How?"

"Two days ago a man named Speedy Thompson came by. He's not a miner, but he'd traded for a boat somehow. He—asked if I'd sell Thor. He's got some dog teams, and he said Thor was worth more than most of them."

Cass's head lifted instantly, and he was touched by the offer. He knew Serena's love for the dog was great, and he said at once, "There's absolutely no way we're going to sell Thor, Serena."

"But we have to—"

"We're not selling him—and that's final!"

Serena felt a gush of relief and said no more. It had been a difficult offer for her to make, and now she whispered, "I can't be much help to you, Cass. I wish I were a big, strong man!"

Cass grunted, "Well, I don't." When she gave him a startled look, he grinned. "There's enough ugly men around here. I need something pretty to look at once in a while."

Serena blinked, because it was the first compliment he'd ever paid her. She lowered her eyes and said nothing but felt pleased at his remark.

As Cass sat there looking at Serena, he began to realize how much the hardness of the trip and Jubal's death had drained her emotionally. Now as she sat very still Cass thought, *I've been feeling so sorry for myself that I've forgotten how hard this must be for her. She loved Jubal, I think, better than Aaron and I did.* He sought for some way to speak his thoughts, but nothing came. He, too, was deeply scarred by the loss of his cousin, and now he said, "Sorry about how rough this is, Serena. I didn't know it'd be this hard."

She lifted her head and smiled tremulously. Her lips looked soft and vulnerable, but there was a smile on them now. Cheered by his words she said, "It's all right, Cass. We'll get through."

Cass admired her courage, but shook his head doubtfully. "If we just had a boat! That's the toughest thing we've got to whip."

The next morning, the two of them rose early, fixed breakfast, and were eating when a voice startled them.

"Ah, we're just in time for breakfast." Two men had stepped out of the murky dawn light, and one of them was wearing a red coat. Samuel Steele looked as trim as though he'd just come for breakfast with the Prime Minister. Serena only had time to wonder how he managed to keep himself so well groomed, when Cass let out a sudden cry and leaped up to grasp the man beside the mountie with a fierce hug.

"Mike Rooney!" He beat the smaller man on the shoulders, and then stepped back, astonishment in his eyes. "Where did you dig this one up, Steele?"

"He's been under arrest, I'm afraid," Steele shrugged. "For brawling and drinking too much." He smiled and said, "Serena tells me you need someone to take the lower part of the sawpit. If you'll stand for his good behavior, I'll release him into your custody."

Cass had been startled by his reference to Serena, since he'd not known that the big mountie had been in the camp. Serena said quickly with some embarrassment, "Samuel stopped by yesterday. I forgot to tell you, Cass." Stepping forward, she put her hand out and smiled. "I'll stand for you, Mr. Rooney—if Cass won't. We need a good Irishman to help us get down this river. Cass has told me all about you."

Rooney grinned sheepishly, then took her hand and shook it. "Well, now, miss, I'd rather be put in the charge of a beautiful young lady such as yourself—than into the hands of that one!"

Steele seemed amused by the incident. His sharp blue eyes fixed on Serena and he said, "Very well, he's in your hands, Miss Stevens. If he doesn't work, come and see me." He touched the brim of his hat and walked away, his step purposeful and long as always.

Cass was delighted, and for the next hour fed the chunky Irishman and listened as Rooney told of his adventures. "I've been stuck in Dyea since I got here. Lost all I had in a poker game, so I've been workin' like a dog as a packer." He sighed and sipped the hot coffee, then looked at the pair. "You need a man, Steele says. Well, look no more, Bucko! We'll make the finest craft on the Yukon River."

Later when they were alone, Cass explained Serena's presence to Rooney. "I didn't want to bring her, but she's done her share," he said.

"Steele told me about how you lost your cousin. Sorry about that, Cass." He saw Cass's lips tighten and knew he'd touched a tender spot. "Well, now, the Lord have mercy on his soul! Now, about this boat, I'm thinking we can build a fine one!"

★ ★ ★ ★

"I never thought we'd see spring again, Sam!" Serena paused beside the frozen lake, took a deep breath, then turned to add, "We'll be leaving here pretty soon, won't we?"

"As soon as the ice breaks up—perhaps a week or so." Steele admired the sheen of the young woman's crisp brown hair and the brightness of her eyes. He'd been in and out of the camp half a dozen times during the winter, but on each return had made it a point to come by and check on the progress of the boat—and of Mike Rooney. "That Irishman, has he behaved himself?" he asked idly.

"Oh yes, Sam! He's really helped us get our boat built." She smiled mischievously, then cocked her head in a way that was most appealing. "I called you my guardian angel once, remember? I still think you're an angel for bringing Mike to us just when we needed him. But you're such a large angel—and I never knew angels to wear red coats."

"What do they wear?"

His response delighted her, since it was only by degrees that the rather sober Superintendent had allowed his reserve to be broken. "Oh, shining white robes and halos, I suppose," said Serena.

Steele suddenly gave her a smile, which made him look much younger. "No, some of them wear overalls and green plaid shirts and have curly brown hair." He reached out and took her hand—something he'd never done before. The action startled her—and brought a deep growl from behind him. He turned and saw Thor with his lips drawn back, exposing sharp white teeth. Casting a wary eye on the large dog, Steele said, "He's worse than a father or brother, Serena!"

Serena laughed aloud, a delightful sound to Steele, and said, "Be still, Thor!" Then she looked down at his large hand holding hers and laughter danced in her eyes as she asked demurely, "Are you holding my hand, Superintendent Steele?"

"Yes. And would like to do a little more." Steele was rather shocked at himself, for he was not a man to flirt with women. But he had discovered that something in Serena Stevens brought out a side in him he hadn't known he'd possessed. Burdened down with heavy responsibilities, he had had little time for romance—and in all his travels he'd not met a woman who had warmed him as did Serena Stevens. "I don't mean to be glib, Serena," he added, still holding her hand. "But I've grown fond of you."

His simple statement warmed Serena, for she admired Steele greatly. His reputation in the world she'd entered was legendary, and she was slightly awed by him. Nevertheless, there was something more than the rather stiff appearance he sometimes hid behind—and now she smiled at him, saying, "We're good friends, Sam."

He released her hand but shook his head. "I hope we'll be more than that."

For a few moments they stood in silence on the shore gazing across the lake. Spring had finally arrived, and the beauty of this northern wilderness was breaking out all around. Nearby a purple pasqueflower poked its hairy stem above the snow. The sun was shining down on tiny forget-me-nots, the pink snakeweed, the delicate blue harebells, and dozens of other wild flowers that opened their petals to soak in the warmth. Sparrows chirped and fought for seeds in spots where the snow had melted, revealing brown grasses from the past year and emerald shoots of the new. The world was warm again, drenched with sunlight and vibrant with color.

Steele and Serena strolled back along the margin of the lake where boat-builders sat and smoked their pipes, waiting for the breakup of the ice. When they got back to where Cass and Mike were putting some final touches on the boat, Cass turned, holding a small brush dripping with black paint. "Well, we've named our boat—come and see."

Serena moved around to the side of the boat and saw the name
THE YUKON QUEEN in bold letters. "Oh, that's a nice name,
Cass!"

"It's you," he replied gruffly. "It's the name Jubal gave you."

Instantly Serena looked up at Cass because it was the first time
he'd mentioned Jubal's name since the accident. "Yes, he did say
that, didn't he?" For one moment the two stood there as though
they were all alone. Each was thinking of the night they'd sat
around a fire and Jubal had been full of life. Sudden tears formed
in her eyes, not only at the poignant memory of Jubal, but also at
the fact that Cass remembered the name Jubal had given her.

"I'm not really a queen," she murmured. "But it's something
to add to our memories of him, isn't it?"

"I guess as long as you and I are alive and remember him, he's
not really gone."

"That's sweet, Cass!" Serena squeezed his arm, and when he
met her eyes, she whispered, "We'll keep him always—you and
I. Won't we?"

Cass would have answered, but even as Serena spoke, they
both heard a sharp crack and a rumble. Cass swiveled his head
around just as a yell went up from the men who watched along
the shore: "The ice is breaking!"

Cass grabbed Serena and gave her a bearlike hug—ignoring a
growl from Thor. She was shocked at the touch, and when he released her, turned with some confusion—meeting the eyes of
Steele. "I—I guess he's excited," she murmured lamely. Somehow
she was embarrassed but covered it by saying, "Sam, we'll be going down the river!"

Steele had watched the pair carefully, aware that they had
been in a world of which he could have no part. Now he shook
off his thoughts and turned to gaze at the river. "Yes, I'm afraid
so," he murmured. At her look of inquiry, he shook his head
doubtfully. "It's five hundred miles down that river to Dawson.
And some of those who start won't make it."

But Steele's solemn words of caution had no effect on the men
and women who set out on that voyage. They never forgot the
date—May 29, 1898—when the ice broke and the great adventure
began. During that first day eight hundred boats of all sorts set
sail for the Klondike.

As Serena looked back from where she sat in the stern of *The Yukon Queen*, she saw a solitary figure wearing a red coat. Sam Steele stood on the shore and watched their departure, and she lifted her hand in answer to his stiff salute. For all his size and strength, he looked rather forlorn, she thought. As he faded from view, somehow she knew their paths would cross again.

★　★　★　★

The Yukon River was crowded with boats of every sort—over 7,000 of them loaded with thirty million pounds of food. Down the river they sailed, in search of gold. There were twenty-ton scows packed with oxen, horses, and dogs. They even saw one-man rafts made of logs hastily bound together. As the days passed, Serena never tired of watching the ragtag armada. Every day she saw different kinds of vessels. There were slim canoes and cockleshells, outriggers and junks, catamarans and kayaks, arks and skiffs. Some of the boats had flat bottoms, while others were curved or wedge shaped. Some of them looked like coffins, and one of them was a strange craft modeled after a Mississippi side-wheeler with two side wheels operated by hand cranks that propelled the craft downstream in a zigzag fashion.

Once, Cass pointed out a boat with a sail made out of women's undergarments, sailed by two women. Serena had sniffed at his jab but had been forced to laugh out loud when Mike had remarked that if the two were in as bad a shape as their underwear, they didn't have much to worry about from the men who passed them by!

After being bogged down in mud for the winter, the trip on the river was delightful. The mountains, with their peaks still frosted, turned to an azure blue, and the sun seemed to bathe the waters of the river in a golden mist at noon and at dusk.

"We'll never see anything like this again," Cass remarked, staring out over the river at the flotilla of boats. "It could only happen once."

Serena followed his gaze, nodded slowly, then remarked, "It's the biggest thing that's ever happened to me, Cass. It'll be something to tell our grandchildren about—I mean—" She halted in confusion, and color flooded her cheeks.

Cass didn't seem to hear, for he was looking ahead, peering through the haze. "Look up there, Serena. I guess that's Miles Canyon."

Mike Rooney grunted, "If ye've got any prayers, this might be a good time to start saying 'em. Everybody says that's a killer of a canyon."

They were soon forced to pull the *The Yukon Queen* ashore, for one glance at the choppy waters ahead warned them that the passage would be very dangerous. Before them stretched a gorge, a narrow cleft in a wall of black rock. The white water leaped high, exposing the teeth of rock seemingly made to tear the bottom out of a frail vessel. When they finally managed to dock, they walked around asking others what they knew about the passage.

"Why, it's suicide!" a tall, rawboned man with a shock of black hair exclaimed. His name was Johnson, and he informed them that most of the first boats to attempt to run the rapids had been wrecked. "I walked around the rapids, and at the other end, it's just pitiful," Johnson moaned. "People who lost their boats and all they had are just wandering about, crying and wringing their hands! Seen some who lost their people, too—which I ain't gonna do! I'm hauling my gear around."

"Is there a road?" asked Cass.

"No, but I'd rather climb another mountain than risk that river!"

For two days the three of them camped on the crowded banks of the river, uncertain and filled with doubt. They found out that over one hundred fifty boats had been swamped and wrecked, and now several thousand craft were bottled up in the neck of the canyon.

In the end, it was Sam Steele who straightened the thing out. The morning of the third day he had appeared with several of his men, and the crowd gathered around him at once. Steele smiled briefly at Serena, then his voice fell on the silence.

"I am taking charge of this passage. No more women or children will be taken in boats. They will walk around by land. No boat will be permitted to go through the canyon until Sergeant Dixon approves it. . . ." He spoke rapidly and at once brought order into the situation.

"Well, I'm glad that redcoat showed up," Rooney nodded vigorously. "He's all sorts of a feller, ain't he, Serena?"

"Yes, I think he is," answered Serena, admiring the way Sam Steele had taken control of the difficult situation.

The next day Serena found time to speak with Steele. "I'm glad you came, Sam," she said quietly.

"Are you? Well, it's worth the trouble then." He asked her to come for a walk with him, and as they moved along the bank of the river, she was impressed at how the men watched the big mountie with awe and admiration. They came to an open spot, and they stood there speaking quietly. "I worried about you, Serena," said Steele.

"Did you? How nice to be worried about me! I'm not used to it, I suppose."

"This is the worst of the river. On the other side, there are two rapids, the Squaw and the Whitehorse—but with care, they're not dangerous. You'll be in Dawson soon."

"Will you be there, Sam?" asked Serena hopefully.

"Yes. I'm to see that you Americans behave yourselves." His eyes were steady and he found himself wanting to say more. But he let the moment go and said instead, "I better walk you back. I've got plenty to check on."

When they got back to the boat and he had left, Cass asked rather stiffly, "He say anything about the rest of the trip?" When Serena related Steele's comment, Cass said with relief, "Good! I'm ready to get off this river."

They made the rest of the trip without difficulty, pulling *The Yukon Queen* ashore at dusk, and leaving at dawn each day. The trip now took on the aspects of a frenzied race, because everyone wanted to be first to get to the mining camp. Finally, on leaving the rapids, they passed into the Lewes, then at last came the moment when they swung around a rocky bluff and saw what they had been striving for.

"That's Dawson," Cass said, standing in the bow with Serena at his side.

They looked out at a great tapering mountain beyond the Klondike River. At the foot of it two rivers made a junction, and spread across this junction stretched thousands of tents, shacks, cabins, warehouses, and other structures. It seemed a little unreal in the shimmering June heat, and as Cass moved to the stern and turned the boat to the shore, Serena said, "Well, Cass, it's a long way from the convent where we first met, isn't it?"

Rooney stared at her, his sharp brown eyes gleaming. "Convent—Miss Serena, I'm thinking that place we're looking at is about as far from a convent as a town can get!"

CHAPTER FIFTEEN

GOLD CAMP

★ ★ ★ ★

The steamship *May West* was a diminutive craft, only eight feet wide and thirty-five feet long. What gave her a claim to fame was the fact that she was the first ship to reach Dawson from the upper river. All winter she had been locked in the ice flow, but on June 8, she steamed into the tent city of Dawson with a triumphant blast of her shrill whistle.

Standing in the prow of the *May West*, Brent Traphagen examined the teeming shore of Dawson with evident satisfaction. He was wearing an expensive black suit, an immaculate white shirt, and a pair of expensive black boots. A large diamond flashed on his right hand as he lifted it to smooth his carefully barbered hair. He was a dandy, but one with a straight-grained nerve. The shoreline was filled with so many boats tightly packed together that men had to leap from craft to craft to reach the shore. Turning to the man beside him, Traphagen said, "We got here just in time, Whitey. Look at all those boats!"

"How do we do it, Brent?" Whitey Dugan wore a plain brown suit, but the gun at his side cost more than his clothing. Dugan constantly caressed the pearl-handled .44 with his right hand. From time to time he lifted it from the tooled brown holster, then let it fall back. He loved no man nor woman, and if he had affection for anything under the sun it was the pistol with the hair trigger. He had used it often, and there was a murderous streak in the albino that would surface again. "You want me and Leo to find a place for the saloon?"

"I'll do that. You two watch our goods. When I find a place to set up, I'll let you know."

Traphagen had planned this journey ever since the news of the gold strike broke out. He was not one to take on an enterprise lightly, so he had come well prepared to relieve every one he could of their hard-earned gold. Stowed in the hold of the ship was the largest tent that Traphagen had been able to buy, along with tables, chairs, a knocked-down bar, and all the furnishings for a saloon. The ship lay low in the water because Traphagen had stowed kegs of liquor into every crevice.

Leaving the ship, he spent the day making arrangements. Space was at a premium, but he managed to find a choice spot on the main street. Dawson was a city of sawdust and stumps and skeletons of fast-rising buildings. Its main street was a river of mud through which horses, whipped on by clamoring men, floundered and kicked. In between them flowed a sluggish stream of humanity. They trudged up to their knees in slime or negotiated the buckboards that were thrown across the black morass.

Traphagen ambled along the high boardwalk that was mounted on one side of the street. The prices of building lots were out of sight, some selling for forty thousand dollars! After some smooth talking, he obtained one by offering five percent of the profits of his saloon, which he called "The Shady Lady." When he had signed the papers with the owner of the property, he returned to the ship and gave the orders to Dugan and Ritter. "Hire what help you need to set up the tent and the fixtures," he commanded. "Whatever you have to pay, we'll take it back with the cards and roulette."

Two days later The Shady Lady was up and running at full tilt. The huge tent was the biggest one in sight, and it was filled day and night with miners who clamored for the whiskey and for a chance to lose their pokes of gold dust. There were "hostesses" as well, for Traphagen had recruited four of them. One of them was a robust and rather attractive woman of twenty-seven who kept the others in line. Her name was Lottie James, and she knew as much about life as her boss, Brent Traphagen. On the night of the opening, she came and sat beside Brent, saying, "You're going to be rich—look at that crowd!"

Traphagen grinned and nodded with satisfaction. "That's why we came here, isn't it, Lottie? We'll be able to retire if we play this thing right." He let his eyes run over her figure and put his hand on her arm, stroking it lightly. "You and I, we're a lot alike."

Lottie turned to face Traphagen. She had a highly colored face, a mass of blond hair, and a pair of steady blue eyes. "Are we, Brent?" She had resisted his advances from the time they'd met, which she knew angered and yet drew him. *He's used to having his way with women—and he expected me to fall into his hands like a ripe apple.* She shook her head, saying, "It's like I told you from the start, Brent. We've got a business arrangement—and that's all."

Traphagen's thin face colored, for he was a willful man, but then he laughed and nodded. "All right, Lottie. Let me know if you want to change the rules." She rose and moved away, and his eyes followed her. "I'll have you before this is over," he muttered, then took another drink and looked over the saloon with a great deal of satisfaction. *I'll have her—and whatever else I want,* thought Brent. *This is where I make it big—and nobody's going to stop me!*

When Whitey Dugan came to sit down, Traphagen said, "Whitey, you're going to become a mining expert."

The albino stared at Traphagen in astonishment. "Me? I ain't digging in no ground!"

"No, not you," Traphagen laughed. He waved his manicured hand over the room in an expansive gesture. "We'll make money out of this—but the real haul will be in the claims. We'll never turn over a shovelful of dirt—but we'll get our hands on some rich claims. Then we'll hire some strong backs to dig the gold for us."

Dugan leaned back and studied his employer. His colorless face showed little emotion, but he was shrewd enough. "That'd be the way, Brent," he nodded. "And right here is where we get word of which claims we'll go for."

"Sure. You're an artist at doctoring the roulette wheel. When we get word somebody's got a good claim, I'll let him win enough to get him excited—then I'll bleed him dry!"

★　★　★　★

Cass shook his head as he walked into the campsite. "It's a madhouse," he announced, waving his arm back toward the forest of tents. "The sooner we get out of here and start prospecting, the better off we'll be."

Serena had been waiting, keeping guard over their supplies—along with Thor's help—while Cass and Mike went to see what the town was like. "Did you hear anything about where the gold is?"

Giving her a look filled with disgust, Cass sat down on a keg of flour. "That's the bad part, Serena. The claims are all staked. At least the good ones close to Dawson are. The men who were already here got first choice."

"You mean—all of us came here for nothing?"

"Looks that way." Cass glanced at the town, saying, "Lots of men are going back. Just plain giving up." Then he stood up and summoned a grin, saying, "But not us, Serena. We'll stay and see what happens."

"Good!" Serena smiled, her eyes glowing. "God didn't bring us here to fail. One of the nuns used to say, 'God doesn't sponsor failures.' And she's right, Cass!" She looked around and asked, "Where's Mike?"

"Sniffing around, trying to find a good spot to go hunting for gold. Oh, I did get a map." He pulled a piece of paper from his pocket and spread it out on the ground. "Take a look at it—this is the Yukon running south, and here we are, right on the mouth of the Klondike River." As Serena bent over the map, Cass pointed out the features of the surrounding country. He was acutely conscious of the smoothness of her cheek and how well her trim figure was set off even in the worn overalls and thick wool shirt.

"See these creeks? This is Bonanza Creek. It's where a fellow named George Carmack made the first strike. And over here is Gold Bottom Creek. See this place called the Dome? It's the biggest producer of all. Gold so rich a man could just pick it up by the handful!"

"There must be other creeks with gold," Serena murmured. "Can't we go looking for them?"

"We'll have to," Cass shrugged. "But we'll have to build a shack to keep our grub and our gear in. This is a pretty rough bunch, I'm afraid, so we'll have to make it pretty secure."

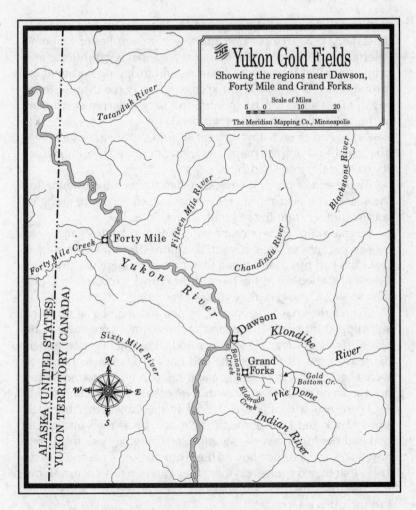

"More cutting boards in a sawpit?"

"No, there's a sawmill operating here in Dawson. I made sure to save enough money before buying supplies to buy enough lumber to build us a small place. When Rooney comes back, we'll let him do guard duty and I'll show you the town."

The construction of the shack went slowly, since the two men had to go for several miles to cut thick posts for the uprights and the rafters. As they moved among the crowds, they kept their ears alert to any news about new claims in the surrounding area. Almost daily, prospectors came into town for supplies or for some entertainment in one of the saloons. And inevitably, after a few drinks, many of them began boasting and dropping pertinent information to those who had a keen ear. Slowly the three of them began to get a feel for the country, and they collected every map of the Yukon they could lay their hands on.

At the end of each day, they sat around the fire after their evening meal studying the maps and trying to refine the rumors that spawned daily into solid facts.

By the end of the first week they had finished the framing for the shack. The next morning Cass said, "Serena, we're going to get the lumber from the sawmill. Come along."

Serena complied at once, pausing long enough to change into a clean pair of jeans and a shirt. She climbed up into the wagon that Cass had hired, and when they passed through the streets of Dawson, she looked at the faces of the crowd, exclaiming, "They look so sad, Cass! Like they've lost everything."

"Guess they have, Serena," Cass nodded soberly. At times he still slipped into moodiness, and at those times Serena knew he was thinking of Jubal. He was lean and trim, and his muscles had hardened from all the work he had done. The planes of his face were sharp and almost angular, and his skin was bronzed by the hot sun as he studied the crowd. "Never saw such a sad bunch!"

There was a deadly air of grief in the crowd that tramped slowly back and forth through the mud. It was the same group that had dared the rivers—shouting and singing back then—but now a strange lassitude bowed them down. Both Cass and Serena knew that they'd sunk everything they had into this venture. Now that they had reached their goal and it had proved futile, they had lost their drive.

"I guess they expected gold to pop up out of the ground," Cass muttered. "About the way I did," he added with a wry grin. "I was pretty green back there in Seattle, wasn't I?"

"We wouldn't be this far if you hadn't pushed us, Cass," Serena said. "And we're not going to be like them!"

"Way to talk!" Cass said. "Now, let's get that lumber and build our little castle."

He drove the wagon to the sawmill, loaded the boards from a

stack, then after he paid the owner, climbed back into the seat beside Serena. "Look at my hands." He held them out so that she could see the dark stains of the sap on both palms. "Green as gourds," he admitted ruefully. "Back home we wouldn't use wood like this to build a doghouse!" He slapped the lines on the backs of the horses, adding cheerfully, "But it'll do until we make our strike—then we'll hire carpenters to build us a *real* house!"

He seemed happy, Serena noticed, and as they were jolted and jounced on the muddy road that led back to Dawson, the two of them laughed more than they had since leaving Seattle. Once she was thrown against him, and as she grabbed him to steady herself, she felt the hard outline of a gun beneath his coat. "Do you have to carry that?" she asked.

"Hope I never need it—but there are some pretty dangerous characters in this place. As a matter of fact, we need to stop and see if we can find you a small gun." Seeing her look of astonishment, he quickly said, "You'll probably never need it—but if Thor or one of us isn't around, you might find it handy. Anyway, we need some canned milk if we can find any. Pancakes made with water aren't so good."

When they pulled up in front of the general store, Cass leaped to the ground, then walked around the wagon and reached up to help her down. Serena was startled, but he grinned and said, "Got to get rid of my trail manners now that we're in town." When she was on the ground, the two of them went inside. "You buy whatever we've got to have in the way of groceries. I'll see about the gun."

Serena moved along the shelves of the store, which stocked everything from canned food to bear traps. She gasped at the prices and chose only what she thought necessary. When she had made her selection, Cass waved over to a counter on which was spread a variety of pistols. He handed one to her to handle first, saying, "See how that feels." As Serena gingerly took the weapon, he said with approval, "That's a Colt .32. Not many of them around. Too light for a man, but just right for a woman. Do you like it?"

Serena held the pistol awkwardly but managed a smile. "I don't like guns—but this one feels comfortable."

Cass paid for the purchases, which included a belt and holster for the .32, then the two left the store. After he'd put the supplies under the seat, Cass said, "It'll be dark soon, but let's take a walk—maybe get something to eat."

"All right."

The two wandered along the boardwalk, looking into the businesses. There was a carnival air about the town, despite the haggard looks of many of the men. Behind false-fronted buildings were concealed dance halls and gambling houses. Already men with megaphones were calling out the merits of the attractions to the accompaniment of tinkling pianos, scraping fiddles, and blaring horns. Serena stole glances inside the saloons, where silk-clad women danced, liquor flowed over mahogany counters, and poker chips clicked on green felt tables.

"Like to go inside?" Cass asked suddenly, a mischievous look in his eye.

"Oh no—!"

"Oh, this place is harmless enough. When you write your biography in forty years, you can give this place a whole chapter. Come on—!"

Serena was curious and, at Cass's relaxed manner, allowed him to lead her into a large frame building with the name Sam Bonnifield's Saloon emblazoned on the front. The large room was lined with tables on two sides, a bar across the third, and a small stage at the end. Two pretty, petite girls were singing in clear, bell-like voices in harmony. They sang "Break the News to Mother," "A Bird in a Gilded Cage," and "I Love Her, I Love Her Just the Same."

Serena was amazed to see tears running down the weathered cheeks of a rough-looking miner who was watching. Cass saw it and leaned over to whisper, "Those sentimental songs take these men back. I'd start crying myself if you weren't here."

After the singing, the Oatley Sisters, as they were called, danced for a dollar a dance with the miners who climbed up on the stage. Several other girls joined them, and Cass said, "I hear this goes on until morning. Don't see how those women can stand up to it!"

Serena was saddened by the faces of the women, for beneath the paint and the wide smiles, she sensed a desperation and unhappiness. "I think I'd like to go, Cass," she said quietly.

He took one look at her face and said instantly, "Sure. Never should have brought you here."

But before they could get to the door, a bulky shape appeared, and Serena felt a heavy hand on her arm. She was turned as easily as if she were a child, and gasped at the power of the grasp. When she quickly glanced at who had grabbed her, fear ran through her. It was the big man who'd been with Brent Traphagen that day they landed back in Skagway—the one named Leo Ritter.

"Now then, missy, you and me are gonna have us a dance."

"Turn the lady loose, Ritter."

Something in Cass's voice caught the attention of the crowd. A silence spread over the room, and Ritter looked pleased. He was a bull of a man, with a swelling chest and a neck as wide as his large head. The muscles of his arms swelled against the cloth of his shirt, and he looked around the room with a broad grin. Turning back he said, "Back off, Winslow. You ain't got your help with you this time."

Cass pulled his coat back to expose the butt of the Colt in his belt. "Ritter, let her go." His voice was quiet, but something in the look of his eyes caused the men behind Ritter to scramble out of the way.

"I don't have a gun, Winslow."

"I do."

"You can't use a gun on an unarmed man. The boys would stretch your neck. It'd be murder, ain't that right, boys?" A mutter went around the crowd, and Ritter's grin grew broader. "Now you just lay that gun down and we'll give the boys a show."

Cass was well aware that Ritter carried no gun and that he preferred to use his massive fists on his victims. He also knew that the man would stop at nothing to get even from their last encounter in Skagway. *He'll get me down and kick me to death—or gouge my eyes out,* Cass thought. He was in a bad spot and knew it. He thought quickly, then said, "Go get a gun, Ritter. I'll meet you on the street."

"This is good enough for me," Ritter said. His smallish eyes glittered and he looked forward to the fight. He had a skull thick enough to withstand even hard blows, and his massive strength was deadly.

Cass suddenly pulled the gun from his belt and slashed the

wrist of the arm that held Serena. Ritter gasped with pain and grabbed his wrist. "I'll kill you!" he roared and actually leaned forward. But the sound of a shot echoed at once and his curses were cut short. He stared down at the floor where Cass's bullet had plowed into the floor between his feet.

"If you like, I can shoot you through both knees," Cass said evenly. "Then you can crawl around for the rest of your life."

Ritter's face paled and he backed up a step. He was abruptly convinced that the young man with the steady blue-green eyes meant what he said. He lifted his hands in a defensive gesture and through clenched teeth said, "I'll see you later—you won't always have that gun!"

"I'll always have the gun—and you'll apologize to the young lady."

Ritter wanted more than he'd ever wanted anything to throw himself onto Winslow and beat him into raw pulp. But Cass's gun was steady, the muzzle aimed at Ritter's heart. "Sorry—" he mumbled, then whirled and shoved his way through the crowd, disappearing through the double doors.

A babble of talk began, and one miner said, "Watch out, Winslow. This ain't over."

Cass nodded and turned to take Serena's arm, but as he did so, a voice called his name.

"Cass Winslow—" A small figure stepped out from behind some men at his left, and Cass grunted with shock.

"Joe! Joe Winslow!" Cass could hardly believe it. Joe looked thinner, but his blue eyes were as sharp as ever.

"Boy, I sure did enjoy that. It was like seeing my dad all over again. You could've passed for Sky Winslow when you backed that buzzard down!"

"Joe—what are you doing here?"

"Why, I'm aiming to make my big strike, boy. Didn't I tell you back in Virginia I'd be at the next big one?"

"You did, for a fact. Man, I'm glad to see you!"

"And who's this pretty young lady?"

"Oh, this is Serena Stevens—come on, Joe, we've got a lot to talk about. . . !"

Cass practically kidnapped his relative, taking him back to camp. Serena was fascinated by the old man and insisted on fixing a meal. She listened as she cooked, learning more about the Winslow family than she'd ever known.

When they sat down to the meal, Joe pitched in and showed her how a good meal should be treated. After a refill and another cup of strong black coffee, Joe shoved his plate back and gave her a sharp look and a smile. "Ain't had no cookin' like that for quite a spell. These fellers are pretty lucky, havin' a fine cook like you."

"Thank you, Mr. Winslow."

"Reckon Joe is what I answer to. Now, let's hear about how you got to this here place. . . ." Cass filled him in on the story while Serena busied herself with washing up the dishes. When Cass finished, Joe nodded and said, "Wal, reckon by now you've been enlightened. Most men will turn tail when they find out there ain't a gold mine under every rock. But I see you folks are stayers."

"Is there a chance, Joe?" Cass spoke up. "I know now it's going to be tough—I'll do anything to find gold."

"Always a chance, Cass," Joe answered. He took out his pipe, got it stoked up, then leaned back to look at his young relative. "Don't put your soul in hock for it—that's the main thing. Lots of men get sour when they don't make the big strike. Don't want that to happen to you."

"How do you keep that from happening, Joe?" Serena asked.

Joe Winslow had listened carefully to Cass's story of Serena Stevens, and he was good at reading faces. Now he said, "Why, I reckon you probably know the answer to that, Serena. It's a matter of puttin' God before gold—or anything else."

Cass suddenly thought of Jubal. He dropped his head and said little more. Later, while he was giving Joe a ride in the wagon back to his cabin, Cass broke his silence by saying, "I don't know if I can do it, Joe—put God first. I know it's right—but there's something in me—I can't explain it, but I've *got* to make it big!"

Joe Winslow looked up at the stars that were glittering coldly in the heavens. He let the silence run on, then put his gnarled hand on the shoulder of the young man. "A man can't hand wisdom to another—like it was an apple or something. We all of us have to find it for ourselves." The wagon rumbled over the deep ruts, and the old man finally said quietly, "But you're a Winslow—and I'm bettin' that before this thing is over, you'll find out a few things about God—and about Cassidy Winslow!"

CHAPTER SIXTEEN

A JOB FOR SERENA

★ ★ ★ ★

If Dawson was like a carnival by night, Serena discovered that by day the settlement became a great bazaar. She roamed the streets, fascinated by the multiplicity of endeavors that mushroomed almost daily. She quickly discovered that thousands who had thrown every ounce of strength they had into getting their gear over the mountains were now determined to sell out—trying to get enough cash to get them back to their homes. The two main streets—Wall Street and Broadway Avenue—were packed with stalls where strange and unusual items could be bought for all sorts of prices.

On a bright July morning Serena wandered down Broadway examining the goods for sale. She saw clothes, furs, plug hats, fresh grapes, opera glasses, safety pins, and ice cream. She was amused at one salesman who offered ostrich feathers and the tusk of a gigantic mammoth. She passed by those who offered to read her palm, massage her back, or fill her teeth. Some stalls were filled with Bibles, complete sets of Shakespeare, and collections of Dickens' novels.

One sign caught her eye, perhaps because it was lettered in purple paint on a lime green background:

DRUGS DRUGS
Rubber boots, shoes, etc.
Bacon, flour, rolled oats, rice, sugar
Onions, tea, German sausage
DOGS! DOGS!

The yapping of half a dozen dogs rent the air, and Serena saw the animals tied to a post. They were large, well-fed animals of all breeds, and when she moved over to pet one of them, a large reddish dog stared at her out of mournful eyes.

"Like to buy them, lady?" A short, very fat man wearing a colorful necktie and a plug hat appeared at her side, his smallish brown eyes studying her carefully. "Make you a good price for the lot. Me name is Mack Mulroy."

"Oh no, I don't need a pack of dogs," Serena said quickly. As she was swarmed by the friendly dogs she laughed. "I love dogs, but this would be too many pets for anyone."

"Pets? Why, these ain't pets, ma'am! These here is trained sled dogs—the best money can buy!"

"Sled dogs?" Serena looked more carefully at the animals and noted that they were all seemingly well fed and healthy. A thought came to her, but she shook her head. "I don't know anything about sled dogs. Why, I've never even driven a sled!"

"Why, bless you, ma'am, there ain't nothin' to it, nothin' at all! You say 'Mush' and they go forward, say 'Gee' and they go right, 'Haw' and they go left. A child of six could drive these here dogs. . . ."

Serena had been fascinated by the dog teams she'd seen since reaching the North. Every time a sled shot by, propelled by a line of bushy-tailed dogs, she'd watched them with great interest. One time she said to Cass, "If Thor had a chance, he'd be a great sled dog leader. He's so strong and smart!" Now as Mack Mulroy rattled off the virtues of the dogs, she was tempted to buy them. *You must be crazy,* she scolded herself. *You wouldn't know what to do with them—and they probably cost a fortune.*

But as Mulroy urged the many uses of a team, she found herself growing more interested. "Why, you don't have to make a thousand-mile trip, ma'am," he nodded vigorously. "There's little outposts all around Dawson, and horses can't make it through the snow up in the mountains. Them miners out there are needing everything from Dawson. You could load up a sled with tins of sardines, for example, and make a swing around the close-in claims. You'd make the cost of this here team in a few weeks, I tells you. . . !"

Finally Serena shook her head. "I just don't have enough money, Mr. Mulroy."

Sensing a sale, Mulroy spoke up quickly. "I'd not be so quick to say that, ma'am. What's yer name, by the way?"

"Serena Stevens."

"Ah, well, Miss Serena, let me put a point on it—" Leaning forward, Mulroy whispered, "I could shave my price a little for a good customer. Let you have the whole lot for a thousand dollars."

"Why, I don't have that much money. The most I could get together would be two hundred dollars."

Disappointment crossed Mulroy's face, but he suddenly grinned. "Now maybe you and I could do a little business together. You pay me the two hundred down, and pay the rest as you drag in the cash. In three weeks you'd own these fine animals and make a nice living for yerself. What do you say now?"

"But—I don't even have a sled!"

"Sled goes with the team. Is it a bargain?"

Serena was not an impulsive girl. She was usually cautious and thoughtful, but somehow this thing seemed to strike a chord in her spirit. Night after night she had lain awake wracking her brain to find some way to help with the endeavor. Cass and Mike had thrown themselves into learning the mining trade, taking lessons from Joe Winslow. She felt useless and longed to do more than cook and keep the tiny cabin neat. Now as she looked at the dogs, a desperate urge seized her. She had been given a little over two hundred dollars by Cass to use for supplies, and the thought of spending it all frightened her.

Lord—can I do this thing? she prayed frantically. She had long ago learned to pray over decisions, but now this one loomed before her. Lord—I want to do this—but I won't if it's not your will—so give me a big "no" if it's not for me. . . . She waited, praying with all her might, aware that Mulroy was watching her with a curious light in his blue eyes.

Finally she said, "I'll have to pray about this, Mr. Mulroy."

"Oh, praying, is it? Why, that's fine! You do that. I'm not much of a praying man meself—but you do your praying, Miss Serena, and if the Good Lord gives His permission, why you and me will do business!"

Serena moved away, her mind swarming with the suddenness of the thing. For two hours she roamed the streets, seeing almost nothing, so intense were her thoughts about the venture. She prayed almost frantically, something she'd never done before. It was as if she banged on the door of heaven with her fists, *demanding* that God give her an answer.

Suddenly she came out of this intense concentration when a large red object loomed in front of her. Stopping abruptly, she looked up to see Sam Steele, who had planted himself in her pathway. "What in the world are you thinking of, Serena?" he asked, amusement in his flickering blue eyes. His cheeks glowed from a fresh shave and every hair was in place, so that Serena wondered again how he kept himself groomed so immaculately. "You're going to step into a well if you don't wake up!"

"Oh, Sam," Serena gave a half-laugh. "I guess you're right. My mind is a million miles away—well, not that far, I guess. But I've got to decide something really big." She was wearing a pair of Jubal's old trousers and a snug-fitting tan shirt she'd bought at one of the shops. She wore no hat and her curly hair blew in the soft breeze, accenting the size of her eyes. She made a pretty picture before him, but the anxiety in her expression drew his concern.

"Want to tell me about it?" he asked, and when she hesitated, he smiled. "Be just like confessing to a priest," he confided. "All sorts of people come to me with their problems. Come along and tell me about this thing. . . ."

For the next hour the two walked along and Steele listened as Serena related her problem. When she was finished, she gave him a rueful smile. "Crazy, isn't it, Sam? I've never driven a team of dogs in my life, and here I am thinking of buying one!"

Steele said thoughtfully, "Driving a team isn't all that hard. You could do it, I'm sure."

"Really?" said Serena, surprised at Steele's comment.

"Yes, but the travel is different. You'd never be safe on long trips. It takes someone born in this country to do that—but what Mulroy said about short trips is true enough." Looking down at her he asked, "Well, has God told you what to do yet?"

"Don't laugh at me, Sam," Serena pleaded. "I want to help— Cass and Mike are working so hard at Joe's mine. If this would work out, I'd feel like I was more a part of the whole thing."

"Well, I say do it then . . . the worst thing that could happen would be if you failed. If you didn't like it, you could sell the dogs."

"But I don't know how to drive a team!"

"But I do," Steele smiled. "And I'm a fine teacher. Why, you'll be mushing along like an old sourdough in no time!"

"Would you help me, Sam?"

Steele hesitated, then said in a different tone, "I'd do anything in the world for you, Serena. Don't you know that?"

Serena looked up, startled to see the intensity of his gaze. She couldn't mistake his expression and could not speak for a moment. Finally she said, "I—I'm not used to anything like that. But if you could help me with this, I'd be so grateful."

"Of course I'll help you. But I bet you're nervous about how Cass will take it. So here's what we'll do. Why don't I teach you how to drive before you tell him? I'll help you get a few hauling jobs—one of them for the government, taking the mail inland. If you can go to Cass with all that done, it'll make it easier for you to tell him, won't it?"

"Oh, Sam! That would be *wonderful*! Come on, let's go buy those dogs!"

As Serena and Steele hurried back along the busy boardwalk, men and women stopped and turned to look at a sight they'd never expected to see. Superintendent Samuel Steele, "The Lion of the North," was being dragged down the main street of Dawson, his serious face filled with laughter as he looked down at the young woman who was chattering like a magpie as she tugged at his hand.

A tall, crusty miner who'd had his differences with Steele stared at the sight in astonishment. Yanking off his cap, he scratched his bushy gray hair and muttered, "Well I'll be a ringtailed sidehill gouger if I ever saw anything like that!" Turning to his companion he shook his head sorrowfully. "This here country's done ruined Steele! He was a good man, but he's plum lost it, Clyde!"

* * * *

"It ain't quite the way you fellers figured it'd be, is it now?"

Stained with mud from head to toe, Cass and Rooney paused and scowled at Joe Winslow, who was watching them with satisfaction. He took his pipe from his teeth and laughed quietly. "If you two ain't a sight! Your own mamas wouldn't know you!"

Mike Rooney glared at the old man. His clothing was so covered with the red mud that no trace of the original color was exposed. His feet were two large lumps of mud, and every time he reached up to wipe the sweat away, he left a red streak across his face.

"Begorra—this is worse than digging spuds!" he snapped. Giving Cass a hard look he said, "See what you've gotten us into?"

Cass looked no better than his companion, nor was he in any better mood. Glaring at Rooney he shot back, "Nobody made you come—go on back to Ireland if you don't like it here!"

The two of them were exhausted, disgusted, and sick of the mine that Joe Winslow had agreed to share with them. When he had mentioned in an off-handed fashion that the three of them would be equal partners in the Glory Hole, they were beside themselves with gratitude. But when they had been introduced to the mine and discovered that the effort required to get at the gold would put a galley slave to shame, their enthusiasm all but faded.

Joe's claim was located in the middle of what seemed to be the aftermath of a huge explosion. All the machinery for placer mining—rockers and boilers, steam engines and pumps, hoses and winches—cluttered the landscape. Joe lived in a fetid cabin about ten feet away from his mine, which was nothing more than a hole in the ground.

"Gold is mebby twenty—thirty feet down," Joe had said nonchalantly. "You fellers can do the digging, and I'll do the teaching."

Cass and Rooney discovered that the permanently frozen ground of the Yukon had to be thawed before bedrock could be reached. And Joe Winslow informed them it was the bedrock that contained the gold.

Winslow had let the sun do the first part of the work, thawing out the topsoil. He'd laboriously scraped away the thawed earth, then let the next layer thaw. But the sun was not enough, so Cass and Rooney cut firewood and built fires over the frozen earth. When the fires had burned out, they then removed the ashes and dug down a few inches. A few days of wheezing in the smoky shaft gave them hacking coughs, and the little dirt they did remove seemed insignificant. They piled all they removed in this fashion in what Joe called a "dump," and wanted to start looking in it for gold right away.

"Nope, we don't do it that way, Cass," Joe rebuked him. "We do our digging, then we take it to a sluice box and take out the gold. Can't be runnin' to a sluice box every time you fellers bring up a shovelful of dirt!"

Cass and Rooney groaned and complained but labored on. Other miners had collected enough dirt to start washing for gold, and the two men sometimes took a break to watch. The sluice boxes were long rectangular boxes into which the gravel was shoveled. Then water from a sluiceway was channeled into it. In the bottom of each sluice box strips of wood called "riffles" were nailed crossways. As the water rushed through, the soil and gravel were carried away, but the heavier gold was caught in the crossbars and matted on the bottom. Every two or three days the water was diverted and the miners did what they called a cleanup, which meant taking the gold from between the riffles.

One afternoon Cass was wearily chopping away at the ice-hard ground, when he heard Joe cry out, "Well—look at this, won't ya! Cass, come up outta that there hole!"

Willing to stop the digging for any excuse, Cass clambered out of the hole. When he got to his feet and looked past Joe, he blinked in surprise. He saw a team of dogs hitched to a sled, and standing behind it—was Serena!

"How do you like my outfit?" Serena cried out. She was wearing a pair of dark green trousers, a light green plaid shirt, and a bright red toboggan cap. Her eyes were alive with excitement and pride as she waved her whip toward the dogs that sat with their red tongues lolling. "Come on, Cass, I'll take you for a ride."

Cass moved forward slowly, eyeing the dogs carefully. He noted that Thor was in the lead position, and then remembered asking Serena what she did while he and Rooney worked in the mine. *Oh, I'm working on a surprise for you,* she'd said.

"Serena, what in the world—"

Serena cut him off as she excitedly started talking. "They're mine, Cass! Aren't they beautiful? That's Thor—then Bob, Skeet, Pap, Red, Tom, and Ollie. . . ."

Rooney and Joe came to stand in front of the excited girl, and finally Cass interrupted her long enough to ask, "Serena, you didn't *buy* this rig?"

"Oh, Cass, I did—but it's all right. I've got a plan for paying for them."

"Doing what?" demanded Cass.

Serena could tell Cass was upset and hastened to explain. "I bought them on credit from a man named Mack Mulroy. But Sam's got me a government contract for taking mail, so I'll be able to pay for them in a month."

"Well, now," Joe said with admiration in his voice. "Now I call that real fine! Can you really drive those beasts?"

"Yes—I'll show you. . . ." There was only a thin crust of snow left on the ground, but enough to allow the steel runners to plane over the surface. Grasping the handles of the wicker sled, Serena cried out, "Mush!" At once the dogs threw themselves against the harness. The sled moved away, bumping over the rough ground. By the use of her voice, Serena steered the team into a wide circle, then back the opposite direction. She and Steele had spent a great deal of time practicing, but she was now confident in her skill, so that when she drew up, calling, "Whoa!" the dogs obeyed at once. Stepping off the runners, she gave Cass an appealing look. "I can do it, Cass!" she said.

Aware that the others were watching him, Cass shook his head. "Well, I don't see how a young woman can go all over this country by herself. It's too dangerous."

"Sam's put the word out," Serena said. "He's posted a notice that anyone who bothers me will be arrested for interfering with the government of Canada and will go to the penitentiary for a long time."

Sam Steele had foreseen this, and when a miner had tried to

force himself on Serena, making lewd remarks, he'd found himself in the iron grasp of the big mountie. When he stood before Steele at the office, the man demanded, "What's the fine?"

"Fifty dollars," Steele had said.

"Is that all?" the miner had sneered. "I've got that in my pocket."

Steele had given him a hard glance and added, "And thirty days on the work crew. Have you got that in your pocket?"

The offender had been sent to cut firewood for the mounties, and the word that quickly spread was, "Don't fool with the mail lady—Steele will rip the hide off you!"

"Who taught you to drive that thing?" Cass demanded.

"Why, Sam did."

For some reason this displeased Cass. He grunted, "You're going to have trouble, I can tell you that."

But Rooney and Joe were pleased with the young woman and praised her for her accomplishment. Serena was glad to hear such nice things, but both men noticed that she was upset with Cass's obvious displeasure. Mike Rooney cornered him later and demanded, "What's the matter with you, Cass? You act like a bear with a sore tail. It wouldn't have killed you to have encouraged Serena. She's just trying to help out."

Cass stared at him but had no answer. "I'm her guardian. Her father asked me to watch out for her. She should have come to me before she got involved in a fool scheme like this."

But as the days went on, the "fool scheme" turned out better than Serena had expected. She made enough from the mail contract to pay for the dogs, and enough left over to buy their food. She was in constant demand for hauling light-weight items to the outer reaches of the Dawson territory, and when no one hired her, she followed Mulroy's suggestion of hauling specialty food items to miners too far out to come to town often. Once she bought a sled load of canned peaches and came back with two pokes filled with gold dust.

She held it up before her three friends, and Joe said, "Easier than digging it out of the ground."

"We split it four ways," Serena said, and despite the objections of the others, she insisted on dividing the dust. "We're partners—and we split even," she smiled.

Cass finally grudgingly came to admire the girl's skill and said so. His praise brought color to her cheeks. "Oh, Cass, I was so glad to find something to do, to help. I—I should have come to you first, but I was afraid you'd say no."

"I would have," Cass nodded, but he smiled at her. "Not the first time I've been wrong. I'm proud of you, Serena—and your dad would be very happy for you."

Serena felt happier in the weeks that followed than she'd ever been in her life. Cass mentioned once to Joe that Jubal had named her the Yukon Queen, and Joe boasted of that to his friends. Soon every miner in Dawson was calling Serena by that name. It caught the fancy of the town, and when a stranger arrived, one of the first things he was told about was the beautiful young woman with the dog team. "Yep, that's the Yukon Queen," they'd say as Serena would come flying by, guiding her dogs. "Ain't she something?"

Serena didn't like the name. "It was something very private, between Jubal and us," she complained to Cass. "I wish they wouldn't call me that."

Cass shook his head. "That's one wish you'll never get," he said. "The whole Klondike calls you that, and they're not going to forget. It's kind of an honor."

But Serena shook her head. "I wish they wouldn't."

CHAPTER SEVENTEEN

A TOUCH OF JEALOUSY

★   ★   ★   ★

Like all other mining camps, Dawson was flooded with reports of new strikes—almost all of them false. Rarely did a week pass without a stampede into the hills based on some tale that spread like wildfire through the town.

Cass was one of those who rushed to Rosebud Creek, fifty miles from Dawson, when an old man reported a strike there. He rushed to the spot, panned gold by the sun by day and by candlelight after dark—but there was no gold there. When he returned, Joe had tried to comfort him. "That's been my life for fifty years, son. Runnin' like a hound dog after some kind of rabbit that ain't there!"

As fall came, Rooney had his fling, making his way to Swede Creek, where he got caught with three hundred others in a sudden freeze. All of them suffered from the terrible cold and two men had their feet amputated as a result, but no one found a trace of gold.

Time and again Cass's hopes rose, only to fall again. The strain of it all took its toll on Cass, and he soon became silent and moody from working at the mine for long hours. He always dreamed of making the big strike somewhere out in the hills, but every time news about a new claim failed to produce gold, his hopes were dashed again.

"He's gone sour," Mike said to Joe one day. "He was a light-hearted lad until we got here. Now he acts like a dog looking for someone to bite."

Joe Winslow took his pipe from between his teeth and shook his head. "Seen it many a time, Mike. Something about gold rots the brain—of some men, that is. Sometimes it's the finding of it that ruins a feller—and sometimes it's the *not* finding it." He replaced the pipe and sent a cloud of purple smoke into the air, his seamed face sober and somewhat sad. "Guess I've thrown my life away chasing the phantom. If I'd had the chance, I'd have lived different."

Mike was silent, his homely face fixed in an attitude of thought. He was very fond of Cass and finally said, "I wish he'd get out of here, Joe. This place ain't no good for him. And you know what? I think he's bothered about Serena."

"Why, thet gal's doin' fine, Mike!"

"Oh, sure, she's made money hauling freight and mail with them dogs—but mebby that's what the matter is. A man like Cass, he's got lots of pride. All he's done is muck around at the bottom of this blasted mine—and she's done so good that every miner in the Klondike knows the Yukon Queen."

"Could be, I reckon. But he's a fool fer thinkin' that way." Admiration shaded the lean features of the old prospector as he added, "She's extra, thet gal is! Ain't never knowed a better one— and purty as a Georgia peach!"

Rooney shot a glance at Joe Winslow. "And that might be part of what's givin' Cass an itch he can't scratch."

"Meanin' whut?"

"Meaning that every time that big mountie comes callin' on Serena, Cass sulls up like a possum. Ain't you noticed it?"

Joe had noticed it but shook his head firmly. "Don't say nothin' to him, Mike. He don't know what's goin' on inside him, thet boy don't. He's like all the other Winslow men, I guess. My pa was the same way. My ma wasn't a good woman, and after she died, he was so mixed up about women, he couldn't even think straight. He told me that himself, Mike. But then when he found a good woman, why, he come out of it."

"I don't see why he don't just come straight out and court

Serena—lots of others have tried, but they've been scared off by Steele."

"Cass is too proud fer one thing," Joe nodded. "He thinks he's got to be a millionaire to impress women. Did he tell you about thet girl back in New York who led him on? Wal, he's been burnt purty bad, and he's not gonna risk it again! It's not right, as I've tried to tell the boy, but he won't listen to reason. A good woman don't look at a man because he's got money—not a good woman that is."

Rooney thought about that, then offered, "I think he feels kinda like a father to Serena."

"Likely—since her pa give him the keepin' of her. Thet's another thing that's got Cass's harness all tangled up. He's all mixed up with that obligation—and whut he feels for her as a man."

That evening the two men saw enacted the very problem they'd discussed. Steele came for supper, seeming to fill the small cabin. His scarlet coat and the riding trousers with the yellow stripe made an impressive picture. Other men looked smaller and somehow colorless beside him.

Serena had surprised them by wearing a new dress. She'd found it in one of the shops, and though it was not new, it was in excellent condition and fit her perfectly. Steele commented on it at once, stopping as he stepped inside the room. "Now that's a pretty dress, Serena. New, is it?"

"Well, new to me," Serena smiled. She felt self-conscious as the three men looked at her. The dress was made of pale silk, a light blue with dark blue ribbons woven into the cuffs and bodice. It nipped her small waist, emphasizing her hips and bust in a fashion that had troubled her, but she had fallen in love with it. Now she flushed slightly, saying, "You all sit down and talk while I set the table."

Steele and the others sat down at the rough table, and Sam commented on the flowers that gave some color to the drab cabin. Serena had found them and made the arrangement, and when Steele praised them, Cass felt angry at himself. *Why don't I ever say nice things about something like that—it wouldn't kill me.*

While Serena took the bread from the oven, filling the room with a delicious aroma, the men talked of the affairs of the camp. It was Joe who gave Steele a sharp look and asked, "What you going to do about Lyle Medford, Superintendent?" Medford was a miner who'd found a good claim on Strawberry Creek, five miles north of Dawson. He'd been a happy man, but had been pressured to sell. When he had refused, he'd been found badly beaten. He'd sold out and left as soon as he was able to travel. "I guess we all know who had Lyle beat up."

Steele gave Winslow a direct stare and stated flatly, "Give me a name and some evidence and I'll arrest him."

"Why, everybody knows it's Traphagen who done it!" Rooney protested hotly.

"Did you witness the beating?"

"Why, no, but—"

Steele frowned, his classic features firm in the yellow lamplight. "Traphagen didn't leave Dawson the day Medford was attacked."

Cass looked up quickly, demanding, "So you checked on him? Then you must know he's behind it."

"I don't know it," Steele shook his head. "I may suspect the man, but it'll take more than suspicions to convict him in a court of law."

"It was one of his toughs," Joe insisted. "Probably Leo Ritter. The way poor ol' Lyle was roughed up, I'd say it was Ritter's work. He's a bully and oughta be shot!"

"Well, I can't jail a man for that—and if anyone shoots him, I'll have to arrest him." He then looked directly at Cass and said, "That's for you, Cass. He's an animal, I agree, and I'd like nothing better than to run him out of Dawson. He tried to get you once, and it's my judgment he'll try again. Don't fight him, not with your fists—and don't shoot him if he's not carrying a gun."

"I'll stop him any way I have to," Cass said. "A man can defend himself in our country."

"This is not your country. If you shot an unarmed man in Canada, you'd stand trial for murder." Steele frowned and shook his head. "I don't mean to sound unfair, but I'm required to enforce the laws of the land."

"We know one thing," Joe put in. "Lyle sold out to Traphagen after taking a beating. And he's not the first. In the old days in California, somebody would have stopped his clock!"

Serena interrupted by saying, "Anybody hungry?" She put a

plate of corn bread on the table, adding, "It's not as good as I'd hoped, but it'll have to do." She brought the rest of the food to the table and then sat down. "Who'll ask the blessing—you, Super-intendent Steele?"

Steele at once bowed his head and asked a brief blessing. When he looked up at Serena, he smiled fondly. "We always asked the blessing in our home. It's a habit I've missed. Thank you for bringing it back."

"We always prayed over the grub at our house," Joe nodded. He took a bite of the roast beef, chewed thoughtfully, then glanced at Cass. "Your ma and pa, they're praying folks, too, ain't they, Cass?"

"Yes, they are," Cass said. He poured milk from a can into his coffee, his eyes thoughtful. "Can't remember ever having a meal that one of them didn't ask the blessing. I guess most Winslows are praying people." He lifted the cup, held it to his lips, then paused. "Except for us mavericks, of course—like me and Aaron."

Serena at once looked at Cass. There was some sort of longing in his tone that she had not heard before. His big hands held the cup loosely, and his eyes were hooded, as though he kept some sort of private thought in his mind. He was wearing a rough mi-ner's shirt with the sleeves rolled up, yet there was a touch of ease and grace about him. His long tawny hair curled over his collar, and his long lips were pulled together in an expression she couldn't read.

Mike Rooney had been watching Cass, too, and the thought came to him, *Cass is a man of God—only he ain't found it out yet*. He himself was far from his home, but he had his own memories of is parents taking their brood to Mass, come rain or shine. He'd led a rough life and now said, "I think of me early days—we went to church every Sunday of me life, I do think." Shaking his head with a touch of sadness, he murmured, "A man is a fool for leaving the best of his life. . . ."

"Not too late, Mike," Serena urged. "You're not too old to go back to those good things."

The meal lasted a long time, for it was more than eating that they required. The harshness of the wilderness in the Klondike made men and women hungry for the softer things of life, so that meals like this with friends were more appreciated than by those who had them regularly.

They sat around speaking quietly, Steele telling a few of his experiences—which made Cass feel like a callow youth. Finally the mountie rose and said, "I hate to leave, but I have to go to Skagway tomorrow. Serena, that was a meal fit for a king."

"I'll go with you to your horse." She wanted to say a word to him, and when they were outside standing beside his big roan, she asked, "Sam, isn't there anything we can do about Cass? I'm afraid he's headed for trouble with Ritter and Traphagen."

"I'll do what I can—but he'll have to keep a lid on his temper." Steele looked down on her face, adding, "You're fond of him, aren't you?"

"Why, yes, I am."

Steele admired the smooth curves of her cheek and suddenly put his hand on it. The touch startled her, and then without warning he bent and kissed her. His lips were firm and gentle, and when he put his arms around her, she yielded to his embrace. There was safety in his strong arms, and she returned his kiss for a moment. The touch of her firm body as she stood in his arms brought a rush of desire to Steele. She smelled of lilacs and there was a wild sweetness in her lips that was like nothing he'd ever known.

"You're a lovely woman, Serena," he whispered, and when she pulled back, he released her reluctantly. "I'm falling in love with you, I'm afraid."

"Why—Sam!" Serena gasped. She was still intimidated by Sam Steele, but his words sent a thrill along her nerves. She tried to think, but his kiss had unsettled her, so much that she knew that she would not sleep for thinking of it.

"You don't have to say anything, Serena," Steele said, a husky edge to his voice. "I just wanted you to know." He turned and stepped into the saddle, then said as he rode out, "I'll remember this night—!"

Serena stood very still. The night air was cold, but she was unconscious of it. Slowly she reached up and touched her lips, and as she did, a warmth came to her, rising inside like a fountain. She was stirred and wondered what she would say to him if he spoke of love again. Slowly she turned and moved to the door of the shack, by an act of will composing her features, hiding the excitement that Steele's kiss and his words had brought. Somehow she knew instinctively that Cass would not approve.

★ ★ ★ ★

Brent Traphagen sat at his customary place—at a private table with his back to the wall, facing the double swinging doors of The Shady Lady saloon. As the roulette wheel spun, the cadence of the ball as it settled into a slot was a pleasant sound in his ears. He scanned the blackjack tables, then his eyes moved to the poker tables, coming to rest finally on Lottie as she smiled at a dowdy miner at the bar.

The place was filled every night and a good part of each day as miners came to town to find an outlet for their appetites. Traphagen ran a smooth operation, as there never seemed to be a lack of liquor and good entertainment. In fact, he had added some more game tables and even had Lottie hire a few more girls.

The saloon had brought in a steady flow of money since the night it had opened. But Traphagen was not satisfied to be just another saloonkeeper. He used the profits from The Shady Lady to buy up claims, and despite the fact that some of them had proved worthless, enough had come through to make him smile as he thought of them.

"Brent—you want me to take the cash over to the bank?"

Traphagen looked around to see Whitey Dugan standing beside his table. "Yes, but first sit down and let's go over this list." When the albino sat down, Traphagen pulled a small book from the inner pocket of his coat, opened it, and read it carefully.

Dugan sprawled in his chair, his pale eyes moving over the crowd restlessly. He cared little for the women and liquor that drew other men. He loved good horses and treated them with a kindness he never showed to any man. A cruel streak ran through Whitey Dugan, and the men of Dawson moved carefully around him with the same caution they would show to a dangerous animal.

"What about Hank Thomson? You make him an offer?"

"Sure. He's scared. I figure one more trip ought to do it."

"Good. He's taking two, maybe three hundred a day out of that mine."

"Want me to rough him up?"

Traphagen considered the lean face of his lieutenant, then shook his head. "Not yet. Steele has got his men watching us pretty close. Just lean on him, Whitey. He'll fold, I think."

"All right. Who else?"

The two went down the list, and finally Traphagen hesitated. "I've been thinking about Joe Winslow's mine."

Dugan shrugged, saying, "Not too rich, from what I hear."

"I've got a feeling about that one. It's right between two of the richest mines in Dawson—Patton's claim and Joe B. Howard's. We can't pressure them, but I think we'd better buy Winslow's right away."

"How much you want to offer?"

"Two thousand."

"He won't take that. He's been grubbing for a year in that shaft."

A wolfish grin broke the symmetry of Brent Traphagen's face. "That's what I pay you for. Get it and you can buy that gelding you've been lusting for."

Dugan's eyes lit up at once. "Now you're talking." He rose and clutched the sack of dust and nuggets. "I'll drop this in the bank, then I'll pay a call on Winslow."

Traphagen nodded at the poke. "Be sure you don't get held up. There's some pretty bad fellows in this camp."

Whitey Dugan's free hand made a smooth motion and came up with the Colt at his side. His draw was so fast that as often as Traphagen had seen him practice it, he was always taken aback by the man's speed.

"I wish some yahoo would try it," Dugan nodded, a hungry look in his expression. As he left the saloon, men drew back and gave him ample room as he moved across the crowded floor, leaving Brent Traphagen smiling to himself as he watched Dugan.

★ ★ ★ ★

The dump beside the Glory Hole had grown steadily, and the few tests Joe had made revealed that the gold content was good.

But Cass had grown heartily sick of the endless task. Week after week he and Mike grubbed away at the bottom of the shaft, and finally he knew he could stand no more of it.

He crawled out of the shaft at noon, giving place to Mike, who had grown to hate the work as much as he did.

"Mike, I'm not going down in that hole again," Cass announced suddenly.

Rooney stared at his partner but was not taken by surprise. "Faith! I been wonderin' how long it'd be before you come to that. Are you going home, Cass?"

"No—I'm going into the hills—way back where I can get some air in my lungs." Staring down with hatred into the black shaft, he snapped bitterly, "I thought I could stand any kind of work, but I was wrong. That's hell on earth, Mike, down in that mudhole!"

Mike knew better than to try to argue with him. "Well, I'll stick it out until cleanup, then I'll have enough money for one big bust at least." His broad face broke into a grin, and he slapped Cass hard on the shoulder. "Save me a place out there, Cass!"

"Sure, Mike." Cass hesitated, then said, "I've never forgotten how you saved my bacon back in San Francisco. Keep hoping someday I can do you a turn."

"Go out there and find us a good creek," Mike nodded. "I'll be there in a week or two, and we'll make our big strike. Where you headed for?"

"I've always thought there was something in the Indian Head Creek." Cass shrugged and laughed self-consciously. "I know some pretty good prospectors have gone over it—and I'm probably wrong. Just a feeling, Mike."

"Well, now, I've learned that a man's feelings are sometimes more to be trusted than some educated book. Go on and I'll be with you soon as I can, Cass."

"Check in at Barney Hodges' shack, at the mouth of the Indian Head. I'll keep in touch with him, let him know where I am."

When Cass returned to the cabin, he found Serena feeding her dogs. They crowded around her, almost upsetting her in their eagerness for the dried fish she was passing out. Cass stopped and watched her, thinking suddenly of the first time he'd seen her. She had blossomed, it seemed to him, and he wondered at the change in her.

Serena was unaware of his presence until she shooed the dogs away and turned to find him watching her. "Oh, Cass—I didn't hear you," she said. "Come on inside and I'll fix your meal."

Cass followed her inside asking, "Where's Joe?"

"He went to buy some new boots. Said his old ones were too far gone to repair." Serena moved around the kitchen, speaking in a lively manner, not noticing that Cass was saying almost nothing. She had grown accustomed to this, but finally after he'd eaten, he looked up at her, a peculiar expression on his face.

"Is something wrong, Cass?" she asked.

"Not really—but I'm leaving Dawson."

Serena moved her head in surprise. "Leaving? Where are you going?"

"Not back home—not yet, anyway," Cass answered. He clenched his fists and looked down at the table, thinking of how to put the thing. Finally he shrugged and lifted his eyes to meet hers. "I can't stand that hole in the ground another day, Serena. I'd rather be poor than live like that. I'm going to the mountains— see if I can find color in Indian Head Creek."

Serena was taken aback, but she realized that all of Cass's friends had seen this coming. "I'll miss you, Cass," she said simply. "Maybe I could go with you?"

"No, there's no cabin, no place for a woman." Cass hesitated, then added, "Besides, you're busy with your team, and—" He faltered slightly, then said, "You have other interests."

A flush of color touched Serena's cheeks, for she knew he was referring to Sam Steele. She met his eyes, however, and shook her head. "I don't want you to go, Cass—but I know you feel you have to do it. I've seen how digging in that mine has dragged you down. But Indian Head Creek is not that far away. I'll bring some supplies and sell them to the men up in that part of the world."

"That'll be something to look forward to," Cass said. Rising from the table, he suddenly said, "I'm leaving as soon as I can get some gear thrown together." He hesitated, then shook his head. "I promised your father I'd take care of you, Serena, and I don't aim to go back on that promise. When I make my fortune you'll have everything you ever wanted." He started to leave, then turned back. "But it won't be the same up there without you."

"I—I'll miss you, too, Cass," Serena whispered. "Don't stay away too long."

Cass felt the awkwardness of the moment and put out his hand. When she took it, he tried to put what he felt into words—but could only say, "Well, I'll be back when I get rich."

"Come back, Cass," Serena said quickly. "Even if you don't get rich."

Cass thought of her as he rode out of Dawson on a horse he'd bought, with a pack mule trailing behind. As the town faded from his sight, he wondered, *What's a man to do? I couldn't bring her on a trip like this.* He found no pleasure in leaving Dawson, and he was acutely conscious that he was alone in a way he'd never been before.

CHAPTER EIGHTEEN

STRIKE ON THE INDIAN HEAD CREEK

★ ★ ★ ★

A gray sky was scored by ominous dark clouds, and Serena looked up at them apprehensively. She had learned to judge the weather well, knowing that her life might depend on it. *Don't fool with no blizzards, Serena,* Joe had warned her. *Them things will sneak up on you and kill you before you can blink!*

Thinking of his words, she looked down at the dogs, gauging their strength. The trip had been a long one, and they were tired. Ordinarily she would have camped out, but something menacing in the look of the sky made her apprehensive. She hesitated only briefly, then made her decision. Going to Thor, she reached down, saying, "Got to make Dawson, Thor—you can do it!" He licked her hand, and reaching into a bag, she drew out a dried fish and gave it to him. "A little bonus—" she whispered, then moved along the line, giving each of the dogs a fish. She patted each of them, murmuring little encouragements to them, then moved back to the sled. She took out a leather case and ate a sandwich, washing it down with lukewarm tea from a wrapped jug.

As she ate, her mind was busy, thinking of the route ahead, the weather, the condition of the dogs, her own fatigue. She wore a fur parka with the hood up and a pair of thick fur gloves. The weather was the enemy—that she had learned—and it had become a game to her, beating the weather at the contest.

Finally she grasped the handles of the sled and cried out, "Mush—mush!" The dogs threw themselves against their harnesses and the sled moved over the thin layer of snow. Serena trotted along behind the sled, sparing the dogs. She'd made a quick trip to the western end of the gold country—against Sam's advice. But she was bored and had laughed at his concern. "I'll be back in time for the dance," she'd promised, referring to a big dance planned by the city fathers.

Now as the sled hissed along over the snow, she let her mind think on Sam. He'd been to visit several times—had kissed her once. But there was a sensitivity in the big man that kept him from pressing her. She knew he wanted her, but she could not make up her mind about herself.

Do I love him—or is it just affection, she pondered. The silence around her was profound, and nothing moved except a far-off eagle that scored the gray sky. She watched his flight, then her thoughts turned to Cass. *Why doesn't he come back? Or at least send a note?* She thought she knew him well enough to know the answer to that. *He's too proud—he thinks he has to have a mountain of gold before he can go to a woman.* He had never mentioned the woman in New York to her, but Mike Rooney had, and she grew coldly furious at the thought of it.

"I hope you choke on your old diamonds!" she spoke aloud, then laughed ruefully as the ears of the dogs went up. "Not you," she said. "You boys are much better mannered than that hussy!"

The sled threaded a gap between two huge rocks that lifted their bulk out of the earth, like twin tombstones, she thought. The air was growing colder and she stepped up the pace, although she hated to work the dogs so hard. *Wait until we get home,* she promised them silently. *I'll give you all a steak apiece—if I have to kill a cow to do it!*

The day wore on, but at dusk she felt relieved when the ragged outline of Dawson came into view. As she pulled into the camp, she was greeted by almost every man she met—"Hey, Serena, where you been?" they asked in one form or another.

"Just a little trip," she returned, and gave them a wave. She'd gotten to know many of them, and Steele's warning and swift action at the first infraction had been potent enough to assure her safety. Many of them tried to court her, but not a man had made rude advances.

They're all so lonesome, she'd said once to Cass. *Most of them are away from their families and so many of them are young.* As she closed in on the cabin where she saw the light burning in the window, she thought of that moment with him. They'd been standing on the banks of the Yukon River, watching the flow, and she'd said, *I guess I'm like a mother to some of them.* And as she called out "Whoa, boys!" she suddenly remembered his quick grin. He'd reached out and squeezed her arm and had said, *You don't look like anyone's mother to me!*

The door opened and Joe and Rooney rushed out, greeting her warmly. "Here, you get inside," Mike said after giving her a hug. "I'll take care of the dogs."

"If we have any beef, give them a good steak," Serena said. "They've earned it today."

"Right!"

Serena moved inside the cabin, savoring the warmth of the small room. Going at once to the wood-burning stove, she pulled off her gloves and held her hands to the heat. "That's good, Joe. The temperature's dropping pretty fast."

"Shore is," Joe commented. "I was startin' to get worried about you." He took her parka and, after hanging it on a nail, said, "You set and I'll get some hot vittles."

Serena sat at the table letting the fatigue of the trail seep out of her. She had been on the trail since dawn, and her muscles protested as she shifted on her chair. When Mike came back in from tending to the dog team, the three ate, with Mike doing most of the talking. Afterward, Joe said, "Girl, you're wore out. Go to bed and sleep the clock around."

"I think I will, Joe." She rose to go to the small room that was hers and paused to ask, "Any word from Cass?"

"Haven't heard a word. Guess he's busy trying to get that strike before the creek freezes."

"Well, good-night, Joe. It's good to be back." She entered the small room, which was no more than nine feet square, then undressed and donned a heavy woolen gown and a pair of thick white socks. She turned back the blankets on the narrow cot, got between them, then let herself relax. Tired as she was, she didn't go to sleep at once. Finally she drifted off—and dreamed of an angel in a red coat. But that dream faded, and she slept through the night without turning over.

When she awakened, it was with a start, for the sound of angry voices broke through her sleep. Confused, she gave a wild look around the room, seeing that the thin, pale light of dawn was breaking through the single window of her room. The voices got louder and she slipped out of bed. Pulling on a pair of boots, she threw on a heavy housecoat that she sometimes wore in the morning and went to the door.

When she stepped into the room, she was startled to see Joe and Mike facing two men who had evidently forced their way into the cabin. Alarm ran through her, for she recognized Whitey Dugan and Leo Ritter at once.

Ritter whirled around, his hand going to the gun at his side, but when he saw her, he grinned broadly. "Well, Whitey, looky here whut we got!"

But Whitey Dugan, after giving Serena a sharp glance, paid no heed to her, turning back to face the two men. "You'd better be smart and sell out, Winslow," he said, his pale eyes fixed on Joe.

Joe was wearing a pair of pants and his red underwear top. He'd answered the knock at the door, thinking it was one of his friends from down the creek. The two men had shoved their way in, and Whitey Dugan had started threatening him at once. They'd been at the house two weeks earlier, but Joe hadn't mentioned it to Mike or Serena. Now as he watched the eyes of the killer, he said carefully, "Go tell Traphagen he'll not get my claim."

"Aw, Grandpa, you don't want to be like that," Dugan sneered. He let his hand brush the handle of his gun, then turned to face Serena. "Why, this is a dangerous place. You wouldn't want nothing bad to happen to that pretty woman, would you?"

A streak of fear ran through Joe Winslow. He himself was too seasoned to be intimidated by Dugan and Ritter, but he knew they were ruthless men. He wished that Serena hadn't come back, but now he became as conciliatory as possible. "I'll talk to Traphagen," he said. "But he won't get this claim for nothing. Go back and tell him I'll have a fair price or I won't sell."

Whitey was enjoying the moment. He'd seen the fear in the old man's eyes, and this was the sort of thing that gave him pleasure. He grinned at Ritter, winked, and said, "Why, we done named a price, Winslow. You're so old you're getting forgetful."

"Two thousand dollars? Don't be funny, Dugan."

"You don't need money, Grandpa," Dugan needled. "You're too old for women—and that'll buy all the whiskey you can drink."

Ritter had been watching Serena, thinking of the last time he'd spoken with her. He carried the memory of how Cass Winslow had backed him down, and now with that festering in him, moved over and took her arm. "I ain't seen you in a time, sweetheart," he said. "Why don't you and me do the town some night?"

Raw anger flared in Joe Winslow's eyes. He moved over to strike at the bully's arm, crying, "Let that girl alone—!"

But he never finished, because Leo Ritter struck him in the chest with a terrible blow of his huge fist. Joe was driven backward, collapsing on the floor. The blow had driven his breath from his body and Serena cried out, running to kneel beside him.

And at that moment Mike Rooney made a terrible mistake. He'd had his revolver strapped on and now he shouted, "You dirty scum—get out of here!"

Serena turned to see Mike reach for his gun, his eyes on the huge form of Ritter. She saw the gun clear the holster, but she also saw the gun of Whitey Dugan leap into the hand of the albino.

"No—!" she screamed, but the explosion of Dugan's gun covered her frantic cry. The shot struck Rooney in the side, driving him down, and as he fell Dugan's lips drew back in a crazed smile and he put another shot in the helpless body of the falling man.

"Mike—!" Serena rose and ran to fall beside Rooney. Picking up his head she cradled him in her arms. Blood ran from his mouth in a crimson stream and his eyes were beginning to dull. He died in her arms, and she began to weep, holding his bloody head against her.

"You seen it, lady," Dugan said. "He pulled his gun. I didn't have no choice." The gunman stood there, watching as Joe got painfully to his feet. "You seen it, too, Grandpa. When you tell your story, make sure you tell it straight. He went for his gun first."

Winslow was breathing painfully. At least one of his ribs, he knew, was broken. The sharp pain shot through him as he came and kneeled beside Serena. He put his hand on the girl's shaking shoulders, saying nothing—for there was nothing to say.

The two gunmen watched the pair, then Ritter mumbled, "Let's get out of here, Whitey." When they were outside, he said, "We're in trouble now. That girl's a friend of Steele's."

"We ain't in no trouble," Dugan snapped. "We came here on legitimate business. They both saw the Irishman pull his gun—and when they say that, no court in the land would convict us. Come on, let's get back and tell Brent about this."

Drawn by the shot, men came running to the cabin to see what had happened. As they entered they stood there looking down silently on the tragic scene. Serena was sitting on the floor weeping, holding the body of their dead friend. "I'll go get Steele," Harry Bonner said. "You'd better let us take care of Mike." He was a tall man with a long face—and had been a good friend of Rooney's. When they had carried the body to a wagon, Harry listened as Joe told him what had happened. His eyes grew bleak. "They'll get by with it, Joe. Mike went for his gun—you and Serena seen it. He knows Steele can't hang him with that kind of story."

"If I was a younger man, I'd settle him myself, Harry!"

Harry Bonner was a tough man, and now he looked in the direction of Dawson. His reply, when it finally came, was mild, but there was a chill in his blue eyes.

"Well, something might happen to them two, Joe."

★　★　★　★

Cass moved down to the shallow end of a pool, stepping from stone to stone. When he came to the shore, he stooped and dug up a shovelful of dirt, then put it into his pan. Squatting down with the pan in his hands, he dipped it into the stream, then gave it a deft circular motion that sent the water swirling through the dirt and gravel. The lighter particles worked to the surface and these he spilled out over the edge. Occasionally he raked out larger pebbles and rocks with his fingers.

Finally he worked the pan until only fine silt and the smallest bits of gravel remained. At this stage he worked carefully. At last the pan seemed empty, with only a very thin layer of black soil on the bottom of the pan. Cass bent forward, his eyes squinting, and in the center of the pan, he saw a tiny golden speck.

"You're here!" he whispered, his voice breaking the silence of the small canyon. "By heaven, you're here someplace!"

Rising to his feet, he stood a long time surveying the walls of the canyon. His blond beard covered the lower part of his face, and his tawny hair hung over the collar of his coat. For weeks he'd moved along this creek, panning gravel and finding nothing—but now he felt certain that he was on to something.

He slowly turned and walked back to his campsite, which amounted to a lean-to built of saplings and covered with fir branches. He moved the animals, finding a scarce patch of dead grass, then built up a fire and cooked his meal—fried fish and beans. He was sick of both, but ate doggedly, at the same time studying the river. He had no training in geology, but he'd listened to men talk and had formed some ideas of his own.

It was the river that created the setting for gold seeking. For hundreds of years it had cut its way from snow-capped mountains to the seacoast, nibbling away at the soil, forming serpentine banks.

Cass pictured in his mind the maps he'd studied arduously, remembering the thousand tentacles that reached back to the very heart of this rugged wilderness. Boulders had grated on one another and gravel had turned to sand, until the river was glutted with silt.

And the rocks and metals had come up through the crust of the earth, to be shaved and washed away. Quartz and feldspar and granite and limestone now reduced to muds and clays had been carried down the river to the sea.

But the gold never reached the sea, since it had a gravity weight nineteen times that of water. It was carried downstream by swift torrents until it reached the more leisurely streams, where it sank and was caught in the sandbars. Some of it, Cass knew, had lain there for centuries, and now the right shovelful of sand could reveal a strip of gold as yellow as a hound's belly.

He drank his coffee slowly, noting that he had enough for one more pot. He was low on food and was gritty-eyed with fatigue. Looking up at the iron-colored sky, he frowned. *Going to snow soon—then I'll have to go back and muck in the Glory Hole. Or go back to the States.*

The thought depressed him, and he was tempted to pack up and leave. But a stubbornness rose in him, and he stood, ignoring sore muscles. Doggedly he moved along the creek, panning and finding nothing. He thought of home and comfort—and he thought much of Serena.

Finally when there was just enough light to barely see the pan, he stopped at the branch of a small stream flowing into Squaw Creek. It was little more than a trickle, no more than two feet across, and he stared at it with jaded eyes. He wanted to eat and fall into his blankets, but shook his head angrily, then bent over and scooped up a pan full of gravel. Kneeling, he began swirling the water in the gravel, his skill at the art so advanced that he did it automatically.

From far off a night bird cried, a lonesome sound that somehow grated on his nerves. He longed for warmth and talk and the sound of laughter. The gravel made a grating noise in the pan, and he worked the mass of it over the side, then swirled the water until only a thin layer of dark soil lay in the bottom. With a sigh he leaned forward, tilting the pan to catch the last rays of sunset.

And then a jolt like electricity ran through him! In the center of the pan he saw a group of glittering specks—more than he'd ever seen before. His hands suddenly trembled, and he had difficulty swallowing. Very carefully he washed the rest of the dirt out of the pan, then stood and peered with eager eyes at what remained.

"By heaven!" he breathed, catching his breath. He saw that not only were there flakes of gold but one nugget. Small as the head of a pin but a nugget—and where there was one, there were certain to be others! *Not enough to be sure—but this washed down from that creek.* He wanted to shout and pan more gravel, but the dark closed in. Regretfully he returned to camp, built up his fire, and made his last pot of coffee. For over two hours he sat there staring into the tiny flame of the fire, and then at the gleaming specks of gold in his pan.

Finally he rolled up in his blankets and went to sleep. But at dawn he was beside the small creek, and shoving past the bushes he made his way ten yards upstream. Nervously he scooped up a pan of gravel and worked it. When he stared at the bottom, he saw three nuggets, and the bottom of the pan sparkled with color.

Cass Winslow went a little mad. He danced in the waters of the small stream, shouting and waving his hands wildly. Tears ran down his cheeks and he found himself shouting, "Thank you, God!" at the top of his lungs. This so amazed him that he halted and stood there, blinking with astonishment.

"I've never thanked God before," he muttered, wondering at himself. "But I do now!" He bowed his head and stood there silently giving thanks. It was a moment he never forgot, and when he began moving up the creek, panning at intervals, he knew that something had happened to him—something very important.

He worked like a fury for six days, then the snow began to fall and he was forced to leave. He packed his gear, and the last thing he did was stake his claim. When he wrote his name on the papers, he paused, searching for a name. A smile came to his lips, and he wrote firmly on the paper, THE YUKON QUEEN. This pleased him, and he studied the words for a long time, then turned and mounted his horse. Gathering the line that led the pack mule, he said, "Got to get back. Joe and Mike need to stake as close to my claim as they can—and Serena, too."

The snow was falling faster, but he was glad for the turn in the weather. He knew no miners would come to pan gold in this inclement weather. "Come on, we've got a quick trip to make," he laughed, and the snow flew as he drove the horse into a fast trot.

On the way back to Dawson, he met up with several of his friends but was careful to say nothing. He knew that as soon as word was out, every inch of ground along the small creek would be staked out. He thought of his close friends, the ones he'd speak to privately so that they could get a head start, and it pleased him.

He arrived at Dawson just after dawn, and half an hour later reined up in front of the cabin. Slipping off his horse, he entered the cabin—and there sat Serena at the table mixing biscuits.

"Cass!" Serena gasped and dropped the spoon, coming to him at once, her eyes wide. "Oh, Cass, you're back."

To Cass's astonishment, she threw herself into his arms and held him fiercely. He put his arms around her, holding her, and he thought, *This is what I've wanted!*

Then she drew back and her eyes were wet with tears. "Hey,

none of that," he laughed. Looking around he asked, "Have Joe and Mike already gone to the mine?"

"Joe has—"

"Blazes! Come on! We've got to find those two!" He laughed abruptly, then picked her up and spun her around. "I've made a strike, Serena—a big one!" He put her down but kept his hands on her arms. "You've got to file a claim, and so have Joe and Mike." His eyes gleamed as he spoke, and then he saw that she was not responding. "What's wrong, Serena?"

"Cass—it's Mike." She saw his eyes narrow and wished that she didn't have to go on. But she knew the kindest way was to be plain, so she put her hand on his forearm and said, "He's dead, Cass."

Cass felt as if the room had become hollow, and the sound of her voice seemed unreal. Staring at her he said harshly, "Tell me!"

Serena told the story, faltering at times, then said, "We wanted to let you know so that you could come to the funeral, but Harry and Tom couldn't find you."

A bleak anger built up in Cass, and his eyes lost their happy gleam. "What's happened to them—Dugan and Ritter?"

Quickly Serena said, "There's nothing to be done, Cass. Sam tried to bring them to trial, but the judge said there was no case. Joe and I had to say that Mike drew his gun first."

The world seemed heavy to Cass. He turned and walked to the window, staring blindly out at the red light of dawn as it fired the tops of the mountains. He stood there so long that Serena finally came to him and turned him around by touching his arm. "It's a dreadful thing, Cass. I still weep for him."

Cass took a deep breath. "I'll see Steele. I can't believe they can walk around after murdering him." Then he tried to smile. "I thought about him a great deal. How we'd have claims together like we'd planned. He was—a good friend."

"Sit down and eat. Afterward we'll go find Joe and tell him about your find. Tell me about it."

Cass told the story of finding the gold deposit, but something of the excitement of it had gone out of him. The thrill of seeing the color in his pan was gone, and he wondered if it would ever come back. Finally he rose, and when she put on her coat and came to the door, he put his arms out and she stared up at him.

When she hesitated, he stepped forward and drew her close, whispering, "This thing has knocked me flat, Serena—but I want you to know, while I was out there alone, I thought a lot about us."

"About us, Cass?" Serena drew back and her eyes were troubled. "I don't know what you mean."

"I mean I care for you." Cass pulled her close and let his lips meet hers. They were soft, but somehow unyielding. He held her for a moment, then lifted his head. Something in her face made him ask, "What's wrong?"

Serena pushed herself back and stood before him with trembling lips. Finally she said in a strained voice, "You never said a word to me about—anything like this."

"I guess I didn't know myself," Cass answered. He saw that her breathing was short and her face was pale. "What is it? Don't you feel anything for me?"

Serena swallowed and tried to speak, but the words were broken. "Cass—Sam has asked me to marry him."

Cass stared at her. He had known that Steele was attracted to Serena but had not thought for a moment that it would come to this. He asked finally, "What did you tell him?"

"I—nothing yet—" Serena stumbled over the words. "I don't *know* how I feel, Cass!"

But Cass's lips had hardened into a thin line. He nodded and his voice was wooden as he said, "I had no right to expect anything else. I hope you'll be happy, Serena. He's a fine man."

Then he turned and walked out of the room. Serena stood there staring at the door, then ran to the window and saw him mount his horse and ride off. She slumped down in a chair, put her head on the table, and began to weep.

Cass went at once to Joe and gave him the news of the strike. The two talked about Mike's death, and Joe told Cass to be careful and not do anything rash. Joe had been saddened by the death of his young friend but said, "Cass, life out here is hard, and life goes on. I'll go out and stake claims for Serena and myself. Will you come along?"

"No, I've got to see Steele."

Later that morning he found the mountie at his office. As Cass entered, Steele rose to greet him, saying, "Sorry about your friend, Winslow. A tragedy."

"Sure. He was a good man. You plan on doing anything about it?"

"Nothing to be done, I'm afraid. The judge ruled it justifiable homicide."

"I see." Cass stared at the officer, saying nothing for a brief time. Then he nodded. "Serena told me about you two. Congratulations. You'll be getting a fine girl."

For once the chiseled features of Steele broke. Showing some embarrassment, he shook his head. "She hasn't agreed yet, you understand. But I have hopes."

"She'll make you a fine wife."

Steele watched as Cass turned to leave his office, his eyes troubled. *He'll never let it go,* he thought. And then he had visions of a nightmare—one in which Cass Winslow shot Traphagen, and the Royal Mounted Police had to arrest him—and hang him if the judge so ordered.

"Don't do anything foolish, Cass," Steele called out after him. But he knew men, and from the look in Winslow's eye, he knew that his advice was unlikely to be heeded.

Cass rode down the main street, pulled his horse up in front of The Shady Lady, and sat there staring at the place. Several men saw him and stood watching carefully. Finally he rode on, making his way to the cemetery, where he found a fresh grave with the name Mike Rooney on a new wooden cross.

Slipping from his saddle, Cass moved to the mound of raw earth and stood there for a long time staring down. Finally he whispered, "Goodbye, Mike—I'm sorry." He turned and mounted his horse, his lips compressed and his eyes bitter at the raw earth of the grave of his friend.

PART FOUR

KLONDIKE JUSTICE

★ ★ ★ ★

Winter 1898—1899

CHAPTER NINETEEN

JOE PREACHES A SERMON

★ ★ ★ ★

The winter of 1898 was hard and bitter in the Klondike. By Christmas the stock of supplies was low and none could be brought in over the frozen rivers. Steele put his men on reduced rations and any man he arrested had to furnish his own provisions. There was no escape from Dawson except by dog sled, and only the most hardy drivers would attempt it. One miner paid a thousand dollars to an Indian to take him out, and both men suffered from frostbite before they reached Skagway.

Life slowed to a standstill as the food diminished and the sun vanished almost entirely. Miners in the hills were hibernating, but so were those in Dawson as well. They lay in their bunks until noon, half suffocated by the glowing oil-drum stoves, then ventured forth into the searing cold, their faces sheathed by heavy scarves.

Many of them were afflicted by scurvy. One of these was Jack London, the young man that Cass had met on the trail heading out of Skagway. He had since learned that Jack wanted to be a writer. London shook his head and told Cass, "I'm getting out of this place, Cass. It'll be something to write about—but it's not worth this suffering!"

"Stick it out, Jack," Cass urged. "There's one spot on the Indian Head that's not claimed. When spring comes, I'll take you down and we'll stake it for you. It'll make you rich."

London was a cynic, but this offer touched him. "Not many men would do that, Cass. Most people look out for themselves. They're like wolves, I think. The weak go down and the strong survive."

"It's up to the strong to look after the weak," Cass argued. He laughed at his own words. "That's funny, Jack, for me to say. My mother and father live like that—but I've been pretty much of a selfish dog."

"Most men are," London frowned. "But I think you're different, Cass. I don't know why. I just do."

Cass left London's shack, worried about the young man. He leaned against the wind, his face numbed at once by the biting cold. By the time he reached the room he'd rented in the Majestic Hotel, he was stiff and his lips could hardly frame a greeting to the clerk. He heard his name called, and turned to see Joe Winslow seated in a chair.

"Been waitin' for you, Cass," he said. "You had anything to eat yet?"

"Not yet. Let's go have something."

Ten minutes later the two men were seated at a table waiting for their food. Joe leaned back and shook his head. "Well, how does it feel to be rich, Cass?"

"Don't know, Joe. I'm about broke to tell the truth." Indian Head Creek had been filled with claims, but there had been no time to get gold out before the freeze came. "May all be a fluke," Cass shrugged. He was looking haggard, and Winslow noted this with interest.

"Nope, the gold's there all right," Joe said. "Enough there to keep us both the rest of our days." His eyes grew warm as he added, "I owe you for that, Cass. Looked all my life and found nothing—but you found it for me. I guess it pays to be a Winslow."

"Sure, Joe."

Cass was depressed and Joe said, "Been wanting to talk to you, Cass. You got a pistol on you?"

With an astonished look on his face, Cass nodded. "Why, yes, I have, Joe. What makes you ask?"

Joe Winslow's lips smiled behind his white beard, and his old eyes gleamed. "Because I'm gonna preach you a sermon—and the mood you've been in, you may want to shoot me before I finish."

A touch of humor gleamed in Cass's eyes. "All right, Joe. Start the sermon. I'll shoot when I've had enough of it."

"Fair enough, boy." Joe leaned forward, growing very serious. "I'm an old man, Cass, and I've seen lots of men die. Some of 'em by rope, some by a bullet or a knife—some jest wore out. But the one thing thet's killed more men than any of them is whut you got."

"I'm not sick," Cass snapped.

"Shore you are. You got something worse than cholera or yellow fever or heart trouble, Cass." He slapped the table with a hard hand, saying, "You got hate in you, son—hate and bitterness—and that's whut's going to do you in."

Cass sat there, his eyes fixed on the old man's face. He was aware that he was bitter, but the words of his relative found no lodging in him. He listened, but Joe saw that there was no response. The food came and the two ate, but when the meal was over, it was Joe who said, "Well, end of sermon, Cass. You can't cram wisdom down a man's throat. Makes me feel bad." He rose and tossed some coins on the table, then gave Cass a regretful look. "I took to your pa, Cass. He's got a lot of sense. Wish he was here to talk to you." His voice turned harsh and he said, "You're walkin' off a cliff, boy—and you don't even know it!"

Cass went to his room, lay down on the bed, and tried to sleep, but it came slowly. He tried to think of Joe Winslow's words, but a whisper inside kept saying, *What about Mike? Is a man supposed to forget his friends? What kind of a man would I be if I let a friend get murdered and did nothing?*

He finally drifted off into a troubled sleep, but when he awoke, he felt tired and listless. He was a man who needed action, and the enforced hibernation made him sullen. He got up and shaved, then went downstairs and left the hotel. For a time he roamed the street, but the fierce wind and blinding snow made it impossible to stay outside. Looking up he saw that he was directly in front of The Shady Lady saloon. He had seen Traphagen twice but had never spoken to him. Now the impatience that churned inside him began to grow, and with a sudden move he shoved his way through the double doors.

Four stoves kept the large room warm, and he took off his

parka and heavy gloves, hanging them on a rack. When he turned he saw Brent Traphagen sitting at a table with three men. The owner was watching him carefully, and at once Cass moved over to the table. "I feel like a little poker, Brent," he said easily.

Traphagen was a suspicious man. His hazel eyes took in the gun at Cass's hip, then shifted to his right. He saw Whitey Dugan standing stiffly at the bar, his pale eyes fixed on Winslow. He noted that Leo Ritter was aware of the situation. Only then did he say, "Sure, Winslow. I'd as soon take your money as anyone's."

Cass sat down, took out his poke, and began to play. He was a fine poker player, a skill he'd acquired despite the warnings of his father. He lost two hands, then began to win.

At some point Whitey Dugan came over and murmured, "Like to take you on, Winslow."

Cass looked into the expressionless eyes of the gunman. They were like marbles, cold and hard. "Sure, Whitey. Have a try."

Brent Traphagen was an expert card player. He knew how to manipulate the deck, but somehow the blue-green eyes of the tall man who sat across from him made him nervous. This in turn made him angry, and he grew reckless. The stack in front of Winslow grew, and as the chips flowed from Traphagen's stack, his temper grew shorter.

As the stakes rose, the three men who'd been in the original game dropped out, leaving Traphagen, Dugan, and Cass facing one another. The stakes rose to highs unusual even for a gold camp. The roulette wheel and the other card games were abandoned as the miners packed themselves in a circle around the single table. Many of them had lost fortunes in this very saloon and found it satisfying to see the owner taking his licking.

Dugan was a poor player and lost hand after hand. He tried a bluff, betting the stakes up to over a thousand dollars; then when Winslow called and tossed down three of a kind, Dugan cursed and threw his cards onto the table. Cass drew in the chips, saying lazily, "Better go find something you're better at, Whitey."

Dugan glared at him and, letting his hand touch the handle of his gun in a habitual gesture, whispered, "I can think of one game I can beat you at, Winslow."

The mutter of voices died out, and Traphagen moved slightly back from the table. "Any game you say, Dugan," Cass said, laying his glance on the albino. He stared long and hard at Dugan, and the knowledge that the other man was probably faster meant nothing to him. The days and nights he'd spent thinking of how Rooney had been shot down had formed a hard core in him, and now he stared at the gunman with a terrifying intensity.

Whitey hesitated, then muttered, "There'll be a time for that."

"No time like now," Cass prodded him. He smiled and said, "Let's make it now, Whitey." A madness of sorts came over him, and he said, "You and your boss like long odds. Two of you and one of me."

"Leave me out of this," Traphagen spoke up. "If you've come for trouble, take it someplace else."

Cass took his eyes from Dugan and put them on the gambler. "You're a dog, Brent—a yellow dog with no insides." He saw Traphagen's face freeze, and he heard a sigh murmur around the room. It was the kind of insult no man in the Klondike could take and keep his reputation. "Take exception to that?" Cass asked softly.

"Not now—but I'll remember it."

"I remember things, too, Traphagen." Cass's voice grew hard, and his body tensed so abruptly that men behind Traphagen moved from the line of fire. "I remember Mike Rooney, who was a better man than you or your dog, Whitey."

"He went for his gun—I had no choice!" Dugan said, his body tense as wire. He longed to go for his gun, but he had never seen Winslow pull a gun. Fast as he was, he liked to have an edge, and now he sensed that death was close to someone in the room.

Cass turned to face Dugan. The silence was heavy, only the sound of men's breathing broke it. Cass stood up, and at once Whitey rose, his pasty cheeks twitching. "All right, Whitey, this time you'll pull first." When the albino hesitated and then turned, Cass's voice lashed at him. "Come on! You've been bragging about how you cut down Mike Rooney. Let's see you go for that fancy gun."

Whitey gasped, and to the shock of every man in the room, he turned and walked stiffly out of the saloon, leaving through the back door that led to Traphagen's office.

Cass turned back and his eyes glittered. "Your hired killer let you down, Brent. But there's still a chance. Go on, pull that gun out from under your coat. I'll give you first shot."

Traphagen shook his head. His face was pale as chalk as he stood up saying, "Game closed," then walked across the room and disappeared through the door Dugan had taken.

A yelp went up from one miner, "They done tucked their tails and run!" Then the saloon exploded with rough laughter and a raucous babble of talk. It was the sort of story that would be told over a thousand campfires in the Klondike, and from that moment onward, Cassidy Winslow was a name known to every miner in the North.

Cass felt the heavy pressure of many hands, heard voices congratulating him on his action, but paid them no heed. He took his winnings and moved to the door, but two men blocked his path, Doctor Winnie Blackmon and Harry Bonner. Blackmon was a short rotund man of fifty who drank hard and did the rough doctoring in the town. "Cass, this isn't over," he warned Winslow. "Those two backed off, but they'll take their try."

"Doc's right, Cass," Harry Bonner nodded, his long face tense. "Don't go by yourself—and watch the alleyways. Dugan can't let this slide. He's lost his reputation, and a killer can't stand that."

"I'll watch myself," Cass assured them.

Bonner looked around, then said, "Come outside, Cass. Got something to tell you." He turned and left the saloon. The wind was whipping sharply down the street, making a low moaning noise, so that Bonner leaned forward to put his face close to Cass's ear. "I got a word about Nate Mullins—you know about that?"

"Yeah, shot down outside of town." Cass gave Bonner a startled glance, then demanded, "What about it, Harry?"

"Well, I ain't got nothin' fer sure, Cass—but I got a friend who says he knows Dugan done the job. Name's Al Drilling."

"He saw it?"

"He won't come out and admit it—but he did at first." Bonner shook his head sadly. "Cass, Al saw it, but he's scared. If he puts the finger on Dugan, and the verdict don't go right, he knows Whitey will gun him down for sure."

"I want to talk to him, Harry."

"Figured you would, but he's a scary sort. I'll have to go with you, Cass. I done him a good turn, and he'll maybe listen to me."

"Where is he?"

"Holed up out on the Strawberry. Be hard to get there in this blizzard. Soon as it clears off, we'll make a little trip to see him."

"All right—and thanks, Harry."

"I liked Mike—as well as any feller I've ever known." Harry's long face grew even longer. "Somebody's going to get his neck stretched for killing that boy. The jury might say it's fer killin' Nate Mullins—but I'm hopin' to spit in his face and tell him we done him in for killin' Mike Rooney."

"He's going down, Whitey is," Cass said coldy. "If we can do it through the law, fine. But if that doesn't work, I'll take care of him."

"Sure, Cass. We'll do it." The two men parted, but inside the saloon a bitter argument was taking place in Traphagen's office. As soon as the gambler had stepped inside, he'd lashed out at Dugan. "Well—what were you waiting for?"

"It wasn't the right time."

"Not the right *time*?" Traphagen glared at Dugan, his eyes wild with anger. "It was the time, Whitey. You let him make a fool out of you. Everybody in the Klondike will be laughing at you."

"He's turned into a killer, Brent—and you don't brace a killer when he's like Winslow was. I'd have taken him, but he'd have gone down shooting."

Traphagen slammed himself down in his chair and was disgusted to see that his hands were trembling. He put them on the desk and said more quietly, "All right—but we can't let it slip by—" He stopped suddenly as the door opened and Leo Ritter came in, his piggish eyes hot with fury.

"Why didn't you gun him down, Whitey?" he demanded. "They're laughing at us out there!"

"We'll get him," Whitey said. "But we'll do it the smart way."

"Let me do it, Brent!" Ritter said. "I can lay out there with a rifle and put a bullet in his brain."

"Do it and there's a bonus in it for you."

Ritter nodded. "He's been pushy, but I'll put him under. I'll pick my spot and he'll die."

Whitey said softly, "Don't miss, Leo. If you do, you're a dead man."

"I won't miss!"

Traphagen lit a cigar, his hands steady again. "All right, get him, Leo. One bullet and we're back in control."

★　★　★　★

Steele and Serena had attended the small frame church and heard Hosea Carmichael preach a fine sermon. Afterward they went to the Majestic Hotel where they had lunch in the dining room. After they had ordered their meal, Steele said, "Fine sermon, wasn't it?"

"Yes. He's a good preacher." Her thoughts, however, were not on the sermon. "Sam, what happened at The Shady Lady?'"

"I only heard it secondhand from Doc Blackmon." He repeated the story, then shook his head. "You've got to talk to Cass, Serena. He's going to get himself killed."

"I've tried, Sam, but he won't listen."

"No, he won't listen to me either." Steele sipped from the glass of water in front of him, then put it down. "I have no doubt about Traphagen. He's a killer and sooner or later I'll catch him. But he can't let anyone humiliate him as Cass did in his saloon. He won't do the job himself, but there are plenty of roughs around who can be hired to shoot Cass."

They talked about the problem until the meal came, and as they ate, Steele saw that Serena was preoccupied. "Serena, I want you to marry me."

Startled, Serena lifted her gaze to meet his. She had spent endless hours thinking of him, wondering if he was the man for her. Now she said, "Oh, Sam, I don't know. I feel like a silly fool, and you deserve better than that."

"I want you, Serena. I know that I love you." Steele put his hand out and she put her own in it. "You don't care for me as much—but I know that will come."

"Will it?"

"Yes, I know it!"

Serena felt the power of his hand and wished she could be more certain. "I don't have any experience with love, Sam," she said quietly. Her eyes were soft, and there was a tremulous look about her lips. "I think marriage is for as long as we live. I—I'm afraid to make a mistake."

"Do you care for me at all, Serena?"

"Yes! But a wife has to give her husband all she has—and I must be certain you're the man God wants me to marry."

Sam Steele released her hand reluctantly. "You're a strange young woman," he said finally. "I don't know what to make of you."

Serena shook her head almost sadly. "So many women would love to marry you, Sam. I'm just a silly girl, afraid of marriage, I think."

"Only natural, considering your background—but I love you very much. I'll be very patient with you."

Serena sat there wishing that she could say yes to this fine man. He was so handsome—and she knew that once he gave himself to a woman, he would honor her.

But there was something in her that caused her to hesitate. She could not identify it, but neither could she ignore it. Finally she said, "Give me two weeks, Sam. I'll have an answer for you by then."

"Fine!" Steele smiled, then added, "I'll find it hard to wait, but if I can have you, Serena, it'll be worth waiting for!"

CHAPTER TWENTY

DEATH AT DUSK

★ ★ ★ ★

"Joe, I don't think there's anything worse than waiting."

The two men were sitting on two chairs as close to the stove as they could get. Outside the temperature had dropped to fifteen below zero, freezing Dawson in its icy grip.

The older man grinned crookedly at Cass, spit at the stove, and listened with satisfaction to the hissing sound that followed. "Why, boy, this ain't *nothin'*!" he snorted. "One time I was trapped in a cabin with Chick Nebergall for three months. Couldn't set foot outside, and by the time we got out we wuz eatin' shoe leather!"

The door swung open and Serena entered, followed by Steele. The mountie slammed it shut and brushed the snow from his shoulders, then stood watching as Serena put some packages on the table. "Sit down, Sam. Have some coffee."

But Steele shook his head. "No, thanks. I've got to get back to the office." He hesitated, then nodded. "I'll see you tomorrow."

As he left the cabin, Joe got up and said, "Set down, Serena. I'll fix a fresh pot. This stuff will cut varnish."

Serena hung up her parka and gloves, then came and sat down by the stove. Holding her hands out to catch the heat of the stove, she smiled at Cass. "I brought you something. If you're nice to me, I'll give it to you."

"I thought I was always nice. What is it?"

Serena pulled an envelope from her pocket. "Letters from home—two of them."

Cass took the letters, opened one and said, "From Aaron." He scanned the lines, then read it aloud.

Dear Cass,

I hope you've struck it rich by this time. All the way home I felt like a traitor, leaving you and Serena alone. But Jubal took some of me with him when he died. Can't explain it, but when a man dies in your place, it makes you feel peculiar. I've wished a million times it'd been the other way around—that I'd saved him. Why God would take a good man like him and let a rotter like me go on living—well, I can't explain it and never will, I suppose.

As soon as I got back, I went to see Jubal's folks. It was the toughest thing I ever had to do. They took it better than I'd have thought. Losing your only son would be terrible—but to lose him in such a way must have been worse. I told them the truth, Cass, that he gave his life for mine. His mother looked at me and said, "It's not the first time someone gave his life for another."

She meant Christ, of course, and I couldn't say a word. Uncle Tom was hard hit, but he pulled me off for a talk before I left. Told me that the only way Jubal's sacrifice would have meaning would be the meaning I gave it.

I left there feeling lower than a snake. And I'm blaming it on God. He could have taken me, but He didn't. Don't write me a sermon, Cass. I've had plenty of those—but none of them explain Jubal's death!

You couldn't write me even if you wanted to. By the time you get this letter I may be dead—but if I'm alive I'll be fighting the Spaniards. Yes, I joined the army and our ship is due to leave in a week. Why did I do it? I don't know. Why do I do anything?

If I don't make it back, remember some of the good times we had. Try to think well of me.

Serena, you're a fine young woman. Don't let a reprobate like me spoil your faith. You take care of yourself and Thor—and I'm leaving you to Cass. He's about as mixed up as I am, but you can see him through.

All my love,
Aaron Winslow

Cass lowered the letter and looked up, his eyes troubled. "Just like Aaron to pull a fool stunt like that." He saw tears brimming in Serena's eyes and shook his head. "I wish he'd come along. I still miss him."

Serena dashed the tears away and rose as Cass read the remaining letter. It was from his father, and he didn't mention the contents to Joe or Serena. They both noticed that he was quieter than usual, and after supper, Joe said, "Well, I'm gonna join that poker game at Shorty's." He gave Cass a strange glance and said no more but pulled on his heavy coat and left.

Silence fell across the room, and it was Serena who finally broke it. "Cass, I'm worried about Aaron. He could get killed and he's not ready to meet God."

"No, I guess not." Cass was whittling on a stick and let three shavings curl and fall to the floor before he looked up to meet her gaze. "I'm not either—I guess that's what you're trying to say."

"I—I worry about both of you."

"Wish you wouldn't."

His brief reply was cold, but Serena insisted, "Why don't you want to know God? You admire Christians. Why, you're proud of your parents, and from what you've told me, your relatives are mostly believers."

Cass moved his shoulders restlessly. He folded the knife, stuck it in his pocket, and leaned back to examine her. "Maybe I'm just not picked out to be saved," he said. "Sometimes I think God chooses people for one thing or the other—some to be good and some to be bad."

"No, that's not right! The Bible says *whosoever* will may come. God wouldn't be fair just to let a person die without having a chance."

"Serena, don't waste your prayers on me. If prayer would change a man, I'd be a Christian. My mother and father have prayed for me all my life—and it's not done any good."

"You don't know that, Cass," Serena said quietly. "It's not too late."

"I can't forget Mike," he said sharply. "Can I be a Christian and revenge his death?" He knew he was being unfair, and when he saw the pain cross her face, he came out of his chair at once. "Sorry. I'm just not much of a prospect for conversion."

Serena rose and came to stand before him. "I know you don't like to be preached at, Cass. I'm sorry."

Cass looked into her face, and then without warning reached out and took her into his arms. Her eyes grew large and her lips parted with surprise. He studied her features, then put his one hand on the crown of curls that he had always admired. She smelled fresh and clean, and he said, "I've wanted to do this for a long time—" He waited for her to draw back, to protest, but she said nothing.

Slowly Cass drew her closer, and a strange restlessness came over him. He had learned to live with his restlessness—those vague wishes—even though he did not fully understand them. But now he knew, for he suddenly realized as he watched her eyes that it was for her that he so deeply longed.

As for Serena, she put her hand on his shoulder. Instinctively, she knew that somehow this man and this moment were important. She watched his face, the recklessly expressive face of a man who loved action—but now a face that revealed a hidden misery. Looking at him, she saw that he was aware of her closeness, that he was straining on the leash of his reserve. She waited for that reserve to break, and when he lowered his head, she met his kiss, fully giving herself to him. His lips were heavy on hers and she felt her own wishes stir.

"Serena . . ." he whispered when he lifted his lips. "You're like no woman I've ever known!"

Shaken by his kiss, Serena lay in his arms for a moment. There had been, despite the roughness of his caress, a tenderness. And she felt a joy, for all the months she had known him she'd sensed that beneath his rough exterior he possessed a gentleness. She smiled at him, and Cass saw the generosity of her mouth, the glow of her eyes, and wondered at it.

Then she drew back and for a moment watched his face. "What does a kiss mean, Cass?"

Her question drew his attention, and despite the fact that her kiss, so freely given, had stirred him, he felt a heaviness. He thought of Steele, and then of how his determination to avenge Mike lay between them, clouding the moment.

"Sorry—it was my fault. I've—been alone too much."

His words struck Serena like a blow. She stared at him unbelievingly, then took a deep breath. Angry at his response, she turned and left him without a word, closing the door with a finality that struck on his nerves.

Cass felt as if he'd been punched in the stomach. Unable to stand the cabin, he yanked his coat from the wall, put it on, then left for his room in town. The wind snatched at him, shifting him off balance, and the cold numbed his face. The scene had drained him, had shown him how deep the bitterness in him lay. And yet as he plowed through the drifts, he remembered the sweetness of her lips and the touch of her vibrant body as she lay in his arms.

★　★　★　★

The storm subsided, like a huge beast that had tired itself, but as Asa Tyler told Cass, "Don't trust the blamed weather. Reminds me of a woman."

Despite his bitter mood, Cass smiled. "Funny thing to say, Asa."

Tyler's lips curled in a bittersweet smile as he remembered a similar conversation when they first hit the trail back in Skagway. "Well, I guess it is—but I've had experiences, Cass. A woman's the best thing there is on this planet—or the worst. They can get nice and soft—like that there storm, but when a man least expects it, why, she puts a knife in his liver."

The two men had been sitting in Jake Dent's barbershop, idly talking and listening to other men. The talk was rough, sometimes of women and big binges, but it always came back to the one mania that had brought these men here from all over the world—gold. They talked incessantly about creeks, rivers, canyons—all the untamed expanse of the Yukon that lay in their minds. They related again the stories of how the first men on the spot had raked in fortunes, and in every voice and every eye was the dream that they would become the next to hit the big strike.

Alex McCarty, a smallish Scotsman, approached Cass as he was leaving the shop. "Like to buy that claim from you, Winslow—The Yukon Queen." McCarty had struck pay dirt three times and now had enough wealth to gamble. His bright eyes gleamed and he whispered, "Pay you ten thousand for it—in dust right now."

It was a good offer, and for one moment Cass was tempted. He stood there, his large stature filling the doorway, then said, "Not today, Alex. I'm kind of interested in that one."

"Might go a little higher—" McCarty called out, but giving a wave of his hand, Cass moved down the walk. The sun was bright, and he shut his eyes against the glare. Remembering that he needed a new razor, he ambled down the street, speaking to those who greeted him until he came to Clarence Howe's General Store. When he stepped inside, he saw Serena standing in front of the counter. He hesitated, thought of leaving, but moved over and greeted her. "Hello, Serena."

His voice touched her, and she turned at once, her lips pressed tightly together. She had been hurt by Cass's rejection and now nodded, saying in a tight voice, "Hello, Cass."

At once he knew what she was thinking. *She's got a right to be angry,* he thought as he stood there uncertainly. *I made a fool out of myself—and she took it wrong.*

When she paid the bill and reached for the sack, Cass said, "I'll carry that for you."

"It's not heavy." Her eyes met his and both of them relived that moment when the world had slowed, narrowing to that one kiss. Serena turned and left the store, leaving Cass to stand there thinking of what a fool he was.

"Need something, Cass?"

Turning to the storekeeper, Cass said, "A razor, Clarence, and I'll have that poke of mine I asked you to keep."

"Sure, Cass." Howe put a tray containing a selection of razors on the counter, saying, "I'll get the poke." Howe didn't trust banks, so he kept his cash in a steel safe in his bedroom. There had been one attempted robbery that ended with two thieves blasted by a double-barreled shotgun. Dawson toughs took the hint and gave the burly storekeeper a wide path.

"Here you are, Cass," Howe said, handing over a thick sausagelike sack. "Like any of them razors?"

"This one is fine." Cass opened the drawstrings of the poke and handed it to Howe. "Take it out of this, Clarence." Most goods were paid for in dust in Dawson, cash being in short supply.

Howe carefully poured a little of the gold onto a scale, eyed it, then closed the sack. "Good razor. Use one like it myself." He was a curious man and asked, "You think your claim will pay off big this spring, Cass?"

"Ought to do well, Clarence," Cass said. He slipped the poke into his inside coat pocket, then added, "Gold mines are like women—or so Harry Bonner says. Don't know what he means by that."

"*I* do!" Howe frowned. "Watch out for yourself, Cass. Dugan won't forget how you rode him in The Shady Lady."

"Sure," Cass nodded carelessly. "Well, I've got to get moving. See you later, Clarence."

As he left the store, the reflection of the evening sun on the snow almost blinded him. He blinked and pulled his hat down on his brow, then turned and moved down the street. He walked slowly, having no place to go, and he thought idly of Howe's warning. *Probably right,* he thought soberly. *All Dugan's got is his pride. He'll make his try, but he'll have to do it in the open. No other way he can get his reputation back.*

The street was almost deserted, since there was little business to do until the ice thawed and the mines and creeks were unlocked. He passed Doc Blackmon and greeted him, but the rotund physician only nodded briskly and hurried on.

Cass turned the corner and headed down the side street where the Majestic was set back. Halfway down the block he stepped in front of a short alley that separated two clusters of buildings. A slight movement caught his eye and alarm touched off a nerve. Swinging around, he caught a quick glimpse of a big man wearing a black coat. He had a rifle, and even as Cass turned, the explosion of a shot rocked the silence of the street, and a blow struck Cass in the left side. It was like being struck by a giant's fist, and he thought with astonishment, *I've been shot!*

He fell backward, but even as he fell another shot echoed, driving snow into his face. He clawed his gun free and, lying on his back, got off a desperate shot. It was all instinct and he expected the rifleman's next shot to strike—but it did not come. Lifting his head, he saw the gunman drop the rifle and grasp his chest. He began to fall and hit the snow face first, uttering a hoarse yell.

Cass got to his feet, his side aching, and at once two men came running. One of them was Harry Bonner. He had his pistol in his hand and cried out, "Where'd he get you, Cass?"

Cass could hardly speak, for the breath had been driven from his body. He touched his left side. "Here—" he gasped.

"Why, that's right in your heart!" Bonner said in amazement. "Let's see—maybe the slug turned and grazed you."

But Cass shook his head. Reaching inside his coat he brought out the tightly packed sack of gold dust and stared at it. "Look at this, Harry—" he said, holding the sack out for the two men to see.

Bonner and the other man stared blankly, then Bonner touched the hole in the center. "This thing caught the slug," he whispered. Slowly the gold began to leak out of the hole, and Bonner said, "I'll take care of this—let's see who did the shootin'."

The three advanced to the form on the ground, and when they rolled the man over, it came as no surprise when Bonner whistled, "Leo Ritter!"

Cass knelt down and lifted the burly form to a sitting position. Blood was pouring out of a wound in the man's huge chest. His eyes were open—and filled with fear. "I—I can't die—" he choked, but he knew that his wound was fatal.

"Why'd you shoot at me, Leo?" Cass asked. He expected no answer, but the huge man was tough enough to gasp a protest— then his eyes opened wide and he cried, "I can't die—I ain't ready—!"

Even as he tried to rise, his eyes closed and he gave one great cough, then lay still.

"Well, I guess he went, ready or not," Bonner said. He looked down with satisfaction on the still form of Ritter and said, "Wish he'd told us who put him up to it. It had to be Traphagen."

By this time a crowd had gathered, and shouts echoed down the street. The people of Dawson, always hungry for a fight or excitement of any kind, spread the word of the shooting quicker than a telegraph.

Serena was moving to her sled when she heard the shot. She hesitated, then finished loading the groceries. But a man came running down the street crying out, "It's Ritter—he shot Cass Winslow!"

Serena felt as if a huge cold fist had closed around her heart. She began to run blindly toward the crowd of men who were moving toward the alley. When she got there, it was packed, but she cried out, "Let me through!" and the men stepped to one side.

She emerged from the clump of men—and then she saw Cass. He was standing beside Harry Bonner, and beyond him she saw the still form of a big man lying on the ground.

"Cass—!" She cried and ran toward him, oblivious of the curious stares of the men who watched. Her breath came in short bursts, and when she reached him, she would have fallen if he hadn't caught her. The touch of his arms brought her to herself, but she clung to him, whispering, "My dear—I thought you were dead!"

Her words struck Cass as hard in one way as had Ritter's bullet. He held her, forgetful of the crowd. She clung to him fiercely, and he thought, *She must care for me*— Then he said, "I'm all right. Come on, Serena, let's get out of here."

They moved away from the alley, with Serena holding fast to his arm. When they were back on the main street, she felt a little sick. Lifting her face she asked, "What happened?"

Cass shook his head. "I was a dead man, Serena. He had me cold. I turned as he fired, and his bullet took me right over the heart." He took the pouch of gold out and showed her the hole. "The bullet went right there—and I got this poke from Clarence right after I saw you. If I hadn't, I'd be dead right now."

"Thank God!" Serena gasped.

An odd look came to Cass's face. "I guess I can say amen to that. Ritter is dead, and half an hour ago he was alive. It should have been me who died, not him." He stood before her, his eyes filled with doubt. "Just before he died, Ritter said, 'I'm not ready to die.' " Cass shook his head in despair. "Somehow I can't hate him, Serena—I feel sorry for him. Why is that?"

Serena wanted to speak, but she knew that this was a question no one could answer for Cass. She put her hand on his chest, looked up at him, and said with tremulous lips, "I—I thought my life was over—when they said you'd been shot." Then she quickly turned her head, adding in a muffled voice, "I must go, Cass—"

As Serena moved away, Cass was surrounded by a crowd of excited men who all wanted to hear the story of the shooting. He hated to speak of it, and when he left, one of the miners said in disgust, "He may be a dead shot, but he's shore the worst story-teller I ever heard."

"Maybe he doesn't like killing a man," another suggested.

"Don't be a fool—he done the camp a good deed—oughta be proud of it!"

But Cass Winslow was anything but proud. He returned to his room and lay down for a long time, thinking about what had happened. He'd thought that he was tough enough to handle such things, but all he could think of was the pitiful cry of the dying man—*I can't die—I'm not ready!*

CHAPTER TWENTY-ONE

A RACE FOR LIFE

★　★　★

Serena awoke with a start. She had been curled under every blanket she had when the sound of a muffled banging noise woke her from a sound sleep. She poked her head out from under the covers, the cold striking her almost like a blow. At first she thought that Joe was up making breakfast, but then the knocking became more insistent, and she heard Joe's voice complaining, "I'm coming—if you can wait until I get my pants on!"

Slipping from the bed took moral courage, for her small room, though it cut off the cruel lashings of the wind that crept around the cabin, was still bitter cold. Her teeth began chattering, and she pulled on her clothes as quickly as she could. By the time she had gotten into her fur-lined boots and pulled on a heavy coat, she heard voices coming from the kitchen. Opening the door, she was surprised to see Dr. Winnie Blackmon standing beside Joe. The doctor was a rotund man and the layers of heavy furs made him look like a huge ball. His face was blue with cold, and fatigue marked his round face.

"What's wrong, Doctor Blackmon?" Serena asked instantly. She had worked with the physician several times, getting him over the snow in her sled to a patient. "Is someone sick?"

"Not *someone*," Blackmon said, speaking slowly and with difficulty through stiffened lips. His parka was covered with grains of ice that glistened in the light of the yellow flame given off by the lamp in Joe's hand. "It's an epidemic of some kind. Up at Forty Mile."

"You came from there in this weather, Doc?" Winslow demanded. "Don't see how you made it."

"Almost didn't." Blackmon shook his head at the bad memory that came to him. "Henri DuPriest just about killed all his dogs getting me back. It wasn't so bad when I went, but this storm's as nasty as it can be."

"Are you going back? Do you want me to take you?" Serena asked.

"I'm not going back—not right now," Blackmon shook his head. Ice had formed on his mustache and he pulled at it with his fingers. "I've got two women here in Dawson who've decided to have their babies right in the middle of this storm. Anyway, I can't do much for those men except give them medicine. There's a young fellow there named Stanley Burcher who got in some time in medical school. He can do what needs to be done—but he's got no medical supplies."

"You want me to take the medicine to Forty Mile?" Serena asked.

"Why, she can't do thet, Doc!" Joe Winslow shook his head vigorously. "Ain't no time for a woman to be makin' a trip like that!"

Serena herself was somewhat apprehensive about such a venture. She had learned the dangers of the trail but had never traveled in such a violent storm. As she thought rapidly of the difficulties, Blackmon caught her worried expression. "I guess you're right, Joe." A heaviness came into his face, and he said gloomily, "All the rest of the dog teams are gone, holed up somewhere, I guess, until this thing blows over." He sighed deeply, then shrugged his shoulders as he turned to go. "I just didn't know any other way to help those fellows."

"Doctor, will they die—if they don't get the medicine?" Serena asked.

"Yes, some of them will."

Serena hesitated for one instant, then said firmly, "Get the supplies ready. I'll be at your office in two hours."

Blackmon stared at her, his brown eyes skeptical. "I don't think you should do it, Serena. That would be a hard trip for a seasoned man—I shouldn't have mentioned it to you."

"God will be with me," Serena said simply. "A long time ago I settled this kind of thing. I asked Him to keep me—and I promised Him to answer every call for help." She smiled and patted the physician fondly on the arm. "You'll see God come through for those poor men. Go along now. I want to get an early start."

For the next two hours Serena worked furiously, going over her gear carefully. She replaced worn harnesses and packed emergency supplies in the sled, including plenty of food for the dogs. As she worked to get ready, Joe Winslow was at her elbow, his face twisted into a worried frown. "This ain't a good idea, Serena," he grunted as she put the last package into the sled. "Are you *sure* the Lord is in this thing?"

"Yes, I'm sure, Joe." She leaned forward and kissed his withered cheek, then stepped back and shouted, "Mush!" sending the dogs ahead in a fast trot. Her voice drifted back as she disappeared into the mist of fine snow: "Pray for me, Joe—!"

The icy crystals bit at her face, and she lowered her goggles to keep her eyes free. The dogs were in fine form, and Thor barked sharply as they entered the streets of Dawson. When she pulled up in front of Dr. Blackmon's office, she saw the lights burning in the window. Calling out to the dogs to stop, she turned and saw two men emerge from the door. As they stepped closer, she was shocked to see that the tall figure beside Blackmon was Cass Winslow.

Blackmon said brusquely, "Got a volunteer to make the trip with you. Come on inside and we'll go over the supplies."

Serena stepped up on the walk, saying stiffly, "You don't have to go. I can make it fine."

Cass had been awakened in his room by Blackmon, who'd explained the situation. "Feel better if that girl had a man along, Cass," he'd said, and Cass at once had agreed to make the trip.

Now he said, "Sure, but on a trip like this any driver would need a backup. I'll try to keep up."

Serena nodded, feeling a gush of relief, for she knew that Cass knew the trail better than she did. She was also aware that if a lone traveler was injured, there was no help in a storm as bad as this one. She was touched by his offer and wanted to say how badly she'd behaved. But Blackmon was calling and she had no time. She went inside and listened carefully to his instructions about the medicine while Cass loaded the medical supplies.

"Still think it's too risky," Blackmon said, gnawing on his lower lip nervously. "Wouldn't like to see you get in trouble out there. You've never been on the trail in a storm like this one."

But Serena said quickly, "We'll be careful, Doctor. There are places to stay all along the river. Cass and I know most of them. If it gets too bad, we'll just hole up until we can go on safely."

"God go with you, then," Blackmon said, somewhat surprised at his use of the term. He was a cynic as far as religion was concerned, but now he felt that it would take God's help to get the pair through.

Cass was waiting when the two emerged, along with a few curious miners on their way to breakfast. Serena moved behind the sled and called out, "Mush, you huskies!" and as the sled moved out smartly, a cheer went up from the spectators. One of them was Mack Mulroy, who said to Blackmon, "I sold her them dogs, Doc!"

"Well, I hope you did her a favor—but the thing doesn't look good." Blackmon stood peering into the swirling snow until the sled disappeared, then shook his head doubtfully and stepped back into his office.

★ ★ ★ ★

"There's McIver's cabin," Cass shouted. He was twenty yards ahead of the dogs, breaking the twelve-inch blanket of fresh-fallen snow with his snowshoes. "We'd better hole up and give the dogs a rest."

"All right." Serena guided the team, and when she pulled them to a stop, Cass went to awaken McIver. After banging on the door, he opened it and stepped inside. He came out to help Serena release the dogs from their harness. "McIver's not here. But there's wood for a fire, and a hot meal sure would help."

They fed the dogs and saw to it that they had protection from the weather inside a small shed, then moved inside. "I'll get a fire going," Cass said, his lips stiff with cold. He handled the kindling awkwardly, his fingers almost paralyzed with the cold. It had been a hard trip, but they had made good time. They could not get lost, for the trail ran parallel to the Yukon River, headed due north. Others had followed this same trail, so even though the storm had kept men and dogs inside, they had no trouble except for the biting cold.

Cass made a small pyramid of sticks and shavings, fumbled for a match, struck it, then touched it to the pile. It caught at once and he squatted in front of the small stove, feeding small bits of fuel until he had it going well enough to add more sizable chunks. Finally he stood up and turned to where Serena was unpacking a canvas bag filled with utensils and food.

"We've been lucky," Cass nodded. He slumped down in one of the two chairs, rubbing his calves. The use of snowshoes threw an unnatural strain on the lower legs, and now as he thawed out, his legs started cramping. Gritting his teeth he looked up and saw Serena watching him. Summoning a grin he said, "Times like this a man wishes he had webbed feet like a duck."

"I couldn't have made it if you hadn't broken the trail for the team, Cass."

"Winslow's Fancy Trail-Breaking Service—we never close," Cass answered; then the muscles of his right calf doubled into a hard knot and he cried out with the pain.

Serena at once fell to her knees and began kneading the tight muscles. She kept her head down, massaging the tortured flesh, and finally when Cass gave a sigh of relief, she looked up to ask, "Better? That happens to me every time I put on snowshoes." She rose and turned back to the sack of provisions. "You rest while I throw something together."

"Guess I will." Cass sat down, closed his eyes, and was asleep before Serena could get the meal started. She took one of the blankets they'd brought and placed it carefully over his long form. For one moment she hesitated, for the urge came to push the hair that had fallen over his forehead back—then she changed her mind for some obscure reason.

She cooked a quick meal, made coffee, then came to touch his shoulder, whispering, "Cass—? Cass, wake up." She saw his eyes open reluctantly, then he moved his legs painfully. "I hate to wake you up, but you need to eat."

"Sure." He stood to his feet, and his tall form seemed to fill the small room. His eyes were weary and his cheekbones high and pronounced against his skin. He unexpectedly smiled, and Serena wished he could keep the sudden warmth that came to him. "Looks good—but you always set a good table."

The two of them ate, then rolled into their blankets, each falling into the narrow bunks and losing consciousness in an alarming fashion. They slept until the fire died down and the bitter cold crept back into the cabin. Cass woke up and rose to build it up again. He didn't go back to the bunk, but slept sitting in one chair with his feet propped up on another. From time to time he fed the fire, keeping the icy grip of the cold out of the small room. Finally he fried some bacon, put some bread in the grease, and made coffee. When it was done, he called out, "Serena—breakfast."

Coming out of sleep was a struggle for Serena, but she forced herself to slip out from under the blankets. "Why, you fixed breakfast, Cass," she mumbled. Her hair was a crown of curls framing her face, and she smiled at him. "I didn't know you could cook."

"Wanted you to get all the rest you could," he shrugged. "But we need to get going. I'd like to make Forty Mile before dark." They sat down and she bowed her head, praying silently, then began to eat. When they had finished, Cass said, "Why don't you pack up here while I feed the dogs."

"Give them a good meal, Cass. They've earned it."

When he stepped outside the cabin, the cold struck him like a fist. He spat and the spittle cracked, freezing instantly. He blinked and shook his head. *If those fellows weren't dying, I'd never try this.* He quickly fed the dogs, harnessed them, and paused to give Thor's head a rough caress. "You son of a gun!" he whispered admiringly. "You'd pull this sled by yourself if you had to, wouldn't you?" Thor uttered a deep-throated *wuff*, then looked up with a lopsided grin on his chops.

Just as he turned back toward the cabin, Serena opened the door and said the gear was all packed. The two carried it outside and loaded the sled. "Have to replace that wood we burned up on our way back," Cass noted. "Wish we could take that stove with us!"

They moved out, glad that the snow had stopped falling. Cass went ahead of the team to break the trail, but knew that his legs would give out sometime that day. The strain of that unnatural stride was too much for a man. But he determined to get as far as he could. All morning long they forged ahead, stopping once to give the dogs a rest. Serena had put hot coffee into a jug and wrapped it in furs. It did not stay hot for long but seemed hot to their senses, so stiffened were they by the wind that cut to the bone.

They forged on until three o'clock, then paused to rest. Cass was having leg cramps again and tried to hide it from Serena. But she looked at him carefully. "You can't go on, Cass."

"I'm all right. If we keep this up we can reach the camp before dark."

But when they started again, it was torture for him. His legs knotted up in agony, and one hour later, he was trudging along in a fog of pain. If he had been clear minded he would have seen the color of the ice across the creek that ran down to the Yukon. The creek was not large, less than twenty feet across, but two hills gave the mouth of it a natural shelter, and this meant that the ice was thinner than that of other creeks they'd crossed. Vaguely Cass was aware that the creek was there, and wearily lifted his snow-shoes to make the crossing. He was twenty feet in front of Thor, who led the team, and reached the middle of the creek before he sensed the trouble. The snowshoes slowed his reflex, but he felt the ice give and he twisted wildly. But the snowshoes became tangled and the ice collapsed suddenly, and he had no chance at all. The icy waters closed over his body, and when his head went under, the shock ran through him. He struggled to the surface, but his feet were hampered by the snowshoes.

Got to get out of here! The thought was a scream in his mind, for he knew that he was a dead man if he didn't get dry. He'd heard a sailor once tell about how a shipmate had fallen overboard into the icy waters of the Bering Sea. *"We got him in less than ten minutes—but he was frozen to death,"* the sailor had said. Desperately Cass struggled, but he knew he'd never get out of the water with the snowshoes strapped to his feet. He kicked wildly, then finally doubled up and with numb hands shoved the snowshoes off. He lunged upward, but the creek was so deep that he couldn't touch bottom. When he surfaced, he grabbed at the ice, but it broke off under his flailing arms. *Not going to make it,* he thought dully.

And then he heard Serena cry, "Here, Cass—put this over your arms—!"

Serena had seen Cass disappear under the ice. She screamed once, then halted the dogs. Her mind raced, and she knew that she'd never have the strength to pull him out of the icy creek. A thought flashed into her mind, and she grabbed the rope that always lay on top of the supplies. She called out, "Gee!" and as the team swung around in a circle, she tied one end of it to the bracing of the sled. Running forward, she fashioned a noose, and throwing herself facedown on the ice, crawled toward Cass, who had risen and was thrashing at the ice. When she called to him, he didn't respond.

The ice gave under her weight, and she knew if she stood up it would collapse. "God—help us!" she cried, then moved to the very edge of the broken ice. "Cass—over your head!" she yelled. His dull eyes seemed to clear, and when she tossed the noose over his head, he managed to work it down. But he was losing consciousness, and Serena screamed, "Mush—mush, Thor!"

Thor leaped forward along with the other dogs. The rope grew tense, and Serena reached out and fastened her hands on Cass's coat. "Mush! Mush!" she kept yelling. Cass's body was drawn to the edge of the ice, but he needed to be pulled *up* Serena saw. With the last of her strength she moved forward, got her arms around his chest and heaved upward.

It was enough! She fell backward and Cass was pulled free. They both went skidding across the ice, and when they hit the solid ground, Serena cried out "Whoa!" stopping the team.

Scrambling to her feet, she saw that Cass was almost unconscious. His lips were blue and his breathing had become very shallow. *Got to get him to shelter!* she thought wildly. Her mind raced, but at the same time she was furiously engaged in getting him on the sled. She guided the dogs by her voice until the sled was beside Cass's body, then she heaved him onto the sled legs first. By pushing and shoving, she rolled his upper body into the sled. She snatched the blankets free, wrapped them around his still body, then ran to take the handles. "Mush!" she cried.

As the sled moved away, she was suddenly taken by a thought. *The mine! Ben Carleton's old mine!* They'd passed it not five minutes earlier. Serena knew it well, for it was a famous mine. It had been one of the first in the territory but had never produced much gold. Now it was a mere hole in the side of a steep cliff beside the Yukon. *It's the only shelter close enough,* Serena thought as she drove the dogs at top speed.

They reached the mine as darkness fell. Serena drove the team right into the dark rectangle that marked the opening. As soon as they were out of the wind, she lit the lantern with numb fingers. The yellow light threw a feeble light on the rock walls, and at once she advanced, leading the team to the end of the shaft, a distance of some forty feet.

Instantly she set the lantern down and ran to Cass's side. He looked dead, and for one moment her heart seemed to stop. But she prayed, "God, don't let him die!" Then she unhitched the sled and simply rolled it over. It took all her strength and she was panting when she shoved it back and ran to Cass.

"Got to get him dry!" she said aloud. The wind howled outside, but the blasts did not reach into the crevasses of the mine. She stripped off his wet clothing, boots and all, then rubbed him vigorously with a dry blanket. He lay as still as a dead man, but finally she felt a twitch. Encouraged, she continued to rub his body until her arms ached.

Finally his eyes opened and he muttered something. Serena at once grabbed some more blankets and wrapped him tightly in them. The cold was bitter, and she had no way of making a fire. She was wet herself from pulling Cass out of the water. A thought came to her, and she unhitched the dogs. They yelped and sniffed around the mine, but when Serena dived into the food sack and gave them all two fish apiece, they gobbled them down.

"Thor, come here," Serena commanded. She went to where Cass lay, his eyes half open. Stripping off her own wet outer garments, she wrapped up in some dry blankets and lay down beside him, getting under the large fur she had thrown over him. Then she pulled Thor down between them. Next she called out, "Bob, Skeet—come here. You, Pap and Red and Tom—come here—lie down. You, too, Ollie—come on!"

The dogs were quick enough to obey, for they were exhausted. The food and the comparative warmth of the cave made them sleepy, and they drew close to the pair, flopping down all around them and going to sleep almost instantly.

Soon the heat of the dogs' bodies made the cold bearable. Serena reached over and touched Cass's face. His eyes were closed, and she saw by the pale light of the lantern that his lips were now relaxed.

"Sleep well, my dear!" she whispered, then fatigue caught her like a blow and she fell into a profound slumber.

★ ★ ★ ★

Serena uttered a faint cry of fear and gave a great start. Something warm and wet and rough was touching her cheek—and when she opened her eyes, Thor's great head filled her vision. His lopsided grin appeared, and he gave a resounding *Wuff!* and licked her face again.

"Affectionate, isn't he?"

The voice was right in her ear, and Serena's head jerked around—to find herself staring into Cass's blue-green eyes. His face was not six inches from hers, and she was suddenly aware of how close he was—and that his arm was under her head!

The memory of yesterday's near tragedy came back, and she put out her hand to touch his face. "Cass!" she whispered. "You're all right!"

"Thanks to you." Cass suddenly kissed her on the lips, and when she would have protested, he said, "Don't say it—I might do it again." Then his face grew serious. "I don't know how you did it, Serena. How in the name of heaven did you get me out of that creek?"

Serena lay still, very conscious of the touch of his body next to hers. She told him how the dogs had pulled him out, making light of her efforts, then said nervously, "I—I can't stay here." She pulled away from Cass, rose, and said, "I'll rig up the oil stove. We can dry the clothes and maybe fix some coffee."

Cass watched as she found the small oil stove and got it going, then made coffee. It took some time, but finally he took the steel cup she handed him and swallowed the hot liquid. It seemed to run through his body like fire, and he coughed, but he drank it all. His wet clothes lay on the earth, and the small stove threw out such a small amount of heat that it took several hours to dry them.

Cass sat wrapped in a blanket, saying nothing. Serena fed the dogs, then got out a pan and opened two cans of beans. Along with bacon, bread, and tea, they had a good meal.

But Serena was puzzled by Cass's silence. He ate slowly, his brow wrinkled, and finally after she'd packed the dishes back in the sled, he gave her an odd look. "I had some bad dreams last night."

"Bad dreams? About what?"

"About Leo Ritter." Cass was sitting beside Thor. The big dog had finally formed a liking for him, and Cass dug his fingers into the thick ruff, his face drawn and his eyes thoughtful. "It's a—a terrible thing to end a human life, Serena. Not a day's gone by but I think of it."

"You were just defending yourself, Cass."

"Sure, I know—but I keep hearing him say, 'I can't die—I'm not ready!' " Cass looked up and pain filled his eyes. "When Jubal died, I got mad at God. But all the time I knew deep down he was all right, that he was *better* off. But Ritter—he went out to meet God and he wasn't ready. I keep thinking if he hadn't died, he might have been saved. Now it's too late."

Serena sat quietly, listening as Cass spoke. He went on speaking for some time, and she grew tense, not knowing what was coming. Finally he fell silent, and she asked, "What about you, Cass?"

Cass looked at her, his lips drawn tight. "When I went down into the water yesterday, Serena, I thought the same thing Ritter thought—I'm not ready to die."

"Would you like to be ready, Cass?"

"Yes—yes, I would!"

Serena's heart seemed to move and she cried out in her spirit, *Lord, give me words—and wisdom to show him the way.* She began to speak of her own walk with God.

He listened carefully, and when she'd finished he said, "I've heard the gospel so many times. But it all seemed too—too *easy.* I mean, from what I understand all a person has to do is turn to God."

"It's easy for *us*, Cass—but it wasn't easy for God." She had retrieved her Bible from the sled and opened it now. "You probably learned this verse when you were growing up: 'For God so loved the world, that he gave his only begotten Son, that whosoever believeth on him should not perish, but have everlasting life.' " Her eyes were warm as she looked at Cass. "If you could just grasp that *one* fact, Cass—that God loves you so much that He sent Jesus to die for you—"

She spoke earnestly, her voice gentle but insistent. She read scriptures and patiently answered his halting questions. The dogs moved around, Thor sometimes thrusting his grinning face to nudge Cass's side. But Cass was not aware of the dog or of anything else. He was trembling and finally said, "I remember what Jubal preached about—that Christ would rise again—and he said that no man needs more proof than that."

"If you believe that Jesus is the Son of God and that He rose again, would you trust yourself to Him, Cass?" When he nodded, she said, "Tell Him so, then." She bowed her head and prayed quietly. She prayed for a long time, and in the midst of the prayer she was aware that Cass was weeping. He was not, she knew, a man to weep easily, and when she opened her eyes and saw that his eyes were filled with tears and that his lips were relaxed—and that there was a peace in his eyes that she'd never seen, she too began to weep. She leaned her head against his shoulder as they sat quietly together.

"I've given my life to Jesus Christ, Serena," Cass said. "I don't know what it will mean—but I'll never turn back. Will you help me?"

And Serena, the Yukon Queen, took his face between her hands. She blinked back the tears and nodded. "Yes! Oh yes, Cass! I'll help you. . . !"

She put her arms around him and held him close, her face pressed against his broad chest.

And Thor, watching carefully, said *Wuff!*—and then grinned and began to scratch his stomach.

CHAPTER TWENTY-TWO

GUNFIGHT AT DAWSON

★ ★ ★ ★

Superintendent Samuel Steele suffered many disappointments in the pursuit of his duties. The territory he covered was enormous, so large that many major crimes simply went unreported. Men vanished, and though Steele knew they had been killed, the bodies were often never found. Dawson had become a boiling caldron of men and women hardened to such an extent that the Royal Mounted Police were kept busy in an endless fight against crime.

At times Steele almost despaired of the enormity of the task, but from time to time the solving of a crime simply fell into his lap—and one of these times occurred a week after Serena and Cass had returned from Forty Mile. That itself had been a trip that had set the Klondike to buzzing. Everyone talked about how the Yukon Queen had risked her life to save the miners from death. Steele had congratulated both Serena and Cass, but something about the pair troubled him—something that he could not quite identify.

"Those two set the country on its ears, didn't they?" Sergeant Reginald Blake said, coming into the superintendent's office late one afternoon. He was a slight young man with bright blue eyes and an alert manner. "Miss Stevens ought to have a medal!"

"I dare say," Steele murmured. He had taken Serena to dinner the evening before and was still puzzled at the change in her. She had been as bright and happy as he'd ever seen her, but as she related the story of her trip to Forty Mile, the name of Cass Winslow was threaded into almost every sentence. Steele had listened to her and approved of the young man's decision to follow Christ—but he had left her with a heavy spirit. He had not attempted to kiss her when he said good-night, and now he realized that she had not mentioned his offer to marry her.

A streak of irritation ran through him, and he said sharply, "Well, what devilment has this town been up to, Sergeant? I wish all these Americans would go back where they came from!"

Blake stared at his commanding officer with surprise, for Steele's calm demeanor was known throughout the territory. However, he had kept track of the big man's goings and thought to himself, *It's that girl—he's getting edgy over her*. But he said only, "Well, they'll leave when the gold plays out, sir." He went over the items that required Steele's attention, and as they spoke a knock at the door interrupted them.

"Come in," said Steele brusquely. The door opened and a middle-aged mountie entered, his face alight with excitement.

"Sir," he said, "I've got something, I think. About the Mullins murder."

The unsolved murder of the miner had grated on Steele, and he demanded, "What have you got, Corporal Maythorne?"

Maythorne fidgeted with excitement, his dark brown eyes gleaming with satisfaction. "I've got an eyewitness to the murder!"

Steele seldom showed excitement, but Maythorne's statement brought him out of his seat. "Where is he?"

"I've got him outside, sir. Shall I bring him in?"

"At once!"

Maythorne went to the door, said, "Come in, please," and two men entered.

One of them Steele knew, and nodded, saying, "Evening, Mr. Bonner."

Right behind Bonner came another man, and Steele waited until the corporal said, "This is Al Drilling, Superintendent."

Drilling was a small man, not over five feet five inches tall. He twisted his hat nervously in his hands, ducked his head, and mumbled, "Pleased to meet ya." He had tow-colored hair, stiff with dirt, and a feeble scraggly beard and mustache that covered a tiny mouth.

"Al's got evidence for you, Superintendent," Bonner prompted. He nudged the smaller man with his elbow. "Go on, tell him what you seen, Al."

Drilling shifted his weight, looking desperately around as if seeking a means of escape. He was as fearful a man as Steele had seen, and now he said easily, "If you have proper evidence, Mr. Drilling, you'll be protected. Have no worries on that score."

It was the right thing to say, for a look of relief washed across Drilling's pale face. "Well—I should've come in before, I guess. But I seen too many men killed to take any chances."

"What did you see?" Steele asked quietly.

"I—I seen Nate Mullins get shot," Drilling blurted out, and then the words seemed to gush from him. It was as if they'd been dammed up, and now they rushed from him in a torrent of relief. "I wuz coming back from town, and when I passed Nate's cabin I heard voices. It sounded like an argument and I didn't want nothin' to do with it, so I jest moved on by. But then I heard a shot and a scream—and when I turned around I seen a man come runnin' out of Nate's cabin. He was holding a gun and I ducked behind a shed. When he got on his horse and rode off, I run to the cabin."

Drilling took out a dirty handkerchief and wiped his forehead with a trembling hand, then held his hands out in a pleading gesture. "Nate was dead, plugged right in the heart. Nothing I could do for him, so I ducked out. I seen there was some fellers comin', so I just stayed back until they went inside. Then I went in, playin' like I'd just got there."

At once Steele asked, "Who was the man who left the cabin? Had you ever seen him before?"

A tremor came to Drilling's lips, and he gave one pathetic glance at Harry Bonner. "Go on, Al, you owe it to Nate," Bonner said.

"It—it was that albino, Whitey Dugan!"

Steele's eyes were fixed on the miner. "Will you swear to that in open court?"

"He'll kill me if he don't get convicted!"

"He'll hang, Drilling," Steele said firmly. "I can't say how a verdict would go in the States, but in my country no jury would bring in any verdict but guilty, and no judge would do less than sentence Dugan to be hanged."

Drilling looked down at his worn shoes, and the three men held their breath. Finally he looked up. "I liked Nate. He was a good friend. I'll do it."

"Fine!" Steele smiled. "I'll turn you over to Corporal Maythorne. He'll take your testimony down."

"What about Dugan?" Drilling asked anxiously.

"I'll have him behind bars by the time you've finished," Steele promised. He smiled grimly, saying, "Come along, Sergeant, we have an arrest to make!"

* * * *

The tinny sound of the piano sprinkled notes over the barroom, but as the massive form of Superintendent Steele appeared in The Shady Lady, the piano player faltered, slowed, then sped up again. The customers watched as the tall mountie moved across the floor and came to the table that Brent Traphagen used for his station.

Traphagen had spotted Steele instantly and now said pleasantly, "Good to see you, Superintendent. Sit down and have a drink on the house."

Steele smiled grimly, his direct eyes fixed on the owner. "I'm here on business, Traphagen."

"We haven't broken any city ordinances, have we? I'm sure we can fix it if we have to."

"Murder is hard to fix." Steele enjoyed the shock that flickered in Traphagen's eyes. "I've got a warrant for your man Dugan."

"A murder? I can't believe Whitey would be involved in anything like that!"

"You're the only man in Dawson who thinks that." Steele glanced around the room, then his eyes came back to the gambler. "I don't see him. Where is he?"

"He got sick about an hour ago. Went to his room, I suppose." He was thinking with lightninglike speed and said, "In the States we have to have evidence against a man before we arrest him on a murder charge."

"He'll hear the evidence when he's in court, Traphagen." Steele half turned, then brought himself back to face the man squarely. "He'll have one chance to escape the rope, Traphagen."

"And what's that?"

"To turn evidence against anyone involved in the killing with him. He can get off with a prison term that way. And you know what? I think he'll do just that." Steele stared hard at Traphagen for a long moment, then said softly, "I'm going to nail you on this thing. You'd better enjoy yourself while you can."

Traphagen waited until Steele was out of the door, then rose and went at once into his office. He shut the door, then turned to say to Dugan who was dozing on a couch, "Wake up!" When Dugan came up with a start, he said, "You've got to get out of Dawson, Whitey. . . ." He quickly related the details of Steele's visit, then shook his head. "He's got something to hang you with. You'll have to get out of the Klondike—out of Steele's territory."

"He's got nothing!" Dugan insisted. He stood there arguing and stopped only when the door burst open and Nick Bolton came rushing in. Dugan's gun leaped into his hand and he swore. "Come in like that again and you're likely to get killed, Nick!"

Bolton stared at him, then shook his head. "It's all over town, about Al Drilling."

"What about Drilling?" Dugan snapped.

"Why, he seen you coming out of Nate Mullins' shack when he was killed!"

"What? How do you know that?"

"Feller who cleans the mounties' offices, he heard it while he was working."

Traphagen made an angry gesture and glared at Dugan. "You told me there were no witnesses!"

"I never seen him!" Sweat popped onto the albino's face, and he gritted out, "Well, he won't be doin' no testifying. I'll fix him!"

"You think Steele hasn't thought of that?" Traphagen said with contempt. "You'd better hit for the States, Whitey."

Dugan leveled his pale eyes on Traphagen. "You'd like that, wouldn't you, Brent. I run for it and the mounties catch up with me. You know they never quit! Steele would follow me to the pit!"

"Go outside and see what's going on, Nick," Traphagen said. As soon as the bartender left, he said, "We've got to be smart about this, Whitey. Steele's been looking for an excuse to nail us—and if we don't watch it, he'll get us both."

"He won't have nothin'—not after I get Drilling!"

"He'll have somebody with him, you can bet on that." Brent Traphagen was a wily villain, thinking of his own skin first. Now he saw Whitey Dugan as a liability. A thought came to him, and he said quickly, "We'll do it right now. Steele won't be looking for anything this quick. He told me that Drilling's making out his story in his office. He'll come out of there, and you've got to pot him."

"By myself?"

"No. You can stand in the alley. I'll get on the roof of the feed store and if you miss, I'll nail him." Traphagen urged quickly, "It's that or a rope, Whitey. Have your horse ready, and as soon as you get Drilling, ride out and head for Shorty's camp. When Steele comes looking for you, Shorty and his bunch will swear you've been there with them all day."

"All right, we'll do it." Whitey gave Traphagen a hard stare, saying, "Don't make any mistake about this, Brent. You're in as deep as me. So you keep them off my back when I make my break."

"Sure, that's the way it'll be. Now, get your horse and stand in that alley. I'll have a rifle upstairs. It can't miss!"

Traphagen moved to get a rifle from a rack, then left his office. He made his way down the alley. Seeing no one, he climbed the outside stairs, until he reached the flat roof. Lying down he glanced over the edge and saw with satisfaction that he had a good view of the alley below. Even as he watched, he saw Whitey come down the alley and take his position.

Carefully Brent lowered the rifle, drew a bead on Whitey's chest, then nodded. "You're too dangerous, Whitey. Sorry about that. You knock Drilling off, and then I'll put you away. Steele will have to be satisfied with that!"

★ ★ ★ ★

Harry Bonner came running up to Cass and Serena, his face glowing with excitement. "It's gonna be all right about Mike, Cass! I got Al to come to town and testify about Whitey shootin' Nate Mullins."

Cass had just stepped out of the wagon and had turned to help Serena to the ground. He turned quickly, his face alert. "What did Steele say?"

"Said that Al's testimony would be enough to hang Dugan," Bonner agreed emphatically.

"I want to talk to Steele," Cass said instantly. Then he turned to Serena, saying, "Why don't you go see about those books we were talking about. I'll meet you at the store as soon as I talk to Steele."

"All right, Cass." Serena had seen some Christian books at one of the larger stores and had insisted that they go look them over. "Don't be too long."

Cass turned and walked down the street with Bonner, the latter telling him excitedly how hard he'd had to work to get Al Drilling to testify. "He was a friend of Nate's, or he never would've done it," Bonner said as they turned into the office of the Mounted Police.

"Is the superintendent in?" Cass asked the corporal.

"Yes, he is—but somebody's with him," Corporal Maythorne said, then he grinned broadly. "He's with Drilling, so I guess he might be willing to see you, Mr. Bonner. We owe you for getting us a good witness." He rose, went to knock on the door, then when a voice answered, he opened the door and stepped inside. "Bonner and Cass Winslow to see you, sir."

Steele glanced up, thought for a moment, then said, "All right, Corporal. I think we're finished here."

Drilling began to say nervously, "But you didn't catch Dugan. He'll pot me sure as the world."

"He's in Dawson, Mr. Drilling," Steele said patiently. "We've got men looking for him. An albino won't be too hard to find. Come along, now. . . ." He led the way out of the office and nodded to the two men. "Dugan's not been found, but we'll get him."

A worried frown crossed Bonner's face. "He'll have heard about this by now. It's all over town about how Al's going to testify against him."

"We'll have to keep a guard on him," Steele said, then hesitated. "I've got all my men searching for Dugan. But you'd better stay here, Mr. Drilling, in headquarters."

Drilling looked around nervously. "All right, but I got to have something to eat. I ain't had nothin' since Harry started out on me."

Bonner grinned. "Come along, Al. Me and Cass will bodyguard you. I'm sort of hungry myself."

"I missed my lunch," Steele said. "We'll go down to Browning's Cafe and get something." He plucked his hat from a peg, settled it squarely on his head, then nodded to the corporal. "I'll be back in forty-five minutes, Maythorne. I want to be informed as soon as Dugan is brought in."

"Yes, sir, I'll come myself."

The four men left the office, turned, and walked down the sidewalk. The snow had partially melted, but there was enough to give a sheen that flickered from the rays of the sun. As they moved down the street, Cass led the way with Al Drilling beside him. Steele and Bonner followed, Bonner asking about the new laws about claim jumping.

"Tell me about Mullins' murder, Al," Cass said. "Did you see Dugan do it?"

Drilling was beginning to sense that he was going to be a very important man in Dawson. His fear of Dugan had faded, for how could the gunman get him with three men such as these beside him? He began telling his story and was gratified to see that Winslow was paying close attention.

Cass listened carefully, and as the small man repeated how he'd seen Dugan come out of the cabin, he was convinced that there would be no problem. "You're doing the right thing, Al," said Cass. A man like Dugan will kill again—"

He broke off, for a figure had stepped out from the recess of an alley not fifty feet away—and Cass instantly recognized the pasty features of Whitey Dugan. He saw that the albino had a gun and was lifting it. *He's got to kill Drilling!* The thought jumped into his mind, and he acted by pure instinct. His gun was beneath his heavy coat, so there was no chance to use it. He threw himself to his right, driving the breath from Al Drilling, who yelled, "Hey—!" as he fell beneath Cass.

At that same moment the report of Dugan's gun sounded, and the shot went exactly where Drilling had been. It passed between Harry Bonner and Steele, and the two stopped at once, staring at the figure who had opened fire.

Cass put himself between the gunman and Drilling. Tearing his coat open, he pulled the Colt and came to his knees. Two more shots rang out, one of them plucking at his sleeve. He leveled the Colt and caught Dugan's chest in the sight. All he had to do was pull the trigger. He saw Whitey fire once more, then lowered his sight and got off his own shot. The slug struck Dugan in the thigh, driving the leg from under the man, who sprawled awkwardly.

But Whitey was not out of action. He yelled with rage and fired again. The shot struck the post beside Cass and then another gunshot made a report. At once Whitey threw up his hands, fell forward, and did not move.

One instant later a gun went off almost in Cass's ear. He looked back to see that Steele had drawn his service revolver. He was aiming up, and when Cass followed the line of the mountie's aim, he saw a man suddenly rise, clutching his chest. He tried to raise the rifle in his hand, but Steele's revolver roared again and the man was driven backward.

"That was Traphagen. He shot Dugan! " Steele exclaimed. He left at a run, disappeared in a door, and shortly appeared on the roof. He looked down at the men below, shook his head, and said, "Dead. How about Dugan?"

Cass and Bonner moved forward at once. Bonner stooped down and rolled the still form over. The white face of Dugan stared upward, but there was no life in him.

"Saved the expense of a rope," Bonner said. He went back and pulled Al Drilling to his feet. "All over, Al," he said. "Nothing to worry about now. Let's go get drunk."

Cass stood looking down at the dead man's face. A few minutes later, Steele came down from the roof and walked up to him. "He was nothing but a cheap gunman, Steele," Cass murmured. "But he wasn't always that. He made a man proud to have a son. A mother loved him, maybe. He must have had something good in him when he was young. Now he's dead—and no one to mourn him."

Steele hesitated, uncertain of how to respond. Finally he said gently, "He made his choice, Cass. Nobody made him become a killer."

Cass met the mountie's eyes. "Could be me. Just one wrong trail, and I could have wound up in his shape."

Right then they heard a woman's voice behind them. Turning, they saw Serena hurrying up the boardwalk, her face pale. "Are you all right?" She addressed both of them, but her eyes, Steele noted, were only for Cass. "I heard the shots and I thought—!"

"We're all right," Cass assured her. He saw that Steele was watching Serena carefully, and remembered that this man loved her enough to offer himself in marriage. He felt cut off and said, "I've got to take the team to get them shod. See you later."

Serena watched him leave, then turned to Steele, her eyes troubled. "I'm glad you weren't hurt, Sam. I wish you didn't have to risk your life all the time."

"It goes with being a mountie," Steele said. He took a deep breath, then said, "Come along, Serena. We need to talk."

Serena looked at him with surprise but took his arm and moved down the street. She didn't know that Cass had not yet turned the corner on the street where the blacksmith was. He stood there watching them walk off together, with Serena led by the mountie's arm.

She deserves a good man like Steele—but I can't stay around to watch it! thought Cass, then he turned abruptly and headed for the smithy.

He got his horses shod, then made up his mind. He went on a manhunt, determined to find Alex McCarty, the man who had offered to buy his claim. After checking out a few saloons, he finally found him in The Golden Fleece saloon. He moved to the bar, took Alex's greeting, then said abruptly, "Alex, are you still interested in buying my claim?"

McCarty's eyes flew open at once. "Why, you're not leaving Dawson, Cass?"

"Yes. What's your offer?"

The two stood there bargaining and finally agreed. "Fifteen thousand and ten percent of all that comes out of the mine," McCarty said. Then he hesitated, his sharp eyes on Cass. "Might get a million out of that claim. You'd be sore at me if I did."

"And you might get less," Cass shrugged. "It's a gamble, Alex.

I'm happy if you are. But I want the money now."

"All right, we'll go sign the papers and I'll get the dust for you."

The two men moved out of the saloon, and as they left, the bartender said, "See him? That's Cass Winslow. Got a big strike up on Indian Head. Sure wish I was him!"

The customer he was serving stared at Winslow, then shook his head. "He don't look happy, Pete. Why wouldn't a man with a big pile of gold look happy?"

"I dunno, Jimmy. Maybe he's got notions." He wiped the bar thoughtfully, then shook his head. "Them things can be dangerous for a man!"

CHAPTER TWENTY-THREE

A TIME TO EMBRACE

★ ★ ★ ★

"What's wrong with you, Cass?" Joe Winslow demanded. The old prospector was watching as Cass packed some of his belongings into a canvas sack. "If you stick it out until spring, you can get rich, maybe."

Cass looked up suddenly, the words of the older man catching at him. "You know, that's an odd thing, Joe. I've wanted to be rich for as long as I can remember. Don't know how much time I've spent thinking of what I'd do if I had a pile of money." He slowly picked up a pair of socks, stuffed them into the bag, then added, "Now it doesn't seem so important."

The older Winslow smoothed his bushy white hair, a puzzled expression on his face. He leaned back against the wall of the cabin, thinking of the past few weeks. Finally he said, "Something's happened to you, Cass. Ever since Traphagen and Dugan got shot down, you been different."

"I don't know, Joe." Cass shoved the last of his clothing into the sack, drew the neck tight, then tied a string around it. He moved slowly, seeming preoccupied with the task, but finally when it was done, he sighed. "Joe, I was pretty filled up with hate. All I could think of was getting even for Mike. I would probably have done it, too, except for that trip Serena and I made to Forty Mile."

"Sure, that was good, Cass! Your people will be happy about your new way."

"Yes, they will—but somehow I haven't been able to get away from the sight of those two dead men—three, really, counting Leo Ritter."

A mule brayed, and Cass listened to it absently. "All three of them dead in just a few months. They thought they'd live to be old men. I don't suppose they gave any thoughts at all to God."

"Probably not," Joe admitted. "They were a tough bunch. But you didn't have much choice. They would have come to bad ends sooner or later."

"Not if they'd found God."

"No, that's right." Joe was watching his young friend carefully. He knew that the restlessness stirring in Cass Winslow was more than a theological problem. Now he asked gently, "You're bound and determined to go home?"

"Nothing here for me, Joe."

"What will you do there?"

"Go back home, help my dad. I've given him and my mother a pretty bad time. I'd like to show them I've changed."

"Thet would be good. You've got good people." Joe Winslow pulled out his pipe, filled it with rough-cut, and put a match to it. He expelled a wreath of smoke, then asked innocently, "Whut about Serena?"

The question seemed to irritate Cass. "What about her, Joe?"

"Wal, didn't you promise her pa you'd take care of her?"

"I thought she was a little girl. She's not, and it looks like there'll be—others to take care of her."

"Steele, you mean? She's gonna marry him?"

"Why not? He's a good man." Cass's voice was curt, and he said, "I'm going back to town, Joe. See you later."

"River won't be free fer a few weeks. Won't be no ship leaving until then."

"I'll be leaving sooner than that, Joe." Cass turned to the old man, then came to him and thrust out his free hand. "Come to see us again, Joe, after you've got your pile made. I'll be in Wyoming with my people. Or maybe I'll go find Aaron—I'd like to talk to him."

"But—how you gonna get to the coast with the river froze?"

"I'll get Dale Troxler to haul me out by sled. Well, so long, Joe."

"So long, Cass, but—" Joe never got to deliver his final words because Cass had moved outside and mounted his horse, riding off with a wave of his hand. The old man considered the horseman as he moved away, then said abruptly, "Blast it all! Thet boy ain't happy!" He stood there with an uncertain air, then grabbed his hat. Jamming it down over his head, he left the cabin, muttering, "I reckon there's one hand in this game ain't been played yet!"

★   ★   ★   ★

Cass was lying on his bed, staring up at the ceiling. He had packed his things and arranged with Troxler to take him out to the coast. Now there was nothing to do but wait. He studied the wallpaper, then closed his eyes. But he could not rest, so he rose and went to the window, staring out at the main street of Dawson.

Ever since he had decided to leave, he'd wondered how to tell Serena, and now he had settled it. He touched the letter in his breast pocket, not satisfied with the words he'd finally put on paper—telling her of his gratitude and congratulating her on finding a man like Sam Steele. And now, his jaw tightened as he thought of the pair.

Suddenly a dog team appeared down the street, and he quickly turned and grabbed his suitcase and left the room. He'd changed the gold dust he'd gotten from McCarty into notes and stopped long enough at the desk to pay his bill.

"Sorry to see you leaving, Cass," Millard Powell, the owner, said. "Bad time of year to travel—but you'll make it."

"Sure. Good luck, Millard."

Cass moved outside and called out, "Here's one suitcase, Dale, but I've got some other—"

And then he halted, for the driver had turned to him. "Serena!" he said, dropping his suitcase. "What are you doing here?"

Serena pushed the parka back and the wind fanned her curly hair. She was pale, Cass noted, and there was some sort of doubt in her that he didn't understand.

"Joe told me you were leaving," she said. "Then Dale told me you'd hired him to take you to the coast." She came to stand in front of him, and her lips trembled. "Why didn't you tell me you were leaving?"

Cass said simply, "I'm just a coward, Serena. Couldn't face up to you."

"You should have told me, Cass."

"Yes, I should." Cass took the letter from his pocket and stared at it with distaste. "I stayed up most of the night trying to say what I felt—but the right words never came." He jammed the letter into his pocket, then faced her squarely. There was a desperate light in his eyes, and he spoke haltingly. "I love you, Serena. Have for a long time, I think. But I was so—so tangled up, I just didn't know it."

"You should have told me that, too, Cass," Serena whispered. She reached up and touched her throat in a feminine gesture, then said, "A woman has a right to know when a man loves her."

"But you and Steele—" Cass halted abruptly, seeking for words. "Well, you're marrying him, aren't you?"

Serena looked at him steadily. "No, I'm not."

Cass stared at her incredulously. "But I thought—"

Serena suddenly reached up and took Cass's face in her hands, her voice breaking as she said, "I'm not marrying Sam because I don't love him." She looked deep into Cass's startled eyes. "I'm going back to the States with you! So get in the sled!"

Cass reached out, hope spreading over his face. "Serena!" he said, then put his arms around her and kissed her firmly.

"Oh, Cass!" Serena whispered. "I thought I'd lost you!"

The two held each other tightly, and then a voice came, breaking through. They looked up to see Superintendent Sam Steele. He was holding on to the arm of a huge miner who was drunk and surly. The miner's face was ugly and scarred and he spat on the sidewalk defiantly.

"Oh, Sam—" Serena cried, her eyes like stars. "You can't guess what's happened!"

Steele smiled slightly. "You're going to marry Cass Winslow." He nodded, amused by her expression, then turned to Cass. "Treat her right, Winslow, or the Royal Mounted Police will be on your trail."

"Steele—"

"I'm a terrible loser," Steele interrupted him. "Get out of here until I can get into a more charitable spirit."

Cass had never admired a man more. He saw the pain in the big mountie's eyes and nodded. "I'll take care of her, Sam." Then he turned to Serena, "Come on, sweetheart!"

Sam Steele accepted a quick kiss on the cheek from Serena and stepped back as she took her place behind the sled. Then at her command the dogs pulled out.

The superintendent watched as they disappeared, then turned and looked at the ugly face of his prisoner.

"Come on, sweetheart," he said gently and, straightening his back, marched down the sidewalk.